P9-DOE-538

PRAISE FOR STARQUAKE

"Bob Forward has the most interesting aliens I never wrote—I wish I'd thought of them!"
—Jerry Pournelle

"Here is a big, roomy mind at play. Join the fun."
—Larry Niven

"How the humans help the space-marooned cheela at the risk of their own lives and how the cheela reciprocate, while Forward unleashes his imagination with two-way time machines, gravity catapults and Kerr metric space warps, is the stuff of an exemplary hard-sf novel. There is no more dazzling a practitioner of the form now writing than Robert L. Forward."
—*Locus*

". . . dazzling, beautifully worked-out scientific extrapolations . . . an adventure that's sure to please fans of 'hard' sf."
Kirkus Reviews

Also by Robert L. Forward
Published by Ballantine Books

DRAGON'S EGG

STARQUAKE

ROBERT L. FORWARD

A Del Rey Book

BALLANTINE BOOKS • NEW YORK

A Del Rey Book
Published by Ballantine Books

Copyright © 1985 by Robert L. Forward

All rights reserved under International and Pan-American
Copyright Conventions. Published in the United States of
America by Ballantine Books, a division of Random House, Inc.,
New York, and simultaneously in Canada by Random House of
Canada Limited, Toronto.

Library of Congress Catalog Card Number: 85-6183

ISBN 0-345-31233-3

Manufactured in the United States of America

First Hardcover Edition: October 1985
First Mass Market Edition: September 1986

Cover Art by Ralph McQuarrie

Acknowledgments

My thanks to my many friends who contributed ideas and helped me in several technical areas. In addition to those who helped in making the neutron star world of *Dragon's Egg* more believable, I want to thank Paul Blass, Rod Hyde, Keith Lofstrom, David Lynch, Lester del Rey, and Mark Zimmermann for additional help on this sequel.

My special thanks to Eve for generating new names for the many generations of cheela that lived, fought, and died on the following pages and to Martha for putting up with a husband constantly off in a brown study.

Prelude

Burrowing through the dark void between the Sun and its stellar neighbors, a tiny visitor came to the Solar System—a rapidly spinning, white-hot, ultra-dense neutron star. A superstrong magnetic field impaled the star from east to west. Reaching out from the rotating star, the two whirling arms of magnetic force whipped at the random atoms floating in space until they were moving at nearly the speed of light. The shocked atoms gave off a pulsating beam of powerful radio waves. Thus, even though the tiny neutron star was too small to be seen in the sky by the naked eye, it had been detected by radio telescopes on Earth long before it arrived at the Solar System.

The neutron star was given the name "Dragon's Egg." When it was first detected, its position in the sky was at the end of the constellation Draco, as if the dragon had left an egg behind in its nest.

The discovery of magnetic monopoles had revolutionized fusion-rocket technology, so it wasn't long before the first "interstellar" expedition reached the star, only some 2120 AU from Earth. Riding in their interstellar spacecraft St. George, the exploration crew approached the visitor carefully, for a neutron star can be dangerous if approached too closely without taking proper precautions.

Although Dragon's Egg was only 20 kilometers in diameter, the surface gravity was 67 billion times Earth gravity, the 8200 K temperature was hotter than the Sun, and the trillion-gauss magnetic field threading through the star at the "East" and "West" magnetic "Poles" was so strong it could elongate a normally round atomic nucleus into a cigar shape. Since Dragon's Egg was spinning at slightly more than five revolutions per second, the rapidly moving magnetic fields emanating from the East and West Poles would cook any humans who approached the star too closely without protection.

To counteract the gravity and the rotating magnetic fields, the scientists on St. George placed Dragon Slayer, their small science capsule, in a 406 kilometer synchronous orbit about the star, where the extreme gravity was canceled by the centrifugal force. Here also, Dragon Slayer would be moving along with the magnetic field and at 406 kilometers distance the magnetic field was no longer dangerous, just a nuisance.

Although the orbital motion of Dragon Slayer canceled the gravity at the center of the spacecraft, the match was not perfect everywhere. The residual gravity tides of 200 gravities per meter were still dangerous, but the exploration scientists devised a solution for that problem. They looped a superconducting cable a million kilometers long around the neutron star. The cable was used to extract electrical energy from the star's rotating magnetic field. The electrical currents in the cable powered a robotic factory that produced magnetic monopoles. The monopoles were injected into eight of the many asteroids that had been collected by the neutron star during its journey through space. There were two large asteroids and six small ones.

The monopoles from the factory condensed the asteroids until they were almost the density of the neutron star itself. Using the gravity interactions between the two larger asteroids, Otis and Oscar, the humans and their computers played a game of celestial billiards that placed the six smaller asteroids in a circular formation in synchronous orbit over the East Pole of the star. Then, using Otis as a gravitational elevator, Dragon Slayer and its crew was hauled down to join them.

Once in orbit, the crew began to map Dragon's Egg. They expected to learn many interesting scientific facts about this dense visitor to their Solar System, but they also found something they had never expected.

Life!

Life on the surface of a neutron star!

The alien creatures, the "cheela," were dense—as dense as the crust that covered the white-hot star. The tiny bodies of the cheela, a little larger than sesame seeds, weighed as much as a human, since they were made of degenerate nucleonic material. The life processes of the cheela used interactions between the nuclear particles in the bare nuclei that make up the cheela, while life on Earth uses electronic interactions between the electron clouds of the atoms that make up humans. Because nuclear reactions take place a million times faster than electronic reactions, the cheela thought, talked, lived, and died a million times faster than the humans in orbit above them.

When Dragon Slayer first took up its position over the East Pole, the cheela were little more than savages and were awed by the laser mapping beams sent down from the middle of the strange star formation floating motionless in their sky. They raised a huge mound temple to worship the new Gods. The humans saw the temple and started sending simple picture messages, one pulse per second. Within less than a day the cheela had developed their technology to the point that they were able to send their first crude, handmade signals to the Gods above them, at 250,000 pulses per second. The humans, finally realizing the immense time difference, worked as rapidly as they could, but nearly a generation went by on the surface of the neutron star before the human laser pulses answered the crude flare signals sent by the cheela below. The human crew used the slower science instruments such as the laser radar mapper for human-to-cheela communication, while the computer dumped the contents of the ship's library directly from the Holographic Memory storage cubes through a high-speed laser communicator to the surface below.

Chief Scientist Pierre Carnot Niven watched as Chief Engineer Amalita Shakhashiri Drake inserted the first of the 25 library HoloMem cubes, *A to AME*, into the communications console.

"A complete education, from Astronomy to Zoology," Pierre mused. "Alphabetical order may not be the best way to teach someone, but in this case it's the fastest."

For half a day the humans were the teachers for the cheela. In that 12 hours, 60 cheela generations passed. These were prosperous generations for the cheela, with the manna of knowledge pouring from the heavens keeping the previously warring clans on the star busy and at peace. After the first half day, the cheela had surpassed the human race in technological development and it was now time for the humans to become the students. Despite their tired bodies and their bewilderment over the rapidity of events in the past day, the humans continued to work diligently at their various science instruments and consoles, while one after another, the HoloMem crystals in their ship's library were rewritten with new knowledge from the cheela.

Leaving

06:00:00 GMT TUESDAY 21 JUNE 2050

Beep! Beep! Beep!

Pierre Niven opened his tired eyes and awkwardly turned off the alarm on his wrist chronometer. Six hours of sleep. He rubbed his hand over his bearded chin. The beard needed a trim and there were probably a few grey hairs peeking through the brown, but there was work to do. A quick bite in the galley, then he would relieve Amalita at the communications console. Both she and Seiko were long overdue for a sleep break. He heard muffled curses from the next sleep rack as Jean Kelly Thomas struggled to put her bed up.

The long day started.

06:05:06 GMT TUESDAY 21 JUNE 2050

Multi-scientist Seiko Kauffmann Takahashi was on the Science Deck working with the star image telescope. The telescope looked at the neutron star with a one-meter diameter mirror in the top of the cylindrical tower of star-oriented instruments that stuck out of the "north pole" of Dragon Slayer's spherical body. The telescope brought a large, bright image down through the hollow center of the tower and focused it on the frosted surface of the star image table in the middle of the top deck. Seiko looked down at the image while the computer looked up at the same image through the array of light detectors built under the surface of the table. When the crew first arrived a little over a day ago, the star image had only a few features in it. There had been the large volcano in the northern hemisphere, and the rough, mountainous regions at the East and West Poles where infalling meteoric material collected. Now, just a day later, the star was covered with a network of super-highways connecting great cities that grew in size even as Seiko watched. Noticing something happening in the outskirts of the capital city, Bright's Heaven, she efficiently took her compact body swiftly through a set of coordinated free-fall twists that put her on the other side of the table, then took a closer look.

"Abdul," Seiko said. "I would like you to observe this. There is a strange phenomenon occurring at the old Holy Temple."

"Just a sec while I reset the neutrino detector," electronic engineer Abdul Nkomi Farouk replied as he pushed himself over to hover above the star image table. Seiko reached up to the ceiling and made some adjustments to the telescope controls. The disk of light on the table expanded to show an elongated twelve-pointed star formation in the southern hemisphere of the neutron star.

Still the largest structure on the star, the Holy Temple had been raised by the cheela nearly 24 hours ago as they emerged from barbarism. Led by the ancient prophet Pink-Eyes (one of the few cheela who could see the visible light from the human's laser mapping beam), the cheela had raised the great mound-temple to serve as a place for worship of their pantheon of gods: the God-Star Bright (our nearby Sun hovering over the South Pole axis of the neutron star), Bright's Messenger (the large asteroid, Otis, in its highly elliptical orbit), the six Eyes of Bright (the six small asteroids in a circle hovering over the East Pole), and the Inner Eye of Bright (the tiny human spacecraft at the center of the ring of asteroids).

After the humans had established contact and convinced the cheela that they were not gods, the Holy Temple had been neglected and was slowly fading away into the landscape. The shape of the temple was that of a cheela at full alert, a long ellipsoidal body, with the long direction aligned along the local direction of the magnetic field, and twelve round eyes perched on short, exponentially tapered eye-stubs. After a hundred generations of neglect, the ancient ruins had degenerated to twelve blobs that used to be eyes and portions of wall mounds that had formed the rest of the body. Now, however, one of the eyes was once again dark and round, while its eye-stub was easily visible in the telescope image.

Abdul thoughtfully twisted one black whisker tip with his fingers as he pondered the scene. "Looks like they're fixing up the Holy Temple. Are they reverting to human worship?"

"Absolutely not." Seiko pronounced her verdict in the authoritative Teutonic tone she had learned from her father. "They are too intelligent for that. Since they now have space travel, they must have looked down and realized that the most visible structure on Egg looks rundown. Unless your neutrino and X-ray detectors have responded to a crustquake recently, it must be some sort of historical renovation project."

"No big quakes lately," said Abdul. "So they must be doing this on purpose."

"It's about time," Seiko *humphed* in disapproval. "That is the trouble with egg-layers, especially those that let the clan Old Ones raise the young. With no direct family ties through parents, they have no personal links to history."

Seiko had had no sleep for the past 36 hours. She looked up to adjust the solar image telescope controls to expand the view. The sudden motion made her head swim. She hit the wrong switch, and the filter that blocked most of the light from the neutron star flicked open for an instant. Her eyes shut against the glare.

"Seiko . . . Seiko . . ."

Seiko opened her heavy eyelids to see Dr. Cesar Wong holding her by the shoulders and peering through the wisps of straight black hair that had fallen forward over her face. Floating next to him was Abdul.

"I told her and I told her she shouldn't have skipped her last sleep break," Abdul said. "Maybe she'll listen to you and take one this time."

"Seiko, my dear." Cesar's deep brown eyes showed concern. "You have driven yourself much too hard. Please take a rest."

"Doctor Wong, I appreciate your concern. But I am not about to abandon my professional responsibility at this critical juncture."

"Well—at least take a break and join with me in a cup of hot coffee in the galley." Dr. Wong took the petite scientist gently by the arm. She allowed herself to be steered down the passageway to the bottom deck. On the way through the middle deck, they passed Amalita and Pierre working the communications console that talked directly to the cheela through the laser communication link.

Pierre was stretched out in free fall, his head and arms inside the communications console, while Amalita was talking to the cheela on the star. The speaker was not a computer-slowed image of a real cheela, but the real-time image of Sky-Teacher, a special purpose intelligent robot that the cheela had built for the job of communicating with the slow-thinking humans.

Pierre was replacing the HoloMem crystal in the side of the communications console. He reached in and removed the small three-sided cover shaped like the corner of a box. The outside was jet black, but the inner surface was a corner reflector of brilliantly reflecting mirrors. He pushed a button and a clear crystal cube about five centimeters across popped out into the room, rotating slowly from the force of its ejection. Pierre left it in midair as he placed another cube into the memory cavity and replaced the mirrored cover. Then he floated over to catch the cube. The corners and edges of the HoloMem cube were jet black, but through the transparent faces could be seen flashes of rainbow light from the information fringes stored in the interior.

06:13:54 GMT TUESDAY 21 JUNE 2050

Leaving Amalita talking to Sky-Teacher, Pierre grasped the HoloMem cube at opposite corners and followed Doc and Seiko through the passageway in the floor to the lower deck and pulled himself over to the library console. He moved carefully, for between two fingers he was carrying all the wisdom that the cheela had accumulated during the past thirty minutes. He placed the crystal in its scanner cavity in the library console, fitted the brilliantly polished corner segment into place, and closed the lid.

Sky-Teacher had said that this latest HoloMem crystal held a large section on the internal structure of neutron stars. Pierre had the computer jump rapidly through the millions of pages until he found a detailed cross section of the interior of Dragon's Egg. The diagram showed that the star had an outer surface that was a solid crust of nuclei: neutron-rich isotopes of iron, zinc, nickel, and other metallic nuclei in a crystalline lattice, through which flowed a liquid sea of electrons. Next came the mantle—two kilometers of neutrons and metallic nuclei in layers that became more neutron-rich and dense with depth. The inner three-fourths of the star was a liquid ball of super-fluid neutrons and superfluid protons.

Pierre scanned the next page, a photograph of a neutron star, but it wasn't Dragon's Egg. He could tell it was a real photograph, since he could see a portion of a cheela on a space flitter in the foreground. His eyes widened and he rapidly scanned page after page. There were many photographs, each followed by detailed diagrams of the internal structure of the various neutron stars. They ranged the gamut from very dense stars that were almost black holes to large, bloated neutron stars that had a tiny neutron core and a white-dwarf-star exterior. Some of the names were unfamiliar, but others, like the Vela pulsar and the Crab Nebula pulsar, were neutron stars known to the humans.

"But the Crab Nebula neutron star is over 3000 light-years away!" Pierre exclaimed to himself. "They would have had to travel faster than the speed of light to have gone there to take those photographs in the past eight hours!"

A quick search through the index found the answer.

FASTER-THAN-LIGHT PROPULSION—THE CRYPTO-KEY TO THIS SECTION IS ENGRAVED ON A PYRAMID ON THE THIRD MOON OF THE SECOND PLANET OF EPSILON ERIDANI.

There followed a long section of encrypted gibberish.

In near shock, Pierre set the library console for automatic transfer of the data to St. George and slowly floated over to the nearby lounge at the center bottom of Dragon

Slayer. Everyone but Amalita was there. Doc was trying to talk Seiko out of taking some W.A.K.E. pills with her coffee, and Abdul was telling Jean Kelly Thomas about the recent restoration of the Holy Temple as she gulped down a quick breakfast after her shortened sleep period while trying to comb out the snarls in her short cap of red hair at the same time. While Jean and Pierre had been asleep, the cheela had advanced from their first orbital flights around their home world to intergalactic travel.

Everyone was sitting on the soft, circular lounge seat, held there by the low outward-going residual gravity forces. Occasionally one of them would look out the viewport below his feet. Pierre jumped up to the top of the lounge and held onto the handle in the hatch door leading to one of the six high-gravity protection tanks built into the center of the ship. He too looked down and out the one-meter diameter window set in the ''south pole'' of the spherical spacecraft. The electronically controlled optical shutter had been set to blacken the port thirty times a second as each of the six glowing compensator masses passed in front of the port. The only light that entered the window came from a single intense spot that was Bright— the Sun, their home—2120 AU away.

Pierre broke the silence. ''It's nearly time for us to leave,'' he said.

Jean looked up, her perky freckled nose wrinkled in puzzlement. ''I thought the plan was for us to stay down here for at least another week.''

''With the cheela doing all the mapping and measurements for us, there is really no need for us to stay any longer,'' Pierre explained. ''You should have read the detailed description of both the exterior and interior of Dragon's Egg in that last HoloMem crystal I brought down.'' He swung down and stopped himself at the doorway to the lounge.

"I had the computer reprogram the herder probes to move us into the path of the deorbiter mass. In about half a day we will be in proper position to be kicked out of this close orbit back up to St. George. Then we can be heading for home instead of looking at it." He looked up at the clock readout on the lounge wall.

"Time to change HoloMem crystals again," he said. He crouched, then flashed a smile at them through his neat, dark brown beard.

"Come on," he said. "There is a lot of work to do to get this ship ready. Amalita and I will finish off the last of the HoloMem crystals, but the rest of you had better start buttoning up the ship; the gravity fields from that deorbiter will turn anything loose into a deadly missile." He jumped upward to the central deck as the others swam through the lounge door and spread out through the ship.

Pierre swung over to the communications console and looked at Sky-Teacher over Amalita's shoulder. The robot cheela was patiently explaining something. Pierre stared in fascination at the image. With the million-to-one time differential, it had not surprised Pierre that the cheela would make a slow-response, long-living robot that could take over the demanding task of talking to the slow-thinking humans. What amazed Pierre was that the robotic creature was so realistic that it had a personality. Sky-Teacher was not robot-like in its mannerisms at all. In fact, it acted very much like a patient, old-time schoolmaster. One could almost hear the friendly smile and the greying hair in the voice. It was a relief to the humans to have Sky-Teacher to talk to. They no longer felt as if they were wasting a good portion of some cheela's lifetime if they made a mistake or paused for a moment.

"We shortly will have filled up all your available HoloMem crystals," Sky-Teacher's image said, its halo of twelve robotic eyes doing a perfect imitation of the traveling wave pattern of a real cheela. "I am afraid that you will find most of this material is encrypted, since we are now the equivalent of many thousands of years ahead of you in development.

"Yet, if it had not been for you, we would still be savages, stagnating in an illiterate haze for thousands or even millions of greats of turns. We owe you much, but we must be careful how we pay you back, for you too have a right to grow and develop on your own. For your own good, it is best that we cut off communication after this last HoloMem crystal is full. We have given you enough material to keep you busy learning for thousands of your years. Then we will both be off on our separate ways, seeking truth and knowledge through space and time. You in worlds where the electron is paramount, and we in worlds where the neutron dominates."

A tone sounded and a small message appeared on the upper part of the screen.

HOLOMEM CRYSTAL FULL

"You are on your own now," Sky-Teacher said. "It is drawing near the time for you to leave. Goodbye, my friends."

"Goodbye," Pierre said as the screen blanked.

He turned to Amalita. "I'll put away the HoloMem crystal, and you start checking out the acceleration tanks," he said. "It's time to go home!"

06:40:10 GMT TUESDAY 21 JUNE 2050

Amalita closed down her console and floated over to a hatch in the wall next to the console. She looked through the thick glass of the tiny port into the interior of the high-gravity protection tank. The inside of the small, one-meter diameter sphere was empty except for a tiny split-screen video console set in the inner wall. In the walls of the tanks were banks of sound generators that produced pressure waves to counteract the gravitational tidal forces they would experience once they had left the haven of the six dense masses that danced in a ring around their spacecraft. Amalita pushed buttons that emptied the air from the tank and filled it with incompressible water. A touch on the controls and the sound generators sang their protective cloak into the chamber. In the exact center of the tank was a tiny check sphere pinioned by the sound forces. She increased the intensity of the sound pulses and waited until the tiny ball glowed a brilliant green. Satisfied that the tank was operational, Amalita punched for a purge and restart, then went around the central column to check out the next tank.

As Amalita left, Seiko came to a halt in front of the tank and started taking off her clothes. She stripped to a bra and briefs, pulled a wetsuit from the locker below the hatch door, and slid her pale body smoothly into the suit, the underwater breathing mask floating quietly above her head in the low gravity. Amalita paused in her check-out of the adjacent tank, looked down at her blouse, blushed, and dove down the passageway to her private locker. Shortly she was back again, and this time the motions of her upper body seemed to be a little more constrained.

By the time Amalita had come around to the hatch that opened downward from the ceiling of the lounge, Abdul was already there. He was down to his underpants. They were the skimpy European "bikini" style. The white satin contrasted nicely with the muscular ebony-black skin. Amalita floated up under Abdul and grabbed him firmly by his naked waist.

"Here, let me give you a hand with your suit," she said, her long, ballet-trained legs and feet locked firmly in the handholds at the lounge door.

"Hey! Cut it out!" Abdul yelled.

"I'm *just* trying to help," Amalita replied sweetly.

"I bet. I know you oversexed Harvard broads. Always trying to find some excuse to paw an MIT engineer. Leggo. I'm big enough to get dressed by myself."

Despite Abdul's protests, Amalita held onto his muscular waist until he got the legs of his wet suit on. Then pushing his arms into his sleeves as if she were dressing a little child, she helped him dress the rest of the way. Her attention bruised Abdul's ego a little, but Amalita didn't care; they were going home, and it was time for a little fun. Grinning from ear to ear, she shot up the passageway to check out the top tank. The hatch for this tank was under the star image table.

Amalita floated over to the table and glanced down for a moment at the image of Dragon's Egg on the white frosted surface. There was now more to see on the star as the cheela technology became capable of constructing structures large enough to be seen from space. The Bright's Heaven jump loop was now visible below. It was already slinging payloads into space. Within ten minutes or so, a space fountain should be pointing straight up into space from the top of the East Pole mountains off on the horizon. Just before she flicked off the image, Amalita saw the Polar Orbiting Space Station of the cheela flash by below like a white-hot tracer bullet.

06:45:10 GMT TUESDAY 21 JUNE 2050

Captain Star-Glider looked up with three of his eyes as the six glowing masses that formed the Eyes of Bright moved slowly by above him. The polar orbit of his space station carried him close enough to the huge formation that he could see the cylindrical instrument tower sticking out from one end of the spherical main hull of Dragon Slayer. The human spacecraft was as black-cold as a prostitute's eyeball and could only be seen by the red reflections from the Six Eyes and the yellow-white glare from Egg below. He shivered at the thought of living in such a cold place and thankfully spread out his tread on the glowing warmth of the yellow-white deck. It took almost a grethturn before the huge circle of glowing planetoids was far enough off from the vertical that it was no longer "above" him. His three anxious upturned eyes stopped their relentless watch and returned to join the remainder of his twelve eyes in the familiar cheela traveling wave pattern.

The wave pattern quickened as Captain Star-Glider tasted a message scrolling across the communications taste screen built into the deck. They would be launching an exploration ark within a few turns, and the exploration crew had been called for a final briefing. The briefing would take place in two dothturns at the meeting area around on the other side of the space station. The jump loop at Bright's Heaven had been busy the last turn sending up one jumpcraft after another with the crew, while the gravity catapults at the East and West Poles had been busy tossing cargo and equipment into the sky. The catapults were ancient, over eight human hours old. Extremely inefficient, even when aided by the inertia drives on the cargo shuttlecraft, they were slowly being replaced. Most personnel transfers now used the jump loops, and soon nearly everything would come up by way of a space fountain.

Although it really wasn't any of his business, Star-Glider decided to attend the briefing. It wasn't often that an exploration ark was sent off to visit some distant star. In fact, this was going to be the last one for quite a while. The Deep Space Exploration Council had decided for budgetary reasons to limit the number of exploration arks to six. The arks would spend a number of greats of turns at an interesting star, then move on to another one. The rest of the Deep Space Exploration fleet consisted of a small squadron of scout ships and a dozen cargo haulers that resupplied the exploration arks and rotated the crews.

The initial exploration was done by the high-speed scout ships that visited candidate neutron stars looking for interesting stellar dynamics or signs of life. One had recently returned to report that they had found life on a neutron star some 12,000 light-years distant. This was the sixth report of possible life, and the first one where the life forms seemed to be intelligent.

Star-Glider had seen the pictures of the aliens when they first appeared on holovid. They were the ugliest things the cheela had seen since humans. The novelty had worn off quickly, however. Star-Glider hadn't heard much about the aliens since and hoped he could learn more at the briefing. He turned the command of the space station over to his first officer, Horizon-Sensor, and made his way along the many centimeters of corridor to the meeting room on the opposite side of his spherically shaped command ship.

When he entered the large, bowl-shaped meeting room, he found it already crowded. Using his undertread to hold onto the slide-stops built into the sloping ramp, he moved down to the high-gravity region near the center of the room. He was nearly a centimeter closer to the miniature black hole at the center of the space station and it felt good to get under a little gravity again, even though it was nowhere near that of the 67 billion gravities of Egg.

Three dozen taste screens were built into the central portion of the meeting room deck. He made his way toward them, his six-pointed captain's badges parting the crowds before him. Normally, his status would have reserved one of the taste screens for him, but since there were 24 scientists and crew members assigned to the exploration ark to be briefed, the four members of the scout ship that had discovered the aliens, and the Deep Space Exploration scientists and managers, he had to content himself with watching one of the intensity-only visual screens built into the low walls of the meeting room. As he settled himself down to wait for the briefing to start, he found he was next to another Space Force captain. Though she was very young-looking to be a captain, she was huge in size, full of vitality, good-looking, and proved to be quick-witted when she switched an eye from the cheela with whom she had been talking. Instantly realizing who he was, she moved her eyes around to his side and lifted her near tread edge to talk.

"Captain Star-Glider?" she said. "I'm Captain Far-Ranger of the interstellar scout ship Triton." She flicked half her eyes toward her companion. "And this is Lieutenant Star-Finder, our navigator. We both have enjoyed your hospitality these past few turns."

"If I had known you were aboard, Captain, I would have invited you to dinner," he replied. "Unfortunately, this station is so large that often I don't even know how many spaceships we have docked, much less how many visitors are on board. I find your aliens very interesting and would like to learn more about them."

"They are just ugly savages," Far-Ranger said, "as you will see from the briefing. But they have some real potential if we can set up communication with them. If you are really interested, perhaps we can get together over a meal after the exploration ark leaves. I took a well deserved leave of a half-great of turns when I returned and I still have a few dozen turns to go.''

"You are my guest, then," said Star-Glider quickly. "Let's make it at turnfeast on Turn 104." Remembering his manners, he nodded three of his eyes toward Star-Finder. "You are welcome, too, Lieutenant."

"Thank you, Captain," she said. "But I am navigating the exploration ark back to the star. Besides, I am sure you and Captain Far-Ranger will have plenty to talk about."

Star-Glider *'trummed* a polite regret. The briefing had started, and all eyes were focused toward the bottom of the bowl as the strong waves from the tread amplifier at the central speaker's pad rippled through the deck. Star-Glider had to look over the topside of Far-Ranger to see the speaker. A few of his eyes glanced down at her deep red topside, then his gaze wandered to take in her full, fleshy eyelids.

One of her near eyes caught him looking at her anatomy. Instead of glaring him down as he expected, the eye slowly and deliberately dipped down between its eyelids and back out again in a long sexy wink. Star-Glider felt his eye-stalks stiffen as he returned his attention to the speaker.

"We will now have a briefing on the alien life forms found on the star by Captain Far-Ranger, Doctor of Alienology," the speaker announced. Star-Glider was impressed when he heard her second title. "You are welcome to use my taste screen," she said as she started to move through the crowd to the center. He whispered an electronic "Thanks," then moved onto the glowing patch in the deck where her undertread had been. The taste screen came to life under his tread as her amplified voice boomed out through the deck.

"When we first arrived at NS 1566 + 74, we did a mapping of the entire surface. We found no obvious artifacts, but an artificial intelligence search routine programmed with an alien artifact interest operator drew our attention to one of the magnetic poles." A picture flashed on the viewscreen showing an enlarged picture of a low chain of mountains with a small cluster of hexagonal markings at the base.

"This is a small village, with individual compounds shaped like clusters of crude hexagons. We were able to get some close-ups with our high resolution scanning array infrared antenna." An artificial-looking picture showed up on the screen.

"The picture is presented in false colors, since we are looking in the infrared portion of the spectrum instead of the soft X-ray visible portion. The moving objects are blurred by the scanning process, but it is obvious that each compound is inhabited by one or two larger aliens, while the central hexagon in each 'family' grouping contains smaller aliens with an occasional larger one. Outside the compounds are low pens that contain large numbers of very small creatures.

"Once we knew where we could get pictures, we sent in a skimmer orbiter with an X-ray camera and a motion compensator. Despite the mountains nearby, we were able to set the periapsis of the skimmer within less than a meter of the surface and got some excellent pictures of the aliens."

A disgusting-looking blob filled the screen. It looked like a Flow Slow in the process of being butchered. The basic body shape was a treadless, eyeless, flattened blob like a Flow Slow, but stripped of its protective plates. Where the plates would have been were ragged sheets of reddish flesh. Into opposite sides of the body, about halfway up, there were stuck two long sticklike objects with

knobs on the ends. The sticks had a joint at the middle
and were slightly bent like the skinny sticklike arms and
legs of the humans. From around the place where the stick
emerged from the blob, there came a large number of long,
wiggly tendrils. The screen flickered, and the image
changed slightly.

"We were able to get five successive pictures as the
skimmer orbited over this individual, so we can recreate
a crude display of motion." The five pictures were played
rapidly on the screen, and the sequence repeated a number of times. The being was rolling along the crust with
the knobbed armlike things sticking out to the sides and
the tendrils pushing and pulling at the crust to move it
along. The ragged flaps of flesh changed color as they
rotated up, over, around, and under the rolling body of
the alien.

"You will notice that the sticks become darker the further they are from the body, leaving the knob at the end
quite dark red. The knobs are moved backward and forward to cover the regions in front and behind the alien,
but they are never used to touch the ground, so they don't
seem to be for propulsion. Here is a close-up of one of
the knobs. It seems to be a sphere with many tiny hexagonal facets. We believe the knobs are their eyes. They
seem to be similar in structure to the eyes of bees or flies
on the human planet Earth. The stick must be a special
bonelike material with high strength but low heat con-
duction to keep the eyes cool."

There were a number of other pictures, including a
unique one showing two of the aliens side-by-side, grasp-
ing each other with their tendrils, their eye-sticks seemingly buried in each other's body.

"We are not positive what is going on here," said Far-
Ranger. "However, if you are thinking what I think you
are thinking, you are probably right."

There was a rumble in the deck, and someone remarked through the laughter, "I guess if you do it with only one eye at a time, you get more deeply involved. . . ."

"The most amazing feature of this alien culture is that there is no plant life. All the creatures seem to be animals."

"Then what is the base of the food chain?" someone asked.

"It took a long time for us to find out, but one of the clues is that there are only two regions where life is found. They are the two magnetic poles. I can't call them the East and West Poles as we do here on Egg, because they are quite close to the spin poles. The star has a lot of material left around it from the original supernova explosion, and there is a constant infall of expanded, neutron-poor, planetary-type material at each pole. In fact, there is so much that I didn't dare risk our scout-ship in flights over those polar regions. The mountain passes are full of tiny eyeless ball-like animals that probably absorb this neutron-poor dust from the surface of the crust and extract energy to live and grow from the process of converting it into normal crustal material. The larger balls are selected out by the intelligent aliens and herded into pens until they are eaten for food. The aliens are evidently still in the hunting-gathering stage of savagery, except that with no plant life, hunting and gathering are synonymous."

Another picture flashed on the screen. It was the carcass of one of the aliens, surrounded by hundreds of tiny carcasses. All had obviously been seared by a super-hot flash of hard gamma rays from the infall of a large chunk of matter onto the star. "It seems that being the one chosen to herd in the food supply can be dangerous. I think that one of the ways we can help these aliens is to keep a watch on the larger incoming chunks and warn them

away from the mountains during the time they are falling.
That should cut their gathering losses. Also, we might be
able to stabilize the amount of infall so they have a constant supply of food. Once we have secured their food
supply, then maybe they will have the leisure time to talk
to us and develop their culture."

Three turns later, it was time for the expedition to
leave. Star-Glider and Far-Ranger said goodbye to Lieutenant Star-Finder, then watched as the interstellar exploration ark, Amalita Shakhashiri Drake, pulled a few
meters away for safety. They couldn't feel the humming
as the spinor warp drive on the ark was activated, but
they could see a segment of the black, starry sky start to
warp as the space between Dragon's Egg and a point some
100 light-years away was nullified. A large red marker star
zoomed in from the distance, so close they could see the
cloudy patches on it. Then the spinor drive reinserted the
nullified space, but this time on the other side of the ark.
The Amalita and the red star zoomed back into the heavens together.

"A hundred light-years in the time it takes to move a
single tread length," said Star-Glider.

"All you need to do is shrink the hundred light-years
until it is but a tread-length long," Far-Ranger said.
"Bright's Oath, my pouch is dry. How about some juice
before turnfeast?"

"Good idea," Star-Glider said. "I have a few bags of
West Pole Double-Distilled in my locker at my quarters."

"Great!" she said, her nearest eye giving him a long,
slow, wink. "You spread the field lines and I'll follow
along behind."

He lead the way to his cabin, the moving bulk of his
conducting body spreading the weak magnetic field lines
stringing through the space-station plates. They were no-

where near as strong as the trillion-gauss fields on Egg so there was no need for him to act as pathbreaker, but he didn't mind having her snuggled up to his trailing edge. As they moved down the roofless corridor, a few of his eyes looked up into the sky to watch the formation of six asteroids pass over once again. Around each glowing mass were tiny specks that glared periodically. They were the herder rockets that kept the condensed asteroids in their proper position around Dragon Slayer. If these ever failed, the humans would be torn apart by the ferocious tides of Egg. He suddenly stopped and all his eyes turned upward.

"What is the matter?" Far-Ranger asked.

"The pattern is wrong," Star-Glider replied. "The pulses are coming at the wrong times. Something has happened to the Eyes of Bright!" For a blink he panicked at the thought of those large objects falling *down* on him. Then reason reminded him they were in orbit. They wouldn't fall, but something was definitely wrong. He flowed around Far-Ranger and headed back up the corridor to the command deck at full tread-ripple.

"The humans are in trouble!" he said. "Follow me!"

Danger

Outside Dragon Slayer, the six dense compensator masses circled, nudged this way and that by the powerful herder rockets. The rockets could not be allowed to get too close to the destructive tides of the ultra-dense masses, so each rocket pushed at a distance using the magnetic fields generated by a collection of magnetic monopoles in its bulbous nose. As each compensator mass reached one side of the ring, a yellow flare of a jet could be seen from a herder rocket, adjusting the orbit of the mass to keep it in its proper path. As the compensator mass came around to the other side of the ring, the opposite herder rocket would fire, pushing the dense asteroid back the other way. The scene repeated thirty times each second, once every two dothturns to the watchers on Egg below.

A jet on one of the herder rockets faltered as a meteorite tore through the fuel feed section, taking out two of the three triply-redundant fuel valves and damaging the third. A fifth of a second later the jet functioned correctly, but the next time it sputtered once again. The compensator mass that the herder rocket was supposed to control started to wander out of its place in the ring. Soon all the masses were wavering slightly as their rockets tried to maintain some semblance of order.

25

"Emergency!!" Dragon Slayer's computer sounded the alarm through the loudspeakers. "A meteorite has damaged one of the herder rockets!"

Amalita was returning from checking the upper tank when the strong gravity tides of the neutron star grabbed her and pulled her back down the passageway where she collided with Jean, who was putting on her suit. The next fraction of a second the two women were separated and jerked toward the outer wall of their spherical spacecraft.

Amalita grabbed a stanchion and held on. "What's the matter?" she yelled at Pierre. Pierre cinched up the belt on his console chair and activated his console.

"A rocket has malfunctioned," he said.

Jean, floating free near Pierre, was slammed again into the outer wall, then flew inward toward the center of the ship, where she held onto the back of a chair. The next part of the cycle her legs were pulled outward again as if she were on a rapidly spinning merry-go-round.

"Can you fix it?" Pierre asked the computer.

"No. The stress crack in the remaining fuel valve is growing," the computer reported. "You have a maximum of five minutes."

"We'll be torn apart by the tides," Jean screamed as the forces pushed and pulled on her body. They became stronger, ripped her from her precarious handhold and slammed her unconscious against the outer wall. At the next cycle, her limp body came flying inward again.

"Got her!" said Amalita, moving quickly from one handhold to another in the lulls between the forces.

"Put her in an acceleration tank!" Pierre hollered. Meanwhile, Doc Wong had made his way around the central column and helped Amalita open one of the circular hatches in the wall. They stuffed Jean into the spherical tank. Jean roused a little as they were putting her in, and Doc managed to get her mask on before they shut the door.

"Air OK?" Doc hollered over the intercom. The figure inside gave a dazed nod, and Doc noted her chest expand in a deep breath. He activated the tank and water droplets splashed over the porthole as the soothing liquid covered the bruised body.

The cheela communication console lit up. The robotic cheela, Sky-Teacher, was back on the screen. Flitting about him in the background, blurred images of live cheela were busily responding to the catastrophe.

"A rocket is failing," Sky-Teacher said. "Are you in danger?"

Pierre spoke quickly to the robotic image as the gravitational forces jerked him about in his harness.

"We've had it," he said. "I'm afraid you'll have to retransmit that last HoloMem directly to St. George. . . . Goodbye."

Pierre noticed a hesitation in Sky-Teacher's response and stopped. He could see a clustering of live cheela bodies to one side of the robot. The eyes and tendrils on that side of the robotic body accelerated into a blur as Sky-Teacher talked to the live cheela at near-normal cheela speeds. A fraction of a second later, the hesitation in Sky-Teacher's eye wave pattern was replaced by its normal rhythm.

"*WAIT!*" Sky-Teacher cried. "We will rescue you!"

"In five minutes?" Pierre shook his head. "Impossible!" Timing the gravity strains, he dove down to the library console to change the rate for data transfer to emergency mode.

06:51:05 TUESDAY 21 JUNE 2050

The young post-doctoral student swayed back and forth as the senior engineer put the final touches on the machine. Although he had gotten his doctorate in tempology and was not a bad engineer himself, Time-Circle knew that making a magnetized and electrified black hole this big was not something to be left to mere scientists. Fortunately, his grant from the Basic Science Foundation had been large enough so he could afford to hire the best engineer on Egg, Cliff-Web.

Engineer Cliff-Web was not afraid to take on "impossible" projects. After stretching his tread as Assistant to the Chief Engineer on one of the first jump loops, he had taken on the design of the first space fountain. Cliff-Web had designed a tower 200 times taller than the diameter of Egg, and not only showed how to build it, but proved that it would make money if it were built. He sold the idea, formed the team, and then went on to other "impossible" engineering projects. Time-Circle had been lucky to have gotten Cliff-Web for his project. But then, he doubted that any other project could have been more challenging and more "impossible" than this one—building a time machine.

It had been almost two human minutes since the time machine project had started. For his doctoral thesis, Time-Circle had proven the feasibility of time travel by sending signals through time. As a result, he had received his Doctorate of Tempology and had been allowed to choose a new name for himself.

His first time machine had only two time communication channels. He had modified a normal black-hole generator so that it used a mixture of protons and magnetic monopoles with high speed and high relative angular momentum. By making the black hole out of both magnetically and electrically charged matter, he had been able to make the rapidly spinning prolate mass open up its event horizon at spin speeds less than 99% of the speed of light. The resultant black hole lasted less than a seth-turn, but by careful timing, Time-Circle had sent a gamma-ray pulse forward in time through one channel and backward in time through another channel before the black hole popped into a tiny blast of radiation.

The Time-Comm machine Engineer Cliff-Web was now building for him would be permanent and could send signals backward or forward to any time where the machine was in existence or until all eight communication channels were filled with messages. It would be a long time before anyone, even the rapidly advancing cheela, could make a time machine that allowed physical travel of living beings, but even a time-traveling message machine like Time-Comm could be useful.

Now, it was finally completed. The construction crew had been sent off to their personal compounds for a well deserved rest, while their robot partners were being re-programmed for their next job as part of Cliff-Web's growing construction empire. Cliff-Web remained to check out the device and make the final adjustments.

Finally satisfied with the results, Cliff-Web slid to one side of the combined touch-and-taste screen.

"It works," he muttered quietly.

"Good," said Time-Circle. "Let me check it out. Hmmm. This is an historic moment, what message shall I use? It has to be short, but it should be significant. I've got it!" His tread moved over the screen as he set up the message.

"*Turn back, O Time*," Cliff-Web muttered. . . . "I read it on the detection screen just as I tweaked the last parameter."

"That is what I just sent!" said Time-Circle. "It works! It works!!"

"I already said that," Cliff-Web reminded him as he pouched his tools and measuring instruments. The gravity wave detector was long and massive, but folded up into a package that fitted nicely into the big pouch in his body that he had developed for instrument transport. At the very last he went over to the corner and picked up the plant that had been sitting there. It was his trademark, pet, and closest companion—a cleft-wort plant. Checking the plant over carefully, Cliff-Web put it into another pouch in his cavernous body.

"You've plugged up the past of one of your four back-time channels," he warned as he left.

Time-Circle wasn't listening. He was preparing a message to himself at the dedication ceremonies for the Time-Comm machine some three turns into the future. As he was sending it, a confirmation message came from his future self.

He had arranged for it to use the same back-time channel that he had used for his test message. His future self reported that the message had been received at the dedication ceremony, and only two sethturns early. The wave pattern of Time-Circle's eye-stubs slowed as he made adjustments to the time-interval circuits. The message utilization code tacked onto the end of the confirmation message indicated that the message was within a few bits of the maximum that could be sent over that distance in time. Time-Circle had the computer make a scroll copy of the coded message so he could later calculate the exact bit-time product, but it looked as if it were close to what his theory had predicted—864 bit-greats. That meant that he could send a message 864 bits long over a time interval of one great of turns, or a one-bit message over 864 greats. Time quantization statistics would cause variations, of course, and one of his research tasks with the machine was to determine those statistical variations.

He didn't want to fill up any more channels with messages until he had done some calculations, so he put a password lock on the touch-and-taste screen, which turned into a blank silver patch in the yellow-white floor as he headed for the door.

The walls around the Time-Comm laboratory were extra high, and thus very thick at the base. As his tread approached the door, a sensor pattern in the floor read the wrinkles in his tread and the inner door slid open. He entered the security port in the base of the wall and felt his body stiffen as a magnetic field penetrated his body and generated a magnetic susceptibility map to compare with the stored version.

"You are carrying a scroll out that you did not have when you came in," a mechanical sounding voice vibrated through his tread.

"It's the instruction manual for the operation of the Time-Comm machine," Time-Circle explained. "I'm going to read it at home."

"Accepted," replied the machine. The magnetic field disappeared, and the outer door opened. Before Time-Circle left, he set the intruder barriers. He couldn't see the barriers, but the top of the tall wall now bristled with alternating north and south magnetic poles. The fields were so strong and the gradients so high that it would take forever to push anything through them to get over the wall. The field strength near the center of the barrier was strong enough to elongate the cells in a living organism until they didn't function properly. He had been told it felt as if you were putting a tendril into the purple-hot flame of a gamma-ray flare. He noticed the fading track of Cliff-Web that indicated he had pushed off down the slanting corridors to the north-east. Time-Circle moved in the opposite direction and headed Bright-west for the Administrative Compound of the Inner Eye Institute to arrange for the dedication ceremonies.

Cliff-Web felt quietly pleased with himself. First the Space Fountain (he could see the tiny spike of light grow-

ing up into the sky over the wall at the end of the long
north-east corridor), now the Time-Comm machine. The
time machine was finished so far ahead of schedule that
the formal turn-on ceremonies were still scheduled for
three turns from now. He wasn't sure whether he would
bother going to them. He hated to have people tell him
how wonderful he was. It made his eye-stubs squirm just
thinking about it. He was anxious to get home to his holovid and his plants. He then remembered his cleft-wort
that he had pouched when he left. He stopped and, forming a manipulator, reached into his pouch and pulled out
the plant.

"There, there, Pretty-Web," he said. "You getting too
warm?" He held the plant up to his eyes and looked it
over carefully. It *was* too warm. It was almost the same
yellow-white on the top as it was on the bottom, and it
was drooping a little between the acute angle of the artificial cleft that took the place of the natural rock clefts
in the mountains where the cleft-wort normally grew.

Now that the plant was out in the open where it could
see the dark blackness of the starry sky, the top surface
cooled off and turned a velvety red-black, while the underside turned a reflective silver. Cliff-Web lifted the
plant up to his own deep red topside and put the base of
the holder into a pouch he formed on his topside. He directed his body to heat the pouch; and the plant, with its
roots in a source of heat and its topside cooled by the
black sky, started to regain its normal circulation and
perked up. The tension threads that wove back and forth
from one side of the cleft to the other tightened, and the
topside corrugations grew more wrinkled, increasing the
emissivity of the top surface. Tiny threads of red light
started at random in the black-red top, and wended their
way down the feeder veins to the dull red stem leading
to the yellow-white base. It was a pretty moving display.

Cliff-Web could almost feel the hum of the plant as it worked to make food.

Relaxed and happy with himself and his plant, Cliff-Web didn't hurry as he pushed his way north-east. Using the walls of the compounds along the street as a levering wedge, he pushed his body through the magnetic field lines that tried to prevent his northward motion.

For a while he moved through the slumlike area of Old Town that surrounded the sprawling grounds of the Inner Eye Institute. Most of the compounds here had their window slides closed, so there wasn't much to see except wall. The intersections were irregular and he found he had gone too far east before he realized he should have taken a north-west tack back a few intersections. The north-west street he had available now was 60 degrees north of east instead of the nominal 30 degrees. Grunting with annoyance at himself, he pushed his way across the intersection, found the south wall of the street and pushed north-west, this time more north than west. A robotic glide-car for hire passed in the sparse traffic and he was tempted to wave it down, but it was going in the wrong direction, and besides, he could use the exercise.

As Old Town changed to the suburbs of Bright's Heaven, the street pattern became more regular. The main thoroughfares ran straight east and west, with the side-pairs of streets angled off at exactly 30 degrees north from east in crisscrossing patterns that formed diamond and triangular blocks. The personal compounds were built right up to the walkway, and the walls had been coated with frictionless tile to allow for rapid motion of pedestrian traffic north and south. Most of the compounds now had their window slides back so Cliff-Web could look into the outer courtyards.

He stopped to admire the plant arrangement in one fence-port. Someone had taken a normal, triangular window opening and had inserted cleft-brackets between alternate courses of bricks, making an ascending staircase of cleft-brackets. A single heavy stem came up from the crust, divided into two branches that went up the sides of the triangular notch, then spread its web over one cleft support after another. Being staggered, each web of the multi-webbed plant was able to see the dark sky and thrive. The top two clefts in the arrangement were not yet webbed, but he could see the little tendrils being trained to make the next step. Surrounding the growing tips were little boxes. He couldn't figure out what they were. He was impressed with the display. As he moved over the nameplate embedded in the walkway in front of the door, he took note of the name. D. M. Zero-Gauss, 2412 North-West 7th Street. Must be a professor at the Institute. He would have to arrange a visit to discuss gardening some turn.

Cliff-Web didn't miss the proper intersection now that he was back again in familiar territory. He tacked northwest past his compound, still a number of diamonds to the north, made the sharp turn to the north-east onto his own street, and headed for home. His compound was one of the largest in the neighborhood. It took up a whole diamond to itself. After he had earned the huge incentive bonus for coming in way under the target cost for the design of the Space Fountain, he had enough stars to his credit that he bought out his neighbors, tore down the walls between the four plots, and expanded his old personal compound. One of his neighbor's compounds had been turned into a workroom, another into a potting yard and heatbed for new sprouts, and the third into quarters for his pets. He whispered a happy electronic whistle into the crust as he approached his compound. Happy noises echoed back.

He was first greeted by Chilly, the genetically miniaturized hybrid Swift. Chilly had slithered up to the top of the compound fence, its tail wrapped around the street-sign post built into the corner, and greeted him with up and down bows of its head. The five sharp-pointed teeth would spring out to show a glowing white maw, then draw back in again as it swallowed. Chilly took a swipe at the cleft-wort plant Cliff-Web was carrying on his back, but Cliff-Web diverted the animal by sticking a manipulator down its gullet. Chilly's razor-sharp teeth, which could have amputated the end of his manipulator in one bite, just scraped the skin slightly and continued to mouth the manipulator as he pulled it free. Cliff-Web paused to let Chilly slide onto his topside and reached through the fence window to pat a few friendly bodies on the other side. He reached his doorway, pulled out his magnekey, unlocked the fence-door, and slid it into the wall. He was immediately surrounded by three Slinks, a half-dozen Slinklings, and Cold, Chilly's mate.

After he said hello to all the Slinks, they took off on their various Slinkish activities, and he had time to look around for Rollo. The ball-like animal was cowering in a corner behind its large, slow-moving cousin, Slurge, a miniaturized Flow Slow. Slurge had gotten into the parasol bed. He would have to speak with his caretaker, Moving-Sand, about that.

"Come here, Rollo," he called, holding out a waving tendril. "Come, Rollo. Come here."

Slowly the ball rolled out from behind the Flow Slow, its multitude of eyes drawn by the waving tendril. Finally it moved close enough for the tendril to stroke it. It rumbled in pleasure, ducking its eyes out of the way of the moving tendril.

"There, there, Rollo," he said. "No need to be afraid. The noisy Slinks are all gone now." The pet, now more relaxed, rolled around his periphery, enjoying caresses from one tendril after another. Just then Moving-Sand flowed into view around the corner.

"I knew it must be you when I heard the commotion. Those Slinks must have vibrated the whole neighborhood by now." Suddenly he noticed the Flow Slow in the parasol bed.

"Hey!" said Moving-Sand. "What do you mean letting Slurge get into the plants! How am I going to keep things in shape here if you don't help?"

Forming a heavy, clublike manipulator, Moving-Sand flowed over to the heavy creature that was soaking up plant juices through its lower tread, and banged it hard on one side.

"Move, you big hunk of flabby rock," Moving-Sand hollered through the crust.

Shrinking as much from the shrill cry on its underside as from the heavy blows on its armored topside, the miniaturized Flow Slow moved off the patch of parasol flowers and back onto the lawn it had been trained to keep in check.

Moving-Sand gave it a few more blows to keep it moving. "Your mail is in your study and your meal is in the oven," Moving-Sand said. "Get it yourself. I've still got a dozen more fountain-shoots to transplant."

"How are the fountain plants doing?" asked Cliff-Web.

"The ones that survived are doing fine," Moving-Sand reported. "They would do better if you had left them back at the East Pole where you found them, where the magnetic field goes straight up and down. I found if I started from seed, picked those with a tilted firing tube and lopsided catcher, and planted them pointing in the proper direction, I could get them to grow. Don't ever expect them to get too large, though. Nope. The catcher would get so lopsided they'd topple over. Got one planted right over there.'' Moving-Sand's eye-stubs twitched to a circular patch of parasol flowers, in the center of which was a tiny fountain of blue-white sparks.

The fountain plant was a highly energetic form of plant life that worked at intense rates just to stay alive. Biologists at the Inner Eye Institute still argued over whether it should be classified as a plant or an animal, since it could only live in highly rich, neutron-poor soil like that found in the East and West Pole mountains.

The central core of the fountain plant was a long thin tube. Its extensive root system pulled in the nutrients and burned them at a terrific rate. The blue-hot temperatures inside were transferred to seedlike particles that were shot up the tube into the sky in a shower of tiny blue-white specks. The specks cooled by radiation and were only dull red by the time they were gathered in by the cup-shaped collector at the base of the plant to be recycled again. Each gamma-ray photon emitted during the short-lived trajectory moved the nuclear equivalent of the photosynthesis cycle one more notch along on the way to make an energized molecule that could be used by the plant to grow.

The fountain plants Cliff-Web had seen in the East Pole mountains often lived less than a turn. They would start from seed in a promising mound of dust, would sparkle for a few dothturns, getting visibly bigger as time went on, then as the nutrient wore out, the firing stalk would start to shoot out larger seed particles. In the last few methturns, the dying stalk would start to wobble while the ejection velocity increased, and the seeds would be shot over a region many centimeters on a side. If they landed on a promising mound of neutron-poor material, the process would start again. Otherwise the seeds would wait until ground tremors or animal motion moved them to the right place.

Cliff-Web had hoped that by supplying adequate amounts of nutrients he could keep them running for many turns at a time. These plants were not designed for a long life, however, and seemed to give up after a half-dozen turns. They were a real delight when sparking, so he just enjoyed the sight for a few methturns, then went across the outer courtyard to his study room in the inner compound.

As he entered the study, Lassie moved off its pad near the wall that backed up to the oven in the next room. The aging Slink moved erratically as it came to greet its master. The Slink was so old it had lost most of its long hair. Cliff-Web was bemused at how much the hairless Slink looked like a wrinkled cheela hatchling. The close resemblance of the two species was probably why the slinks were the favorite pets of the cheela. Practically every cheela kept one, and the latest trend was to name the animals after hairy, four-legged human pets such as Lassie, Trigger, Peter, Bossy, and Tabby.

Cliff-Web went to his work station, and the silver touch-and-taste screen activated as soon as his tread moved onto it. As a major engineering contractor, Cliff-Web had the latest in intelligent terminals. He read his computer net messages, dictated some replies to his roborespondor program, arranged for the final billing for the Time-Comm machine, then turned to his scroll delivery. He had been gone for a long time, and even though computer messages had replaced most personal message delivery services, there still were a large number of message scrolls in his scroll wall.

Made of strong, crisscrossing plates built into the wall of his study, the scroll wall held those documents that were either too important or too bureaucratic to trust to the computer net message service. Suspecting what it was, Cliff-Web reached for the largest scroll and pulled it from its diamond-shaped hole in the wall. A glance at the outside showed he had guessed right. It was the formal request for plans for the design of the inertia drive engine to replace the failing rocket in the asteroid protecting the humans. Strengthening his manipulator bone to compensate for the weight of the multi-foiled document, he lowered it carefully to the floor where the springy metal foils distorted into an ellipsoidal shape, just waiting for the flick of a tendril to flatten out at the desired sheet. Although there was a copy for him to look at in his message files, Cliff-Web still liked to stare at the crust when he was thinking, so he formed a tendril and, poking it in the central hole of the scroll, pushed down.

The slight bit of pressure added to the strong gravitational field of Egg caused the metal foil to flatten out, revealing the top page. It was the Request For Plan for the giant inertia drive. Cliff-Web scanned the first page and didn't like what he saw.

"May Bright set!" he swore. "It's been over two greats of turns since we promised the humans we would rescue them. I thought the Slow One Interaction Laboratory would have done more by now! This Request For Plan is only for a preliminary design effort. They should have done that study in-compound a great of turns ago."

Having stared down at many such documents in his career, he inserted another tendril about two-thirds of the way through the stack. The "flow-plate" foils that the bureaucracy had inserted between the cover sheet and the meat of the document rolled up again into a tight ellipse. He let a few more pages roll up, back-rolled one page, then cursed again.

"Suck a Flow Slow! They only budgeted 144 great-stars for this contract! They must be expecting us to add eggs to their pen."

He let a few more pages roll up until he got to the listing of the work items required. He didn't curse this time, because he had seen the same thing happen too many times before.

"... and the only difference between this 'preliminary' design effort and a 'full' design effort is that we don't have to submit firm price quotes as part of the final report." He moved his tendril and let the pages roll up quickly one after another as he scanned them. His eye-wave motion slowed and his tread *trummed* nervously as his brain-knot thought of an alternate approach to the problem.

"That might work," he said to himself. He let the scroll roll up and put it back into the scroll wall as he moved onto his touch-and-taste communicator. He was about to set up a conference call to some of his chief engineers out in the field when a slow *gonging* sound penetrated the crust. His pendulum clock was marking the end of the turn with the slow tolling of the twelfth dothturn. He checked his nuclear chronometer—the ancient pendulum clock was still keeping perfect time despite the large crust-quake a few turns ago. No use calling anyone now. Everyone on Egg was settling down to their main meal of the turn. He would get something to eat himself and make the call at dothturn one.

Lassie followed him to the meal room as he left the study. Lassie may have been old, but she wasn't dumb; it would be her mealtime too. Moving-Sand had prepared a good turnfeast. A small pan with a loaf of ground eye-anchor and spices surrounded by a dozen small parasol root-nodes was warming in the oven. He lifted the lid of the cooler built into the meal-room floor and found a fresh salad of petal-leaves with hot sauce made from crushed North Pole stinger-fronds. He also extracted a cooled bag of singleberry wine. It was from the north slopes of the Exodus Volcano and was supposedly one of the best.

He was busy thinking about the new project and normally would have just dumped the contents of the food
plates into an eating pouch and gone back to his study,
but this turn he decided to stay in the meal room and enjoy
the excellent turnfeast. He put the plates on the temper-
ature-controlled segments in the floor next to his eating
pad and settled his large body down. He moved two of
his eating pouches around until they were next to each
other and in front of the two dishes. A manipulator held
the bag of singleberry wine above both pouches and
squirted streams into one or the other as the taste called
for.

The eye-anchor loaf was superb. There were still a few
excellent flank slabs in the freezer that were even better,
but he was glad that Moving-Sand had settled for the
cheaper cut, since he would rather have the slabs when
he had company. After all, it wasn't often that one had
prime cheela meat for turnfeast.

He was fortunate that he still had most of his bonus left
when the carcass went on sale, otherwise Fountain-Petal
would have been eaten by non-clanners. She had been
killed in a terrible glide-car accident caused during a crustquake. All dead cheela carcasses belonged to their clan
and were sold at auction to augment the clan tributes that
were used to cover the expenses of raising the clan hatchlings. Since, on the average, there was only one cheela
carcass per lifetime for every cheela, even the tough,
stringy meat of an Ancient One was more expensive than
the best animal meat. Only a rich person could afford to
buy more than one eye-segment of the typical carcass.
The meat of an accident victim in her prime was nearly
priceless to the indolent wealthy who seemed to spring
up in modern affluent societies. Cliff-Web brought honor
back to his clan when he outbid a combine of feast pad
operators for all twelve eye segments of Fountain-Petal.

The clan tribute was lowered by a dozeth for a great after the sale.

The bag of wine was dry, the platter of ground eye-anchor muscle was empty, and Cliff-Web was poking at the remains of his hot-cold salad when the crust vibrated with the complex melody of the half-dothturn chime. It was still too early to set up a conference call to his engineering team, so he let Lassie suck at his dishes, then moved slowly into the entertainment room. He didn't want entertainment, however; he wanted news—news about the humans and their predicament. He wanted to see what the average cheela on Egg knew (or cared) about the precarious predicament of the Slow Ones above them.

He turned on the holovid and focused his eyes on the empty space between him and the silver screen covering the floor and two walls of the corner of the room. A scene appeared, floating in space. It was a new prophet, treading the ancient phrases of Pink-Eyes, the First Prophet, promising sexual ecstasy to all. Cliff-Web vibrated his eye-stubs in annoyance at this additional example of a degenerating modern society. Already there were some modern males who were renouncing their clans to avoid the tribute needed to raise the hatchlings. After all, they didn't generate eggs that needed hatching and raising. The next thing you knew, female cheela would be aborting their eggs because they got "tired of carrying them." They should be thankful they weren't human females who had to take care of their offspring after they were hatched.

Cliff-Web had a modern holovid set with full computer accessories. The computer was not quite as intelligent as a robot, but nearly as good. It kept copies in its molecmem of all the programming that had passed through its 144 channels in the previous six turns and could retrieve older programs from its permanent memory.

"What news programs have mentioned the humans?" he asked.

"None in the past six turns," replied the computer. "There was a science news program on an educational channel 36 turns ago that mentioned that Sky-Teacher, the special purpose robot used for talking to the humans, had been deactivated for modernization and repairs since the human communicator Pierre Niven had left the communications console. Its place had been taken by an automaton, but Sky-Teacher would be back before the humans missed it. The broadcast was sponsored by the Slow One Patrons."

"The whole public and bureaucracy are Slow One Patrons," said Cliff-Web. "They treat the humans as if they were just another animal to protect. They say, 'The humans are *so* slow and *so* stupid, *we* have to take care of them.' Yet they *aren't* taking care of them! The humans are in danger, and we cheela are trying to save a few stars by delaying work and underestimating costs." He gave a muttered curse and moved off to his study. It was still two grethturns until dothturn one, but if he knew his chief engineers, they were already through with their turnfeasts and back at their consoles.

He activated a conference link and gathered his engineers together to prepare a response to the Request For Plan. Web Engineering would probably lose money on the contract, but that didn't bother Cliff-Web. The combined clans of Egg might not care much about the humans, but Web Engineering did.

06:51:19 GMT TUESDAY 21 JUNE 2050

Dr. Cesar Wong lifted his eyes from the porthole looking into Jean's protection tank and peered at the control board in the wall. The tell-tales indicated that three tanks were now occupied and that Jean, Abdul, and Seiko were temporarily safe from the rapidly varying tidal forces. Pierre was still in the library on the lower crew deck, but should be back soon to get into his tank. Cesar slowly made his way around the central column to his own tank, being careful not to lose control of his limbs to the tearing gravity forces. Amalita's tank was next to his, but she was not there and not in her tank. He looked around with concern. The main deck was empty.

"Amalita!" he called. There was no reply, but he heard sounds of heavy breathing coming down the passageway from the Science Deck. He started up the passageway rungs to see what was going on.

Normally, when the compensator masses were doing their job, the central portion of the Dragon Slayer was in nearly free fall. Only near the outer walls did the gravity field become large enough to give a sense of up and down. Now, however, the compensation was way off, and the gravity forces on the upper and lower decks were substantial. The average field was nearly two Earth gravities and slowly getting stronger, while the variations around that average sometimes exceeded two gravities for a millisecond or so. The variations did not act long enough to build up large velocities, but they made it difficult to navigate the rungs. He turned around so that the gravity was pulling him "down" the ladder to the "upper" Science Deck and climbed down to stand next to Amalita, who was sitting on the ceiling, trying to struggle into a spacesuit.

"I'm going to repair the herder rocket by replacing the valve with a redundant valve from another rocket," she panted.

"You'll be killed!" he said, his eyes growing wide with concern.

"We'll *all* be killed unless somebody fixes that rocket," she said. "I may not make it, but I'm going to give it a good try."

"I admire your bravery," said Dr. Wong. "But if you would only stop to think, you would realize that bravery is not going to be enough." He bent down and made her look at him.

"The herder rockets operate in the region halfway between us and the compensator masses, which are at 200 meters from the center of the ring," he said. His voice took on a commanding tone. "What is the magnitude of the tidal force at 100 meters from one of those masses?"

Doc Wong watched Amalita's eyes glaze over as the superfast colloid computer under the brown ponytail raced through the mental calculations.

"133 gees per meter," she said. Her eyes blinked as she returned to the task of putting on her helmet. "But it is compensated by the neutron star tides of 101 gees per meter. . . ."

"Leaving 32 gees per meter," said Doc. "The joints in the herder rockets are designed to stand those strains, but you'll have to admit that your joints can't."

As he took the helmet from her unresisting hands, a bright streak of light flashed across the star image table above them. The cheela Polar Orbiting Space Station had shot by them once again.

06:52:19 GMT TUESDAY 21 JUNE 2050

Captain Star-Glider was waiting at the docking port as the small jumpcraft maneuvered closer to the space station. It was carrying a two-star admiral, and custom demanded that the captain of the station be there to greet such an important visitor. He wasn't sure why the admiral was coming. It might be that he was on his way out into space, but Star-Glider was not aware of any imminent deep space launches. He suspected that the visit might involve him, since his tour of duty as station commander was about over and it was time for him to move on to a new command. While he waited, he allowed four of his eyes to watch the Six Eyes of Bright pass over, only a kilometer away. It was now over four greats of turns since the meteorite had struck the rocket and the compensator masses were now noticeably out of line. He idly wondered what the bureaucracy of the Combined Clans was doing about it, for he had heard nothing in the holovid news reports.

The jumpcraft docked smartly on a flat spot on the side of the spherical space station.

"Welcome to the Polar Orbiting Space Station, Admiral Milky-Way," Star-Glider said, his tendril brushing his six-pointed captain's star in salute. "What brings you so far from the warmth of Egg?"

"Well, I *could* say that I've come on a surprise inspection," the admiral answered. Then his tread rippled with laughter as he noticed the nervous twitch in Star-Glider's eye-stubs. "But actually I've come to see you about a private matter. Can we retire to your quarters?"

"Certainly." Star-Glider was slightly puzzled. Usually a change of command was made by a public announcement. He led the way down the corridors and they entered his quarters. He had left the holovid on and the viewblock contained a close-up of a single cheela eye. It was a cool, deep red and the eye-stub below it was thickening as it drew the eye down below the plumpest, sexiest eyeflap on Egg. The holocamera pulled back to show the rest of the female cheela as she continued her slow ripple across the stage, winking one eye after another as she sang the slightly risqué song, "Twine Thine Eyen About Mine."

Slightly embarrassed, Star-Glider moved over to the control patch to turn it off, but the admiral blocked his way with a tendril.

"Don't do that," he said. "Let her finish her song, it's one of my favorites." He moved over to a resting pad and flowed himself out to enjoy the show. Star-Glider perched on the other pad with half his eyes on the viewblock and half on the admiral. The song came to an end, and with it the show. Star-Glider moved out a portion of his tread and turned off the holovid.

"A perfectly delightful creature, that Qui-Qui," Milky-Way rumbled. "I find her an excellent antidote for egg-tending fever. Every time I see those twelve luscious eyeflaps, I feel like a hatchling again." He shuffled his tread a bit, then reached into a pouch and pulled out a message scroll. Instead of rolling it over to Star-Glider, he held onto it as he talked.

"As you probably realize, your tour of duty here is coming to an end. You have done an excellent job and could stay on here for another tour if you so desire, but you have been recommended for another position. It is not one of the normal command posts, but is a unique one-time mission that requires someone with your breadth of experience in large space operations. It will be an onerous post at times and will require a long-term commitment on your part. Longer than the usual four-great tour of duty. For those reasons, we are not just going to assign you to the post. Instead, I came up here to talk to you candidly about the positive and negative aspects of the position and give you an opportunity to turn it down."

"I don't mind committing myself to an extra-long duty tour, if it is the right kind of post," said Star-Glider. "But what is so onerous about the job?"

"You will be given full responsibility . . . but almost no authority," Milky-Way explained. "In fact, most of the work of the commander of this special mission will be to beg and plead and cajole to get enough authority to carry out the mission he has the responsibility to perform. In this case, by authority I mean money." He rolled the message scroll across the deck.

"It was over four greats of turns ago that a meteorite struck one of the rockets herding the Six Eyes of Bright and placed the humans in danger. At that time it was estimated that it would take about five human minutes or ten greats of turns before the circular formation of the Six Eyes became so deformed that the gravity tides would tear the Inner Eye spaceship apart. Shortly after that, even the isolation tanks would be unable to protect the humans.

"When the accident happened, the President of the Combined Clans made the commitment that the people of Egg would undertake a mission to restore the rocket and save the humans. But the initial public enthusiasm for the project rapidly wore off. It was a full two greats of turns before even a design study contract was issued—and *it* was inadequately funded. The Web Construction Company has completed the design effort and come up with a technically feasible approach. They tried to keep the costs down, but the mission is going to require a significant increase in the space budget and the Legislature of the Combined Clans are clenching their treads and procrastinating to avoid having to appropriate the funds."

Star-Glider pushed on the scroll and it flattened out on the deck. He lowered an eye to read it.

"A promotion to admiral!" he said.

"Yes. Six more points on your star if you take the job," said Milky-Way. "And I can almost guarantee another star if you can ride the Swift without getting eaten."

Star-Glider hesitated.

"You will earn every one of those six points if you take the job," said the admiral. "You will have to go on holovid shows and attend clan gatherings to regenerate public enthusiasm for the project. You will have to get to know most of the members of the Legislature of the Combined Clans and become so close to the members of the legislative sub-group on Space, Communications, and Slow One Interactions that they will think of you as a hatchling mate. Above all, despite provocation, you will have to keep calm, make no enemies, and never lose your temper. Can you do it? *Will* you do it?"

"Yes!" Star-Glider responded emphatically.

"Congratulations . . . Admiral," said Milky-Way. "I happen to have brought along some dozen-pointers with me." He fumbled through his pouches, then pulled out a board with a half-dozen stars on it. While Star-Glider remained motionless in the middle of the room, the admiral circled him, pulling six-pointed stars out of the holding sphincters in Star-Glider's body and inserting shiny new twelve-pointed stars. When he completed the circuit he asked, "Care to change your name, too?"

"No. I still like the one I chose after I graduated from the academy."

"Well then, Admiral Star-Glider," said Milky-Way. "Let's assemble your crew for an announcement."

Admiral Star-Glider turned over the command of the space station to First Officer Horizon-Sensor and returned with Milky-Way to the surface of Egg. He had been in orbit for over a great of turns and was looking forward to going to his clan gatherings again.

The pilot on the jumpcraft used a short burst of inertia drive to drop them out of their polar orbit. He timed the deorbit push so that their perigee occurred near the East Pole. As they approached the strong magnetic field region above the pole, stubby superconducting wings unfolded from the slender jumpcraft. Tilting the winged space-craft as it flew through the slippery magnetic field lines, the pilot transferred momentum to Egg through the East Pole fields and switched from a polar orbit to an equatorial orbit. There was no change in the jumpcraft's speed since the interaction with the magnetic field was essentially lossless. The maneuver took them within a hundred meters of the thin metal stalk of the Space Fountain. The tower was now fifty kilometers high and loomed above their trajectory. Star-Glider made sure he was on the top-side as the turn was made. The view was excellent. He could even see the small construction elevators moving up and down the lengthening shaft.

06:52:20 GMT TUESDAY 21 JUNE 2050

The young roustabout felt uneasy. Normally he wouldn't mind at all being squeezed in an elevator between two plump-lidded females. A little squeeze and tickle would help pass the dothturn-long drop to the surface. This time, however, one female was his gang-chief and the other was the shift supervisor. This was his first shift up on the Space Fountain since he had started his apprenticeship at Web Construction, and he was trying to make a good impression so they would let him have more high tower time.

The two supervisors talked shop under his tread, and he suffered in silence as he tried to find some place for his eyes to look that wasn't eyeflap or topside. Six of his eyes watched the three pairs of rapidly moving streams of superconducting rings shooting up through holes at the corners of the triangular-shaped elevator. The other six eyes stared out into space toward the distant horizon where he could see blotches and lines that were cities and roads leading westward toward Bright's Heaven.

A glowing speck swung around the tower a hundred meters away and shot off into the distance. It was probably a jumpcraft headed for the Jump Loop. The elevator came to a stop at the 60 kilometer platform. The platform was bare except for the deflector magnets surrounding each of the six pairs of ring streams. The upgoing elevator that rode the other three streams had just left the on-shift replacement, and they waited while the shift instructions were passed.

"Keep a few eyes on the deflector for stream three-up. It's getting warm, and Topside says they are getting too many pushouts," the off-shifter reported. "I sent down for a spare."

"Got it right here," said the on-shifter, pulling a bulky box from a cavernous workman's pouch. "I'll have it fixed in no time. Have fun in Swift's Climb."

"I expect to. See you in a dozturn."

Heavy-Egg knew about pushouts. That was his job on the Topside Platform. The six up-streams were scanned by some sort of detector when they came topside. Any rings that were bent or too hot got pushed aside into a rejection bin where they slammed into a magnetic stopper. You didn't want bad rings going into the turn-around magnets. They could cause a lot of problems. Heavy-Egg's job was to hook the ring out before the next one was rejected so they wouldn't bang into each other and get dented. The magnetic field in the stopper was so strong it would burn his skin if he left his manipulator in it too long. It was hot and noisy work, but he enjoyed it. Each of the rings he saved was worth more than he made each turn. They were made of monopole-stabilized metal, the only thing on Egg that didn't blow up in free fall. The last dozturn shift he figured he had saved Web Construction enough money to pay him for a whole great of turns, and he hadn't allowed one banger.

They reached the bottom of the tower and the off-shift crew shuffled off the elevator and headed for the chutes. Heavy-Egg stopped to feel the crust at the top of the East Pole mountains. It was humming with power from the constant stream of rings that were accelerated in long circular tunnels at the base of the mountain and shot upward in a fountain of metal.

Heavy-Egg flowed into the chute-car. This time he arranged it so that the female next to him wasn't his gang-chief. Her name was Glowing-Tread, and they became real friendly as the chute-car rocketed down the mountain passes in a semi-enclosed superconducting chute that kept the magnetic field out. They braked to a halt in the outskirts of Swift's Climb and headed for the nearest pulp-bar. The pulp-bar had some private pad rooms and some couples headed directly for them, dropping some stars in the bartender's cash pouch as they passed.

It was still a few methturns to turnfeast, so Heavy-Egg and Glowing-Tread treated each other to a few bags of fermented pulp from the petal-pod plants. They were into their third bag when Heavy-Egg's favorite holovid show came on. It was the "Qui-Qui Show," starring the sexiest female entertainer on Egg. The males whooped and stamped the crust in rhythm while the females made jokes about the shape of her eyeflaps.

"If she put all twelve eyes on one side, her tread would leave the crust," muttered Glowing-Tread, drawing a few laughs.

"My eye-balls say you have the same problem," said Heavy-Egg, making the first move. She turned all twelve eyes around to look at him, and his eye-stubs grew stiffer as she winked one after the other in a fairly good imitation of Qui-Qui's famous ripple-wink.

"Like this?" she said, leaning heavily on him and letting her fleshy eyeflaps rub against his topside edge. "It's a good thing you are there to lean on or I might topple over and bruise something."

They got real friendly again, and she even let him reach into her heritage pouch to feel her clan totem. However, the totem wasn't familiar—so she wasn't a member of one of the out-clan families related to his clan. She was willing to rent a pad-room and go further, but Heavy-Egg still felt a strong allegiance to his in-clan and its out-clan families. Any egg he might be responsible for must end up in his clan hatching pens. There were already too many clanless hatchlings on the streets.

Heavy-Egg parted reluctantly with Glowing-Tread. She found someone else and went off to turnfeast with him. Frustrated, Heavy-Egg invested a few stars in a private holovid screen room and watched the rest of the Qui-Qui Show.

Qui-Qui was of his in-clan, and he had actually seen her at a clan gathering. Of course she had been surrounded by admirers. His dream since he became old enough to realize that females were different from males was to have Qui-Qui lay his egg. He knew it would never come true, but that didn't stop him from dreaming.

The Qui-Qui Show was finally over. Heavy-Egg played it back again using the automatic replay feature while he pouched a turnfeast meal without seeing or tasting it. Most of the rest of the off-shift crew were going to take a few turns of break-time, but he made his way back up to the top of the mountain and reported to the Web Construction scheduler. There was always some roustabout who got too lazy or too full of pulp to make it back to work on time. He was lucky; there was a Topside job open. He grabbed it eagerly, for the only thing that he liked better than thinking about Qui-Qui was the nearly sexual thrill of working on the tower, where the tiniest slip meant instant death.

Heavy-Egg enjoyed work, and often wondered what it would feel like to be a human and have to spend a third of your life unconscious. He had heard that humans would fall asleep even when their lives were in danger. He then remembered hearing long ago on the holovid that the humans were in some kind of danger and wondered if any of them were asleep.

06:53:21 GMT TUESDAY 21 JUNE 2050

Amalita crawled slowly along the passageway ladder from the Science Deck to the Central Deck, her muscles fighting the high outward-going residual gravity tides. She was careful at each step to maintain a tight three-point grip with feet and hands on the rungs as the varying forces from the errant compensator mass alternately tried to pull her up and down the ladder. As she passed the protection tank containing Seiko, she looked inside. Seiko had her eyes shut, and her limbs hung limply in the water. She was sound asleep.

"I guess thirty-six hours of strenuous activity is enough even for a super-human like her," Amalita muttered. She clung to the handholds near the communications console. Pierre was strapped into the seat.

"If only Dragon Slayer had some means of propulsion," she said to Pierre.

"It'd have to be faster-than-light propulsion to get away from the neutron star before the tides tore us. . . ." Suddenly something clicked in Pierre's mind. In special relativity, faster-than-light travel was equivalent to time travel—and he knew the cheela could travel faster than the speed of light. Pierre turned back to the console screen.

"Sky-Teacher," he said. "You can travel faster than light. Do you have time travel?"

"Yes," said Sky-Teacher. "A Doctor of Tempology communicated through time two minutes ago, just after your accident."

"Then send a message back in time and get someone to deflect the meteorite!" said Pierre.

"Unfortunately, our time machines don't allow communication with times before the machine is first turned on," said Sky-Teacher.

"Then we've had it," said Pierre, his body jerking about in his console chair. "The hull won't last more than two minutes."

Rescue

An intermittent buzzing sound radiated through the crust. Cliff-Web tried to ignore it and continued with the pleasurable task of setting out tiny parasol plants in a border around his back garden to replace the old ones that had gone to seed. He pulled up the old plants and put them in a pile for Moving-Sand to haul away, then replaced them with the new little shoots. They were a new variety he and Moving-Sand were developing from a mutant form he had discovered on his last engineering job.

The normal parasol plant had twelve supporting rods that grew up and out from the single tap root to support the reddish, cool concave top surface that radiated to the sky. These shoots had twenty-four rods. The doubling was not simple, however, but was more like two plant skeletons trying to exist under the same skin, for the glowing pollen tips of the cantilevered rods alternated in sex and color. Normal parasol plants slowly pulsed with time, the pollen tips turning from deep red-black to a bright white-hot glow, then back again. The two sets of tips on the double parasol were out of phase. While one set was dark, the alternate set was bright, producing a pleasing blinking effect.

The buzzing persisted.

"Moving-Sand," he hollered into the crust. "Can you answer that for me?"

"You get it. I'm busy cleaning out the Slink rooms," came a voice from the rear of the compound.

With a shrug, Cliff-Web emptied out his gardening pouch, wiped his manipulator on a wiper, dissolved the stubby, bony arm back into his body, and made his way to his study. The buzzing grew louder as he entered the room. Lassie was still resting in the warm corner of the room. He glided onto the taste-plate in the floor, and a portion of his undertread touched the *ANSWER* square on the screen. It was Admiral Star-Glider, head of the Slow One Rescue Expedition. The picture was speckled with white spots again. He would have to call the video-link company and get them to find the bad spot in the X-ray fiber cable to his compound.

"Turn on your holovid to the public services channel," said Star-Glider. "The legislature is winding up its debate on the funding for the Jumbo Bagel. There should be a tally soon, and then we will be able to start work."

"Seeing" Star-Glider through the ultrasensitive taste buds built into his tread, Cliff-Web turned some of his eyes toward a silvery screen set in one wall of his study. He formed a tendril and, reaching to a small console set into the floor, touched some panels. Brief scenes flashed in front of the screen as the planar phased-array antenna embedded in a corner of his compound switched its reception beam to receive a stream of modulated gamma rays coming from a direct broadcast satellite hovering to the west of the Eyes of Bright.

Four of his eyes looked upward at the pattern of six glowing asteroids hovering over Bright. The pattern was badly askew.

"The Six Eyes are already way out of their pattern," said Cliff-Web. "We should have been up there to fix that long ago. After all, we promised we would."

"Well, politicians like to make promises," Star-Glider replied. "But when it comes to appropriating money for it, they seem to feel they can take their time, especially in cases like this one, where there is no real urgency. We have plenty of time."

"We did have plenty of time when the accident happened," Cliff-Web reminded him. "But the politicians have fooled around for six greats of turns trying to find a cheaper way to do it. My engineers and I have done our best, but there is no way we can build that giant inertia drive engine and get it up into space for less than a billion stars, and the longer they wait, the more it is going to cost. How are the humans taking it?"

"According to Sky-Teacher, they are becoming panicky. He can tell by the overtones in their speech."

"What is the present estimate of the time to failure?"

"It's hard to tell. We have an eight body gravity model that can predict the future positions of the ship and asteroids with respect to Egg fairly accurately, but the real unknown is the strength of the spacecraft hull. The humans are in the process of climbing into their acceleration protection tanks, and they should be safe there for a while. But, I would like to get the rocket fixed before the hull fails so the humans can take the whole ship back up when it is time for them to go. I would guess we have at least two human minutes."

"That gives us four greats of turns," Cliff-Web said. "I should be able to get the drive built in less than two. *If* we get the money." He turned his attention to the three-dimensional scene floating above the floor in front of the silvery holovid screen. The legislators had gathered in a large depression in the center of Bright that served as a meeting compound. The place wasn't used very often lately, since most large gatherings for business and entertainment were carried out through multiple communications linkups rather than in person.

This was the last session of the legislature before the recess for elections, however, and it was traditionally held at the meeting compound. The last item of business left in this great's session was the appropriation of the money to build the giant scale inertia drive engine needed to replace the failing engine on the human herder rocket. The large, doughnut-shaped device had been dubbed the "Jumbo Bagel" by the holovid newscasters. The name came from the engine's resemblance to a confection eaten by the humans. One of the legislators was speaking, and the holocamera zoomed in on the waving eye-stubs as the speaker's pad amplified his tread motions.

". . . I, for one, don't want to go back to my clan just before election and say that we are going to have to raise taxes just to save a bunch of ignorant Slow Ones who were too dumb to build their spacecraft correctly. Let them rescue themselves, I say!"

"I'm sure my esteemed colleague in the third sextant of the chamber didn't really mean that," another speaker chided. "We certainly can't blame the Slow Ones for being ignorant. They live so slowly that there is no chance they will ever catch up with us. Yet they are not animals. We cannot ignore their plight and just let them die. After all, they did help us once."

"But that was long ago. Back when we were still but savages. We have paid them back in full by filling up their memory crystals with all the advanced technology they could possibly use. We even cleaned out the black holes in their Sun to stop the ice ages they would otherwise have to face. We owe them nothing, I say. Space explo-

ration is dangerous. People—humans and cheela alike—
are often killed by unforeseen accidents. These Slow Ones
knew they were on a risky mission when they volun-
teered. They were unlucky and will have to accept their
fate. Why should we empty our pouches to save them
from their own foolhardiness. I will vote *No!*''

"He can't be serious!" Cliff-Web exploded in anger.
"We can't let those humans die when we could easily save
them! He must be playing to the voters. Is there really a
chance that those fools won't give us the money?"

"If it comes to a tally this turn, the appropriation will
probably pass, although it will be close," Star-Glider calculated. "What I am afraid of is that they will decide to
put the tally off until after the elections. We will then have
a large number of newly elected clan representatives and
we will have to go through the whole round of re-edu-
cating and re-justifying. It could cost us a full great of
turns, and time is getting short. . . .''

Another cheela moved to a speaker's pad. She had to
be leader of the fourth sextant since she came from the
frontmost pad of that sextant. Her body was large and
firm and she had great presence. The wave-pattern in her
eye-stub motions moved slower and slower as she drew
the attention of the assembled legislators.

"The legislator from the first sextant and the legislator
from the third sextant are both competent people. They
have both looked at the same set of facts yet can't seem
to agree. I am sure that there are others of you with similar
differences of opinion. I would like to propose a com-
promise position. I recommend that we return this ap-
propriations scroll to the hole in the scroll wall that it came
from, and pull it again when the elections are over. By
that time we will have more information from our ac-
countants and engineers and we can make a more knowl-

edgeable decision. Perhaps by that time, they will have found a less costly way of carrying out the project."

"The humans are in danger, we must act now if we are going to do any good at all!" said a tread from the first sextant. The leader of the fourth sextant paused, formed a pair of tendrils, reached into a pouch, and pulled out a scroll. She placed it on the floor where the gravity held it flat. Lowering one of her eyes near the ground, she proceeded to read.

"Record of the reports to the Legislative Sub-Group on Space, Communications, and Slow One Interactions. Dated Turn 112 of the 2875th great of turns since Contact. A progress report from the Commander of the Slow One Rescue Expedition, Admiral Star-Glider." She skipped over a portion, then continued.

"I quote Admiral Star-Glider. 'Our analysts estimate the tides will be high enough to tear the hull of the human spacecraft by 2880. The humans can survive in the tidal protection tanks until perhaps 3010.'" she continued. "In a later section . . . 'From the time a start is authorized, our engineers estimate that it will take about two greats to make the inertial drive engine and install it in the human rocket.'"

"We have time. In a few turns it will be just 2876. The humans will be safe for at least four greats, and we only need two greats to complete the task. Surely we can defer a decision for a short period while we go through elections."

The leader of the first sextant moved swiftly forward to a speaker's pad. "The distinguished leader of the fourth sextant neglected to continue the quote of the Commander of the Slow One Rescue Expedition. Would she please read the next portion of the report while she has it so conveniently under tread?"

Her eye-stubs twitching in annoyance, she continued reading. "'If there is a delay in the start of construction, however, the actual cost may exceed the present estimated cost. To maintain the schedule, a number of fabrication steps will have to be taken in parallel. There is a possibility of error and costly rework may be necessary.'" She raised her eye from the scroll, "Yes, there is risk in delaying the start, but there is risk in starting now and not looking for a less expensive solution. As leader of the fourth sextant, I press for a tally on holing the scroll."

"That does it," Star-Glider muttered. "Once a leader of a sextant presses for a tally, debate stops until the tally is taken. I'm glad she was at least made to read the part about the extra expense, but she covered herself well. This is going to be close. If the tally were yes or no to appropriate the money, then we would probably win, because no one wants to go on scroll as being willing to let the humans die. But there are a lot of yes tallies that would be just as happy to put off a decision until later."

The view on the holovid zoomed back to show the legislators moving to their pads, where they touched their tread screens to indicate their tallies. In a glowing rectangle inset in the center of the holovid block, Cliff-Web could see the tally. It had reached 114 *Yes* and 112 *No* for holing of the scroll when two more legislators scurried down the ramps and the total was tied at 114 each.

"There is one legislator missing!" Admiral Star-Glider exclaimed.

"I see someone in the back."

"Bright's Curse!" Admiral Star-Glider quickly identified the missing cheela. "It's Talking-Tread of the fifth sextant. He's bound to tally for holing the scroll. But he's only got three sethturns to get to his voting pad."

They watched the legislator moving down the ramp. He was one of the senior legislators, and his pad was down near the center of the meeting bowl.

"One sethturn left," Star-Glider whispered. "Just 12 blinks . . . 8 . . . 7 . . . 6 . . . 5 . . . 4 . . . 3 . . . 2 . . ." A gong rang out and the tally remained tied at 114 *Yes* and 114 *No*.

"A tie tally is no tally," the tally counter announced.

"We've won!" shouted Star-Glider's image so loudly that Cliff-Web felt his tread tingle. "Pack your pouches. I'll see you at the East Pole Spacecraft Assembly Plant."

"Won?" Cliff-Web said. "They haven't even started to take a tally on the appropriation. How can we have won?"

"Considering how easy it is on the brain-knot of a legislator to postpone things, that last tally was an overwhelming victory. Take my word, when they finally do get around to voting on the appropriation scroll, it will be 3 to 1 in our favor."

But Star-Glider was wrong. With the leader of the fourth sextant pressing for a tread tally, the vote was unanimous.

Cliff-Web turned off the holovid and returned to his gardening. It wouldn't do to leave the border unfinished, and he needed the little bit of peaceful relaxation that came from working the soft crumbled crust with his manipulators before he went off to take personal charge of one of the larger engineering projects his company was undertaking.

The gardening finished, he returned to his quarters and started to stuff his pouches with the things he would need during his long trip away from the compound.

"Moving-Sand!" he called. "Where are my engineering badges and body paint? There's bound to be some formal ceremonies and I will have to wear them."

"They are still in your travel bag," said Moving-Sand, bringing the bag to him. "You never unpacked from the last trip. I took out a bunch of dirty wipers that had so much dirt and food stains on them you could use them for compost. There are clean rolls of wipers and some glow-jewels in the lower left hole of your dressing wall."

"Just put the wipers in the bag," said Cliff-Web. "The glow-jewels can stay. This is a job, not a party."

"You *will* take the glow-jewels," Moving-Sand insisted. "You'll be visiting the space stations and Topside Platform. *You* may not think much of yourself, but you're a celebrity to those people. There will be receptions, and you should look like the owner of one of the largest private companies on Egg." Moving-Sand pulled the radioactive jewels made of neutron-fat uranium crystals out of the hole in the dressing wall. He gave them to Cliff-Web, who watched the jewels for a while as they sparkled with gamma-ray emission from the spontaneously fissioning uranium nuclei, then tucked them into his travel bag. He opened a pouch in his side and tucked the travel bag away in his body. He would have to take it out again when he took the Jump Loop transport. They only allowed a small amount of pouched baggage in the main cabin of the jump-craft.

He went to his study, pouched a few instruments and technical scrolls, then gave his robotic office secretary instructions for handling messages. Lassie, having seen her master leave many times before, moved slowly from her resting pad and came over to have him pat her on the eye-stubs. As Cliff-Web patted the balding Slink, he made soft electronic whispering noises to her, while at the same time talking to Moving-Sand with his undertread.

"It will be at least a half-great before I can take time away from the project to come back for a visit," he said. "It could be that Lassie will die while I'm gone."

"I'll take care of her," Moving-Sand promised. "The rest of the Slinks will be glad to have something besides Flow-Slow meat in their meat-bins."

"Don't feed her to the Slinks," said Cliff-Web. "She has been my faithful Slink since engineering school. I will eat her myself."

"I can't understand you!" Moving-Sand sounded disgusted. "Here you are rich enough to eat prime cheela steaks every day and now you tell me you want to suck old, stringy Slink meat."

"I do," said Cliff-Web. "But perhaps you're right about it being old. Better make ground meat out of the tougher cuts." He gave Lassie one last pat, picked up his mascot plant Pretty-Web, and flowed out the door, through the courtyard, and out to the street where a robotic glide-car was waiting to take him to the Jump Loop.

He slid onto the waiting plate of thick metal between the front shield and the rear power unit, and the transparent superconducting shell closed over him. The glide-car rose a few microns and sped down the street, riding on the traveling ripples of magnetic field that it generated in its base plate.

The passenger terminal for the Jump Loop was on the outskirts of Bright, not far from the ruins of the ancient Holy Temple. There was some restoration work going on there, and Cliff-Web could see the large crust-moving machines working on an eye-mound. The job was one of the few that Web Construction had lost. He and his engineers were used to high-technology jobs and always ended up losing on price for crust-moving projects. The glide-car came to a halt, and Cliff-Web inserted his magnecard in the slot. The glide-car subtracted 8 stars and 64 greths and released him from his temporary transparent prison.

The terminal was in a tough part of town, so he moved quickly across the street toward the door marked IN. Just as he activated the automatic door with his tread, a small youngling burst through the opening going the wrong way. He was filthy and his decorationless hide had more scars than most soldiers. Holding the door open with his tread, he jabbed a sharp metal pricker at Cliff-Web, who rapidly reversed his tread ripple.

"That's right, you fat egg-sucker. Move back and you won't get hurt." He looked back through the door. "Crumpled-Tread . . . Speckle-Top . . . Move it!" he hollered. "The Clankers are right behind you!" Two more street urchins burst through the door; they were even smaller than the gang leader. The littlest one had some costume jewelry and an embroidered wiper she had obviously stolen. She was no more than a hatchling, and Cliff-Web could look down on her topside to see that "Speckle-Top" was indeed covered with spots of different emittance than the rest of her body. The speckled pattern extended to her eyes, some of which were pink instead of the normal dark red.

Crumpled-Tread gave the gang leader one of the two travel bags he had snatched, and the three street urchins took off in opposite directions. Cliff-Web heard a banging on the closing automatic door and stepped on the activator mat to open the door and let the Public Peace Officer out. Her twelve eyes took everything in at a glance, and she took off after the gang leader, who was still trying to stuff a heavy travel bag in a pouch. Cliff-Web watched her go, but it was obvious that the officer, weighed down with her weapons, badges, and communicator, was not likely to catch the fleet youngling.

Cliff-Web had been appalled by the size of the smallest thief. In his clan hatchery, a hatchling this size would still be playing with the Old Ones, hearing the ancient stories of the clan heroes and their exploits.

The little one must be what the social workers called a "dump hatchling." Its mother was probably a clanless prostitute who left her egg at the local dump. If the egg wasn't eaten by scavengers, the little hatchling had a reasonable chance of living, since newly hatched cheela could feed themselves and there was plenty of food at the dump. Older hatchlings would take the dump hatchlings under their mantle and then teach them to steal for them.

Just thinking of the poor, unprotected hatchling with its ugly speckled top brought a surge of protective emotion through Cliff-Web's body. He wanted to find that poor hatchling, throw his protective mantle over the ugly scarred body, and feed her, and love her. He wanted. . . .

Cliff-Web shook himself and drove back the feeling. He couldn't allow his hormones to turn him into an Old One yet. He had a job to do. He flowed through the door and entered the terminal, all business. He found the gate and went through, his magnecard confirming his reservation for the launch. Since the jump-fare was a major expenditure, they had a tread-reader at the gate that verified he was the true owner of the card.

As he glided onto the long, slender vehicle, an attendant assisted him in depouching his travel bag. Now significantly thinner, he made his way up the narrow aisle and slid sideways into his slot. He raised the panel that would keep his body from slipping out into the aisle during acceleration, pulled out a scroll, and started reading it the hard way in the cramped quarters. He scanned a small portion while he used his tendrils to unroll one end while he rolled up the other.

The jumpcraft left on time, and he put away the scroll to watch as the clear superconducting shields moved up to enclose the compartments. The vehicle slid down a chute to the start of the Jump Loop proper. The Jump Loop looked like a flattened pipe that traveled along the crust for a while, then slowly raised itself up off the crust into the sky in seeming defiance of the tremendous gravity of Egg. Cliff-Web's aisle mate was a youngling that looked as if he had just left the Combined Clans Engineering Academy in Bright. He was wearing his engineering badges, and they looked newly made.

"Sure looks impossible, doesn't it," said the youngling.

"As if it might fall down," Cliff-Web responded.

"Don't worry," the youngling reassured him. "Everything is perfectly safe. You see, what is holding it up is what you can't see, the super-high-speed band traveling inside the pipe. There is a big underground electromagnetic linear motor in a tunnel to the east of here that is pushing the belt up to high speed and feeding it into the pipe."

They felt a bump as the nose of the vehicle started to tip up and they were pushed to the back of their slots.

"We just passed over the bending magnet that deflected the belt upward," the youngling engineer explained. "The belt is traveling at nearly a quarter of the speed of light and would go into orbit if it didn't have to carry the weight of the pipe."

"Oh. Really?"

"Yes," said the engineer. "But don't worry, we're not going into space. The pipe rides on the moving belt using superconducting guides and soon bends the belt over so it is traveling above the surface of Egg. Here we go. Feel the acceleration as the vehicle magnegrips start to couple to the belt?"

They sank even deeper into their slots as the vehicle started to climb up along the pipe on two tracks of superconducting glide-ways while extracting energy from the high-speed belt inside the pipe. They built up speed, flattened out at 10 meters and moved swiftly down the 2 kilometer long pipe. To their left was an identical pipe carrying the belt on its return journey to the terminal they just left. A silver sliver shot by on the left track, glowing slightly at the nose.

"That's an orbital jumpcraft returning from space," said the young engineer. "The real problem with the jumpcraft is slowing down enough to land. Unlike Earth, the atmosphere on Egg is too thin for aerobraking. Magnetic drag won't work either. It will just melt the jumpcraft. To slow down, they glide along the pipe and put the vehicle energy into the belt. We will take some of that energy back when we leave. Since we don't need to accelerate that much, we will probably transfer to the eastward belt at the half-way station."

At the one kilometer point, a switch in the guide-ways sent them in a small loop that turned them to the east. Cliff-Web, having ridden the Jump Loop many times, was able to feel the tiny increase in gravity on his body as the gravity-field generators built into the base of the vehicle were activated. The magnegrips grabbed the belt, and they started accelerating.

"They're supposed to turn on the gravity first!" the engineer explained, his eye-stubs twitching nervously. "When we leave the end of the loop and fly off, we're in free fall. The gravity has to be on or we'll blow up!"

"I'm sure the pilot is taking care of things. I understand the gravity generators are quite expensive to operate so he is probably waiting until the last blink." The vehicle flew off the end of the pipe at a quarter of the speed of light, and they both expanded vertically as the gravity dropped to a mere million gees.

"Doesn't feel like much, does it?" The youngling was obviously relieved. "But it's enough to keep our electrons from going into orbits around our nuclei and causing our nuclear molecules to break up."

The sub-orbital flight one-quarter of the way around Egg only took them two methturns at their near-relativistic velocity. But during that time Cliff-Web heard all about the youngling's new job working on the Jumbo Bagel.

"This will be the biggest inertia drive engine ever built, and probably the biggest that will *ever* be built. But Web Construction is the biggest construction company on Egg, and they are big enough to do it. I was sure lucky to get my first job with them. They treat their engineers right if they work hard, and that's what I'm going to do. I'm assigned to the team that will build the launch cradles for the engine segments. Those are the. . . ."

"I think we are coming to Swift's Climb," said Cliff-Web.

The young engineer looked ahead. "The Jump Loop here is shorter than the one at Bright's Heaven," he said. "They only used it for sub-orbital flights. The one at Bright's Heaven can accelerate vehicles up to half the speed of light, more than enough for escape from Egg."

The pilot was using thrusters as he lined up the vehicle with the two long streaks hovering above the crust. Swift's Climb was a blotch in the background with a rectangular street grid that turned random as the city slowly climbed the foothills of the East Pole mountains to the resort areas hidden in the upper valleys. High above them loomed the Space Fountain, a metallic streak that disappeared into the sky many kilometers overhead.

"That's another project my company is working on," said the engineer. "Isn't it amazing? It's sort of a vertical jump loop, but it uses a stream of rings instead of a belt."

They decelerated down to ground speeds as the vehicle coasted to a halt inside the terminal. The young engineer was already out in the aisle, pushing his way to the travel bag bin. Cliff-Web followed behind, taking his cleft-wort plant out of his pouch and letting it cool off to the sky.

The youngling looked at the plant with interest. "That plant looks just like the one that Web Construction uses on its signs," he said. "Well, it was nice talking to you. What will you be doing in Swift's Climb?"

"Oh, I'll be working on the Jumbo Bagel, too," said Cliff-Web.

"You will? What division are you in? Launch Cradle?"

"No. I take care of long-range planning and finance."

"Oh. Well, I guess someone has to do the scrollwork. But the real fun is in the engineering. Eye you some turn," he said as he pushed his way off through the strong vertical magnetic field that permeated Swift's Climb.

Cliff-Web felt old as he flowed into the rear slot of the chauffeur-driven company car that was waiting for him in the street.

"Administration Compound," he told the driver. "Wait! I've changed my mind. Take me to the Spacecraft Assembly Plant. The scrollwork can wait."

While the glide-car was making its way through traffic to the plant on the outskirts of Swift's Climb, Cliff-Web made a call through the mobile communicator to Star-Glider at the Combined Clans Space Center.

"I've pushed the contract through the bureaucracy at Bright's Heaven and the Space Center," Star-Glider reported. "It is ready for your tread-print. Where shall I bring it? I want to get started."

"We've already started. Why don't you meet me at the assembly plant? I want to see the mock-up before they tear it down to make room for the real thing."

The Web Construction Spacecraft Assembly Plant was right on the launch base grounds not far from the Space

Center headquarters building, so Star-Glider was there before Cliff-Web arrived.

"Have a nice jump?" Star-Glider asked politely.

Cliff-Web paused. "It was . . . interesting," he finally said. "Let's go see the mock-up."

The scaffolding surrounding the mock-up could be seen in the distance. They entered through the security gate, then a small glide-car took them on a tour around the giant circular structure.

"I had the engineers do a full-scale mass model on the mock-up so that we could get the stress scaffolding built correctly. Although the engine will operate in space, we have to assemble and stress it on Egg so that we know it can withstand the operating stresses when we turn it on in space."

Star-Glider looked up to see a cheela gliding across a narrow beam high above him as easily as if she were on the crust.

"How high up is she?" Star-Glider asked.

"The thickness of the engine is 48 millimeters," Cliff-Web told him. "So the top of the scaffolding must be about 60 millimeters."

"I don't mind looking down from orbit," said Star-Glider. "But I would never have the nerve to try that."

"Few cheela do. We find the best ones are from the White Rock Clan. They spend most of their hatchling time playing around steep cliffs."

The glide-car stopped near a break in the structure. One segment of the mock-up had been pulled aside.

"The engine will be built in twelve segments," said Cliff-Web. "After stress testing, the segments will be launched separately and reassembled in space."

The glide-car moved through the gap in the doughnut-shaped engine and they could see the complex of energy extractors, stress negators, and vortex generators that would manipulate the vacuum itself and extract energy from it, then use that energy to give inertia to the vacuum so that it could be used as reaction mass for the thruster to push against.

The glide-car stopped near the scaffold elevator, and they took it up to the top viewing platform. Their bodies safely protected behind barriers, they looked down at the 144-millimeter diameter "bagel" with a bite taken out of it.

"In a great of turns the mock-up will be replaced with the real thing," Cliff-Web told him.

"Let's get that contract signed and get going," said Star-Glider. "The gravity tides are starting to cause noticeable distortions in Dragon Slayer."

The fabrication of the twelve segments of the Jumbo Bagel was finished on time, but the stress test brought out a flaw in the design. A power connector failed when the superconducting shield was activated.

"There are 144 connectors in each segment, and there are twelve segments," said Cliff-Web. "The rework will take a minimum of 12 cheela-greats and put us 24 turns behind schedule."

"I'll go to the Budget Sub-Group of the legislature and ask for an increase in funds," Star-Glider promised. "I warned them this kind of thing could happen if they delayed on the start. How much do you need?"

"Nothing," Cliff-Web replied. "I'll pay the difference out of my own pouch. Just explain to them why we will be late."

A half a great later the last of the segments were loaded into the spherically shaped launch cradles that were half scaffolding and half spacecraft. The sphere was hauled to the middle of an open field and placed into a depression at the center. Buried under the ground was a gravity catapult that first levitated the sphere about 100 millimeters above the crust so the inertia drive engines could be activated. Then, engines thrusting, the sphere was tossed into space by a short burst of gravitational repulsion from the gigantic coils buried in the ground.

"From zero to one-third the speed of light in a blink," Cliff-Web remarked "yet because gravity forces were used, there were hardly any stresses."

"Amazing for a machine that old," Star-Glider said. "Well, shall we follow it up?"

"I want to inspect the progress on the Space Fountain first," said Cliff-Web. "I'll see you at the East Pole Space Station."

Admiral Star-Glider took advantage of the launch of a newly commissioned scout ship to experience being catapulted into space. The gravity catapult wasn't used for ordinary travel anymore since it cost so much to operate. Cliff-Web checked out the work on the Space Fountain, jumped back to Bright's Heaven, spent a few turns gardening and playing with his pets, then it was back to the Jump Loop for a long jump up to the East Pole Space Station. He and Star-Glider went out on a small cruiser to inspect the installation of the Jumbo Bagel on a converted cargo carrier. They got there just as the last segment was put into place.

"In a few turns my job will be done and yours will start," Cliff-Web said.

"Good," Star-Glider said. "We're just in time. We have started to see some damage in Dragon Slayer's pressure hull, but it is still intact. The humans have abandoned the communications console and are retreating into the protection tanks."

06:54:00 GMT TUESDAY 21 JUNE 2050

The gravity tugs were getting worse. A metal drinking flask broke loose in the galley and came shooting up the passageway from the deck below. It flashed by Amalita and headed for one of the science electronics consoles set in the outer wall of the main deck between the portholes. The drinking flask smashed into one of the knobs on the console, and soon there were three missiles shooting back and forth around the main deck—a dented metal bulb and two sharp plastic knob halves.

"That does it," Pierre declared. "It's too dangerous out here. Let's get into the tanks!"

"But once we're in the tanks, there's nothing we can do to save the ship," argued Amalita, hanging onto a stanchion. Cesar didn't argue with Pierre and soon was shutting his hatch door.

Pierre pointed at the outer wall of Dragon Slayer, which was twisting noticeably under the extreme gravitational forces.

"Once the pressure hull goes, those tanks will be the only thing that will keep us alive," he replied. "In you go." He opened the hatch to her tank and held it open for her.

Reluctantly, she opened the locker door beneath the hatch, took out the breathing mask, and put it on. Just then the metal drinking flask came flying in toward them. Amalita fielded it on the fly, tucked it inside the locker, latched the door shut, and climbed quickly into the tank, adjusting her mask as she did so. Pierre checked her tank, then as the water splashed up on the porthole, he made his way around the central column, trying to stay as close to the center of mass of the ship as possible to keep the gravitational forces down. Just before he closed his own hatch door, he noticed that the latching mechanism for the metallic shields over one of the outside portholes had failed and he could look out and see the deadly neutron star whirling by the porthole five times a second. Fortunately the glass was still holding pressure. As he was closing his hatch door, he saw a cluster of bright, star-like objects appear just outside the porthole.

06:55:05 GMT TUESDAY 21 JUNE 2050

"Holy Egg!" exclaimed one of the cheela crew as the small armada of cheela spacecraft drifted in between the large glowing condensed asteroids. Engines working continuously to compensate for the constantly changing gravity field pattern caused by the out-of-position asteroids, the spacecraft settled into a synchronous position some fifteen meters out from the hull of Dragon Slayer. They were near one of the viewing ports where the metallic shield had been drawn back.

"Break out a flitter for me," commanded Star-Glider.

"Yes, Admiral!" replied his second-in-command, Captain Bright-Star. Her tread '*trummed* a command into the crystalline hull of the spaceship where it was picked up by the flitter launching crew on the opposite hemisphere of their spherical spaceship.

"May I accompany you on another flitter?" Bright-Star asked with an electronic whisper.

"Certainly. It is not often we get a chance to look at a human in the flesh. I understand they look very strange since the X-rays penetrate right through them and you can see the manipulator bones inside them. In fact, I'm sure most of the crew would like an opportunity to see the Slow Ones. Break out some X-ray illuminators and take them over to that porthole to illuminate the inside."

With the X-ray illuminators in place, the crew could see through the heavily tinted, fuzzy glass. The main deck was empty except for two large, jagged objects floating slowly by. They were nearly transparent except for a bent piece of metal embedded in a hole in one of them. Using the map of Dragon Slayer obtained from the archive files, Star-Glider was able to identify the hatch door to Pierre's tank. The hatch door was half open, and in the hatch Star-Glider could see a strangely shaped and colored blob. It was Pierre's head. At the center of the blob was a relatively dense violet structure with four holes in it. The bony skull was covered with blue-white flesh, while the top and bottom had faint yellow-white strands of hair.

"Why doesn't he close the hatch door?" Bright-Star asked.

"He is. It just takes a long time for the Slow Ones to do *anything*," Star-Glider replied. "If you come back in a few turns, you will be able to see that the hatch door is shutting. But it will take a dozen turns before he gets it closed and latched."

Another flitter joined them. Riding on top was Watson-Crick, Professor of Humanology at the Inner Eye Institute and Chief Scientist on the expedition.

"Admiral Star-Glider," he began. "I recognize that our original plan had been to study the humans and their spacecraft after the herder rocket has been fixed. But with all the humans in the protection tanks but one, and only the head of that one available for analysis, I was wondering if you might allow us some research time now, before Pierre closes his hatch door."

"You wouldn't be asking if the legislature had only moved ahead on this project more quickly," said Star-Glider. "We would have been here two minutes ago and had three humans to study."

"It is really too bad," Watson-Crick agreed. "Our modern instruments are much more sophisticated than the ones used the last time cheela had the opportunity to analyze a human."

"When was that?" Bright-Star asked.

"Over a thousand greats ago," Watson-Crick replied. "Could we have a dozen turns, Admiral?"

Star-Glider considered. "I'll give you a half-dozen. Then we'd better get on with the main purpose of the mission—fix that rocket and rescue the humans."

The humanologists were greatly disappointed that all they had to study was a human head, and *it* was over two meters from the porthole. But they did what they could and were finished when only five turns were up.

06:55:06 GMT TUESDAY 21 JUNE 2050

"Well," Star-Glider prompted as soon as Watson-Crick told him they were finished. "A whole human second has gone by. Let's get busy and rescue them. Head out to that malfunctioning herder rocket, then ready the cargo ship to put its replacement engine in place."

Bright-Star tapped the message into the hull with her undertread. Soon the giant cheela spacecraft, as big as a basketball, smoothly moved out toward one of the six glowing red masses surrounding Dragon Slayer.

The tiny glowing ship approached to within a few meters of the gigantic stainless steel girders that held the failing rocket engine to the main body of the herder rocket.

"Be careful," Star-Glider warned. "Don't get too close. That stuff is as fragile as a Tiny-Shell hatchling."

"Launch the cutters and collectors," *trummed* Bright-Star, and a collection of smaller spheres emerged from depressions in the side of the large spherical cruiser. The smallest of the tiny ships were one-cheela flitter spheres, not much bigger than a cheela body. Each cheela brandished a long dragon-crystal cutter. As large as swords, they were especially designed for this mission.

They approached the girders at selected joints and proceeded to slice through the hard steel of the beam as if it were fog. Other cheela directed larger robotic spacecraft in a zig-zag pattern through the thrust chamber of the sputtering rocket engine. The extreme gravitational tides of the black holes inside the cheela spacecraft tore the steel chamber into incandescent threads, the material compressing and sucking down onto the surface of the spacecraft where it disappeared in a flash of light, leaving a tiny lump of degenerate matter on the surface of the sphere that rapidly spread out into a thin incandescent sheet. With the rocket chamber removed from the herder rocket, it was time to install the replacement engine that the cheela had brought with them.

"Bring up the cargo ship," said Star-Glider. "But, take your time and do it right, we have a whole turn before the rocket is due to fire again."

The cargo ship moved up into the void at the rear of the herder rocket where the engine had been. The cargo ship, a sphere 360 millimeters in diameter, carried embedded in its surface the 144-millimeter doughnut-shaped engine. Both were dwarfed by the gutted remains of the 10-meter diameter herder rocket body.

"Engine in position," Bright-Star reported.

"Release engine and remove cargo ship," Star-Glider commanded.

The Jumbo Bagel and the cargo sphere separated. As the sphere moved off, violet force beams shot out from tiny bumps on the glowing white doughnut, to grasp the girder cut-off points on the frame of the herder rocket.

The violet beams varied in brightness as they brought the rocket under control. The tiny, but massive, engine was now installed.

Star-Glider felt the sethturns tick away on the chronometer at the top of the console under his tread. When the proper time came he gave the order.

"Activate inertia drive."

The violet traction beams holding the engine brightened, and there was a warping of space emanating from the hole in the doughnut. The star field to the rear of the herder rocket wavered. After a long wait of nearly a dothturn, the engine cut off, its job on this cycle of the rotation done. They would have to wait for eleven more dothturns before the engine would be called on again, so there was little to do but clean up and wait. Then there would begin the long tedious process of checking out the operation of the engine for a number of cycles before the expedition left the engine operating on its own and returned to the surface of Egg.

Star-Glider was pleased. The mission had been a success. Three of his eyes focused on those of his first officer.

"Announce a rest-turn, Bright-Star," he whispered. "And pierce the pulp-bags!"

But before the captain could 'trum the official command, the admiral's electronic whisper had been picked up by the bridge crew. Soon Star-Glider heard subdued tappings echoing throughout the spacecraft. He flipped a tendril at the captain, silencing her before she started to 'trum the command into the deck. The two listened with their treads. They heard a rustle of eager treads hurrying toward the recreation area where the pulp-bags were stored. The wave-pattern of Star-Glider's eye-stubs developed an annoyed twitch. Bright-Star knew what was coming and picked up the sensitive edges of her tread as a roar shook the crystal hull undertread.

"BUT FIRST!!!" came the Swift-stopping shout from the Admiral's tread. "An INSPECTION!!! A wet-eye-ball inspection!"

A shocked silence followed throughout the ship. The only sound coming through the hull was the throb of the idling inertia drive engines.

"Look at this place!" 'trummed Star-Glider as he moved about the bridge, his tread tossing up bits of trash and dust, his tendrils flipping at offending insignia on junior officers that weren't held exactly horizontal to the local vertical.

"How can I expect the rest of the crew to keep this place ship shape when the bridge looks like a Flow Slow wallow!" He glided over a display screen in the deck, then exploded again.

"What Tiny-Shell-brained offspring of a Slink dribbled pulp juice on the screen?!? The taste of those spots burns my tread. I want that screen cleaned and I want this ship cleaned until I can put a wet eye-ball on any spot without blinking!!"

He stormed off to his private quarters and slammed the sliding door. He waited a few methturns, then concentrated on the vibrations coming through the hull. There was a subdued murmur as Bright-Star and the rest of the officers spread throughout the ship. Then there came the shuffling sound of the crew as they started the long overdue cleanup of the ship.

Star-Glider formed a tendril, inserted it into a pouch in his side, and pulled out a magnekey. He inserted the key into a slot in the side of his locker, slid open the door and pulled out a small bag of West Pole Double-Distilled, the best on Egg. Carrying the bag, he shuffled tiredly over to his resting pad, his body seeming to deflate as he relaxed his command posture and spread out on the soft decorated mat. He put the bag of pulp in his drinking pouch and with a powerful squeeze from his pouch muscles, broke the bag and started to squeeze the pungent juice through the thin membrane at the back of the pouch. He fluffed up his manipulator pillow, formed a small holding manipulator and laid it on the pillow. He then used a tendril to extract one of his twelve-pointed star-shaped admiral's insignia from its holding sphincter in his side. He brought the star near his drinking pouch, spit some pulp-juice on it, transferred it to his holding manipulator, and proceeded to buff it to a high polish with a well-used rag. To help pass the time, he flicked on his holovid and watched the final segment of the *Qui-Qui Revue*. Qui-Qui was a little past her prime, but she was still the sexiest female on holovid.

06:55:07 GMT TUESDAY 21 JUNE 2050

"The cheela must have fixed the herder rocket," said Amalita from her tank, her voice altered by the breathing mask. "There is still no rocket exhaust, but the gravity tides are getting weaker."

Pierre shifted his glance from Amalita's image in the upper left of his split screen to the view seen by the one remaining outside camera.

"I noticed some activity at the rear of the rocket just a second ago and now there is a brightly glowing framework where the engine used to be," said Pierre.

Amalita activated the miniaturized engineering control panel in her tank and zoomed the camera in to focus on the rear of the herder rocket. Five times a second the star field in back of the rocket wavered. Slowly, the wandering compensator mass was moved back to its correct position and once again began to coordinate its motion with that of the others, the invisible warping of one of its herder rockets contrasting with the brilliant rocket blasts from the rest.

Soon the humans in the tanks could no longer feel the residual tidal tugs and their ears stopped sensing the ultrasonic beams that had protected them from the pulls at their extremities.

"I guess it's safe to come out," Pierre said looking at the five faces in the split screen display inside his tank.

"What about Seiko?" Jean asked.

Pierre looked at the screen next to the one that held Jean's image. Seiko still had her eyes closed and was breathing very slowly.

"I recommend we let her sleep," said Doc Wong's image from the screen below. "I'll keep a watch on her in case she has trouble with her breathing mask."

"Last one out of the water is a wrinkled prune!" Abdul was already starting the purge of his tank.

"Wait!" said Amalita. "Let me go out and check first for problems. The interior pressure monitor is holding steady, but there may be leaks or weak spots." From her console she canceled Abdul's purge command and started her tank draining instead.

"Put on your space suit before you go wandering around the ship banging on walls," Pierre reminded her.

"Of course." Amalita opened the hatch and listened carefully. Hearing nothing unusual, she pulled herself out of the emptying tank into the main deck area and ottered up the passageway to the suit storage locker.

Quiet

When the Rescue Expedition returned from its successful mission, the Commander of the East Pole Space Station arranged a formal reception for Admiral Star-Glider and his staff. Admiral Milky-Way and a number of the sextant leaders from the Legislature jumped up for the occasion.

Cliff-Web dutifully shined up his engineer badges, painted his body in a pattern of silver and yellow that Moving-Sand had assured him was stylish, plugged his remaining holding sphincters with glow-jewels, and suffered through the event.

The reception started at turnfeast and lasted three dothturns. The foodmats were covered with enough food and drink to gorge a Flow Slow. There was a whole roasted hatchling with its pouches full of triposter-nut stuffing and tastefully garnished to cover the accident scar, cubes of Flow Slow marinated in a pungent sauce that Cliff-Web didn't care for, a chopped fruit he hadn't seen before, topped with pickled Tiny Shell eggs, and baskets piled high with tiny bags of sparkling juice from White Rock City. Cliff-Web took two and broke one in his eating pouch. The delicate flavor of the distilled pulp juice was heightened by the spurts of energy from the fissioning uranium nuclei added just before the distillate was bagged. Cliff-Web stayed until Admiral Milky-Way climaxed the event by a promotion ceremony for Admiral Star-Glider. Three sextant leaders and three Space Force officers formed a circle around Star-Glider and each replaced a single twelve-pointed star with a two star cluster. Star-Glider took the opportunity to choose a new name for himself. He was now Admiral Steel-Slicer.

Cliff-Web decided it was time to leave when Schuler-Period started making eyes at him. She was at least two pulp-bags past her limit and was trying to get him to come to her quarters to sample her locker. She wasn't bad looking and would have been fun to tread, but he made it a point never to get involved with government officials. He did too much business with the government. He slipped away while she was admiring Steel-Slicer's new stars.

A dothturn later, stripped of his reception finery, he was at the launch deck of the space station, waiting for a Web Construction Company shuttlecraft to pick him up. The launch deck was on the Egg-facing side of the spherical space station. He looked out at his glowing home world and tried to make out the cities below. At 406 kilometers distance the cities were blurred patches on the yellow crust, and the only thing that showed up was the cool patch of the East Pole mountain range with his Space Fountain rising up from it.

The top of the Space Fountain stopped at 405,900 meters, while the East Pole Space Station was in synchronous orbit at 406,300 meters. The space station was located slightly to one side of the Space Fountain so he could not only see the nucleus of what was to be the Topside Platform, but the long stalk that held it up over the East Pole mountains. As he watched, a glowing dot rose from the platform below him. It started to drift off to the west, but thrusters brought it back under the space station. The speck grew larger, turned into a Web Construction shuttlecraft, and settled on the launch deck. Cliff-Web rec-

ognized the pilot as Heavy-Egg, one of the shift supervisors for the Topside Platform crew. With the two
stations this close together, it didn't require a trained
space pilot to move from one to the other. Just another
example of how the Space Fountain was going to revo-
lutionize space travel on Egg.

Cliff-Web moved along the curved ramp that allowed
his body to transition from the gravity field of the black
hole in the center of the space station to the field of the
tiny black hole in the center of the four-cheela shuttlecraft.

"How is the job going, Heavy-Egg?" Cliff-Web asked.

"Like a greased Swift, Boss," Heavy-Egg replied, lifting the shuttlecraft vertically out of its dimple in the
launch ramp area. "We're way ahead of schedule. We
stopped 100 meters short of top-out three turns ago. I've
got the crew making Topside Platform look decent for the
topout ceremony. The Chief Engineer says there's going
to be a bunch of big badges from Bright's Heaven and the
Space Force coming for it."

Cliff-Web was not looking forward to another formal
reception, especially one he would be paying for; but it
was all part of doing business. They berthed in a hemispherical cradle near the middle of a 50-millimeter flat disk
covered with busy workers engaged in the long task of
expanding the disk into a large, 200-millimeter diameter
platform that would have low walls to divide the deck into
offices and compounds for the operations crew, and shops
and eating places for the passengers and tourists. This was
the top of the three decks in Topside Platform where the
passengers and cargo would be transferred from the Fountain to various space stations and spacecraft and back
again.

Cliff-Web and Heavy-Egg glided off the spherical shuttlecraft onto the flat deck.

"It sure feels good being on a flat surface again after all that time in space on curved decks," Cliff-Web remarked.

"I know what you mean," Heavy-Egg agreed. "I never did trust them black holes. I like to be under Egg gravity, even if it is kind of weak."

"During top-out just make sure you stop your crew after 100 meters," said Cliff-Web. "The gravity from Egg will still be strong enough to keep us together. But if you go 300 meters more, the gravity will drop to zero. . . ."

"And *whoosh!* We get as big as humans."

"Become a cloud of plasma, is more like it," said Cliff-Web. "Things are progressing well here on Topside, let's take the elevators to the middle deck."

They went to a special freight elevator reserved for the operations personnel. The tread pad in front of the elevator door recognized Heavy-Egg's tread and let them board. They stopped at the middle deck and moved off into a cavernous room. The deck beneath their tread vibrated with energy. The bottom of the deck above was not cooled to simulate sky, but was only covered with silver paint. It helped some, but even though he was an experienced engineer, having something overhead still bothered Cliff-Web.

There was a loud clang from nearby.

"Still getting pushouts?" Cliff-Web asked.

"Three or four per turn," Heavy-Egg answered. "The Chief Engineer makes us save them and send them to Quality. An up-deflector on platform 200 caused some trouble, but that got fixed. Now Quality says we are just weeding out bad rings."

They moved over to a massive tube that rose out of the deck, curved into a large arc that touched the ceiling overhead, then came back down to penetrate the deck again. Six of them were equally spaced around the center of the deck. In a bin near the tube was a glowing-hot ring suspended in a magnetic field. A young roustabout was fishing out the ring with a hook. As soon as the ring was placed on the deck, she sucked her manipulator inside her body to cool it off.

"Bright's Turd!" she swore. "That eye-ball-sucking catcher field is *hot!*"

She hadn't sensed their approach on the noisy deck, but now saw them coming with one of her eyes. She didn't know who the stranger was, but from all the metal hanging off him, he must be some sort of big badge. She pulled her still stinging manipulator out and picked up the ring.

"I'll get this right over to Quality, Supervisor," she said.

"Just a blink, youngling," said Cliff-Web. "I want to feel it." The young roustabout looked at her supervisor, who flicked his eyes at the deck. She put the ring down and the big badge flowed over it.

The ring was large, half the diameter of a cheela. Made of highly polished monopole-stabilized superconducting metal, it was a precision part in a precision machine. The ring was subject to terrific accelerations as it was thrown upward at nearly half the speed of light. Any flaw in the polished surface could cause local heating and the possibility of the loss of superconductivity.

"No dents, but there is a hot spot on the outside and a tiny stress crack," said Cliff-Web. He flowed off the ring and the youngling picked it up and took it off. Cliff-Web then moved over to the side of the up-pipe and peered through a view port in the side. Illuminated by the glowing metal of the room-temperature pipe, the procession of cold silvery rings blended into a seemingly solid bar that waved slowly back and forth to show that it was a moving stream. The rings had started at nearly half light-speed at the surface, but as they drifted upward, they lost speed from the intense pull of Egg and the tiny tugs at each deflector platform. They were still going at one-twelfth light-speed when they reached Topside Platform.

Cliff-Web peered upward where he could see the black nothingness of the cold bending magnet that turned the rings around and sent them back down again. Cliff-Web watched the stream carefully for a while.

"Very steady flow," he finally said. "Every acceleration bucket must have a ring in it."

"At last break-turn in Swift's Climb, the Base Plant Supervisor bragged they were at three elevens."

"The entire crew is doing an excellent job," Cliff-Web remarked. "I'd like to ride it down."

"We got some spare lifts," said Heavy-Egg. "I'll get one set up. I'm almost at break-turn, so I'll take you down."

They took the elevator to the bottom deck. This would be the transfer point for passengers, so the ceiling was cold black with simulated stars. The lifts on the Space Fountain rode the streams up to this deck, while the streams of rings continued on to the turning magnets above them on the middle deck. The passengers and freight transferred to smaller elevators that took them to the top deck, while the lifts were detached from the streams, pulled back from the hole in the platform and stacked until a down-going lift was needed.

As Cliff-Web watched, a lift was removed from a stack, placed on glide-rails and moved out on support arms until its deflection coils surrounded the tubes carrying the flowing streams. Each lift used three stream pairs for safety. The support arms were pulled back, and the lift bounced lightly as it shifted its load to the streams. A roustabout hurried over with a ramp to cover the crack between the platform and lift. Cliff-Web waved him back with a flip of his eye-stubs.

"Save it for the crust-crawlers," he said, gliding over the six-micron-wide crack. He tried to keep his eyes focused off in the distance, but some of them insisted on looking down at Egg, 406 kilometers below his tread.

The things a boss must do to maintain respect, he said to himself.

Heavy-Egg activated the lift controls. As soon as they cleared the bottom deck, the pipe covering the ring stream ended, and they could see the reflection of Egg's glowing crust in the silvery flow. Except for the first 100 millimeters, where a vacuum pipe was needed to keep the weak electron and iron vapor atmosphere of Egg from heating the rings, there was no solid structure in the tower, not even a skeleton framework, just flowing rings.

"If you don't mind, Boss, I got a few chores to do while I take you down," Heavy-Egg said.

"The job comes first. It would be different if I were a paying passenger."

"I got to finish the checkout on this lift and later on down deliver a part to Platform 40."

"What kind of checkout?" Cliff-Web asked.

"The stream selector controls," Heavy-Egg replied. "Right now we ride on all six streams. Drag on the up-streams and push on the down-streams. I just got to check that we can turn off a coupler if a stream gets rough and the automatic doesn't do it."

Cliff-Web wasn't worried. He knew this part of the design well. The lift could theoretically levitate on just one stream, although, if it were badly unbalanced, the torque rebalance requirement could cause problems at the next deflector platform. Two or three streams were more than adequate for a smooth ride. He watched with interest as Heavy-Egg turned off one coupler after another and checked the response of the other five couplers as they took up the load. Then Heavy-Egg turned off all three down couplers and rode only on the up-streams. He reversed the controls and they switched to riding the downstreams only without a noticeable glitch in the motion.

"No problems there," said Heavy-Egg. "We're coming up on Platform 40."

Hearing the decimal number for the platform at 40 kilometers altitude made Cliff-Web's eye-stubs twitch. *Every* engineering measurement on Egg used the base twelve numbering system *except* distance. They had inherited meters, kilometers, and millimeters from the humans and seemed to be stuck with it despite many attempts to switch to a non-metric length system where the units were in easily calculated multiples of twelve.

Heavy-Egg brought the lift to a smooth stop. A small crew was busy repairing a redundant deflector on stream four-up. Cliff-Web glided over to the edge of the platform. The gravity acceleration on the platform was now significantly stronger, about one sixteenth that on the surface of Egg. He looked out over the barrier. At 40 kilometers altitude he could make out the outline of Swift's Climb and see the kilometer-long streak of the Jump Loop on the east side which he would shortly be using for the jump home. He hadn't heard anything from Moving-Sand, so Lassie was still alive, but he wondered if she was still mentally alert enough to remember him.

It was nearly turnfeast when Cliff-Web returned to his compound. As the front door slid into its recess he was engulfed with a swarm of happy snuffling Slinks. Even Lassie was there, having dragged herself from the mat next to the oven as soon as she had heard his familiar scuffle as he came up the street. Lassie's cluster had grown with the addition of a clutch of hatchlings. They had never seen Cliff-Web before, but that didn't stop them from joining the happy throng, leaking from both intake and output orifices in their hatchling eagerness. He twirled them all around the eye-rims again and again, until, finally satisfied, they rumbled off. Rollo must have forgotten him, because he was back hiding behind Slurge, which was just managing to push its way through the magnetic fence that bordered the tasty patch of parasol plants. Cliff-Web flowed over to the miniature Flow Slow, and, forming a large bony manipulator, gave Slurge a hard rap on the armored plate just below one of its tiny eyes.

"Back on the lawn!" he hollered.

Slurge retracted its eyes from the side toward the parasol patch. Without the constant reminder of the tasty plants coming to its almost nonexistent brain-clump, it quickly forgot about the garden and started back in the other direction onto the lawn, where it continued its methodical munching and sucking. With the Flow Slow moving in the proper direction, Cliff-Web had time to look at the arrangement of his garden. Moving-Sand must have had some success breeding the fountain plants, for there was a tall one in the center of the circular patch with six more arranged in a hexagon around the central one. All seven were sending up healthy showers of sparks. He then finally noticed something odd. If he had not just come from the East Pole he would have noticed it earlier. All the showers of sparks were going straight up into the air. That was really unusual, for the magnetic declination in this portion of Egg was nearly a quarter-pi off vertical.

"Moving-Sand!" he pounded into the crust.

From off on a distant corner of the compound came a gruff reply. "About time you came back."

The ancient tracking senses built into the super-sensitive undertread of Cliff-Web instantly triangulated the position of the sound and placed Moving-Sand in the northeast corner of the potting compound. With his attention riveted on that portion of the surrounding territory, his tread could now pick out the motion of someone else with Moving-Sand. He flowed across the outer courtyard to the opposite side of the large compound.

"That is an amazing display of fountain plants," Cliff-Web said as he rounded the potting compound wall. "One of those plants looks as if it has been growing for a half-dozen turns or more. How did you accomplish that? And how did you get the fountains to go straight up?"

"She helped a little," said Moving-Sand, his eye-stubs twitching in the direction of the stranger. She was a large, slightly over-bulky female who was obviously well past her egg-bearing prime, but still not quite ready to quit and tend hatchlings. The normal motion of her eye-stubs switched to the converging wave greeting pattern as she spoke.

"I am Zero-Gauss, Doctor of Magnetics at the Institute," she said. "I specialize in the study of the interaction of magnetic fields on plants."

"Then it is your compound that has the cleft-wort trained to climb the staircase of supports on the window."

"Yes," she replied. "When Moving-Sand came over to inquire about my technique, I learned that you had a large collection of strange plant forms. We have had such an interesting time while you were away. I've explained my various tricks in using magnetic fields to train plants and animals, and Moving-Sand has supplied me with a number of new types of plants that you collected in your various journeys around Egg. They are not only lovely additions to my garden, but some of them are proving valuable in my research at the Institute."

"I noticed that you two have really improved the performance of the fountain plant in the front circle bed," Cliff-Web said. "What did you do?"

"I brought over a large superconducting coil with a persistent current in it, and we buried it in the crust below the root system. We tilted it so that the direction of the combined magnetic fields of the coil and Egg is vertical. That way, the jet of sparks from the fountain plant can rise straight up as it does at its home location at the East Pole.''

"Was a lot of work. But it did the trick," said Moving-Sand grudgingly. "That fountain plant has lasted more than a dozen turns and is still growing. Best I could do before was three turns. Was hardly worth bothering to plant them.''

"I guess even plants thrive best when conditions are similar to what they are familiar with," said Cliff-Web.

"Not necessarily. In my research laboratory at the Institute," Zero-Gauss explained, "I have found that many plants grow faster and healthier if there is no magnetic field at all.''

"No field at all?" Cliff-Web's engineering curiosity was aroused. "What do you do? Put them at the center of some Helmholtz coils and cancel out the magnetic field of Egg?''

"I do use a pair of large Helmholtz coils to start with," she replied. "The coils only zero out the field at the center, however. Even a few microns away the cancellation is poor enough that the plant is affected. Between the coils I have built a special room lined with superconducting shielding where I have completely eliminated the magnetic field of Egg over a large enough volume that I can carry out tests on dozens of plant samples at the same time.''

"I don't understand." Cliff-Web's eye-stubs were twitching in a confused manner as his engineer's brain tried to imagine how one could make such a room. "I suppose you could make a room with a floor and walls made out of high quality superconducting plate, but even if the walls were extremely tall, the fringing fields would come in over the top. That wouldn't work at all.''

"I didn't mean a regular room, open to the sky,'' Zero-Gauss explained. "My laboratory is under the crust and has a domed cover of superconducting plate over the top, like the 'ceilings' or 'roofs' the humans use on their living and working compounds.''

"You wouldn't catch me working in that place,'' Moving-Sand muttered. "I don't trust things over top of me.''

"The dome is artificially cooled to simulate the cold of the sky,'' said Zero-Gauss. "That helps me a lot when I'm working in there. Since it is as dark as the sky, I can't see it, so it is easy to pretend it isn't there.''

"That must be an amazing structure,'' said Cliff-Web. "I presume there are pillars and double-arches holding up the domes like those in the human cathedrals. How big is it?''

"It is thirty millimeters square and has a post every centimeter. The top of the dome is five millimeters up,'' she replied. "Would you like to see it?'' She hesitated, then added, "We limit direct access, since each entry allows a little more magnetic field to leak in. However, we have an array of remotely controlled video cameras that will let you look at any portion.''

"I would like to see it,'' Cliff-Web told her. He led the way back from the potting rooms through the gardens to the front door of the compound. Slurge was quietly trimming the lawn, and Rollo and the Slinks were gone. As he activated the compound door, the area was suddenly full of Slinks. Using his body to block the Slinks from getting out into the street, Cliff-Web escorted Zero-Gauss out the door, for the first time touching the large female.

Moving-Sand came up to chase the Slinks from the doorway and *trummed* after them. "You can't go now.

You just got here. You haven't even read your message file. You must have six dozen messages to answer."

"I'll get to them later," Cliff-Web answered as he led the way down the slidewall toward the Inner Eye Institute.

"One of them is from the Rejuvenation Selection Committee," hollered Moving-Sand. Cliff-Web paused, then continued on down the street, silently thinking.

Zero-Gauss got his attention with an electronic whisper that tickled his backside. "I am impressed. The committee only started announcing the names of those that were being selected for the rejuvenation process a dozen turns ago. You must be up at the top of the list."

"It must be a long list," he said.

"No," she said. "I know of only one scientist at the Institute who is on it. Don't forget, the process is so time-consuming and costly that they are only able to undertake one rejuvenation every three turns—only four dozen cheela in a whole great of turns. It must be tough having to make the decision of who are to be the lucky few who are going to be allowed to live a second life while the rest of us will have to die when our time comes."

Cliff-Web was too embarrassed to reply, and they moved along the slide-walls in silence, switching leads at each tack. As they came to the next intersection they switched places again so that Cliff-Web was spreading the field lines again. Snuggled up to his trailing side, Zero-Gauss tried to break the silence with a whispered comment.

"You certainly have an unusual personal robot," she said. "It is one of the most lifelike robots I have ever seen. Yet most personal robots are programmed to be deferential and polite."

"Moving-Sand is one of our newest models. I'm checking it out before we go into production. As for his personality, being owner of a large company, I meet nothing but deferential and polite people. I wanted something different at home to keep my brain-knot from getting too big for my hide. I programmed Moving-Sand's personality after the Old One that raised me in the clan hatchery."

"Good idea," said Zero-Gauss. "Keeps you thinking like a hatchling. When I can afford a personal robot, I think I'll do the same."

"Anything to keep the egg-tending syndrome from starting," said Cliff-Web. "Gardening helps, too."

"That was one of the reasons I chose plants and small animals for my research," said Zero-Gauss. "Of course, all that may be unnecessary now that we have rejuvenation."

The rest of their journey to the Inner Eye Institute was carried out in silence.

06:55:20 GMT TUESDAY 21 JUNE 2050

While waiting for Amalita to finish her careful inspection of Dragon Slayer, Pierre reopened conversation with Sky-Teacher through the link to the surface of the neutron star.

"I want to thank you for saving our lives. If there is anything we can ever do to repay you. . . ."

"I have studied the speculation past literature of the human race in order to better understand you," Sky-Teacher responded. "It is amusing to me that your present offer coincides with that in the ancient fable by Aesop about the lion and the mouse. At one time in the distant past, you did help us, and we appreciated it. We hope that we have been of some help in correcting your recent predicament. As for the future, it is difficult to see how you, with your limited technology, could be of *any* help to us, but we appreciate your thoughts. If everything is in order once again for you to leave, I will once again say goodbye."

With the last words, the screen went blank again.

06:56:20 GMT TUESDAY 21 JUNE 2050

It was turnfeast, and Time-Circle shuffled listlessly past the foodmats in the faculty dining compound. He took a few staple items from the wide selection, stuffed them in a carrying pouch, picked up a large bag of unfermented pulp juice and made his way to the eating area. Over the topsides of some diners already enjoying their turnfeast, he saw three eyes up on stalks waving at him. He cheered up a little and made his way over to join the newest member of the faculty club, D. C. Neutron-Drip, who had received a Doctorate in Crustallography and chosen a new name only three turns ago.

Time-Circle had taken part in the ceremony as the senior representative of her in-clan family and had given the clan approval for the name change. The two were the only members of their clan at the Inner Eye Institute, since the clan home was far from Bright's Heaven at the East Pole. He knew from her age that she wasn't from one of his eggs so he didn't have to be concerned about his relationship with her. Now that she was no longer a student, he intended to get to know her better.

Neutron-Drip moved over as he approached and spread out to share the resting pad with her. Reaching into his pouch, he pulled out his food and set it on the eating mat.

"What an uninspired turnfeast you have there," said Neutron-Drip, her eye-stubs waving back and forth in disapproval. "Three ground-meat loaves, two crunch-fruits, and a bag of pulp juice. Turnfeast is supposed to be a feast, not a refueling stop." She formed a manipulator, picked up a small portion of baked Flow Slow egg covered with a tangy pulp nut sauce and held it before his eating pouch.

"Here," she said. "Try this, maybe it will cheer you up."

He took the morsel, very much aware of the feel of the strange manipulator in his eating pouch as he did so.

"It *is* very tasty. I may have to go back and get some for myself," he said, his eye-stub pattern assuming a more normal wave-pattern as the taste of the nut sauce penetrated the back of his eating pouch.

"I thought that would cheer you up," she said. "What is bothering you?"

"My research project," he replied. "It used to be fun, but now it is giving me nothing but trouble."

"Is there something wrong with the Time-Comm machine?" she asked.

"It could be something wrong with the machine or it could be I don't understand the theory well enough yet. Either way I don't get any money for a new 24-channel machine until I figure out what this one is doing. This first machine only has four channels each way and it takes forever to get any data. I even had to turn down a graduate student last turn. He was eager to do research on time communication, and I would have loved to have a bright youngling to work with, but I honestly couldn't allow him to spend the next dozen greats waiting to collect enough data to complete a doctoral project."

"I know the student," said Neutron-Drip. "It was Eager-Eyes. He came to me after you turned him down. He and I are going to set up a crustquake detector array around the East Pole mountains. With any luck, his thesis should establish the basis for a theory to predict East Pole crustquakes."

"With a decent-size crustquake every three or four turns at the poles, at least he will have some data to analyze." Time-Circle sounded dejected. "But why bother predicting crustquakes? Except for a few accidents when a high-speed glide-car hits the ground during a big quake, the only thing a crustquake does is crack a few compound walls or underground utility mains. At least we don't have the problem of a "roof" overhead the way the humans do."

"You sound just like the grant committee. Always wanting to know, 'What good is it?' " She drew the edges of her tread back. "What good is a new hatchling?"

"I'm sorry," he said. "I'm just feeling pessimistic about everything."

"Tell me about it," she said, drawing closer.

"In the beginning the project was fun," he began. "I had two bright graduate students. One doing the experiments and one working on the theory. We sent messages back and forth in small increments of time—just a few turns at first. Then we set up a series of progressively larger jumps until we were sending short messages over a whole great of turns. We could code the messages in such a way that the essential data was certain to get through, while the remainder of the message contained codes that allowed us to determine the number of bits the channel was able to pass. We showed that the number of bits the channel could handle was inversely proportional to the distance in time the message was sent. Except for slight statistical variations, the bit-time product was always 864 bit-greats."

"So you could send a yes-no answer over 864 greats of turns," she said.

"Or 124,416 bits over one turn," said Time-Circle, his tread *trumming* out the familiar train of numbers. "Then, as the climax to both of their doctoral projects, we simultaneously sent messages on the three forward-time channels to times two, three, and four greats into the future. The fourth channel we always keep clear in case an urgent message needs to be sent.''

''Four greats is a long time to wait before you can finish your thesis,'' she said.

''We didn't have to wait at all,'' said Time-Circle. ''Somewhere there was a minor calibration error between the forward-time channels and the back-time channels. *Before* we sent out the test signals, we received a response back from the future saying that all the signals had been received and giving the number of bits that had made it through each channel. They all agreed with the theoretical prediction of 864 bit-greats.''

''But suppose you had then decided *not* to send the test messages into the future?'' she asked.

''One of the students suggested that,'' he replied. ''But I had already trod their edges on that subject early in the project. Until we have a theory for these machines so we can understand the implications of creating a paradox, we can't afford to take a chance. *My* guess is that every major paradox causes a bifurcation of the universe. But it would take a good theory to suggest an experiment that would *prove* that bifurcation had taken place.''

''And you have a good theory?'' she asked.

''Until a few turns ago, I thought I did,'' he said dejectedly. ''Now, I'm not so certain.''

''What happened?''

''After the success with the three multi-great transmissions, I had no trouble getting the grant committee to authorize the construction of a 24-channel machine with a greatly increased channel capacity in each channel. Getting the money approved took a while, and while the preliminary design work was underway the time came for the first of the transmissions to be received, the one sent over two greats of turns. The two ex-students as well as members of the grant committee were there as the message came out of the machine from two greats in the past, and they watched as I measured the bit count and sent the confirmation back to myself in the past. I should have quit then."

"What happened?"

"Since I now had two channels free in each direction, I decided to show the committee how the Time-Comm machine worked by sending a message *six* greats into the future. As I prepared the message for the forward-time channel, I was a little surprised that the back-time channel had not already indicated the message had been received. Thinking that the differential calibration had drifted off so that the back-time channels were now shorter than the forward-time channels, I sent the message off six greats into the future and waited for a reply."

"And?"

"It didn't come," he said. "I didn't find out what had happened until a great of turns later, long after the grant committee had decided to hold up on the construction of the new machine."

They had finished eating, and the faculty dining compound was nearly empty.

"You have to get back to your work," he said. "I can't do anything until the next channel clears a few dozen turns from now, so you spread the fields and I'll snuggle along behind and tell you the rest of the sad story."

She headed across the grounds of the Institute and he switched to a soft electronic whisper that tickled through her hide.

"I was really dejected until the time came for the reception of the three-great-long message. That came through on schedule, and I sent the reply through the back-time channel. Almost as soon as the reply was on its way through the channel into the past, the channel was full again with a message from the future, *eight* greats away. At eight greats time distance, you can only send 108 bits of information, so the message was brief. Both the six great *and* the eight great messages had been received, but the response to the six-great message had been blocked by some spontaneous emission in the back-time channel."

"Spontaneous emission?"

"That bewildered me at first. My time communication theory, although based on the quantization of space and time, didn't predict any spontaneous emission of signal energy in the channels," he said. "I brought in a bright theoretical student, and we soon found a third-order effect that could produce spontaneous emission of a bit pair that travels simultaneously backward and forward in time for a short period, then emerges in the receiver. Even though the 'message' is only one bit, that is enough to keep the channel from being used by any other message. It is only supposed to happen once every dozen generations or so, and it had to happen just as I needed that channel to impress the committee."

"Did your new results get the committee to resume the work on the 24-channel machine?" she asked.

"They were just as suspicious of the coincidence as I was," he said. "They decided to wait until we saw the noise in the channel and could learn more about it than could be sent with 108 bits. Sure enough, about 72 turns later, out came a single bit and the channel indicator registered 'Channel Occupied' for almost two greats when suddenly the back-channel was empty and a forward-channel was 'Occupied.' Neither transmitter had activated. I analyzed and re-analyzed everything and was about to approach the committee for restarting the construction of the new machine when the final blow fell."

Neutron-Drip stopped moving, and her edges flowed back about his in a semicircular embrace.

"Last turn I responded to an alarm and found that another back-time channel has noise in it. What is worse, it was not a single bit, but three bits with a nonsense meaning. The chance of spontaneous emission of three bits is infinitesimal. The machine has a noise source. And until we understand it, we shouldn't spend money on a larger machine. But with only four channels, it will take forever to find out what the problem is."

"But once you find out, you can send a message back to yourself with the answer . . ." she started.

"There you go, creating paradoxes again," he said. "If it were possible, I would have already done it, and I wouldn't be here whispering my troubles into your trailing side." He moved around her and pushed off across the compound.

"Enough of my problems," he said. "How about showing me how you are going to set up that net around the East Pole to trap crustquakes?"

06:57:52 GMT TUESDAY 21 JUNE 2050

Qui-Qui was surprised when she received a letter from the rejuvenation selection committee. She sent her acceptance message at once, then called her manager, Grey-Stone.

The picture over the video link was that of a small middle-aged male painted in the bright diagonal stripes that went out of fashion 20 greats ago. The already rapidly moving eye-wave pattern became even more agitated as he recognized his famous client.

"What problem have you got now?" said Grey-Stone. "You never call me unless you've got a problem."

"No problem at all," said Qui-Qui. "It's good news. I have been selected by the rejuvenation committee for treatment. Of course, the treatment takes a half-great."

"A *half-great!*" came the loud reply over the video link. "You don't have a half-great free on your schedule until 2899!"

"I do now," she replied. "I go west for the final interview and tests two turns from now. Unless they find something that disqualifies me, I start treatment immediately after that."

"But your contracts . . ." Grey-Stone said.

"Renegotiate them," she replied. "Just remind them they will be getting the experience of an old, flabby Qui-Qui in the body of a young, firm Qui-Qui."

She watched the traveling wave motion in Grey-Stone's eye-stubs slow to almost a complete halt as he pictured the image she had created.

"At twice the original fee!" he finally said.

"That's why I have you for my manager," she replied with a rippling overtone in her tread. "There is nothing too audacious for Grey-Stone."

She paused, and her eye-stubs stood still while she rippled her bountiful eye-flaps in her famous gesture of shocked, innocent bewilderment.

"Of course . . . it could be . . . ," she said, the ripples of her eye flaps coming to a stop. "That . . . the treatment leaves me flat." She flicked off the video with a chirp of amusement as Grey-Stone's eyes stood straight up in shock.

Qui-Qui programmed her housekeepers to keep her three compounds in shape while she was gone and took the Jump Loop to the West Pole Rejuvenation Center. She had been assigned there to be close to her clan home of White Rock City. At the Rejuvenation Center she had no problem passing all the physical examinations. The last step was a final interview with the senior physician in charge of the Center, Sabin-Salk. During the examinations, Qui-Qui had had plenty of time to think. Now she had some questions.

"What I don't understand," she said, "was why I was selected instead of some scientist or writer or musician or politician?"

"According to our evaluation, you happen to be one of the best cheela ever laid on Egg," Sabin-Salk said matter-of-factly. "You are an expert in communication with other cheela. With a different background or training you too could have been a writer or a musician or a politician, perhaps even a scientist. In fact, if it weren't that you are too honest to deceive people, with your intelligence, good looks, and charisma, you could probably even convince people you were a god and start a new religious cult."

"But all I am is an entertainer," she protested.

"I don't think even you believe that," he said. "To the average holovid viewer you are nothing but twelve big eye-flaps. But those who have talked with you know that behind those eye-flaps is one of the tightest brain-knots on Egg. You have a lot of friends in large compounds. Your choice was no accident.

"Now, let me take you around the treatment facility and show you what you must undergo. The procedure will not be easy." They entered the first compound where there were a couple of robotic attendants and a lot of exercise equipment.

"First we must exercise you and feed you until you have built up a good supply of flesh in your body. The dissolver enzymes will use that as the building material to produce support structures in the intermediate plant body. Those support structures must be of high quality or they will break in the strong gravity of Egg."

Qui-Qui noticed someone exercising under the guidance of a robot in the far corner of the room. It was a large male, almost as large as she was. The robot spoke something to the male, who muttered curses as he increased the tempo of his exercise.

"Who is that?" asked Qui-Qui.

"It is Engineer Cliff-Web. He owns Web Construction Company."

Qui-Qui's eye-wave pattern slowed in puzzlement. She obviously didn't know who Cliff-Web was.

"He was the one who built the Space Fountain and the Jumbo Bagel space motor to rescue the Slow Ones," said Sabin-Salk.

All of Qui-Qui's eyes turned to look in awe at the engineer.

"I was selected with someone that important?" she said.

"Actually, he was in the first selection list," said Sabin-Salk. "But he is quite a bit older than you and, having been involved with scrollwork much of the time, he was in poor physical condition. He was in the exercise phase for almost 40 turns before he had sufficient muscle tone. Two more turns of starving, and he will be ready for treatment."

"Starving!" Qui-Qui gasped. "I thought you said we were fed."

"You are fed during the build-up phase," Sabin-Salk explained. "But we must have your well-muscled body starving and near exhaustion before we inject the animal-plant conversion enzymes. They then activate the dormant genes in you that were left after our evolution from the dragon plants long ago." He paused and observed her carefully as he continued. "I warned you that it would not be pleasant. If you would rather not take the treatment.
. . ."

"No. I want to go ahead with it," said Qui-Qui. Her eye-stubs wavered to a halt as she asked her next question. "Will I still be conscious during the burning part?"

Dr. Sabin-Salk looked bewildered, so she continued.

"I am of the clan of the Ancient One Swift-Killer, the first cheela in recorded history to undergo rejuvenation. In the hatchling pen I was told how she struggled to climb the East Pole mountains to send the first message to the humans. After sending the message, her exhausted body was severely burned by the heat from an infalling meteorite. The burning caused her body to revert spontaneously to the dragon plant form, where the damage was mended. Later the dragon plant reverted back, and Swift-Killer found she had a new, young body."

"Swift-Killer was extremely lucky," Sabin-Salk stated. "Most cheela who have tried the burning approach to rejuvenation died. The only function of the burning was to shock the body and get it to produce the animal-to-plant conversion enzymes. We do not burn you. Instead we manufacture the enzymes artificially and inject them into you. They dissolve everything in the body except the nerve tissue and the outer layer of skin. That liquid is then used to make the plant."

They left the still exercising Cliff-Web and moved on to the next compound. A large array of small machines stood in one corner of the compound, each with two tubes that connected to two larger collecting lines that led to two large tanks. A single robot was tending the machines.

"Those machines produce both the animal-to-plant and the plant-to-animal enzymes," said Sabin-Salk. "It takes all those machines about 18 turns before we have enough for one rejuvenation."

"Only one patient every 18 turns?" exclaimed Qui-Qui. "Surely you could handle more than that!"

"We will," Sabin-Salk told her. "As more of the enzyme producing machines are produced, we will increase the treatment rate to at least one per turn. It will take some time though, since the other centers are also awaiting machines."

"They don't look very large," said Qui-Qui. "You would think there would be plenty of money available for the production of rejuvenation machines. I guess they are complicated inside."

"The problem isn't money or the difficulty of making the machines," said Sabin-Salk. "The process for producing the enzyme requires the use of a rare catalyst. It is a neutron-rich isotope found only in trace amounts in the lava shield from the Exodus volcano. Since the volcano is still quite active, mining the lava is extremely hazardous. It will take a dozen greats before we have enough of the catalyst to reach full capacity. Let us go on to the 'garden.'"

They moved to the next compound. In the center of the compound were two very large dragon plants. They were of the single-root, inverted-canopy type similar to a parasol plant, but much larger. One of them was still growing and had a small crowd of robots and two live cheela attending it. The cheela had large medical badges in their hides with extra stars and colored spots to indicate their advanced degrees.

"That is what you will look like in 30 to 36 turns if you do your exercises properly." Sabin-Salk motioned to the plants with a flick of his eye-stubs.

"Who were they?" Qui-Qui asked in a subdued electronic whisper.

"*Are* they," Sabin-Salk corrected. "You would know them if I told you, but our policy is not to identify the plant form to strangers. Cheela do not mind being pointed out if they are wearing their body paint and badges, but you put all that aside when you are a plant. The larger plant is almost ready for reconstitution. We will let it mature for two more turns, then inject the plant-to-animal conversion enzyme. The reverse process only takes a few turns. The plant support structures are turned into fluid and used to rebuild the body. At the very last stage, the old outer skin peels off and the newly formed eyes come out from under their eye-flaps.''

"Is everything the way it was before, except younger?'' asked Qui-Qui.

"Everything except the brain-knot and the rest of the nerve tissue, since they are not touched by the animal-to-plant enzymes. Except for a blank period during the rejuvenation process, the memory and brain function of the new body is identical to that of the old.'' He paused and deliberately looked off in the distance as he continued. "Since you are a professional holovid performer, I am sure you are interested in what your new body will look like. I can assure you and all your loyal holovid viewers that the rebuilt body will use the same genetic tri-string that made the original Qui-Qui, and the new Qui-Qui will take up just as much volume on the holovid as the old one.''

A directional call signal vibrated through the crust that tickled the outer edge of Qui-Qui's tread as it focused in on the position of Sabin-Salk.

"An Elder from your clan has arrived to approve the final scrollwork,'' Sabin-Salk said. "If you will follow along behind, I will spread the way to my office.''

06:58:06 GMT TUESDAY 21 JUNE 2050

Zero-Gauss had left the faculty dining compound after a nourishing turnfeast and headed for her underground magnetic-field-free laboratory. She passed by some students who stopped their conversation to allow their treads to listen to her. She seemed to be simultaneously talking to herself and emitting squeaks.

"I have a delicious piece of baked Flow Slow egg for you. I wiped off most of the sauce so it shouldn't be too hot," she said as she formed a manipulator, reached into a holding pouch to extract the tasty morsel, then put the manipulator into another pouch. As the orifice of the pouch opened, a fuzzy little Slink hatchling tried to climb out, but was distracted by the sight of the food. It grabbed it eagerly and tried to stuff it all into its too-small eating pouch.

"A little too big for you, Poofsie?" she asked. Her manipulator sliced the bit of egg into smaller pieces, which were greedily devoured by the hungry hatchling. She closed the orifice just enough to keep the animal inside while allowing a small hole so he could keep a few eyes waving about outside to see where they were going.

She entered a small compound that was the top of her unique research facility, which contained subcompounds for her office and those of her graduate students. A second compound a short distance away contained the machinery that operated the underground machinery and provided the cooling for the simulated sky hanging beneath the strong superconducting roof of the laboratory. The second compound had a very unusual structure in one corner—a rectangular box made of thick metal with a door in one end and a covering over the top.

She went to her office and glanced through her computer net mail. There was nothing important, so she paid a visit to a compound containing two of her graduate students.

"How are the plants doing, Careful-Mover?" she asked one student.

"We did have one fountain plant die," Careful-Mover replied. "It shot seeds all over the room as it did so. But it had lasted 46 turns, which is close to a record."

"Did you get all the seeds picked up?" Zero-Gauss asked.

"Yes. And in the process, Fuzzy-Crust and I found another 'hot spot' in one corner," said Careful-Mover.

"Is it bad?" Zero-Gauss asked. "I'd hate to have to go through the process of pumping out the whole lab again so soon."

"It was 100 gauss right on top of the hot spot," Careful-Mover answered. "But it's quite small, and a few millimeters away it fades into the background variations of a few gauss. There were a few plants near the corner so we just moved the containers to another part of the room."

Zero-Gauss turned to Fuzzy-Crust.

"I have a replacement for Peter," she said, pulling the tiny ball of fuzz and eyes from her pouch.

"Poofsie, meet Fuzzy-Crust. He will be taking good care of you from now on," said the professor, forming a little nest on the floor with the edge of her tread and dropping the animal into it. The Slink tried to climb over the edge, but Zero-Gauss kept it in place by rippling her skin underneath the tiny tread. The Slink stopped and looked up at Fuzzy-Crust with all twelve of its dark red eyes. The student brought an eye down to look at it.

"So now it will be Flopsie, Mopsie, Cottonball, and Poofsie," said Fuzzy-Crust. "You found an excellent replacement. It looks just like Peter."

"These genetically pure strains of laboratory Slinks all look the same," said Zero-Gauss. "I just chose the one that looked the smartest."

"You should have chosen the dumbest one," said Careful-Mover. "Peter was smart and look what happened to him. He figured out how to open his cage and died of overeating. Set my zero-gauss horticulture thesis back half a great.''

"I'll make sure the cage is locked this time," Zero-Gauss promised. "Do you have anything else for me to take down?"

"A batch of seedlings," said Careful-Mover. "They are waiting in the storage pen next to the elevator."

Zero-Gauss checked the video monitors that showed every corner of the underground nursery and animal pens, made a mental note to check a few plants that looked like they needed attention, then made her way to the elevator in the facilities compound.

Next to the elevator was a dressing subcompound with high walls. She stripped off her six metal professor badges, took off her jewelry, wiped off all her body paint, and emptied out all her pouches, even her heritage pouch containing her clan totem. The totem was made of clay fired in the ancient manner and had a baked-in magnetic field. She rolled the totem in a wiper and put it into a drawer with a combination lock. Now, as naked as the day she was hatched, she opened the door to the dressing room and looked out. Electron-Pusher, the facilities operator, was waiting discreetly at the operations console around the corner.

She moved softly to the holding pens and loaded up her pouches. Poofsie went into a small pouch and the plastic pots containing the seedlings sprouting in non-magnetic soil went into her carry-all pouch. Now quite bulky, she faced the open door of the elevator. The elevator did not have a cooled ceiling, and it took all her nerve to make her tread move her body under the heavy metal roof. Once inside, she forced her eyes to look at the floor and calmed down. She activated the audio channel of the video link.

"You may shut the door, Electron-Pusher," she said.

"Door shutting, Professor," said Electron-Pusher. "What is the biggest diameter you're carrying?"

"Nothing bigger than my brain-knot," she said.

"We only need three pump-walls then," said Electron-Pusher. There was a whining noise, and the back wall of the elevator moved toward Zero-Gauss.

"Here comes the first wall," he said. "Let me know when everything is through."

The heavy superconducting metal wall stopped in the middle of the room, and a small circular orifice opened in the door a little way off the floor. First, Zero-Gauss emptied out her pouches and arranged the seedling pots near the wall. Then she stuck a manipulator through the tiny hole, grabbed a handle on the other side, narrowed herself down as small as she could, and slipped herself through the hole. The iris on the hole followed the outlines of her body, dilating as the brain-knot went through, then finally shrinking down to the diameter of the trailing manipulator that held the squirming Poofsie firmly in its grip.

While her body resumed its normal flattened shape, her manipulator was busy transferring plants from one side of the wall to the other. That done, the orifice closed tightly and the superconducting wall continued across the elevator to the door, compressing all the magnetic field lines in front of it. The elevator door opened briefly, and the field was pushed to the outside. A second wall approached from the back of the elevator and the process was repeated. The only difference now was that the first wall was made non-superconducting before the final expulsion stroke. After the third wall had passed, Zero-Gauss went over to a control plate in the floor and pressed in a code. A probe rose out of the floor into the middle of the room.

"A good pump," she said over the audio link. "It only registers 2800 gauss."

"Close enough to zero for the chamber lock to handle," said Electron-Pusher. "Ready to fall?"

Her eye-wave pattern developed an annoyed twitch at his stale attempt at a joke. He had probably gotten a squeal out of one of her graduate students sometime in the past at the thought of falling down under the ground. Now he repeated it every time they went down.

"I am ready to descend," she said, her tread firmly rapping the metal plating of the floor. She didn't quite get the right "Senior Professor" tone in the 'trum. It is a little hard to sound authoritative when you are naked.

"Yes, Professor," said Electron-Pusher, and the elevator began its slow descent beneath the crust.

At the bottom, the magnetic pumping procedure was carried out again using the pump-walls in the lock leading to the low-field chamber. All the residual magnetic fields possible were pumped into the elevator, which used barriers that alternated between normal conducting and superconducting states to trap the fields. The elevator then rose again to the surface where the trapped fields were expelled to the outside.

Zero-Gauss stopped by the dressing alcove, slapped on some neutral body paint, plugged in six professor badges made of metal-colored plastic, and, now decent, moved out in view of the video cameras scanning the chamber. The ceiling was a comforting black. She, Poofsie, and the plants were all glad to be out of the stifling closeness of the elevator and locks.

She started with the animals. Three of the nine segments of the field-free room held multiple breeding pairs of all the major animals on Egg with the exception of the two that were larger than a mature cheela, the ponderous Flow Slow and the carnivorous Swift. These were represented by miniature genetic hybrids about the size of a Slink.

She had a number of different types of Slinks. In addition to three sets of brightly colored but stupid food Slinks bred with flesh of different flavors, there were some highly trained herding Slinks bred for intelligence. Now, with the addition of Poofsie, she had two sets of a laboratory strain especially bred with bodies that responded like the body of a cheela to environmental changes.

She had a lot to check in the laboratory. After having gone through the long, laborious task of getting into the laboratory, she was in no hurry to leave. There was at least two turns of work to do, what with taking the animals through physical checkups as well as intelligence tests. They had restocked the food lockers in the dressing alcove the last time they had pumped out the room, so she would just refuel at turnfeast from them. Besides, someone had to check the quality of the nuts and fruits on the food plants.

Steel-Slicer was looking forward to his return to the Polar Orbiting Space Station. Many things had happened since his last visit there. He had retired from active duty, was elected to the Legislature of the Combined Clans, and had been selected for rejuvenation. He was still entitled to wear his two-star Admiral cluster badges, so he put them on for his visit.

Far-Ranger had also just finished her rejuvenation and was about to warp back out into interstellar space. She had invited him up to attend her "warpfeast" before she left.

The robotic glide-car hummed through the run-down east side of Bright's Heaven and slid to a stop in front of the entrance to the Jump Loop terminal. Steel-Slicer slid his magnecard into the payslot, and the glide-car released him. As he flowed to the walkway he noticed a small, wiry, scarred, and badgeless youngling slumped against the wall nearby. The youngling's eyes were casually, but attentively, watching everything going on around him, especially the traffic in and out of the automatic doors to the terminal. The terminal was in a rough section of town, so Steel-Slicer moved quickly across the street and through the *IN* door.

Once inside, he relaxed a little and headed for the baggage queue, where he unpouched his small traveling kit. There was a little time left before the jump so he moved through the crowded terminal toward the pulp-bar. He started to circle around a small, heavily speckled female who had all eyes on the tough-looking male to whom she was talking. Suddenly, without seeming to look where she was going, the female backed away from the tough, and Admiral Steel-Slicer found himself half-enveloped with speckled female flesh.

"Excuse me," Steel-Slicer said as he tried to move away.

"I don't mind if you don't," said the nubile female as she brought a number of her eyes around and draped a few speckled eye-flaps on his topside. "Besides, you're a lot handsomer than that rough-tread over there." She flicked her eye-stubs at the tough, who glared at them. Steel-Slicer noticed that the speckled pattern on the female extended to her eye-balls. Some of them were pink instead of the normal dark-red.

The Admiral tried to extract himself, but found that the female had formed a number of tendrils and was holding him by his two-star Admiral's badges. Other tendrils, hidden by their bodies, started tickling him.

"Want to have a little fun?" she said in an electronic whisper that sent tingles through his body. "I know a nice quiet little pad-place nearby."

Steel-Slicer started to turn down the offer when he was jolted by a slap from a heavy manipulator.

"Leave my flapper alone!" said the tough, glaring at him.

Stunned by the shock, Steel-Slicer didn't notice the loss of two of his star-cluster badges as the freckled female pulled away.

"I got them!" she hollered, and started for the *IN* door at full tread ripple. The tough was right behind her.

"Stop!" shouted Steel-Slicer as he finally noticed his loss. He started after them. The tough pulled a sticker from a pouch in his rapidly retreating trailing edge and waved it menacingly.

"Go suck your eye-balls, Spacer!" yelled the tough.

"Here comes a clanker!" warned the speckled female as they approached the door. The door was opened by their confederate outside, and it almost shut before the peace officer arrived; but he squeezed through the crack and took up the chase.

Steel-Slicer halted when the peace officer took off after them. He stopped, a little embarrassed, and shifted a star cluster partially to cover the bare place on his hide. It was doubtful the officer would catch the thieves. Since it was time for his jumpcraft to leave, he turned and headed for the boarding area.

"That egg-eating clanker got through!" shouted Speckle-Top. "Scatter! We'll sell the stuff later!"

She pushed down a side street that led toward the old temple grounds, where she knew there were plenty of places to hide. Luckily the clanker had followed Crumpled-Tread. She was the one with the stolen badges so even if the clanker caught him, they would have to let him go.

Her street-trained tread heard the rapid movement of two other clankers coming, so she hurried, trying to keep the noise of her tread-ripple down. At the entrance to the old temple grounds she squeezed her skinny body through a quake-crack in the ancient outer perimeter fence. Dodging some workers carrying out restoration work, she rushed past one of the newly restored "eyes" of the ancient monument and made her way to a small crust-rock at a point where the base of the "eye-stub" met the wall that formed the "body" of the temple. Behind that rock was an ancient tunnel that she discovered a few turns ago. She had noticed a tiny hole in the wall after the huge crust-moving machines had passed. Looking for a safe place to hide stolen stuff until it could be sold, she had found that the hole opened into an underground tunnel heavily lined with an old-fashioned type of thick metal superconductor.

When originally built in the days of Pink-Eyes the prophet, the superconductor had kept the magnetic field of Egg out of the tunnel so the High Priests of Bright could travel quickly from the outer sanctuary to the top of the Inner Eye mound, where they would miraculously appear to the crowds below. The tunnel was now clogged with pinned magnetic flux that was strongly coupled to the walls.

Speckle-Top pushed her way through the flux lines until she was inside, whereupon she rolled the rock back to hide the entrance. She relaxed as the magnetic field pinned her body solidly to the surrounding crust. She was a little apprehensive about being underground, but felt sure that the clankers would never find her in her secret hideout.

* *

The end of the shift finally turned around, and Heavy-Egg dismissed his crew. He watched them crowd onto the lifts and head for the surface of Egg and the pulp-bars with more speed than he had seen out of them all turn.

"Last lift, boss." Hungry-Pouch was holding the lift steady.

"Wait for me," said Heavy-Egg. "Got to see the chief."

He took the elevator to the upper deck of Topside Platform and made his way to the compound that was the office of the chief engineer of Topside Platform. His crew had barely made their quota today, and he finally had to take some action. He didn't mind a little squeeze and tickle during the shift, it helped make the turns go by; but when he had found Yellow-Rock treading Easy-Flow behind the elevator shaft, that was the pod that toppled the plant. He wanted them replaced.

The door to the chief engineer's compound was open. Heavy-Egg flowed in with a determined tread, then stopped. A young stranger was in the office, and the chief engineer was listening to him deferentially. The youngling had badges bigger than the chief engineer's badges.

"Shift Supervisor Heavy-Egg," said the stranger. "It's good to see you again." Seeing the bewilderment in Heavy-Egg's eye-wave pattern, he added, "I'm your boss, Cliff-Web. I've been 'rejuved'—I think they call it now. Do you have a problem?"

"It can wait until next shift," Heavy-Egg said, reversing his tread-ripple. He moved back out the door in a daze and made his way to the bottom deck. Yellow-Rock avoided his glance as Heavy-Egg flowed onto the lift, took over the controls from Hungry-Pouch and started the long trip down the Space Fountain to the surface.

* *

Time-Circle was feeling lonely again and was looking for someone to talk to. Another of the channels in his time machine had become clogged with noise. He wandered over to the other side of the Inner Eye Institute and visited the Crustallography compound; but Neutron-Drip wasn't at her computer, so he went looking for her in the laboratory. All he found was Eager-Eyes, busy treading a touch-and-taste console. On either side of the console were two highly flattened spheroidal bowls that represented the east and west hemispheres of Egg. They were shaped according to the old-style maps where distances were marked off in tread lengths. They were flat in the regions near the magnetic poles where the cheela treads were of minimum size, and more curved near the magnetic equator where the horizontal component of the magnetic field stretched out the cheela's tread. Now that the cheela had space travel, they realized that Egg was spherical; but the ancient shape was still useful for the crustallogists, for most of the activity in the crust took place near the poles. The maps flickered with lights showing the crust-quake activity. A bright blue spot would appear on the map, then shift down in color as the intensity of the quake died.

"I was looking for Professor Neutron-Drip," Time-Circle told Eager-Eyes.

"I'm right here," came a muffled voice. The voice seemed to come from under Eager-Eyes' tread.

"She's on-site at the East Pole," Eager Eyes explained. "I'll switch the picture to the visual screen on that wall over there. Things are happening fast, so I had better keep working with the touch-and-taste screen.

"I came over to see if we could have turnfeast together," said Time-Circle. "I didn't realize you had gone."

"The trip wasn't planned," replied the image of Neutron-Drip. She was moving among an array of acoustic transceivers that were picking up data from the distant seismic instruments buried under the crust around the East Pole.

"I jumped over early this turn to make sure the transceivers stay on scale. I think there is a big quake coming. But I can't be sure, since this is the first time anyone has tried to record the quakes prior to a big one."

"Things really started to happen just after last turnfeast," Eager-Eyes reported. "I was watching the signals coming in from the array around the East Pole, when I began to see ringlike patterns."

"Not only that," said Neutron-Drip. "Although they started small, the magnitude of the quakes has been increasing nearly exponentially for the last ten dothturns as they close in on the root of the East Pole mountains."

"Exponentially!" Time-Circle was clearly impressed.

"I expect a 'Trimble-tremblor' anytime soon," said Neutron-Drip. She noticed the confused twitch in his eye-stub pattern. "The East Pole mountains will drop a few millimeters, and the length of a turn will increase slightly. The human Nobel Laureate Trimble was the first to predict them accurately from her observations of the Crab Nebula neutron star."

"You might be in danger! You must leave at once!" Time-Circle shouted.

"Too late now," Neutron-Drip responded. "Keep collecting the data, Eager-Eyes!" she commanded. Suddenly the viewscreen went blank.

Time-Circle shifted his gaze to the bowl that showed the eastern hemisphere. The East Pole mountains were surrounded by flash after flash of bright blue light. Suddenly the whole East Pole exploded in a blue glare. There was a pause, then a smooth ripple spread out from the focal point. It reached Swift's Climb . . . and the display went out.

Time-Circle *now* understood why three channels in his time machine were blocked with noise. He raced out of the lab and across the Institute compound. There was one clear back-channel left. If only he could get a message back in time to himself, he might be able to warn the rest of the population on Egg. As he pushed his body through the clinging magnetic fields coming from the crust, he fought off the specter of despair. After all, "he" that was here on this time-line, struggling to reach the time machine, had received no warning message from the future. His present time-line was doomed, but perhaps he could create a paradox—a bifurcation—that would save the "he," and the rest of Egg, on some other time-line. He struggled on.

Quake!

Deep within the root of the East Pole mountains, a thick block of crust groaned audibly under the great stress of the billions of tons of matter piled up for centimeters overhead. The stress peaked to the ultimate limit, then with a loud crack, a block of crust broke and a long rip propagated through the striated undercrust. The mountain peaks, now unsupported, dropped a full twenty millimeters in the intense gravity field of Egg. The shock wave from the fall of the mountain range spread out from the East Pole at nearly the speed of light, striking first at the town of Swift's Climb.

Walls cracked and communications were cut off as the crust lifted and fell. Neutron-Drip felt her eye-stubs flutter as the crust rolled beneath her. She kept watching the overloaded instruments and willing them to get back on scale so they would record the remainder of what had to be the largest crustquake in cheela history.

A little while later the surface wave passed through the Inner Eye Institute in Bright's Heaven. Time-Circle's already panicked brain-knot screamed mentally as the crust raised up underneath his tread. He slowed to a self-conscious deliberate slide as the wave passed under him and the crust dropped again, having done little to him or the well-constructed compounds of the Inner Eye Institute.

The magnetic fields of the star, frozen into the moving crust, waved back and forth a little, causing electrical currents to flow in Time-Circle's body and exciting the electrons and random nuclei in the tenuous atmosphere until they were moving fast enough to generate electron-positron pairs. The counter-flow heat exchangers in the base of his eye-stubs increased their cooling capacity to extract the heat that had been generated in his eye-balls by the flowing electric currents. As his eyes cooled to their normal dark red, he could see the decaying X-ray fluorescence as the remainder of the positrons generated by the atmospheric currents found an electron to annihilate with.

More slowly now, Time-Circle continued on to the Time-Comm compound to check his machine. Although the crustquake was a large one, he was sure that Cliff-Web had designed the machine itself to survive the shock. But perhaps the quake had disturbed the control console, and that was what was causing the strange noise signals.

The lift carrying Heavy-Egg and seven of his crew was passing level 50 when a flare of light from the atmosphere below signaled the start of a crustquake. A couple of methturns later the hum of the up-deflectors changed pitch as the accelerators on the ground compensated for the twenty-millimeter drop of the crust underneath them.

"That was a big one," Heavy-Egg thought, as his tread felt the change in pitch of the vibrations in the deck.

There was a loud *clang*. A pushout, the first in many turns, was hanging in the catcher, the extra strain having proved too much for the ring.

The shock waves from the crustquake penetrated to the center of the neutron star where they were bounced back and forth by the density differences between the various layers. A number of the bouncing shocks met each other at one of the boundary layers and concentrated their energy in a very small region. The extra pressure was just enough to initiate a phase change in the material, and it shrank in volume. Once started, the phase change spread at nearly the speed of light. An inner layer of star almost a kilometer thick changed density and shrank by two meters, leaving the outer layers of the neutron star unsupported. The outer layers fell, and the crustquake became a *Starquake*.

The gigantic starquake rose to the surface and shook the crust like a Swift shredding a Flow Slow. The crust alternately buckled and spread, sending anything loose moving across the surface at high speed to smash into walls, plants, or cliffs. The magnetic fields embedded in the crust shook along with the crust and accelerated the electrons and ions in the thin, tenuous atmosphere. The atmosphere heated up until it reached a temperature of a billion degrees. Electron-positron pairs were created, only to annihilate again to produce a continuing flood of X-rays. The X-rays bounced off the high speed electrons in the super-heated atmosphere and with each bounce increased in energy until they were a deadly, penetrating glare of gamma rays.

Time-Circle felt the crust drop beneath him once again. Unlike the first time, the dropping motion didn't stop. The whole world around him was dropping and dropping. The gravelectromagnetic fields in the Time-Comm machine lost control of the spinning black hole at the heart of the machine. The black hole converted back into energy, blowing up the Time-Comm compound and Time-Circle.

Neutron-Drip had been expecting a second series of shocks as the crustquake circled around Egg and returned again. It returned early. She was still trying to understand why the quake seemed stronger than before, when she found herself sliding helplessly at high speed toward the array of instruments she had been tending. The sharp edges on the instruments cut her to ribbons.

Zero-Gauss was in her underground laboratory. She was picking up some pellets that had missed the catcher on a fountain plant during the initial crustquake. The starquake hit and she and all the plants and animals were swept across the metal floor to one corner of the room. The support pillars buckled, and the roof fell in.

A pulsating sheet of fire flickered over the surface of the neutron star, generating a high-energy blast of radiation that spread out into space. It only took a millisecond for the high-energy ultraviolet, X-rays, and gamma rays to reach Dragon Slayer in its synchronous orbit above Bright's Heaven. The stronger of the gamma rays sheeted through the tough hull of the spacecraft, through the thin protection of Amalita's spacesuit, and irradiated her body with three times the lethal dose. The ultraviolet radiation bounced off the star image telescope mirror, burned through the protective filters, and poured unimpeded down on the star image table, flooding the Science Deck and Amalita's eyes in an ultraviolet glare.

Amalita's eyelids closed too late over cloudy-white corneas and started to blister under the intense radiation. Following on the heels of the electromagnetic radiation pulse came a three-pulse burst of kilohertz gravitational radiation that whipped Amalita's body back and forth, breaking three joints and snapping her spinal cord at the neck. The last memory stored in Amalita's dying brain was of the stinging pain in her eyes.

Qui-Qui was still recuperating from her regeneration and was taking it easy at West Pole mountain resort. She was playing with her new toy, a custom built, high powered, personal flyer. There were less than a dozen on all of Egg, for they cost much more to operate than intercity glide-cars and weren't any faster. A glide-car, however, couldn't go *up*.

The flyer had a gravity repulsion drive for operation near the surface, an inertia drive for high altitude, and superconducting wings for gliding on the magnetic field of Egg. It was expensive, it was extravagant, but it was fun!

She took off from the resort and jumped over some nearby foothills to find a small deserted valley. She took the flyer up to speed on the gravity drive and hit one-twelfth light-speed before she had to switch to inertia drive and zoom up over the mountain at the end of the valley. Turning off the repulsor drive and flipping out the wings, she put it into climb on the inertia drive and watched the energy reserves in her accumulators drop. Her manager would complain about the recharging bill, but she had plenty of stars saved, and there would be lots more now that she was young again.

Qui-Qui was at 25 meters altitude when the starquake hit. Fortunately, she had been looking up at the West Pole Space Station when the atmosphere lit up. As it was, before she could pull them in under her eyeflaps, two of her eyes had spots that didn't go away for nearly a turn.

She had trouble believing the altimeter when it varied from 24 to 26 meters every few methturns. All the communicator channels were silent with the exception of some lonely navigation beacon somewhere that proved that her set was working. She knew it was a crustquake because of the glow in the atmosphere, but it must have been a huge one and it was still going strong.

She would be safe as long as she stayed up out of the atmosphere while the crust was moving. She set the flyer on autopilot with a minimum power trajectory. The plane slid out its superconducting wings and started gliding slowly down the magnetic field lines, extracting lift when it could from the slow variations in the fields as they followed the motion of the rolling crust below.

The jumpcraft carrying Admiral Steel-Slicer was starting its jump to orbit when the starquake pulled the support structure out from under the Jump Loop. High-speed ribbon sliced through the outskirts of Bright's Heaven as the pilot fought the jumpcraft clear. The jumpcraft didn't have enough energy to make it into orbit and arced over into a trajectory that ended in the middle of the West Pole mountains. One by one the pilot lost the sight in eight of his twelve eyes from the X-ray glare as he tried to find the West Pole Jump Loop for an emergency landing. It wasn't there. He snapped out his superconducting wings and, using the last of his onboard emergency propulsion reserves, managed to bounce the jumpcraft off the West Pole magnetic field into an elliptical orbit.

"Periapsis 5 meters and apoapsis 90 meters, Captain Light-Streak," the copilot, Slippery-Wing, reported. "Coming up on periapsis now."

The altimeter fluctuated wildly as the undulating crust passed by a few meters below them. Moving at orbital velocities, they shot under a slowly moving flyer high above them. The underside of the flyer glowed brightly from the glare below.

"I'll circularize the orbit with magnetic lift to give us a chance," Light-Streak said. "But it won't be long before we run out of power and the gravity generators fail, leaving us in free fall."

Slippery-Wing concentrated on her instruments and tried not to think of what it would be like to die by slow disintegration.

* *

Speckle-Top felt the bump of the first crustquake, then the ups-and-downs of the big crustquake that came after. The ups-and-downs went on and on. Turnfeast time came, and she was hungry. The big quake was probably keeping the clankers busy, so she started to squirm out of her hiding place. When she reached the rock covering the entrance, she put part of her tread on it and listened. The only noise was that of stones rubbing against one another as the crust moved up and down. She pushed the rock aside a little and peeked out. The glare left streaks in her vision. She pulled the rock back and retreated into the blackness, hungry and cursing.

Heavy-Egg, his senses extra-alert because of the crust-quake, tucked his body into the lift console station, formed extra manipulators to take over the controls in case any of the automatics stopped working, and continued to monitor the hum of each of the six deflectors holding up his lift platform. He slowed the speed of their drop to give the deflectors more margin.

"Snatch that pushout, Metal-Pusher," he said.

"It's still hot, Boss," Metal-Pusher complained.

"I said 'snatch it'," said Heavy-Egg. "That was a big quake, and it'll be back around soon. Quality won't like it if you bring them in a pair of bangers."

There was a grunt, a curse, and a clang as the hot ring was dropped on the deck of the lift.

The up-deflectors started to change pitch again.

"Here it comes," Heavy-Egg said, six of his eyes on the instrument panel and six eyes on the six streams of rings above them, glittering in the glow from Egg. The pitch deepened and deepened as the up-going rings came further and further apart. The deck vibrated with anxious murmurs from the crew. Heavy-Egg watched the instruments carefully. The automatics were shifting the load from the troubled up-streams to the stable down-streams. The pitch continued to deepen, then become erratic.

The up-deflector indicators were fluctuating rapidly as the deflectors attempted to straighten out the ragged stream of rings. There was a clang as another pushout appeared in the catcher. Metal-Pusher was ready and tried to snatch it, but his hook was knocked from his manipulator by another ring that banged loudly into the first. Three more rings followed.

"We're losing it!" Heavy-Egg shouted.

The up-going streams slowly pulled away from the down-going streams, destroyed their deflectors, and like three ragged knives, sliced through the triangularly shaped lift. Two of the streams were soon out away from the platform, but the third was making its way right across the middle. Bodies tried to compress to make room on the crowded lift for the deadly stream. A scream of terror turned into a scream of pain as the rings tore off one side of Yellow-Rock and continued on to cut their way through the platform.

Three of Heavy-Egg's eyes watched in horror as the platform was cut in two. As the last connection through the decking was severed, the voices of the five members of the crew on the other section were cut off. That section had only one deflector, and with no connection to the computer in the control console, the single deflector couldn't compensate adequately. The section tilted, then fell away to the crust below.

Heavy-Egg turned his attention to his remaining section. It was the smaller of the two pieces even though it had the control console and two deflectors. Besides the console operator there was only room for two, and one of those was the dying Yellow-Rock. The down-streams now started to show some variations. The automatics reached their limits of control and the platform tilted badly as pushout after pushout banged into the catcher. Yellow-Rock screamed again as he started to slide off the slippery deck.

"I got you," said Hungry-Pouch. She already had a good grip on the barrier rail with a number of manipulators and now was trying to hold onto Yellow-Rock's limp body by grabbing his eye-stubs and jamming pairs of manipulators into his pouches. Their bodies slid closer to the edge, tilting the platform further.

"Let him go," Heavy-Egg shouted. "He's good as dead anyway."

"He's my buddy! We hatched under the same mantle!" Hungry-Pouch explained. "I'm not letting go! You just get this Bright-Afflicted lift level."

"You can't save him!" Heavy-Egg shouted again, fighting the controls. "Let him go!"

There was a grunt, a sliding noise, and the deck came back to level. Heavy-Egg was alone on the platform.

The lift was now down to where Level 30 should have been, but there was nothing there. There were no up-streams anymore, and he was riding on two of the three down-streams. The glare from the ground was becoming brighter, and he had to shield his eyes to watch the controls. He was dropping the lift as fast as he dared, but he needed to know how much down-stream he had left to work with.

He stuck one eye out for a quick look upwards. In the seared after-image he saw three long streams and a lot of dots drifting off to one side. The larger dots had the hexagonal shapes of the 10 kilometer level platforms, but some were the triangular lift platforms. The tiny dots he didn't want to identify.

He risked another look with a second eye to where Level 20 should have been. The X-ray glare was brighter now. As he pulled the painful eye back in under its eyeflap, he resigned himself to having the image burnt into that eye-ball permanently. The three down-streams were definitely shorter, but he should be able to make it to the surface. It was a good thing he had risked a look, for one of the two streams he was using was bent and ragged toward the top.

He used both down-streams for another methturn, then just before Level 10 switched to the one good stream. Rotating the platform around the good stream so it was out of the way of the ragged tail on the second stream, he continued down to the surface. When the altitude indicator showed he had a meter to go, he slowed down. He sacrificed another eye in a look over the side to see a glaring mountain of rings piled up where Base Level had been. There wasn't much time left, so he dropped quickly down the last few centimeters, hit the pile of rings, and slid down and away from the rest of the incoming stream. The lift platform coasted to the bottom of the pile of rings and stopped.

He was alive! And nothing worse than a couple of seared eyeballs. For a long time he stayed on the platform, his eyes tucked under their eye-flaps. After the crust movement had slowed down a little, he peeked out to find that the atmosphere was still flickering with X-rays, but it wasn't too bad this high up in the East Pole mountains. He made his way across the slippery rings until he had his tread once again on firm crust.

He looked up and found the tiny spots that were the East Pole Space Station and the Topside Platform. Topside, having lost its support from the fountain, had drifted off into its own elliptical orbit. Heavy-Egg was wondering what was happening to the people on Topside now that they were in free fall with no black holes to provide gravity. It must be horrible to go that way. He was glad he was on Egg where he was safe.

A strong aftershock rumbled up from beneath the East Pole mountains. The shock became more concentrated as it reached the peak of the mountain. Traveling with the shock was a sheet of X-ray flame. Growing brighter every meter, the flame roared up the valley and burned Heavy-Egg's eyes off.

Both Cliff-Web and the chief engineer paused as their treads noticed the change in the everpresent hum in the deck.

"Crustquake," said the chief engineer. "I thought I noticed an increase in the light reflected from the East Pole Space Station a little while ago."

They continued their discussion while the hum slowly varied in pitch as the ring-streams compensated for the motion of the crust below. The variations had almost faded from their attention when the pitch changed again. The note dropped lower and lower and kept dropping. All their eye-stubs came to alert as they felt the platform start to drop out from under them. A staccato of muffled bangs from an overload of pushouts sent them both out the door and across the deck toward the elevator to the machine deck below. Topside Platform wobbled as it lost the upward force that had been holding it in place. The noise from below became louder. Then, through the deck in front of them shot a deadly stream of high-speed metal rings.

"Get everyone to the launch area and on a shuttle!" Cliff-Web shouted. The chief engineer pulled out an emergency communicator from a pouch, placed it on the deck and put his tread over it. His amplified voice blasted its way throughout all three levels.

"Everyone to the launch area. Topside is going into free fall. Repeat. Everyone to the launch area and onto a shuttlecraft."

"All three up-streams are out of control." Cliff-Web looked around as his creation was sliced into pieces by the errant streams.

Treads gripping the rough spots on the deck, they made their way to the launch area. The atmosphere above the deck was already full of tiny flakes of dirt that were coming apart and expanding into tenuous plasma. Three shuttlecraft waited in their launch cradles, and some of them already had a few workers on top of their curved surfaces. Cliff-Web's eye-balls were starting to itch as he moved up the slippery curved ramp to the safety of the shuttlecraft with its black hole gravity field.

"Shall I lift off, Boss?" the shuttlecraft pilot asked. "There's all kinds of junk starting to fall off Topside onto us."

"Not yet," said Cliff-Web. "We're in no danger of falling, and it will be a long time before Topside decomposes into non-degenerate matter. Who's missing?"

"Nearly everyone from the lower decks," the chief engineer replied. "Wait, here comes the elevator!"

Through the deck the distant whine of motors could be heard. Way off in the distance a crowded elevator rose through the center of the platform. A cursing flood of roustabouts swarmed from the elevator toward the launch deck. Driven by the itching madness in their disintegrating hides and daring only to poke out an occasional eye from under their eye-flaps, they rushed blindly toward the launch deck.

"Stop! Sto . . . !" the first one cried as she became aware of the gaping slash that blocked their way. Her tread tried to reverse on the slippery surface of the decomposing deck, but the pressure from behind was too much. Her cry stopped abruptly as she slid into space.

Instead of falling, however, she free-falled across the gap; and her voice returned, louder and cursing, as her mangled tread clung tenaciously to the jagged metal on the other side.

"Jump!" Cliff-Web shouted to the others who were milling nervously on the other side of the chasm. "You will just float over."

The itching grew worse as flakes of skin billowed in a cloud around the stranded crew as they tried to overcome a lifetime of habit and deliberately throw themselves over a precipitous cliff.

"I'll do it if you will," Hard-Way told Shiny-Tread.

"Last one over eats Tiny Shell ploops." Shiny-Tread moved away from the crack, then tucked his eyes under their flaps, smoothly rippled up to speed on the increasingly slippery deck, and launched himself into orbit. Hard-Way followed right behind. She was larger and stronger than he was, and her greater strength gave her a longer leap over the void.

Once he had jumped, Shiny-Tread felt an amazing sense of well-being, as if he were back in his egg. His body contracted into a ball, distorted by the muscular tread that still twitched as it tried fitfully to make contact with something solid. The itching of his hide grew more intense. He pushed out an eye-ball to look. He could see the platform floating by below him, Hard-Way balled up high above him, and the crowded shuttlecraft ahead. He would have passed over the shuttlecraft and out into space, but the gravity of the black hole in the shuttlecraft reached out and pulled him in. He landed heavily on the topside of the chief engineer.

"I'm sorry, Chief," Shiny-Tread mumbled as he clumsily climbed down off his boss's topside onto the curved deck. But no one paid him any attention. Even the chief engineer's eyes were turned upward as sorrowful sounds murmured through the deck. Shiny-Tread looked up.

"Hard-Way!" Shiny-Tread shouted. "Come back! COME BACK!!"

They watched in silence as Hard-Way sailed high over the launch area and off into the distance. They saw one of her eyes pop out for a look, then her tread start to move futilely in an attempt to return. The cloud of particles floating around Hard-Way increased and cut off their view.

"You will have to jump slower or go around . . ." Cliff-Web told the crew.

"We'll have no hide left if we try to go around," said Many-Rings, a new shift supervisor. "We've got to cross." She formed manipulators and grabbed onto three of her crew nearby.

"Hold on, you lumps of flab," she said. "I'm going to play jump loop." She brought out most of her eyes and, concentrating carefully, stretched her body out into a long bridge and grabbed the opposite side. She moved her rear manipulators off her crew and attached them to the edge of the deck. Then she pulled in her eyes and tried not to think of what she was doing.

"Get across, you Tiny-Shell-brained offspring of a Flow Slow!" her trailing tread roared. The crew gingerly crossed over on the makeshift bridge, pulled their valiant supervisor over to safety and soon were all crowded in the protective gravity of the shuttlecraft. Some of the crew had lost so much hide they were starting to ooze through the muscle tissue underneath.

There was a rumble from below, and the deck lurched as Topside Platform started to break up.

"Raise shuttle," Cliff-Web ordered. "And take us up to the East Pole Space Station. We'll have to take a jump-craft or catapult-lift down and start helping get things restored back on Egg."

Captain Far-Ranger was discussing her warpfeast plans with the chef on East Pole Space Station when Egg flared up. When the light became too bright to look at, she knew there was trouble and headed for the Command Deck. Once there, she stayed in the background and let the station commander, Admiral Hohmann-Transfer, run things.

"Communications Officer, any transmissions from the surface yet?" Hohmann-Transfer asked.

"None from the surface except a single navigation beacon," Lieutenant Giga-Byte replied. "But two vehicles are sending transmissions. One is the jumpcraft in the abort orbit. The other is a personal flyer at the West Pole. The West Pole Space Station has been unable to make contact with the flyer. They don't have transmitters for the flyer band."

"How is the jumpcraft orbit?" Hohmann-Transfer asked.

"The pilot was able to circularize the orbit. But they are running low on power to operate the gravity generators."

"How much time do they have?"

"Less than a turn," said the Comm Officer.

"If only we had a vehicle that didn't depend on a ground launcher for the energy to get up and down," said the admiral.

"We do," Far-Ranger interrupted. "My interstellar scout ship is designed to operate around neutron stars. It can't land and take off, but I should be able to drop down, match orbits with that jumpcraft, then make it back out to synchronous orbit on my drives."

"That will save at least three of them. Maybe more if we can crowd them in."

"If we empty the food lockers and cargo hold, I can probably carry a whole jumpcraft load," said Far-Ranger. "I'm sure the passengers wouldn't mind a dothturn or two in the freezer."

"First Officer!" roared Hohmann-Transfer. "Get a crew and empty that scout ship! Navigator! Prepare a trajectory and dump it in the scout ship computer!"

"I'll have plenty of time for calculating my trajectory myself while my ship is being off-loaded," Far-Ranger politely reminded her.

"Of course," said Admiral Hohmann-Transfer. "My apologies."

06:58:07.1 GMT TUESDAY 21 JUNE 2050

A half-turn later Far-Ranger threw her scout ship at the horizon of Egg. Pushing her inertia drive to its limits, she matched orbits with the slowly sinking jumpcraft.

"If I didn't need my last four eyes to watch my instruments," Pilot Light-Streak said over the communications link. "I'd say, 'It's good to see you.' Any ideas on how to transfer the passengers?"

"Your artificial gravity is planar, while my black hole gravity is spherical," Far-Ranger said. "An osculating tangent is the only solution."

Far-Ranger slowly lowered her orbit until her spherical scout ship was above the orbiting jumpcraft. The copilot Slippery-Wing and two of the passengers had removed a section of the magnetic shielding that covered the passenger section of the jumpcraft, and Far-Ranger put her scout ship just above the hole. One by one, the passengers were hoisted, prodded, or pushed up from the flat deck of the jumpcraft to land, upside down, on the curved deck of the scout ship.

"Up you go!" said Admiral Steel-Slicer, who had been tossing his fellow passengers up to Slippery-Wing above. He reached for the next available body and found he had the pilot of the jumpcraft.

"Thank you for your help, Admiral," said Light-Streak. "But you are next."

"But your eyes . . . ." Steel-Slicer protested.

"I am captain of this jumpcraft," Light-Streak responded, "and I will be the last one off her."

"Of course," said Steel-Slicer. "My apologies. You take the end of the safety line then." Having had plenty of low gravity experience, he bunched one half of his tread around a fixture, used that purchase to slap the other half on the deck, and somersaulted from one ship to the other. Using his four remaining eyes, Light-Streak watched the performance with amazement.

With the admiral gone from the deck, Light-Streak was cut off from conversation. He looked up at the admiral and Slippery-Wing on the curved deck above him. The admiral was pulling insistently on the safety line, while Slippery-Wing was gesturing to him and curling up the edges of her tread. Then Light-Streak finally let loose his tread from the deck and felt himself being drawn upward to safety on the overcrowded deck.

Admiral Steel-Slicer flowed into the jammed control deck of the scout ship and slid in back of the busy scout ship pilot.

"Am I late for the warpfeast?" he asked.

"Admiral Hohmann-Transfer commandeered all the food." One of Far-Ranger's eyes gave a slow wink. "But I saved a few bags of West Pole Double-Distilled." She touched the screen under her tread, and the scout ship shot up into the black of space.

"You sure look good in that new body," whispered Far-Ranger.

"I could say the same about you," he whispered back.

"Somebody is going to have to go out and take the bad news to the rest of the exploration fleet," she said. "And since I have the only scout ship at Egg, it looks like it's my job. I can't take my regular crew. The journey will take too long and they are too old. Know anything about navigation?"

"When I was a cadet I could outnavigate anyone," Steel-Slicer replied.

"We'll see," said Far-Ranger.

06:58:07.2 GMT TUESDAY 21 JUNE 2050

"I don't see how things could be any more disastrous," said Admiral Hohmann-Transfer as she started off the meeting in the main meeting room. It was just after turn-feast, and Cliff-Web was still sucking on a Tiny Shell, trying to get the last morsel out from the spiral cavity. The commander had immediately ordered half-rations when she heard they had been marooned in space.

"We first have a report from Captain Fixed-Star, Space Operations, East," Hohmann-Transfer announced. An aging captain moved to the speaker's treadle and activated a display on everyone's taste screen.

"Our total space force consists of three space stations—East Pole, West Pole, and Polar Orbiting. Nominal permanent crew is twenty-four each. We lost a number of those who happened to be on the ground during the starquake. With no contact from Space Operations Headquarters on Egg, and with retired Admiral Steel-Slicer off on the call-back mission with Captain Far-Ranger, Admiral Hohmann-Transfer, as ranking active officer, is Acting Commander of all Space Operations.

"In addition to the assigned space force personnel, we have 16 civilians on East Pole Station who are refugees from the Space Fountain. There are six explorer ships, four cargo ships, and eleven scout ships out in deep space on exploration missions. Our total inventory is 287 personnel, three space stations, six explorer ships, six cargo ships, twelve scout ships, four jumpcraft with no jump loops to jump to, two catapult-lifts with no catapult to drop to, and three shuttlecraft with no Space Fountain to shuttle to."

"Don't forget the humans," said Cliff-Web. "They are only a quarter-orbit away."

"The Slow Ones will certainly be of no help in our present crisis," warned Admiral Hohmann-Transfer.

"They were once," Cliff-Web said. "And they may be again. For instance. Do our technical libraries on the space stations contain the construction plans for a gravity catapult?"

A young ensign high in the rear spoke shrilly into his vibration pickup. "I doubt it, sir. That technology has been obsolete for dozens of generations."

"The humans have that information, and other 'obsolete' information stored away in their memory crystals. I would count them as part of the 'inventory' if I were you, even if they are slow."

"Then it is 287 people and six humans," Fixed-Star said, in obvious annoyance.

"That is 293 'people' worried about what has happened on Egg," Cliff-Web insisted. "I'm worried too. What *has* happened on Egg?"

"Our next report is from Lieutenant Staring-Sensor, Egg Resources Monitor," said Admiral Hohmann-Transfer.

"According to Doctor of Crustallogy Shear-Wave, our expert on crustquakes, what happened on Egg was *not* a crustquake, but a much more severely damaging phenomenon called a 'starquake' by the humans. Such a thing occurs only rarely—even at human timescales—so we never expected it to happen to Egg. During a starquake, if the ground movement doesn't kill you, the electromagnetic heating will, and for those still left alive, the gamma-ray radiation levels are lethal."

Staring-Sensor moved his tread, and a map appeared on everyone's screen.

"We have carried out a preliminary survey of the surface of Egg. All major structures are down, including all jump loops, gravity catapults, and the Space Fountain."

"It will take a half-dozen greats to get a jump loop or space fountain built," said Cliff-Web. "When do the authorities think they'll be able to get the gravity catapults back in operation?"

"We are trying to contact the pilot of the flyer," said Lieutenant Shannon-Capacity. "Other than the flyer, we have detected no signs of life on Egg."

Qui-Qui had brought her flyer down to a soft landing outside West Pole Mountain Resort. When she had first come to the resort, she had made arrangements to berth the flyer at a local repair garage for the resort's robotic glide-cars. The mechanic was not there to attach the tie-bolts that kept the flyer from sliding around during crust-quakes, so she had to do that chore herself. She found the mechanic inside his machine shop, impaled on a sharp piece of heavy equipment. She moved away in horror and went to the video link to call the butchers. The link was dead.

The glide-cars at the garage were piled into a heap in one corner of the compound, so she had to make the trip by her own tread. The streets were deserted and the crust was silent except for the low rumbles coming up from deep in Egg. She passed by compounds with cracked walls. Through the cracks she saw nothing but death. Flattened cheela bodies that had flowed through partially opened doorways, many with eyes cooked and hide blistered. Pet Slinks imitated their masters in death, their hairs singed off.

Any plant of any size had either toppled or been sheared off at the root, while the smaller plants and ground cover looked limp and lifeless. It took her a while to find the compound for the peace officers, for there was little need for them in this exclusive resort area. The peace officers were dead too, and none of the equipment in the office seemed to work. She finally left and returned to her flyer. When she turned on her communications set, a voice blared through the deck.

". . . anyone on Egg. Please reply on Channels 1, 12, 36, or 144. West Pole Space Station on an all-band call to anyone on Egg. Please reply on channels. . . ." The voice sounded squeaky and hurried since time moved faster on the orbital space stations than it did on the surface of Egg.

She switched her set to channel 36 in the flyer band. "This is Qui-Qui in Flyer 7. I have landed at West Pole Mountain Resort near the West Pole Rejuvenation Center. Everyone in West Pole Mountain Resort seems to be dead. All the video links are gone, too. I'd appreciate it if you would call Bright's Heaven and have them send a mechanic to service my flyer. I've got to get back by next turn to start rehearsals for my show."

She then waited for the long two-grethturn interval while the signal traveled the 400 kilometers or so up to the West Pole Station and back.

"Flyer 7," came a voice. "This is Lieutenant Shannon-Capacity. You are coming in weakly. Did you say your name was Qui-Qui? *The* Qui-Qui? I'm sorry, but I can't call anyone for you. As far as we know, you are the only one on Egg with a working free-space transmitter."

Qui-Qui became concerned. "Do you see any signs of life anywhere? If it isn't too far, I could fly there and find them." She had two grethturns to worry as she waited for a reply.

"Wait. I'll check with the Space Operations Commander," he said. A few sethturns later a harsh harassed voice rasped through the deck.

"You there! This is Admiral Hohmann-Transfer, Commander of Space Operations. We have an extreme emergency. As of now, I am commandeering your private flyer in the name of the government of the Combined Clans. We will need it to restore contact with the remaining authorities on Egg and start the recovery process. Let me speak to your pilot.''

"*I* am the pilot," she said and waited for the reply.

"Bright has cursed us all!" Hohmann-Transfer shouted. "Here we are in the middle of the biggest catastrophe to hit Egg, and I get stuck with a stupid, big-lidded *entertainer*." Suddenly the admiral's voice shifted to panic.

"We've *got* to find somebody else on Egg," she said. "If we can't find somebody to rebuild a jump loop or a gravity catapult, we'll be stuck here in space until we die! We've got to find somebody else. We've *got* to find somebody else."

Qui-Qui turned off the communication set. "Well, Quick-Quieter," she said out loud to herself. "It looks like you're through with acting for a while. This is the *real* thing. As the admiral said, 'We've got to find somebody else.'"

She thought about using the flyer, but decided against it. Until she found a way to recharge the accumulators, she would save the energy for the communications set. There were a number of towns nearby that she could check out on tread, including the home town of her clan. She hoped she would find someone alive there. Subconsciously twitching the clan totem in her heritage pouch, she thought of all her close friends in the clan—the elders, the hatchlings, the *eggs*! The thought of her clan's eggs and hatchlings lying unattended moved her to instant action.

Within sethturns she had the flyer skimming along the surface to White Rock City, the home of the White Rock Clan. She knew exactly where the clan hatchery was, since she had left an egg there only two greats of turns ago.

The sight at the clan hatchery wrung her brain-knot into knots. In the hatchling pen were the tiny bodies of innocent, defenseless hatchlings that had been thrown against the wall to burst and fall to the crust like overripe singleberries. Those bodies that had been cushioned by the dying Old Ones were covered with fatal blisters, while the juice in the blisters was cooked until it was nearly solid. Hoping against hope, she went to the egg pen and laboriously rolled the dead Old One off the eggs he had been tending. It was only two turns since the starquake, so the eggs should have survived without being tended. She looked the eggs over carefully, then, awkwardly forming a hatchling mantle, she tucked them under her. There was no damage and no blisters, but no life. She twitched the clan totem in her heritage pouch and went out to search the rest of White Rock City.

Marooned

The hunger-twinges in Speckle-Top moved from one eating pouch to another. They got so bad she began to think about the old days in the dump when the garbage sleds from the centertown eating places would come. It was long past turnfeast and she *had* to get something to eat. The trouble was, the crust around her was too quiet. The clankers would hear her for sure when she pushed the rock away from the end of the tunnel. So she moved to the tunnel entrance and stuck one eye through a crack between the rock and the wall.

"Bright's Curse!" she whispered as she pulled her eye back in—a clanker was out there. But there was something wrong with her. Putting her eye back out to watch the reaction of the clanker, she moved the rock slightly. A rasping sound radiated out through the crust, but the clanker didn't move. Growing bolder, she pushed the rock aside and flowed out into the still sparkling atmosphere.

Keeping her eyes half-shielded under their flaps, she went over to the clanker. The large body had flowed into a wide oval. A few dull yellow-red eyeballs hung out over their fleshy eyeflaps and the large clanker badges had fallen from their holding sphincters.

"Too tender to stand a little crustquake, you slink-treading egg-sucker?" Speckle-Top picked up a clanker badge and stuck it onto her decorationless hide. The badge was heavy, but felt good.

"It looks better on me than you, you eye-ball-sucking father-lover," she said as she flowed up on the carcass of the clanker and took the rest of her badges. In one pouch she found an electronic lash. Speckle-Top's hide had tasted the lash the first time she had been caught and had been foolish enough to try to run away. Ever since, she just let the clankers lead her away when they caught her doing something wrong. She flowed off the dead clanker and turned on the lash. High voltage currents flickered across the crust. She swept the lash under the tread of the clanker. The first sweep produced some reflex reaction in the edges of the tread, but even that stopped as the lash played its aura over the dead body.

"Just let any clanker try and get me now!" she bragged, waving the lash around. "I'll fry their treads and eat them for a 'tweenfeast snack!" She pouched the lash and moved on toward the center of town, the huge badges almost dragging in the crust. The silence bothered her. Ever since she had hatched in the dump on the other side of town, her tread had felt the constant rustle of tread and hum of machine coming through the crust. Now there was nothing, not even the high-pitched whine of the Jump Loop. She finally thought to look up to where the Jump Loop should be, hanging in the sky. It was no longer there.

"That must have been a slider of a quake!" she whispered to herself as she moved slowly on, her street-wary tread alert.

When turnfeast came again, she was no longer hungry. She had loaded her pouches full of strange-tasting foods taken from shops guarded by flowed shopkeepers. Her stuffed hide now glistened with badges of every kind, including the two-star admiral badges she had stolen from the space-trooper. Her speckles were covered with splotches of fluorescent body paint inexpertly applied, and around each eye-stub was one or more expensive glow-jewel eye-rings stolen from a jewelry shop. Her tread felt a sound off in the distance.

"A clanker!" She moved quickly to a narrow alley between two store compounds. Once in the alley, she took off the heavy badges, hid the eye-rings in a pouch, and listened carefully with her tread. There seemed to be only one thing moving and it sounded like a Slink. Feeling a little lonely, she moved off to find the source of the noise. As soon as she started to move, the noise changed direction and headed straight toward her, moving rapidly. Soon, down the road, she could see a Slink, moving as fast as its tread could ripple.

"Hello, Fuzzy-Pink." Speckle-Top greeted the Slink as it came up to her, its furry top turning reddish-white from exertion. Speckle-Top liked animals and she formed a tendril to reach out and pat the fuzzy hide. The Slink dropped a small scroll on the crust and, avoiding her pat, moved off away from her and waited, its eyes looking first at her, then at the scroll. Speckle-Top moved by the scroll to pat the Slink, but it circled around behind her, picked up the scroll, and put it down next to her tread again.

She gave up trying to pat the Slink and used her tendril to push down on the scroll as she had seen done on the video in the holovid shop displays. The scroll flattened out on the crust. There was some writing on it. A few of the words she knew, like "IN" and "OUT," but the rest she couldn't read. The Slink moved restlessly back and forth as she tried to decipher the message. Suddenly she recognized another word. It was "HELP." She paused. Whoever she helped would probably wonder where she got all the expensive body paint and call the clankers.

"Sorry, Fuzzy-Pink," she said, letting the scroll roll up on the roadway. "Get someone else. I got to take care of me."

She started off to enter a food shop along the road. The Slink picked up the scroll, raced ahead of her and put it down in her path, its twelve eyes looking intently at her every motion. She tried to go around, but the Slink moved quickly to block her way. She stopped to rumble a laugh into the crust and reached out again to pat the animal. It dodged and started making quick trips off down the road in the direction it had come, stopping to see if she followed, then running back to repeat the motion. It made anxious little chirps in the crust as it moved.

"All right, Fuzzy-Pink, I'll come." She followed the Slink off down the roadway, her tread alert for the sound of a clanker.

The Slink led Speckle-Top toward centertown. When they came to an entrance of a large compound it entered one of the gates in the compound walls. Speckle-Top hesitated, because this was where all the big-badge thinker types worked. A few times she and her gang had thought of sneaking in to see if there was something to steal, but the clankers had kept them out. Seeing her pause, the Slink came back to fetch her, its chirps becoming more and more anxious sounding. She moved inside the compound and heard a faint voice off in the distance, calling. Something was wrong. The voice sounded as if it were coming from inside the crust. She scrubbed her tread hard and waited for the next call. The direction to the voice was definitely downward. Feeling very insecure, Speckle-Top followed the Slink toward the voice until it stopped some distance ahead and intensified its chirps. They were answered by a voice.

"Rin-Tin-Tin! You're back!" Zero-Gauss said as she spotted the pink ball of fuzz at the top of the ramp. "I do hope you found someone to give the message to." She placed part of her tread against a side wall and raised the level of her tread vibrations. "Hello out there! Help! I'm trapped in a hole! Help!! Help!!!"

Rin-Tin-Tin raced away and soon was back. This time a young cheela eyeball was peeking over the back of the Slink. The eyeball quickly retracted.

"Bright's Spew-hole!" Speckle-Top said as she drew her eye in under its flap and tried to forget the terrifying image. With the rest of her eyes she looked at the nice flat crust all around her and tried to calm herself. She tried to talk to the grown-up in the hole but found her tread was clenched tight to the crust. She loosened her tread and, keeping her eyes from looking too often at the missing place in the crust, she finally was able to answer.

"Hello, there," Speckle-Top said, her tread still shrill from tension. "How did you get down in that hole?"

"By elevator," Zero-Gauss replied.

"Elevator?"

"It is a machine for going up and down. But it won't work without power, so I guess I'll have to stay here until they get the power fixed. Could you please tell your creche-teacher or some adult I'm down here and have them send some help?"

"I don't have any spew-wiping creche-teacher." Speckle-Top said in an annoyed tone of voice. "I take care of myself!"

"I'm sorry." Zero-Gauss was a little shocked at the vulgar language. "I couldn't see you, and I thought you were a youngling. I'm stuck down here with some hungry research animals and I need to get power restored to my elevator in a hurry. Could you please find a peace officer or someone to notify the authorities?"

"I'm not finding no spew-licking clanker for nobody," said Speckle-Top. "Besides, they're all dead. Everybody is dead. You and Fuzzy-Pink are the only things alive I've seen anywhere in Bright's Heaven.''

As they talked, Speckle-Top slowly lost her fear of heights and moved over to one corner of the square hole in the ground until she and Zero-Gauss could see each other while they were talking.

''You *are* a youngling.'' Zero-Gauss felt her protective instincts rising as she saw the skinny, besmirched young cheela. ''What happened to you? You are all covered with paint. Are any of your clan left to take care of you?''

Speckle-Top hesitated a little before answering. ''No.''

''Then I'll be responsible for you until we can find a member of your clan. My name is Zero-Gauss. I am a professor at the Institute. But first we've got to get me and the animals out of here. They are getting awfully hungry, and I don't want them eating my research plants.''

She ducked back under one of the massive leaning roof-plates and came back with an empty animal cage. Then she pushed her body up the sloping ramplike intersection between two fallen roof plates at one corner of her devastated underground laboratory and added the cage to the row already there. Holding onto the cages with part of her tread, she stretched herself out until she had one eye perched up above the top of the hole right next to Speckle-Top. Now that she was close enough, she could see that Speckle-Top was one of those dump-hatchlings from West-heaven. That explained the filthy language. Rin-Tin-Tin pushed its way between them to get a pat, now that it had done its duty.

''I can't get any more than one eye up here,'' said Zero-Gauss. ''I've tried and tried for the last two turns, but I can't get enough of me out to pull the rest of me up. I need more cages or something to climb on. You should be able to find more cages in that compound over there next to the elevator building.''

"I don't know." Speckle-Top patted the top of the Slink and drew it close to her for a hug. "It sounds like a lot of work."

"Rin-Tin-Tin's friends are getting awfully hungry," said Zero-Gauss as she pushed the bottom portion of her tread through some cage bars and poked Flopsy, Mopsy, Cottonball, and Poofsie to make them chirp.

"Well," Speckle-Top said reluctantly. "Can't let Slinks starve. Come, Fuzzy-Pink. Show me the cages."

Zero-Gauss and the animals were up on the crust before the next turnfeast. Zero-Gauss found the laboratory food supply for the animals and reluctantly agreed to let Speckle-Top feed the animals while she explored the compound of the Inner Eye Institute and the surrounding city. It was worse than she had thought. Not only were all the rest of the cheela dead, but all the plants and animals, too. She had gone to the zoo and visited the cages of the giant north hemisphere Flow Slows and Swifts. All dead. The only Flow Slows and Swifts left were her hybrid miniaturized pets. She found a few seeds in some gardening stores, but wondered if they had survived the blizzard of penetrating radiation that seemed to have cooked everything else. Fortunately, the packaged food in the food stores was edible. They and the animals could survive on that until they could get some crops planted and harvested.

When Zero-Gauss returned to the Inner Eye Institute she found that Speckle-Top had arranged the cages and some boxes to make a compound for the animals and was happily playing with them.

When the big-badge professor came back, Speckle-Top's sharp eyes noticed that she had taken off the cheap plastic badges she had been wearing in the hole and had replaced them with expensive metal ones. Speckle-Top shook off the pile of Slinks that had been clambering all over her and, shoving back an inquisitive mini-Swift, she left the compound she had made. The eye-waves on the big-badge grown-up had a twitch that showed she was worried about something.

"Whole species gone. Wiped out!" said Zero-Gauss. "All we have left is the collection from my laboratory, and it is so *limited*."

"Looks to me like we got lots of everything," said Speckle-Top. "The stores are full of food, and when we want something special, we can eat one of your food Slinks. What is the taste of the striped ones?"

"No!" Zero-Gauss was nearly panic-stricken at the thought. "We must not eat them. They are the last ones on Egg. I must breed them to keep the species alive. The plants, too. They are the only ones left. I have to save the plants, too."

She went to the edge of the hole and looked down at the dozens and dozens of plants many millimeters below. They would survive there for a time, but they or their seeds must be laboriously hauled up on the crust if they were to be available for future generations, if there *were* any future generations.

Speckle-Top had come up beside Zero-Gauss as she peered down the hole at the plants. The feeling of the immature body next to hers caused the collapse of Zero-Gauss's last defenses against the Old-One syndrome. She spread out a hatching mantle and covered the scarred, paint-smeared, speckled topside of the ugly youngling.

Speckle-Top had seen adult cheela do many strange things, but it was a new experience for her when the professor developed a long ridge just underneath her eyeflap bulges. The ridge became a sheet that slid up over her speckled topside.

A strange feeling came over her. It wasn't the intense feeling she got when playing eye-ball games with Crumpled-Tread, but a relaxed, warm, *safe* feeling. She could finally relax the eternal vigilance that had kept her alive since her first terrifying days in the dump with the wild Slinks hunting her.

Someone was now taking care of her. Someone was now watching out for her. She pulled all her eyes in under their eyeflaps, contracted her body into a small egg-shaped ball under the hatching mantle and rested. She liked the professor and the professor liked her. She liked the animals and they liked her. She wondered if this was what it was like being part of a clan. She decided she would stay if the professor wanted her to.

06:58:08 GMT TUESDAY 21 JUNE 2050

The last place Qui-Qui checked was the Rejuvenation Center. As she expected, everyone was dead there, too, even the "dragon plants," snapped off at their roots. The large rods of dragon crystal that had supported the plants now lay glistening on the crust. She moved past a motionless robotic body on her way out and stopped as she felt an electronic tingle.

"Emergency! Emergency!" a metallic voice whispered. She moved closer to the robot. The body of the robot didn't move, but the electronic tingle became stronger.

"Emergency! Emergency!"

"The emergency is over," Qui-Qui's tread vibrated through the crust. The robot continued its alarm as if it hadn't heard her. She switched to whispering herself.

"The emergency is over," Qui-Qui whispered, using her body to set up oscillations in the sea of electrons around them.

"Emergency! Crustquake! Activate Plan Two! Call Doctor!" said the robot.

"Stop!" commanded Qui-Qui, who owned a dozen personal robots. "Emergency Over! Restart! Report Condition!"

"Three-greths functional," said the robot. "I must report to a medical doctor. A failure has occurred."

"Stop! Restart! Emergency over! Tell me how to activate communication links to Bright's Heaven."

"I must report to a medical doctor," said the robot. "You are not a medical doctor." It fell silent.

Qui-Qui was puzzled. The robot's eyes were useless. How did it know she wasn't a medical doctor? She went back to the main offices, found the remains of M.D. Sabin-Salk, pulled off his ornate badges, and replaced her glow-jewel decorations with badges. She went back to the robot, but didn't get too close. She could have done a good imitation of M.D. Sabin-Salk's tread accent, but she had never heard him whisper. She did the best she could.

"Tell me how to repair the communication links to Bright's Heaven!" she commanded.

"Open box," said the robot.

Qui-Qui was bewildered. She looked around, then saw a large metal box in one corner of the room. The room wall had suffered a large dent where the box had slid into it. She went over to the box and read the badly faded label. It was another robot! According to the label, it was a maintenance robot for the next bank of enzyme machines that were due to be sent to the rejuvenation center. She undid the latches and slid off the heavy lid. Twelve glassy eyes raised up from a Slink-sized dome and looked around. The top of the dome had the design of a cleft-wort plant.

"Energy!" it said. The end of the box fell away and the robot glided out on its undulating underside. It paused by the damaged robot to exchange information, then moved into the enzyme machine room, where it found a partially full accumulator and reenergized itself. Qui-Qui followed it. The robot ignored her and started to lift an enzyme machine back onto its base.

"Stop!" she said. "Repair the communication links to Bright's Heaven."

"That is not my function," said the robot. "My function is to maintain the Rejuvenation Center in operational condition."

"Reset!" she commanded. "The Rejuvenation Center cannot operate without doctors. All the doctors are dead. You must get new doctors. The doctors must be called from Bright's Heaven. You must repair the communication links to Bright's Heaven so the doctors can be called."

The robot paused in its repair of the damaged enzyme machine. It moved to the main offices, found one of the video link consoles, and opened it. It carried out a few tests, then moved to the next console. Since none of them were operational, it then took out a part from one console, other parts from another console, more from a third, and put them in a fourth. It left the room for a while and came back with a small energy source to power the console. It went through its testing routine again.

"The communication link is repaired. Bright's Heaven does not respond." It returned to its work of fixing the enzyme machine.

Qui-Qui tried the video-link console. She had made so many long-distance calls in her life that she knew all the screen blotches and tread murmurs that indicated the condition of the various portions of the links. The call probably made it to the central exchange at White Rock City, but the fibers were dead from there to Bright's Heaven. She tried to get the robot to go to White Rock City to fix the central exchange, but it refused to leave its assigned duty station and the enzyme machines. She finally gave up and set out for White Rock City herself to pick up her flyer.

As soon as the flyer was activated, the acoustic coupler to the deck vibrated the floor with a recorded message.

"Qui-Qui! Respond on channel 36. Qui-Qui! Respond. . . ."

The communications set was already on channel 36 so she activated the transmitter.

"Qui-Qui here," she said. After two long grethturns there was an eager reply.

"Lieutenant Shannon-Capacity here, Qui-Qui. Are you all right? I'm switching you right over to the admiral."

The harsh voice came rasping through the deck. The admiral sounded even more harassed than the first time.

"Your behavior is inexcusable!" said Admiral Hohmann-Transfer. "From now on I want you to make contact every turnfeast and midturn. Do you understand? Where have you been?"

"I was trying to find somebody else," said Qui-Qui. "I was not successful. Were you?" She then went through another long wait.

"No," said Hohmann-Transfer. "What am I going to do? We are doomed!" There was another long pause. "If only we had someone else than a *stupid* entertainer."

The link to the admiral clicked off. Qui-Qui was about to turn off the power when she heard Shannon-Capacity again.

"There is someone else who wants to talk to you," he said.

". . . Hello? . . is this Qui-Qui? . . ." came the voice. "I . . . ah . . . I met you some time ago . . . didn't really *meet* you really . . . I saw you when you were going through the Rejuvenation Center . . . my name's Cliff-Web . . . run a construction company . . . or used to."

Qui-Qui had been through this before. Another male overflustered by her large eyeflaps.

"I remember *you*," she said in her best stage tread. "The doctor said you needed to do some extra exercises. I didn't think so. You looked fine to me." After another long wait, Cliff-Web replied. He had regained his composure.

"You looked fine to me, too," he said. "And I bet you're looking even better now after rejuvenation."

". . . I wish we had video," Shannon-Capacity interjected.

"It's been twenty turns since the starquake," Cliff-Web continued. "And you're the only one we've been able to contact. I've talked to the few people here on the space stations who know you and I've done some research in our library, limited as it is. You produce your own performances, manage your own finances, control dozens of personal staff including a dozen robots, and pilot your own flyer. You are *not* stupid."

He hesitated before continuing, "Do you think you can become an engineer?"

"Sure," she replied. "With the right teacher and enough time. Why?" The answer from Cliff-Web came two grethturns later.

"The admiral is basically right. We're stuck up here. We don't have any spacecraft that can land on Egg under its own power without crashing. We can't build a lander because we have no tools and no raw materials to work with. We need something to 'catch' one of the spacecraft we have. The jump loops are down, but it might be possible to reactivate one of the gravity catapults if they aren't too badly damaged.

"My plan is to use the robots on Egg," Cliff-Web explained. "With the two grethturn communications delay from synchronous orbit to the surface, it will be impossible for us to direct them from up here. But if you can help control them, we can send down the information needed for them to make repairs to the catapult. First, however, we have to find those robots and gather them at one of the poles. Can you do that?"

"I've already found some," said Qui-Qui. "They are just as dead as everyone else. Except for one. I found him in a box at the West Pole Rejuvenation Center. He works perfectly, except he only wants to work on keeping rejuvenation machinery fixed. I tried all the robot control tricks I could think of, but the best I could do was make him fix the video link machines. Unfortunately, it was the only functional robot I saw. I'm afraid we can't use robots to repair the gravity catapults." Although disguised by the squeaky sound caused by the gravitational time shift, Qui-Qui could hear the overtones of dejection when Cliff-Web's voice finally returned.

"I'll have to think of something else," said Cliff-Web. "Well, goodbye for now."

"Goodbye, Engineer Cliff-Web," Qui-Qui said in her most pleasant tone. "It has been a real pleasure talking to you. I hope to see you in person *real* soon."

She spent the next two grethturns thinking of the many greats of turns she faced being all alone.

When Qui-Qui's gravitationally red-shifted voice finally reached Cliff-Web, it had been lowered from her normal contralto range to a slow, husky tone normally only heard in the privacy of a love-pad room. Cliff-Web stammered a reply. ". . . ah . . . Yes. I've really enjoyed . . . been a pleasure . . . talking with you . . . ah . . . Qui-Qui . . . really nice. . . ." The link went dead.

Two turns later Qui-Qui returned to the Rejuvenation Center wearing a full panoply of M.D. badges. The maintenance robot had repaired the auxiliary power generator and had gotten one enzyme machine working. Once that was done, it had allowed itself to work on lower priority items and had cleaned out all the bodies and tidied up the place. It was now trying to get a second enzyme machine working. She slipped into the main office and tried to read the files to find out how the Center worked so she could do a better job of playing a doctor. There was no power to the memory banks, so she went back and complained to the robot. It took him two turns, but he finally got the main office memory powered and running.

She then found that the memory files were blank. They had been erased by the radiation during the quake. She went into M.D. Sabin-Salk's old office compound and took down a few scrolls from his scroll wall. Except for some very faint markings at the very center of the scroll, they were blank too. She reported her findings to the West Pole Space Station.

"Why are you still at the West Pole?" Hohmann-Transfer was annoyed. "You should be out looking for robots or something useful!" Her harassed voice changed to one of near panic as Shannon-Capacity told her the bad news. "I could expect computer files to go, but scrolls, too?"

"Even taste-plates," said Qui-Qui. "There used to be an ornate taste-plate sign in the crust at the entrance to the Center. It's now tasteless." The delayed reply back from Hohmann-Transfer was worse than useless.

"Civilization is destroyed! What shall we do?!?"

Qui-Qui didn't bother to reply. She turned off the communicator and returned to her battle of wits with the robot. First she got it to reconstruct most of the files for the operation of the rejuvenation center from its internal memory. She then read those and figured out a way to get the robot to recharge the accumulators on her flyer. She ordered it to bring the accumulators in from the flyers as "urgent cargo" and put them next to the accumulators that were used as standby power to the enzyme machines. She then sent it off on a "repair" in the main office while she switched cables and charged up the accumulators. Then she made the robot haul the "urgent cargo" back to the flyer. She was now ready to go anywhere on Egg. But there was nowhere to go.

06:58:09 GMT TUESDAY 21 JUNE 2050

Heavy-Egg finally came to his senses. He dimly remembered the shrieking pain in his eye-balls. It now was a dull ache. He stretched his eye-stubs to make sure his eyes weren't hidden behind their eyeflaps, but he could see nothing. He listened with his tread, trying to figure out where he was. All was silent around him. The only sounds were the thumping of his fluid pumps and faint rumbles from deep inside Egg.

Pieces of memory started to return. He remembered blindly wandering around on the top of the East Pole mountains, mad with pain. Finding the drop chute. Creeping, falling, sliding down through the darkness. New pain as he hit a broken section of the chute. Cries for help into the crust until his tread was raw, but no help came. Then the hunger pains grew stronger than the burn pains. He had finally found food. A chunk of food was in his manipulator, ready to go into his eating pouch. He was starved. But for some reason he had not eaten.

He felt something underneath his tread. It was the body of another cheela. He moved his tread around, feeling the dead body—it was a large female. There were long slashes in the body torn by a crude blade. The sharp piece of metal that had caused the slashes was in one of his manipulators. The chunk of food was in another. He formed a set of tendrils and reached out to touch the food. It was smooth and round and soft and leathery . . .

"An egg!!!" he cried, his tread grating the crust with its vibrations. "I nearly ate an egg!!!"

He went mad again.

Eye-stumps waving erratically, he put the egg back in its mother, then stumbled across the deserted street. He found a store with an open door. It was a pulp-bar. Pushing his way past the body of the barkeeper he found the cache of pulp-bags. He couldn't read them, but after sucking a few bags dry he didn't care. The dull pain in his eyes went away. He felt good. He loaded his carrying pouches with as many bags as he could carry and weaved his way back out into the street.

"Hello!" he called. No answer.

"Got to keep on moving. Got to find *somebody*."

He moved his overloaded body laboriously down the street and found another open door. This one led to a repair shop. Maybe he could find a good knife. He found lots of tools, but no knife. He picked up a tool from its holder next to the mechanic's work-pad. It was a welding torch. It used tanks of liquids that were mixed to produce an ultra-hot flame. The torch was on automatic and it immediately formed a long flame that flickered toward Heavy-Egg's hide. He screamed in insane panic as he felt intense heat once again. His pouches vomited bags of distilled pulp, and he dropped the torch which licked at a bag that burst into a bright violet-white ball of flame.

"I can see!!!" Heavy-Egg said as the singed end of one of his eye-stumps gave a weak response to the intense flood of light. Entranced by the light, he madly added bag after bag of pulp to the growing blaze. The equipment in the shop caught on fire and drove him out into the street.

Then the tanks of welding liquid blew up in a tremendous explosion.

The next time Qui-Qui checked in on the communicator, there was some good news.

"Staring-Sensor at the East Pole Space Station has detected a large fire and explosion in Swift's Climb at the base of the East Pole mountains," said Lieutenant Shannon-Capacity. "It could be a signal or it could be a delayed reaction to the starquake. So far, it is the only sign of life on Egg."

"Then it is our only hope," said Qui-Qui. "I'm heading for Swift's Climb. I'll take the flyer, but I'm not going to fly, it wastes too much power. I'm going to travel close to the surface where the gravity repulsors have plenty of mass to push against. In that mode I could travel around Egg a couple of times without emptying the accumulators." She paused, "Sure seems like a terrible waste though. Here I have this terrific toy that can fly about in the sky and I have to use it as a dull crust-glider."

Leaving the robot tending its rejuvenation machine, Qui-Qui lifted the flyer on a low altitude, minimum energy flight profile, and headed for the East Pole. Meter after barren meter passed under the flyer as she traversed the glowing yellow-white crust.

Avoiding the wreckage of the Jump Loop spread over the crust, she brought the flyer down in a flat space in the outskirts of Swift's Climb. Finding nothing to tie it down to, she made sure that the machine was left far from anything solid in case there was another crustquake. Before leaving the flyer she made a call to the East Pole Space Station floating overhead and waited for the reply.

"The blaze occurred in the eastern section," said Staring-Sensor. "It's the old section of town right at the bottom of the superconducting chute that was used by the

Web-Con workers on the Space Foundation project. Just find an east-west road and head for the mountains."

Just then another voice entered the communication link. It was Hohmann-Transfer.

"At all costs you *must* protect our flyer," the admiral warned. "The fire may have been caused by looters. You are to take weapons with you and report in every doth-turn."

"I have no weapons, and it will take me two dothturns just to get to the east side from here," said Qui-Qui. "Besides, one fire does not a band of looters make. I will report in when I get back."

Qui-Qui did begin to feel a little uneasy as she made her way through the deserted town. She moved quietly and stopped often to listen. Finally she heard a voice. It had the high tenor pitch of a male tread. The voice sounded drunk and off-key. As she moved along the streets, tracking down the voice, she recognized the tune. It was *her* song, "Twine Thine Eyen About Mine."

She came to an intersection and looked down the street. Wandering blindly from slide-walk to slide-walk was a filthy, drunken, heavy-set male. Where his eye-balls should have been were oozing sores on the ends of stumps. Shreds of skin hung from his blistered hide. Shocked by his condition, Qui-Qui stood still in the middle of the intersection as he weaved his way closer. Her first reaction was that of revulsion. It changed to pity as she realized the pain and suffering he had gone through even to survive, while she flitted around in a luxurious flyer. He was coming to the third verse in the song, and she softly blended her deep contralto voice into his.

". . . Be my friend, be my lover,
Be my tread, be my cover.
Twine thine cyen about mine."

The male's voice trailed off as hers became louder.

"I must *really* be going mad!" he said out loud to himself, throwing the half-finished bag of cheap pulp juice into the street.

"No. You're not," said Qui-Qui, moving toward him.

"Is this the way you die?" he said, still not sending his tread vibrations in her direction. "All my life I have longed for Qui-Qui. Now I imagine she is here."

"I *am* here," said Qui-Qui in her unmistakable voice. "I am *really* the Qui-Qui you have longed for and I have come to take care of you." She moved alongside Heavy-Egg, gently twined three eye-stubs about his wounded stumps and led him off to a hospital she had noticed a few blocks away. As they moved along side-by-side, she sang to him.

At the hospital she cleaned his hide, anointed his blisters, bandaged his eye-stumps, and filled his eating pouches with decent food. Then she made love to him.

She concentrated on the bulk of the body of the male and ignored the lack of eye-balls. His tread massaged her topside with quivering delight, while his twelve eye-stubs wound tighter and tighter around hers until they were coupled eye-flap to eyeflap. The orifice at the base of his eye-stubs opened and droplets of fluid from his body fell into her waiting eyeflaps. A long yearning in each of them was finally satisfied. Qui-Qui relaxed under Heavy-Egg's limp body as the droplets made their way through her body to her eager egg-case.

TIME: 06:58:11 GMT TUESDAY 21 JUNE 2050

Pierrre's hands and feet had been pulled through the water and slammed against the walls of the tank by some unimaginable force as the viewscreens had turned dark. For three long seconds alarms had rung throughout Dragon Slayer as the computer tried to repair its damage and return to operation. The multiple screens built into the walls of his tank finally lit up again.

"Report status," he said.

"Starquake on Dragon's Egg," the computer responded. "Systems suffered damage from gamma rays and gravitational waves. Status 82% operational."

"We have received a significant dose of radiation," said Cesar from his portion of the multiple screen. "Those of us in the tanks have received 120 rems. Half-fatal dose is 500 rems."

"Amalita!" Abdul shouted. "Amalita! Answer me!"

There was no answer.

"Something is wrong," said Abdul. He started to purge his tank.

"I am the doctor," said Cesar. "*I* will check on her."

"The surface of Egg has suffered severe damage," Seiko said. "All activity has ceased. I have activated the scanners."

"All communications with Egg are gone," said Jean. "We do have contact with the East Pole Space Station." Her face on the multiple screen was replaced by that of a flickering cheela, checking in every tenth of a second.

"Any life below you in Bright's Heaven?" Staring-Sensor asked.

"No," said Seiko. "Saw thermal flare at East Pole."

"We know," said Staring-Sensor.

"High energy vehicle from West Pole to East Pole," said Seiko.

"We know."

One of Seiko's screens showed a flashing circle overlaid by the computer on a scanner display of Bright's Heaven. "Patch of new vegeta. . . ."

"*Where!?!*" Staring-Sensor interrupted.

"Inner Eye Inst. . . ."

Seiko stopped talking. The cheela had gone.

"Doc!" said Pierre. "Have you found Amalita yet?"

"Yes," said Cesar. "She's dead."

"I don't think we'd better take a ride with Otis until we get things straightened out here." Pierre commanded the computer to cancel the planned change in trajectory for the deorbiter mass. It would be nearly a day before the asteroid worked its way around to where they could call it again.

06:58:20 GMT TUESDAY 21 JUNE 2050

Qui-Qui reported in at the flyer. She had brought Heavy-Egg along with her. She could have traveled faster alone, and gone back to pick him up in the flyer, but neither wanted to be separated from the other.

"Where have you been!" Hohmann-Transfer exploded when the call from the flyer was transferred to her. "I was worried sick that you'd done something stupid, and we'd lost our only operational vehicle on Egg. What took you so long?"

"I found a survivor, Admiral. He needed medical attention. His name is Heavy-Egg. He was a shift supervisor on the Space Fountain project. He would like to talk to Cliff-Web."

"I want to tell him I'm sorry we lost the Fountain," said Heavy-Egg.

After the long wait, it was Cliff-Web's voice that answered. "*I'm* glad to hear another one of the crew survived. As soon as we get down from here, we're all going to start building the Fountain again. It is sure a relief finding an experienced construction worker on Egg. We've got a lot to do. The first thing is to have you look at the gravity catapults at the East Pole and tell me their condition. Then we can start working on repairs."

Qui-Qui let him handle the reply.

"I wish I could, Boss," said Heavy-Egg. "But I don't have any eyes left."

"Heavy-Egg was the only one left alive in Swift's Climb," Qui-Qui explained. "So far there are only two of us."

"There may be more," said Staring-Sensor. "The humans reported a patch of vegetation at the Inner Eye Institute in Bright's Heaven. The Polar Orbiting Space Station has now confirmed the report. It has been decided that you should try there next."

"And this time keep in touch!" It was Admiral Hohmann-Transfer. "The constant worry has aggravated the chronic inflammation in my eating pouches. You *are* going to let the engineer be the pilot for the flyer now, aren't you Qui-Qui?"

"I'm blind, Admiral," Heavy-Egg reminded her.

Qui-Qui shut down the communications link and raised power on the flyer. Then she glided above the road that led directly west to Bright's Heaven. The broad highway had buckled in many places and was littered with the remains of glide-cars. She knew Bright's Heaven well and brought the flyer to a landing close to the Inner Eye Institute. Side-by-side, holding eye-stubs, they glided onto the Institute grounds. Plants were everywhere.

There was every possible variety of plant one could imagine, but only a few of each type. Qui-Qui picked a few of the ripe fruits, and they both enjoyed the fresh taste after turns of packaged food. The plants obviously had been freshly transplanted, for the trays they had been in were stacked nearby. They both listened with their treads, but could hear nothing but some food Slinks in a distant pen. As they moved by a low-walled office compound, Heavy-Egg came to a halt, his sensitive tread having detected something.

"There is someone muttering nearby."

They made their way into the office compound and found someone busy at a writing pad. She was old and wore a circle of scientist badges around her body. Qui-Qui couldn't quite remember what the symbols stood for.

"Hello?" Qui-Qui said tentatively.

"Let me finish this line." The scientist finished her writing and then turned the attention of her eyes to them.

"I am Zero-Gauss, Doctor of Magnetics here at the Institute. I'm glad to see someone has finally come to get things running again. We are in terrible shape here. Did you know that all the scrolls and molecmems in the library are blank? I have been doing what I can, trying to reconstruct all my research notes, but what with taking care of the plants and animals I just don't have enough time. I'm so tired. All I want to do is tend eggs and hatchlings until I die."

"You can't do that!" said Qui-Qui.

"Why?"

"Not yet, at least. We three are the last ones left alive on Egg," Qui-Qui explained. "If the race is going to survive we will have to lay eggs, many eggs."

"I'm too old and tired for egg-laying," said Zero-Gauss. "Besides, we are not the only ones left. There is one other."

Zero-Gauss's tread sent off a directional call. "Speckle-Top, darling. Please come here. We have company."

07:02:06 GMT TUESDAY 21 JUNE 2050

Now that things had settled down into a routine, Qui-Qui was only supposed to check in on the communicator every dozen turns. Hohmann-Transfer was in a meeting when she called this time, so Shannon-Capacity transferred the call to Cliff-Web.

"We just had another hatchling last turn," said Qui-Qui. "That makes eleven now. Pretty soon Heavy-Egg can start education classes to train the junior engineers you need. Zero-Gauss is finally resigned to the fact that she had to give up working on her research notes to tend eggs. She still thinks it's obscene hatching her own eggs, but being a genetics expert she understands the importance of having as diverse a gene pool as possible, so she does 'her duty' as she calls it and still lays eggs as well as hatches them."

Qui-Qui giggled before she continued with her next sentence. She still felt embarrassed using the obscene words in polite conversation. "She is also keeping track of the 'mothers' of the hatchlings, so we can avoid inbreeding as much as possible." She giggled again. "No problem identifying Speckle-Top's 'children.' Her speckles sure breed true.

"Speckle-Top is a genius with the animals. She can just look at the animals and tell how they are feeling. The herds are multiplying rapidly, and Zero-Gauss finally let us have some fresh meat four turns ago. I'm getting pretty good at tending the plants. The grounds of the Inner Eye Institute are now full of fruit and nut bearers, and I am starting wild patches outside the city."

"I've got some good news, too," said Cliff-Web after the long wait. "We were finally able to establish contact with the rejuvenation robot at the West Pole Rejuvenation Center by sending commands with a tight X-ray beam from West Pole Space Station. The robot has been unable to restore more than one enzyme machine, but within five greats there should be enough enzyme collected for the rejuvenation of a male or a small female."

"Wonderful!" exclaimed Qui-Qui. "I can take Heavy-Egg there and get his sight back. Then you'll have someone who can tell you what is wrong with the gravity catapults, and I'll have someone to help share the burden of tending plants.''

07:03:32 GMT TUESDAY 21 JUNE 2050

This time Qui-Qui activated the communicator early. Her voice was solemn. ''Heavy-Egg has just flowed. I guess the strain on his body was too much.''

''Our last engineer gone! We are doomed!'' came the wail from Hohmann-Transfer. ''We might as well give up.''

''*I'm* not giving up,'' said Qui-Qui. ''Let me speak to Cliff-Web. I want the next assignment for Heavy-Egg's beginning engineering class.''

As she waited for Cliff-Web to respond, she mentally began to go over the parentage of the oldest of the younglings in the creche-school. If they were to keep the small group on Egg growing until the females became old enough to lay eggs on their own, she and Speckle-Top would have to start teaching the older males something other than reading, computing, farming, and engineering.

Sacrifice

Qui-Qui had left her engineering class working on their lessons and was now out in the fields teaching the farming class how to tell ripe nut-pods from immature ones. Through her tread she could hear a loud commotion from the hatchling pens. Zero-Gauss, now very old, was always having trouble keeping the large numbers of hatchlings under control while still tending the eggs. Qui-Qui left her farming class and rushed to the hatchery.

"Weak eyes . . . weak eyes . . . speckle-hides have weak eyes." The high-pitched sound of the taunting treads came from a group of unspeckled hatchlings who were keeping three speckled hatchlings from getting to the food troughs.

"I'll show you who's weak," one of the speckled ones said, then rushed at her tormentors and managed to glide up on top of one of the males and started jabbing at him with a sharp crust-rock. Zero-Gauss was busy with a hatchling just emerging from an egg and could only shout at them from the egg pen.

Overworked, frustrated, and angry, Qui-Qui rushed at the brawling hatchlings and sent all of them sliding across the crust with swift slaps from a manipulator.

"That will be enough of that!" she said fiercely, her dark eyes blazing down at them over her large eyeflaps.

175

"You will stop fighting and eat quietly." Some still whimpering from the slaps, the hatchlings gathered around the food troughs and ate their midturn meal. Zero-Gauss finally came in from the egg pen, pushing a new hatchling in front of her to the food trough.

"I don't know what to do," Zero-Gauss said tiredly. "It seems like every turn they fight more and more. I keep tellling them we all have to work together, but they won't listen to me."

"Maybe it will become better when some of the younglings become old enough to help us," said Qui-Qui, who then checked in on her engineering class before going back out into the fields. The younglings there were now arguing.

"Don't pick that one, stupid," a speckled youngling said to a non-speckled one.

"Why not. It looks perfectly ripe to me."

"It's got ground-slug eggs in it."

"How do you know?"

"It's obvious," said the speckled one. "Just look at its color compared to the good one next to it."

"I don't see any difference," said the non-speckled one.

"That's because you only have 'common' eyes." The speckled one extended its four pink eyes with obvious pride. "We speckle-hides have 'special' eyes that can see things you plain-hides can't. That's what makes us so special."

"You're not so special," said the non-speckled one raising his pull-pike that he used to bring down fruits from the taller plants.

"That's enough of *that*," Qui-Qui hollered from a distance. "You younglings are acting just like a bunch of hatchlings."

07:12:02 GMT TUESDAY 21 JUNE 2050

While Hohmann-Transfer was busy with her scrollwork, some of her eyes noticed that one of the stars in the sky was rapidly growing in size. She let the scroll roll up and went to the command deck as the star grew larger and larger. By the time she got there, she could see the yellow-white speck in front of the star. It was the last of the large interstellar exploration ships, the Abdul Nkomi Farouk. Now, all that were left out in interstellar space were a few scout ships.

"East Pole Space Station calling Abdul," said Hohmann-Transfer. There was nearly two methturns delay while the signal traveled across the 30 kilometers that separated them. During the wait the spinor warp drives on Abdul were turned off and the star receded back into the heavens, while the ship stayed in orbit around Egg.

"This is Captain Searching-Eye of the interstellar exploration ship Abdul reporting to base as ordered. Captain Far-Ranger and Admiral Steel-Slicer were given the last positions of our two scout ships and were still searching for them when we left Herc X-1. What is the status of things on Egg? We are all concerned."

"Terrible," said Hohmann-Transfer. "We are reduced to depending upon the capabilities of an *entertainer*, and she has been able to do nothing for two dozen greats of turns. I am calling a general meeting as soon as you get here."

The main meeting bowl on East Pole Space Station was jammed with bodies. The larger assembly rooms elsewhere on the station were also crowded with concerned spacers watching the video links to the main meeting bowl.

"It has now been two dozen greats of turns since the disastrous starquake destroyed civilization on Egg," Hohmann-Transfer began. "I have done the best I can with the inadequate support from the surface, but the situation continues to look completely hopeless. The one engineer we had left on the surface flowed before we could save him. We are now reduced to training our own engineers with an entertainer as the teacher."

"She is doing a good job under the circumstances," said Cliff-Web. "The problem is that without robots and other labor-saving machines, everyone on the surface has to spend a good deal of his time just keeping himself alive. We give them as much advice as possible, but the two-grethturn time delay in the communication link doesn't help."

"How much longer will it be before they will be able to get a gravity catapult into operation?" someone asked.

"It all depends upon whether Qui-Qui can keep things under control down there and keep the classes going," said Cliff-Web. "If she can, then by selecting out the ones most competent in gravitational engineering and keeping them free to go to classes, we should soon have someone competent enough to go to the gravity catapult sites at the East and West Poles and tell us how bad the damage is. *If* the damage is not too bad, then it will only be another one or two dozen greats until we have trained a batch of engineers who can fix the damage, repair a power plant to run the catapult, and get it into operation."

"You are talking about generations!" exclaimed Hohmann-Transfer. "You didn't tell me that before! We can't wait that long!"

"I told you, but you wouldn't listen," said Cliff-Web. "And we have no alternative but to wait as many generations as it takes."

"But we're getting older all the time. Without rejuvenation we will all be dead before they finish!" said Hohmann-Transfer. "You will have to make some rejuvenation machines."

"You forget we are limited to the materials that we have on hand in the space stations and spaceships. I have had my engineers look into the problem. We could easily rework some of the metal in the less essential portions of the ships into machines to produce the rejuvenation enzymes. But the actual process requires the use of a rare metal isotope. In the whole space fleet there is just enough to make two machines, each capable of making enough enzyme for one person every three dozen greats. Basically, only two people can be kept alive by rejuvenation."

"Then the rest will have to die!" said Hohmann-Transfer. "What is the use of fixing the gravity catapult if there are only two people left to save?"

"We can't allow the space contingent to die off to two people," said Cliff-Web. "The cheela on the ground have lost all their scrolls and all their technology. We need to keep the space contingent at full strength. Since we don't have rejuvenation machines to make young cheela out of old ones, we will have to make younglings the old-fashioned way. I understand that it's not bad, once you get used to it."

There were a number of amused rumbles from the audience, but they went right under the tread of Hohmann-Transfer.

"I don't understand," she said.

"I am recommending that the medicos take selected personnel off their contraceptive drugs. Can't you just see it?" he said, his eye-stubs sweeping around the large meeting bowl. "We could put the egg pen down here at the bottom of the meeting bowl, with the hatchling pens stretching up the sides, and the creche-schools around the top.''

It was ultimately decided to proceed with the building of the two rejuvenation machines. It would be important to have some continuity as the collection of space stations and spaceships were converted into a space colony. After much debate, Hohmann-Transfer and Cliff-Web were chosen to use the rejuvenation machines. The rest of the cheela were allocated one egg each, for the space stations could not handle much more than a doubling in the population. Many cheela went through many greats of serious thought before they finally decided on their ''egg partner.''

07:15:16 GMT TUESDAY 21 JUNE 2050

Qui-Qui was called to the communicator by one of the scribes, Quick-Writer.

''I am still copying a section of a maintenance manual for auxiliary power generators,'' Quick-Writer told Qui-Qui when she arrived at the flyer. ''They inserted a message to you a few methturns ago asking that you come.''

Qui-Qui waited while Quick-Writer finished writing down the last words of the maintenance manual on the scroll in his neat script from the dictation 406 kilometers above. Quick-Writer then activated the video link. Some diagrams appeared on the screen. He copied them quickly, for the video link was extremely wasteful of energy. As soon as he was done, the link was switched back to audio only. There was a pause, then Cliff-Web came on the link.

''Our new Space Council has come to a decision,'' said Cliff-Web. ''We feel that it is now time for you to go to the West Pole and undergo rejuvenation. Now, I know what you are probably thinking—that Zero-Gauss should be the one to go, since she is older. The problem with that is the rejuvenation robot has been unable to get more than one enzyme machine going. If we send Zero-Gauss now, then you can't go for some 36 greats. By then you would be close to 90 greats old and might flow before you could be rejuvenated. We decided we couldn't afford to lose you. You are the only one with the mixture of drive, determination, optimism, and charisma that is needed to keep the surface younglings concentrating on our joint goal, reunification of the clans of Egg. The vote was 288 to 1. I needn't tell you who the 'one' was. As soon as you can, you are to travel to the West Pole, undergo rejuvenation, then return bringing the rejuvenation robot and the enzyme machine. The robot will be useful in getting some power generators running at Bright's Heaven and possibly repairing some of the other equipment.''

Qui-Qui acknowledged the message, then turned the communications link back to Quick-Writer. He started writing again as the dictation continued.

It took a few turns for Qui-Qui to get things organized so that she could be gone the half-great it would take for her to undergo rejuvenation. One of the engineering students, Coulomb-Force, removed the communicator and an accumulator from the flyer so the education of the classes could continue.

Zero-Gauss was relieved that it wasn't she that had been chosen for rejuvenation, for she wanted nothing more than to be with her little ones. Now that there were adults to help take care of the older hatchlings and run the creche-classes, she had nothing to do but hatch eggs and tell stories of the old days before the starquake.

As the flyer carrying Qui-Qui zoomed down the old road toward the West Pole, it passed by a large herd of food Slinks. Speckle-Top was with the herd, teaching her herding class. Everyone in the class had speckles and at least one pink eye. She was teaching them things that were not found in the textbooks, like how to look at an animal with your special pink eyes and tell where it hurt, and how to approach an animal so that it would think you were a friend.

As Speckle-Top watched the flyer pass, an old worry began nagging her brain-knot. Every turn they came closer to fixing one of those gravity machines they kept talking about. Then down would come the spacers and with them their laws. Then after that would come the clankers and their lashes. Speckle-Top didn't want the spacers to come; she liked things the way they were.

07:15:32 GMT TUESDAY 21 JUNE 2050

Eighty turns later, Qui-Qui returned from her rejuvenation in her flyer, bringing the rejuvenation robot and the enzyme machine with her. She glided to a landing near the Inner Eye Institute. No one seemed to be around, so Qui-Qui got out to attach the flyer to the tie-bolts. She heard a slithering in the crust, and her eyes saw a number of miniature pet Swifts approaching. She didn't recognize any of them. She had a little bit of food in a carrying pouch and took it out. She formed some tendrils to pat the animals and called them to her.

The pack of Swifts saw the food, and their slither turned into a charge. Their maws opened, and sharp teeth snapped out into ripping position. Roaring with hunger, they rushed at Qui-Qui. She threw the bit of food to one side to distract them, then made a dash for the flyer. The robot watched impassively as she flowed rapidly aboard the flyer and slammed the magnetic shield shut, a manipulator dripping juices where she had fended off one of the beasts.

Hurt and a little frightened, Qui-Qui became concerned. Something had happened while she was gone. She raised the flyer, flew over the frustrated pack of Swifts, and moved slowly down the streets. The plants that once had flourished on the grounds of the Inner Eye Institute looked untended. All the fruits and pods had been stripped. She came to a compound in the middle of the Institute that looked sealed off. The doors were shut and rocks were placed outside so that it was difficult even to get to the door to open it. The sliding window panels were shut too, and bars were placed across many of the openings. Along the top of the wall was a makeshift coil of wire. Tiny curlicues of light appeared in the middle of the coils as stray nuclei from space spiraled to their death in the super-strong magnetic fields.

A sliding panel in a barred window moved aside slightly, and a single eye-ball peeked through. The panel was thrust aside and Quick-Writer thrust half his eye-stubs through the bars and waved frantically at the rapidly moving flyer. Qui-Qui raised the flyer up over the walls and brought it down inside the closed compound. She was greeted by eight of her former students. Three of them—Quick-Writer, the scribe; Coulomb-Force, the electromagnetic engineer; and Newton-Einstein, the gravitational engineer—were the older ones she had left in charge of the classes. Of the three dozen that had been in advanced classes when she left, there were now only five.

"It was terrible," said Coulomb-Force. "Right after you left, Zero-Gauss flowed. Then things got worse."

"Actually," said Quick-Writer. "Things were fairly stable while we went through the ritual of butchering

Zero-Gauss and distributing her meat. Most of it went to the hatchlings, since she loved them so. After the ritual distribution, however, things did get worse. Speckle-Top told me to turn off the communicator."

"Why?" Qui-Qui asked.

"She said we shouldn't be paying attention to voices from the sky," interrupted Coulomb-Force. "Then she started to destroy the communicator, but I said she might get shocked and I would do it for her. I just disconnected it from the power source. Later I got some parts from a store in centertown and smashed them up, then hid the communicator."

"She also told the students that they didn't have to attend classes anymore," said Quick-Writer. "Most of them cheered and went off to play games. A few came to me and asked if they could learn on their own. There were eight. Three were killed in the fights."

"Fights!?!"

"They were terrible," said Coulomb-Force. "It only took a few turns of nobody working before the food got short. Some of the plain-hides tried to kill a food Slink and got into a fight with the speckled-hides."

"It ended with most of the plain-hides being driven off to the east," said Quick-Writer. "They stripped the plants before they left and managed to hold onto some herds of food Slinks. We went with them at first, but decided our first duty was to the future of Egg and came back to where Coulomb-Force had hidden the communicator. Speckle-Top and the rest of the speckled-hides didn't bother us as long as we kept out of sight."

"They obviously didn't like us, though," said Coulomb-Force. "So we started fortifying this compound. How do you like my magnetic barrier?"

"Is that the coil across the top of the wall?" Qui-Qui asked.

"Yes, I've been collecting superconducting wire since I was a hatchling, and it finally found a good use. It sure used up the energy when I charged it, but it keeps us safe from speckles and Swifts alike."

"I was attacked by a pack of Swifts when I landed," said Qui-Qui.

"There are a lot of wild animals now," Quick-Writer told her. "All the pets that people used to have are now on their own. I also notice that the young miniature Swifts and Flow Slows are bigger than the older ones. The hybrid miniaturization process must be a temporary one, since the new generations seem to be reverting."

"Where is Speckle-Top now?" Qui-Qui asked. "I didn't see anyone around when I flew in."

"She knew you would be returning shortly," Quick-Writer replied. "I guess she didn't want to meet you eye-balls to eye-balls, so she and the rest of the speckled-hides left a dozen turns ago. They headed north, taking the food Slinks with them."

"We had better get the communicator operational again," said Qui-Qui. "I should tell this to the spacers."

"They already know all about it," said Coulomb-Force. "I set up the communicator as soon as we secured this compound. Newton-Einstein is using it now. I think he is getting instructions from Engineer Cliff-Web."

"Follow me and I'll take you there." Quick-Writer led them through a maze of wall and passages. "Don't go that way," he said, pointing with his eye-stubs at what looked like the main passageway while turning to his left into what looked like a storage alcove and climbing over some bags of dried nuts.

"Why?" asked Qui-Qui.

Coulomb-Force didn't answer, but picked up a heavy nut from a burst bag and rolled it down the corridor. The nut flashed into an incandescent glare of purple-hot plasma.

"Cliff-Web suggested it," said Coulomb-Force. "Of course it is more spectacular on a small object like a nut, but it is enough to turn a large cheela into dinner."

They worked their way through the maze to the inner compound where Newton-Einstein was at the communicator.

"Yes. She just arrived," said Newton-Einstein. "I will give her the directions."

Qui-Qui was hoping to hear the familiar voice of Cliff-Web again, but Newton-Einstein had obviously finished the conversation and wasn't willing to wait another two grethturns.

"Greeting, Teacher Qui-Qui," Newton-Einstein said, his eye-balls seemingly locked on her newly restored eye-flaps. "Rejuvenation has certainly treated you well. I would be glad to take lessons from you *any* turn."

Qui-Qui now regretted the necessity that had required her to mate with some of the young nubile males so long ago. They grew up so quickly and now seemed so brash.

"What were the directions from the spacers?" she asked, ignoring his remarks.

"Cliff-Web now feels that I am properly prepared to evaluate the condition of the gravity catapults on Egg. He suggests that we start with the ones at the West Pole, since they were furthest from the epicenter. Shall we go?" He moved closer and extended an eye-stub out to her.

"We will bring Coulomb-Force along with us," said Qui-Qui, taking charge once again.

"Why?" Newton-Einstein asked. "He knows nothing about gravitational engineering. Besides, he is needed here to keep the power generators running."

"I brought a robot to take care of the power generators," Qui-Qui explained. "You forget that a gravity catapult also needs a power plant. While you are checking out the status of the gravity catapult, Coulomb-Force can be finding out if we have some way to run it.''

"If you say so." Newton-Einstein was obviously disappointed that he wouldn't be taking the trip alone with Qui-Qui.

"Show me the rest of the compound." Qui-Qui started off down a corridor that had alternating stripes of dust and hard rock on the floor. "Then we should be on our way." Quick-Writer hurried to block her path.

"We don't have this one activated," said Quick-Writer. "But you should learn what those alternating stripes in the dust mean when you come across them in the maze."

"Another shock treatment?" asked Qui-Qui.

"Worse," said Quick-Writer. He pressed a portion of a picture on the wall in a coded pattern to activate the trap.

"Careful," warned Coulomb-Force.

"Sooner or later we are going to have to learn to do this with our eyes under flaps," said Quick-Writer. He didn't pull in his eyes, but moved quickly over the striped pattern on the floor, his tread developing an exaggerated ripple that allowed his tread to touch the hard crust, but bridged over the undisturbed dusty portions. Safely on the other side, he rolled a nut back across the path. An explosion from a tube buried in the crust at the middle of the striped pattern sent a heavy weight up into the sky, trailing a thin, tough fiber. The weight fell back down, just to one side of the firing tube. It sank deep into the crust, carrying the end of the fiber with it. The sides of the hole glowed from the impact.

Qui-Qui looked at the two holes in the crust connected by a tough fiber, then looked at Quick-Writer.

"Those Zebu barriers are all through the compound,"
said Quick-Writer. "Only the outer ones are activated all

the time. If the high speed weight doesn't damage your brain-knot, then the fiber will stitch you to the crust until we get there to cut you loose.''

Quick-Writer deactivated the barrier, and Qui-Qui tried to cross with the required exaggerated ripple. She made it across with only one buzz from the training monitor.

Before they left, Qui-Qui took the flyer up on a high trajectory to look around. There were some large herds off in the distance to the north, but no danger nearby. Coulomb-Force obviously enjoyed the experience of flying, but Newton-Einstein came down with all twelve eye-balls tucked under pale eyeflaps.

Leaving Quick-Writer in charge of the compound, Qui-Qui, Newton-Einstein, and Coulomb-Force set off for the West Pole, gliding just above the crust. One of the gravity catapults was not far from White Rock City. Qui-Qui had been taken to the catapult site for a visit when she was in creche-school.

As they approached the site, Coulomb-Force had Qui-Qui stop. ''There is a major power conduit running alongside the road. The conduit joined the road just a meter or so back. I think it came from that power plant over next to those foothills.'' He flicked his eye-stubs to the north.

''We might as well look at it while we are here,'' said Qui-Qui. She turned the flyer to the north, raised the elevation to a few centimeters so she would pass easily over the deserted homes and office compounds, and headed for the artificial mound off in the distance.

The power plant was in surprisingly good shape. During the starquake, the crust motions had bounced back and forth through the chaotic pattern of mountain roots at the West Pole and had nearly cancelled out at the site of the plant. Qui-Qui was so pleased with their find that she went back to the food lockers in her flyer and brought out a bag of sparkling wine to help pass away the time while they waited for the West Pole Space Station to respond. While they were traveling over the surface, Cliff-Web had orbited to the West Pole Space Station to keep the communications delay down.

"I'm glad to hear that most of the power equipment looks in good shape," Cliff-Web said. "The first thing to do is to connect the power circuits of the flyer to the control console. Hopefully we will find some power units that were shut down by the safety monitors before the units were damaged by the starquake. Let me know what the status board says and what you plan to do before you activate anything. We don't have any ground power experts up here, but our spaceship power plant engineers may have some suggestions."

It took most of the rest of the turn to maneuver the flyer into the power plant compound and activate the control console. There were a few blinking bright blue-hot lights that indicated unit failures, but most of the board glowed a cool red under the word *READY*.

"The pressure readings on four of the power wells are above minimum," Coulomb-Force reported. "The other two read zero. Must be breaks in the casing, because the pressure cap connectors have no cracks. I'm going to activate well number 2, run the flow through the distribution manifold to motor-generator number 2 and see what happens."

There were no objections from above, so Coulomb-Force pressed the *ACTIVATE* button on the console and the pressure cap on power well 2 opened and allowed the high-pressure, neutron-rich fluid from deep inside Egg to flow to the distribution manifold. The valves held and the pressure gauges on the manifold rose. He then activated another button and the flow surged into the motor-generator. A deep rumble vibrated through the crust and rose to a steady hum.

"We have power!" Coulomb-Force shouted. "We are on our way!"

Qui-Qui reported the good news through the communications link, then switched the power circuits connecting the console to the flyer so the accumulators would be charging instead of discharging.

Two more bags of White Rock City sparkling wine and a friendly three-way tussle in the cushioned, but cramped, back compartment of the flyer left them all exhausted. It was a full turn before they left the power plant, the flyer following the power conduit to the site of the gravity catapult a few meters away.

"The catapult looks all right to me," said Newton-Einstein as they raised the flyer up and circled above the gigantic torus lying half-buried in the crust.

"Wouldn't it lose the ultradense fluid in the pipes if the power failed?" Coulomb-Force asked.

"No," said Newton-Einstein. "The fluid is really monopole stabilized black-hole dust. It is highly magnetic and the tubes are made of high temperature superconductor. Even without power, the tubes keep the black-hole dust contained."

They landed outside the catapult control compound and went in.

"We're in luck!" Coulomb-Force was looking over at a glowing light above a large power breaker in one corner. "The conduits from the power plant are intact, and we have power! Let's activate the console and check out the status of the catapult." He closed the tripped power breaker and the console lights went on. The board was a steady deep red except for a blinking blue failure light in one corner.

Newton-Einstein glided to the console, and the wave motion in his eye-stubs came to a complete halt as he read the engraved inscription above the blinking blue-hot light.

Worried, Qui-Qui flowed over next to him.

"What's the matter?" she asked.

"There was a leak; the ultradense dust is gone."

They went around the outside of the catapult and found the leak. There was a small funnel-shaped hole in the crust near the base of the foundation where the jet of black-hole dust had dropped into Egg, pulling the crust with it.

"The catapult must have been working when the star-quake hit," said Newton-Einstein. "The dust was circling the torus at high speed and all of it shot out of the hole. If it had not been operating, we would have only lost one loop's worth. We could have patched the leak and operated the catapult on the rest."

"Well, there are three more catapults here at the West Pole," said Qui-Qui. "Let's go look at them."

"I hope their power plants are working," Coulomb-Force said. "I don't think we could count on the inter-connect power conduits to be unbroken over those long distances."

They didn't even bother to stop at the next gravity catapult. A major break in the crust had torn the large torus into two half-circles. Two turns later Newton-Einstein reported up to the West Pole Space Station. "None of the gravity catapults are operational at the West Pole. We will have to try the East Pole."

It was Qui-Qui who reported in from the East Pole. Coulomb-Force and Newton-Einstein were too discouraged.

"As we suspected, the machines here were even more damaged. Not even one power well remained pressurized. We will just have to learn to make monopole stabilized black-hole dust and recharge the gravity catapult at the West Pole after we fix the leak. It will take us a few greats, since you are going to have to dictate to us in detail how to go about it; but we'll keep working at it."

The three waited patiently for the reply. It was from Cliff-Web, now back at East Pole Space Station. "I'm afraid that it is going to take a little longer than a few greats. No one uses monopole stabilized black-hole dust anymore. It hasn't been made for over two dozen generations. We have no information on it up here, since it is an obsolete material. With the library records erased down there, we are going to have to get what information we can from the humans and that will take many minutes, perhaps as much as an hour. Even that information will only be general knowledge. I and the other engineers up here will have to expand that into detailed instructions of how to build the machines to produce and stabilize the black-hole dust, try them out up here on prototypes, then dictate the information down to you. All that will take considerable time."

Ignoring the dejected looks of Coulomb-Force and Newton-Einstein, Qui-Qui tried to put a cheerful trill in her tread as she replied. "You had better get busy talking to the humans, then. It always takes them forever to do *anything*. And while you are at it, ask them to send you a capsule history of what they called the 'Dark Ages.' By knowing how their learned people maintained islands of knowledge while surrounded by ignorance and barbarians, I may learn things that will help me cope with the situation here. Also, does anyone up there know any magic tricks?"

They returned to the maze at Bright's Heaven. Slowly the information trickled from the HoloMem crystals in the human console to the East Pole Space Station, where it was studied, checked out, and sent on down to the surface below. By the time Coulomb-Force died, he had managed to construct a few more free-space communication sets. Young scribes, chosen for the honor because of their neat script, copied the information from space, and the manuals and textbooks were passed on to others who attempted to build and operate the machines described with their inadequate tools and resources. There were long periods when no information was being dictated, so many of the scrolls were decorated by the bored scribes with elaborate fluorescent illustrations in the spaces along the edges and within the technical diagrams.

Qui-Qui spent most of her time in the flyer, gathering food and recruits. She was known to the clans around as the glowing God of Youth and Knowledge, the Mother of Egg. She could fly through the sky and talk to the stars. She was forever beautiful and never died.

Qui-Qui would arrive at each clan cluster flying high above in the sky in her flyer, circling until each individual in the tribe had seen her. She would then skim low to the surface and hover the flyer above the ground next to a large rectangular stone altar that the clan had erected and piled high with food offerings. While her acolytes were transferring the food offerings to the flyer on one side, the God of Youth and Knowledge glided out on a nearly invisible crystallium platform on the other side. She seemingly floated in space, while above her flickered brightly colored curlicues of light from compact ion generators she had pouched in her topside.

Qui-Qui would ask to see the hatchlings and younglings. Then seemingly out of nowhere, she would materialize gifts for the young ones. There were educational toys, special treats (full of important trace elements) to eat, and beginner scrolls to read. Just before the younglings be-came adults, they were treated to a ride on the flyer back to the Maze Temple at Bright's Heaven, where they were tested. Only a few were chosen to stay. The rest returned to their clans, awed by what they had seen. Once every three dozen greats, Qui-Qui retired to a special room at the sacred center of the maze for a half-great and came back restored to youth.

08:26:37 GMT TUESDAY 21 JUNE 2050

The last three scout ships came in from deep space together, and Far-Ranger reported to the Space Council. "We found them almost at the core. Plenty of neutron stars, even some with life. But none had progressed past the savage stage. Life is too easy on the typical neutron star. With no competition, there is no need for intelligence. I guess we can thank the humans for arousing curiosity in us so long ago."

"How are things on Egg?" Steel-Slicer asked Hohmann-Transfer.

"Terrible," she said. "It has been over a whole human hour since the starquake and things are only getting worse. I'm tired of it all. I'm tired of making decisions. I'm tired of fighting to keep us going. I'm tired of life."

"Perhaps you should rejuvenate early," Admiral Steel-Slicer suggested.

"No, I'm tired of rejuvenations, too. You can have my rejuvenation. I resign. You take over. I'm going to tend eggs." She pulled the twelve-pointed stars off her hide, gave them to Steel-Slicer and headed off to the main conference bowl, now the hatching pen and creche-school.

09:31:11 GMT TUESDAY 21 JUNE 2050

After generations of use, the old flyer stopped flying despite the best efforts of the engineers in space and on the ground to keep it running. The clans now had to bring their food offerings to the Maze Temple. There were more clans now, however, and many stayed near the Maze

Temple where they traded food for labor-saving machines. The clans farthest away became forgetful, drifted away from the influence of the God of Youth and Knowledge, and reverted back to savagery.

Qui-Qui still flew in the sky on special occasions, but now she was levitated above the Maze Temple by gravity repulsor fields from the small prototype gravity catapult her acolytes had managed to make. It only used dense nucleonic fluid, however, for the manufacture of monopole stabilized black-hole dust had proved elusive.

The turns passed.

Barbarian

He came from the north, subjugating all in his path. His name was Ferocious-Eyes, the Terrible One, and he rode on the back of a giant Swift. He was small, but his wiry, heavily speckled body was more than a match for any of the warriors in his army, for they feared the ferocious glare from his twelve pink eyes more than they did his whip-sword.

As a two-great-old hatchling, just barely able to talk, he had been abandoned on the north slopes of the Exodus Volcano by the elders of his food-short clan. Without even one sharp-seeing "common" eye, the heavily speckled one would be useless for work in the fields. The hungry hatchling had found the nest of a pair of wild Swifts before the Swifts found him. When the Swifts returned, he was sitting, satiated, among the tattered remains of one of their eggs. Raised by the Swifts as one of their own, he soon was participating in raids on the herds of the clans around them.

Many turns later, now a youngling, he rode into his old clan compound on the back of one of his nest brothers, flicking the whip-sword that he had invented by tying sharp shards of dragon crystal onto a long strand of woven fibers. Unreachable on his perch high above the ravenous five-toothed maw of his mount, he was invincible. He

197

slashed the leader of the clan to shreds, fed him to his mount, and took over the clan. Until that time, he had no name. Now he took one, Ferocious-Eyes, from the awed whispers he could hear as he rode through the compound.

Three dozen turns later Ferocious-Eyes was satiated. His eating pouches were satiated with food; his brain-knot was satiated with stories he had commanded from the Old Ones; and his ego was satiated with compliments from the fawning cheela competing for the scraps of food he discarded. His desire for power was not satiated, however, for he would never forgive the cheela race for abandoning him because he was too speckled.

Ferocious-Eyes picked out three of the cheela in the clan, the speckled ones that had the most pink eyes, and taught them how to ride Swifts. It was easy for the speckled ones, for with their pink eyes, they could see subtle color changes in the hides and eyes of the Swifts that allowed them to read the moods of the dangerous animals. Ferocious-Eyes left one of his new warriors in charge of the clan and took the rest of his small army to conquer the next clan.

The pattern of conquest of the Terrible One was simple. His army would surround a clan compound, then he and a small group of bodyguards would ride into the compound. He, personally, would challenge the leader of the clan. If the leader was foolish enough to attempt to duel, he soon was meat for Ferocious-Eyes' Swift. The army would stay long enough to feed themselves and their mounts, disarm and subjugate the clan, pick and train some recruits, then move on, leaving one or two of their number to keep the clan under control. At some of the first clan compounds they had experienced resistance, but any opponents left alive after the battle was over had all but one eye lopped off and were set free to bring a warning to the next clan.

The Terrible One, now at the head of a small roving army, had six captains who each led a dozen mounted picked warriors. They were supported by a much larger army that extracted food and supplies from the subjugated clans and transported it by long lines of porters that stretched from the West, North, and East Poles to wherever the army was. The lines were now converging on the northern outskirts of Bright's Heaven.

"We are coming upon Bright's Heaven, O Terrible One," said Falling-Quirrl. "The home of Qui-Qui, the God of Youth and Knowledge. She lives in a Maze Temple protected by magic. It is said that no one but her has been able to find the way to the center of the maze."

"She is no more a god than I am," said Ferocious-Eyes.

"But they say she can talk to the stars and fly in the sky. They also say she is forever beautiful and never dies."

"She can do no more than the ancient ones that lived before the big crustquake," said Ferocious-Eyes. "God or not, I bet the juices will still come out when you throw one of your quirrls down on her."

His Swift roared and snapped at the Swift carrying Falling-Quirrl. They both had to slap their mounts on their sensitive eyes before they could quiet them down.

"The Swifts are getting hungry," she said.

"We'll stop here and kill a Flow Slow to feed them." Ferocious-Eyes slid down off the tail of his mount. His tread slapped the crust in a loud command.

"Where is that slave carrying the sparkling wine?" he demanded. "I'm thirsty!"

"The Terrible One is just north of the city," the messenger reported. "They have stopped to eat and feed their mounts."

"The Terrible One," mused Qui-Qui, suddenly very tired. The rejuvenation robot had been pestering her to undergo yet another rejuvenation, but she had been putting it off as the news of the Terrible One had been coming in.

"It seems like history on Egg is following the history of Earth. We even have our own Attila. Only instead of Attila-the-Hun, Scourge of God, he is Attila-the-Speckled, Scourge of Bright."

"We had better leave," said Linear-Spring, one of the mechanical engineers. "The Terrible One is irresistible."

"No," said Qui-Qui. "If he is anything like the Attila-the-Hun of Earth, he will not stop until he has conquered all of Egg or dies. If we leave, he will just follow us. We will stay and fight."

"But he has six dozen mounted warriors with him, and dozens and dozens more in reserve."

"We *must* stay and fight." Qui-Qui picked up a pricker and a long pike. "And he cannot be allowed to win, for if he does, then the Dark Ages will surely fall on Egg, as they once did on Earth."

Ferocious-Eyes moved unopposed through the deserted city of Bright's Heaven. He stopped his army when they came to the Maze Temple. He and Falling-Quirrl circled all around the outside wall. There were a few windows in the high wall, but they were barred and the sliding panels had been shut tight. Every few millimeters there were portholes—some at crust level and some at eye level. Through a few ports they caught the glimpse of an eye-ball looking out at them. Along the top of the wall there ran a spiral of metal. Occasional flashes of light appeared in the loops.

"Those must be the 'magnetic barriers' our newest slaves told us about," said Falling-Quirrl.

"It is strange that something that is not hot and glowing can burn." Ferocious-Eyes suddenly whipped his Swift and rode directly at the wall between two portholes, flicked a tendril at the top of the wall and rode away again.

"It burns," he said, sucking the tip of his tendril. "We can't go over."

There was only one entrance to the Maze Temple. It was large, and because it had no door or bars it looked ominous. The entrance opened into four narrow corridors that immediately took sharp turns as they branched off into the maze. The corridors were too narrow to allow a Swift to pass.

Ferocious-Eyes gathered his warriors.

"Falling-Quirrl. You and your warriors will dismount and prepare to enter. Three into each corridor. Arm yourselves with short swords and prickers for close combat. The rest are to ride your Swifts up to the wall on either side of the entrance and fill those portholes with pikes and quirrls. If they can't see, they can't fight."

The picked vanguard of the Speckled Horde arranged themselves in a rough line, one sharp-seeing 'common' eye always watching their commander. He unpouched a pair of limber-swords and waved them in a complex pattern.

"Attack!" he shouted.

They charged, the mounted warriors rapidly outdistancing Falling-Quirrl and her dozen warriors on tread. As the Swifts moved across the bare ground, they began to roar and swerve to one side or the other despite the efforts of their masters to keep them under control. From a porthole in the wall an eye-ball was watching.

"The undercrust magnetic barriers are bunching them up into the firing lanes," Weber-Gauss reported to the control room. "Let loose the terror tops!"

Ferocious-Eyes suddenly heard high-pitched screams arising from all along the outer wall of the maze. Through the holes at crust level there emerged a stream of spinning screaming objects that danced across the crust. They were wide at the top and narrowed down to a tiny point at the bottom. By some magic means they were able to stay balanced on the tiny point instead of falling over as one would expect.

Sticking out from the whirling body of the screamers were sharp knives that slashed long gashes in Swift and warrior alike. Panicked by the high-pitched screams, the Swifts bolted and the warriors fled.

One of the screamers came straight at Ferocious-Eyes. He watched it come, then gave it a flick with the tip of his whip-sword. The screamer changed course and curved around his nervous mount. Ferocious-Eyes rode to meet the fleeing Falling-Quirrl.

"I said for you to attack! *Look* at me!"

Falling-Quirrl stopped instantly and all her eyes went up on rigid stalks. Ferocious-Eyes rode up to the nearest eye-ball, formed a pincer manipulator and slowly crushed the eye-ball.

"Attack," he said.

Falling-Quirrl gathered her warriors and led them back toward the waiting entrance to the deadly Maze Temple. The Swifts refused to approach the wall, and all the warriors were forced to dismount and make their way on tread across the open ground.

More of the spinning screamers came from the wall, but the surprise was gone. The speckled warriors continued their advance. They tried to dodge the screamers and stabbed at them with their pikes and swords to knock them over, but the strange random motion of the screamers across the crust and their rigid resistance to being pushed over caused many casualties. The remaining war-

riors finally got close enough to the wall that most of the
screamers now shot out past them.

"The terror tops have them bunched into the firing-tube
target areas," Weber-Gauss reported to the control room.
"Initiate ripple-barrage on areas one through eight."

A series of explosions from inside the Maze Temple
caused the advancing warriors to hesitate and look all
around for danger. They saw nothing, then died, as heavy
weights struck at them from out of the sky and pierced
them from topside to tread. The limber-swords swinging
about Ferocious-Eyes were still flashing the "attack" pattern, so they pressed on.

"They are now in the range of the flame throwers,"
reported Weber-Gauss.

Jets of violet-hot flame came from some of the eye-level
portholes and swept back and forth, leaving pools of flam-
ing liquid and screaming blistered warriors. One warrior
who managed to reach the wall between two portholes
slid a shield over a flame hole between bursts. The flame
thrower backfired and an explosion behind the wall sent
flames and pieces of bodies flying through the sky. The
speckled one moved in front of the porthole and repeat-
edly jabbed the end of a pike in the hole to keep it from
being reused. One after another, the flame throwers fell
silent as porthole after porthole was blocked by a crust-
rock or pike guarded by a singed, sliced, and angry speckled warrior.

Only six of Falling-Quirrl's warriors made it to the entrance. She sent two each into three of the corridors, then
she entered the fourth alone.

"The pressure sensors indicate seven targets." Mega-
Bar was monitoring the indicators on the maze map in the
west wall control room. "There are two each in the dead-
end corridors and one entered the main maze trail."

"Let them pass over the first traps, then reactivate those behind them," said Neutron-Gas. "That way we can get them coming or going."

Falling-Quirrl moved slowly along the narrow corridor. She jabbed a pricker into every porthole before passing and looked carefully for traps. The point of her short sword poked hard into the crust in front of her before she put her tread on it. When she reached the striped section of corridor, she was especially careful. She prodded the ground and walls with her sword and pushed her shield ahead of her with the front portion of her tread weighing it down. Nothing happened, and she passed over.

In the distance she heard a crackle and a scream. It sounded like Nasty-Scar. Almost immediately there was a sharp explosion and another scream. She came to another striped area and started across it using her shield under her tread again. There was a loud explosion and a dented shield flew up from under her shocked tread. The shield came down on top of the wall, pushed down on the magnetic barrier until it glowed and hummed, then fell back down into the corridor, nearly hitting her.

Ferocious-Eyes waited and waited for Falling-Quirrl and her warriors to emerge. Finally they did, their bodies pushed one-by-one out of the entrance by a little machine that just fit neatly between the narrow corridor walls. Three had been burned by a strange flame that cooked holes through their bodies, and three had deadly puncture wounds that went from tread to topside.

The last one pushed out was Falling-Quirrl. Ferocious-Eyes sent the butchers to pick up the body, but they brought her to him, for she was still alive despite the large oozing holes in her. Two-thirds of her body was paralyzed from damage to her brain-knot, but she was able to talk with the rest of her tread.

"They have traps that they can turn on and off. I passed over one on the way in. It got me on the way out. I played dead. They stabbed me only a few times through a hole in the wall, then left me. They are weaklings, unused to killing. I would have made sure with a thrust to my brain-knot." She held out her dented shield.

"My shield struck the 'magnetic barrier' and was not burned. Maybe with many shields or one large one, we can keep the barrier from burning us."

Ferocious-Eyes tried her shield on the magnetic barriers in the open areas outside the wall. He found that he could indeed pass over it if he narrowed his body down so that it stayed on the shield. Other shields didn't work, however. They interrogated some of their new slaves from the local clans and found out that what was needed was a special metal called a "superconductor." The slaves were sent into Bright's Heaven to scavenge sheets of this "superconductor" to make into shields.

Turnfeast came, and it was time to feed the warriors and their mounts. There was plenty of meat for the warriors, as the butchers had been busy after the battle. The Swifts didn't get cheela meat, however. It was too good to waste on them, and besides, it wouldn't do for them to learn that their riders were so tasty. The Swifts got Flow Slow meat from the herd that traveled with the army.

Ferocious-Eyes was bored, so he decided to kill the Flow Slow himself instead of letting the butchers do it. One of the butchers scampered up the trailing edge of the animal to the top and drove the Flow Slow straight at his leader.

Ferocious-Eyes, pike sticking straight up, waited as the Flow Slow moved ponderously toward him. It was a huge one, twice as tall as the walls around the Maze Temple. He watched carefully as the square plates of bony armor, each as large as a shield, flowed over the top of the creature and down. He fixed on a weak spot between the moving plates, rushed forward to insert the pike into the chink, then reversed tread to get out from under as the Flow Slow impaled itself on the pike and flowed.

Ferocious-Eyes left the butchers to their work. As he moved away, his eye-stubs were waving slowly in deep thought. Instead of joining his warriors feasting on their comrades, he merely snatched a roasted eye-stub from the carcass of Falling-Quirrl and sucked on the eye-ball as he made his way to the area where the slaves were working on producing superconducting shields. He stopped and looked in disappointment at the eye-stub. He had unfortunately grabbed the eye-stub with the crushed eye-ball, so the eye-ball hadn't squirted juice out into his eating pouch when he had sucked on it.

Ferocious-Eyes was in a bad humor when he arrived at the slave pens. He called the slave in charge of the armory away from his meager turnfeast.

"Do you see that large Flow Slow over there?" he asked the slave, his eye-stubs pointing to a herd grazing nearby. "The big female."

"Yes, O Terrible One," the slave replied.

"Instead of making shields out of the 'superconductor' metal, I want you to make metal covers for the plates on that Flow Slow."

"Don't ask me to do that, Terrible One," said the slave. "A Flow Slow is dangerous if it is angry, and it will surely be angry if we try to nail plates to it."

"You have three turns," said Ferocious-Eyes. "After that it will be an eye for each turn you are late." He tossed the disappointing eye-stub to the crust and returned to the turnfeast to get another. The slave picked up the discarded food, but somehow the eye-stub didn't taste as good as he had thought it would.

"It has been five turns and he still doesn't do anything," said Qui-Qui. "The warriors circle around out of range of the Terror-Tops, keeping anyone from going out or coming in, but they don't attack. They must be planning something, but what? Levitate me with the gravity machine. Maybe I can see something."

"We will have to turn off the power to the defenses to activate the machine," said Weber-Gauss. "But we should be safe enough if we make it short."

A dothturn later, the speckled warriors surrounding the Maze Temple went on alert as a deep humming started in the crust. The hum rose to a whine, and out of the middle of the Temple the God of Youth and Knowledge ascended. She went up ten centimeters and stopped. Coming toward her from the outskirts of Bright's Heaven was what looked like a huge robot. No. It was a Flow Slow, covered with metal. On top was a tiny speckled creature.

Following the armored Flow Slow was the Speckled Horde, recuperated from their wounds and back at full strength. Qui-Qui felt her spirits sink along with her body as the gravity machine brought her back down again.

Ferocious-Eyes wasted no time with preliminaries. Either the Flow Slow would conquer the Maze Temple for him or it would fail. Riding on its topside, he rippled backward as the metal-covered plates moved forward underneath him. His two bodyguards kept the Flow Slow moving and on course with occasional pricks between the armored plates. They moved over the outer magnetic barriers with ease, the crust giving off bolts of electricity as the coils failed under the increased magnetic pressure.

He waited while his warriors silenced the flame throwers along a section of wall, then urged his gigantic metal mount forward. The falling plates of superconductor, backed by the massive weight of the Flow Slow, pressed against the ultra-strong magnetic barrier along the top of the outer wall. The coils of wire hummed as the barrier resisted the pressure, then the atmosphere sparked with energy as the coils collapsed.

Bellowing from the pricks of the tiny ones riding on its topside, the armored Flow Slow pushed over the outer wall, toppling it into the next wall of the maze. The Flow Slow continued on and entered a secret room, reachable only by a subterranean tunnel. It was one of the control rooms for the outer maze defenses. Quirrls from the bodyguards on either side of Ferocious-Eyes pinned the acolytes to the crust.

The Flow Slow moved over the bodies and crashed through another wall, heading for the center of the Maze Temple. One bodyguard was struck by a falling weight that had been fired upward from a tube in the corridor through which they passed. The strong thread tied to the weight dragged her off the top of the Flow Slow. She fell to the crust and burst.

Ferocious-Eyes pricked the Flow Slow to drive it harder as it breeched the next wall. They were now in a large inner room that held a number of acolytes. He could hear their treads talking rapidly, but they didn't seem to be speaking to one another. A flickering image of a strangely bloated cheela floated in the center of a magic window embedded in the floor.

"Attila has managed to ride a Flow Slow right over the walls. He is penetrating deep into the maze." The speaker looked up as the wall came down. "Attila is here! We are lost!" He started to run, but was trapped and crushed along with the others as they tried to flee through the one exit from the communications room.

Three more walls and the Flow Slow reached the center of the complex. Ferocious-Eyes stopped the Flow Slow and looked around. In the center of the room were a jumble of boxes connected with heavy tubes. Against one wall was the most beautiful female cheela Ferocious-Eyes had ever seen. She was carrying a pike and what looked like a pricker, but it was hard for his eyes to make out something that small.

"You must be Qui-Qui," Ferocious-Eyes said. "The cheela who never dies." He inserted a quirrl into a specially trained throwing pouch. "Let's see if your magic can protect you from a quirrl." The quirrl flashed down through the air and buried itself deep in the crust just in front of Qui-Qui. He started to reload, when she rushed forward to slash him with her pike. He brushed back his bodyguard, twirled his whip-sword forward and cut the end off the pike. The return flick cut a slash across Qui-Qui's topside. She didn't feel it.

With her pike gone, Qui-Qui retreated to the jumble of pipes and valves that made up the central power distribution system for the maze complex. The power generator itself was hidden in the old underground laboratory of Zero-Gauss.

She tried to goad Attila off his nearly invincible perch. "And you must be Attila-the-Speckled," she said. "I hear you are called 'Ferocious-Eyes.' 'Weak-Eyes' would be more like it after missing big targets like these." She flapped her lower eyeflaps at him. "Come and get me, my little speckled hatchling child."

The insult of being called a "child" nearly made Ferocious-Eyes lose control, but he calmed himself down. Whip-sword flickering in front of him, he prodded the Flow Slow from behind and forced it into the jumble of tubes and boxes. Qui-Qui clambered away. The Flow

Slow mounted a box. The large valve inside gave way and gigantic surges of power burned through the huge body. The Flow Slow died and spread out, breaking other power connections. The automatic defenses of the Maze Temple collapsed and the Speckled Horde rushed in. Qui-Qui was crushed against the wall by the spreading body of the Flow Slow.

Ferocious-Eyes slid down off the dying Flow Slow and approached Qui-Qui. Suddenly a section of the wall slid aside and a dome-shaped metal object appeared. It moved and talked and seemed to be alive.

"Are you ready to undergo rejuvenation?" the robot asked.

"No!" shouted Qui-Qui, her tread muffled by the crushing body of the Flow Slow. "Don't talk to him! Reset! Stop! Deactivate circuits!"

"I cannot obey that command," the robot replied. "I must keep the rejuvenation machinery running."

Qui-Qui didn't answer. The robot moved over to her and examined her body with its sensors.

"She is dead. She waited too long for rejuvenation." The robot turned toward Ferocious-Eyes. It moved around him, sensors in operation.

"You are in excellent muscle tone, ready for instant rejuvenation," said the robot. "Would you like a young new body?"

"Yes!" Ferocious-Eyes kept his eyes on the moving, talking magic dome of metal.

"First we must prepare the records for the Combined Clans Rejuvenation Board." The robot pulled a scroll out of a compartment. "Name?"

Ferocious-Eyes thought for a moment. A new body deserved a new name. A name like no other.

"Attila," he stated proudly.

10:13:14 GMT TUESDAY 21 JUNE 2050

The Space Council met in a compound that had the bright globe of Egg hanging directly overhead. The glow from Egg no longer had any warmth in it.

"We have lost a good friend and a great teacher and engineer," said Cliff-Web.

"And our only contact with the surface," Admiral Steel-Slicer added. "It looks as if we are stuck up here until Attila loses control. If only there were some way to kill him, like dropping something on him."

"We could deorbit a projectile easily enough," Cliff-Web said. "But once the projectile built up speed, the magnetic field of Egg would tear it apart into a cloud of plasma that would dissipate before it got to the surface. To do any damage we would have to deorbit a large mass. We don't have the mass and we don't have the energy to deorbit it. Besides, we would be killing whole clans of innocent slaves just to get one person."

"It's going to be a long, long time before civilization is rebuilt again to the point where they can bring us down," Steel-Slicer said, resigned.

"We will just have to figure out a way to get down to the surface without their help," Cliff-Web said.

"It's going to be tough," Steel-Slicer said. "None of the spacecraft that we have was designed for landing on the surface. Is there some way to fix up some kind of atmospheric or magnetic drag brake?"

"Egg doesn't have enough atmosphere to help much," Cliff-Web replied. "I could design a magnetic drag brake using metal of the right conductivity; but unlike atmospheric braking, the kinetic energy gets turned into heat inside the metal brake. At high deceleration levels the brake would melt. At low deceleration levels we have the problem of supplying gravity for the crew. Besides, magnetic braking becomes less effective at lower velocities. Braking can take some of the energy out of the vehicle, but it would still be going much too fast to land."

"How about adding some sort of propulsion for the final phases?" Steel-Slicer asked.

"The inertia drives on the scout ships are energy efficient, but their thrust-to-weight is so low they can't be used for landing," Cliff-Web replied. "One of the jumpcraft could conceivably be modified to use old-fashioned antimatter rockets for the landing phase. But even if we could make the tons of antimatter needed to heat the propellant, we just don't have the hundreds of tons of propellant needed to land a jumpcraft with its heavy gravity generators. We are mass limited."

"We will just have to find some mass somewhere. Would it help to sacrifice one of our space stations?"

"I'm working on another idea. We could use one of the compensator masses around the human spaceship. They could make do with just five. The idea is somehow to use one of those masses as a 'first stage' for our lander. We can store the energy we need on the mass so we don't have to carry it on the lander, then transfer the energy to the lander through some kind of launcher."

"Are you thinking of a launcher like a jump loop?" asked Steel-Slicer.

"They are too long to fit on the mass," said Cliff-Web. "I was thinking of a large gravity catapult sitting on the mass. We would somehow put the mass in an elliptical orbit around Egg that would take it down almost to the surface. Just at periapsis, the gravity catapult would launch the landing vehicle in the direction opposite to the orbital trajectory and leave the lander stopped, stationary, a few meters above the surface."

"It would be an easy landing from there!" said Steel-Slicer. "We could land a crew of engineers and then build our own gravity catapult so the rest of us could come down."

"I was hoping to get two berries off a singleberry bush," Cliff-Web said. "I think we can design things so that our lander *is* the gravity catapult. Saves time."

"You can't fly a gravity catapult! A gravity catapult only generates gravity forces when the ultra-dense mass currents are increasing. How are you going to drive the pumps? A long power line back to the mass?"

"You also get gravity forces when the mass currents are decreasing," Cliff-Web said. "But you shouldn't really think about the changes in the mass currents. What really makes the gravity field is the increase or decrease of the gravitomagnetic field inside the torus. I think we can design a gravity catapult that requires no outside power to operate. It will have changes in the fields without changing the speed of the mass currents, just their direction. In fact, this sounds like a good project for my new gravitational engineering seminar." He went off to meet his class.

10:13:26 GMT TUESDAY 21 JUNE 2050

"It is time for the team reports again, class," said Cliff-Web. "How is the design for the lander coming? Who is Team Leader for the lander?"

One of the students in the back spoke up. "The basic design is finished. We will have two long, thin multi-channel tubes that wind around the torus in multiple layers to make the interior field more uniform. The lander will take off with one tube empty and the other fully charged with high speed black-hole dust that will produce a gravitomagnetic field at maximum strength counterclockwise. Then when we want gravity repulsion force we use a diverter valve to switch some of the mass current from the channels in the first tube into the second tube, but going in the opposite direction. The reverse current will cancel some of the gravitomagnetic field inside, which is equivalent to decreasing its strength. The decreasing gravitomagnetic field will make a gravity repulsor field that will keep the lander levitated above Egg.''

"What is the hover time?'' Cliff-Web asked.

"Only three methturns, so far,'' the Lander Team Leader replied. "Now that we have the basic design, we are going back and cutting weight. Out goal is six meth-turns levitation time, which should give us nearly a greth-turn for a landing.''

"Keep working,'' said Cliff-Web. "Launcher Team?''

"We had the easy job,'' another student reported. "The launcher is basically like the gravity catapults on Egg, but bigger. Our real effort has been on making the gravity repulsion field at the center as uniform as possible to min-imize strains on the lander during launch. The size became awfully large though, twenty centimeters. I don't think we are going to be able to put it on one of the human compensator masses. We will need the larger deorbiter mass. I think the humans call it 'Otis' after the human that built the first space fountain.''

"It wasn't a space fountain, it was an elevator,'' Cliff-Web explained.

"What is an elevator?'' asked the student.

"Never mind. Launch Base Team?''

"While the launcher keeps getting bigger, the base keeps getting smaller,'' said a third student. "We've formed a joint study team with an astrophysics class taught by Plasma-Sheath, Doctor of Astrophysics. We are learning the realities of particle and plasma physics, while they are learning the fun of being a gravitational engineer. Our team now has the name 'Planet Busters.' We went out in a scout ship and took a look at Otis. The surface is too far down in the fuzz. We are going to have to use monopoles to shrink it and make it denser. Fortunately, the humans kept their monopole factory running, so they have plenty in storage."

"You are all doing good work," said Cliff-Web. "You have 24 more turns to finish your team report, then I think Plasma-Sheath and I had better talk to the humans before we go any further."

10:13:32 GMT TUESDAY 21 JUNE 2050

"We have a call from East Pole Space Station, Pierre," said Jean. "It's Cliff-Web and an astrophysicist named Plasma-Sheath. They are dumping some detailed information through a data channel, but they also want to speak with you."

Pierre stopped his checkout of the ship's computer and switched his screen to the communications channel, where two cheela appeared on the screen. Cliff-Web was the smaller, although large for a male. The other wore badges on her hide with a starburst in the center. Pierre was becoming better at identifying the sexes, although Plasma-Sheath made it easy with her big lower eyeflaps.

"We have found a way to get back down to Egg," Cliff-Web began without preliminaries. "Since we are very short of everything in space, we would have to borrow some mass and monopoles from you. Unfortunately, your ring masses are too small; only the deorbiter mass would do. We would shrink it with monopoles until it turns into a miniature neutron star, then use that as a base to construct the lander and its launcher."

Pierre was puzzled. "I don't see how you can do that. Even if you could shrink it so the surface density equals that of a neutron star, the equation of state is unstable and it will collapse into a miniature black hole.''

"We are aware of that," said Plasma-Sheath. "By injecting only one type of monopole into the deorbiter mass, we can increase the center density by the formation of monopolium, but the monopolium atoms will have a tendency to repel each other since they will have the same magnetic charge. It is hoped that in this way we can keep the shrinking of the deorbiter under control and keep it from collapsing into a black hole.''

"Sounds risky to me," said Pierre. "Are you sure of your calculations?''

"No," replied Plasma-Sheath. "But it is a risk that we must take.''

Suddenly another cheela appeared on the screen. Pierre recognized the two-star clusters on the hide of Admiral Steel-Slicer, leader of the space cheela.

"That is not what concerns us," he said. "We not only want to use the deorbiter mass as a base to build our gravity catapult, but to deliver the catapult to the surface of Egg. We will have to divert it from its normal orbit.''

"That's all right," said Pierre. "All we need is its gravitational field, and it makes no difference if it is a degenerate asteroid, a miniature neutron star, or a black hole. The external gravity field is the same. Just make sure you put it back in its elliptical orbit when you are through so we can use it to get back up to St. George. You aren't going to be using it for too long, are you? We only have supplies for a few weeks since this mission was designed for eight days.''

"That is the problem." Steel-Slicer was now alone on the screen. "It is possible that the compensator mass will be destroyed in the process of placing the gravity catapult on Egg.''

Pierre paused for a few seconds in shock, then quickly realized that he was wasting the equivalent of weeks of time of the cheela whose blinking image indicated he was checking in at the console every fifth of a second.

"Without the deorbiter mass, we would be stuck here. . . . What are the odds?"

"We are constantly trying to find another way of doing it," Steel-Slicer replied, "but right now the odds are 12 to 1."

"Well," said Pierre. "That's not bad."

"There is an 11 in 12 chance that the deorbiter mass will be tidally disintegrated while delivering the gravity catapult to the surface of Egg and only a one-twelfth chance it will survive. It all depends upon how the orbital and tidal dynamics couple into the interior vibrational modes of the deorbiter mass during the actual transit."

Pierre paused a few seconds again, but this time his brain was not worrying about the cheela.

"There is Oscar, the other large asteroid mass that was used to put the deorbiter mass into its elliptical orbit. Couldn't you use that?"

"With our limited resources, we do not have the power to alter the celestial laws for large, low-density masses," said Steel-Slicer. "That asteroid is well on its way out of the Dragon's Egg system. The best we could do is bring it back in about six months. That is equivalent to eternity for us."

"Hmmm." Pierre considered the options, then said, "I think I'd better talk with Commander Swenson and the rest of the crew."

They gathered in the viewport lounge to discuss the question. Doctor Wong blackened the viewport in the floor as they entered. No one objected. It would be hard enough to make a decision without having the bright yellow image of Sol flickering through the port.

"Commander Swenson says the decision is up to us," Pierre replied. "Her only conditions were that there be a secret ballot and that the decision to let the cheela use Otis be unanimous."

"It would be a lot easier to say 'Yes' if the chances were better," said Jean. "Eight percent is not very good odds."

"Eight and a third percent," corrected Seiko. "We must also remember the number of intelligent beings involved. By putting our five lives at risk, we prevent the demise of an entire intelligent civilization."

"I just don't like the way we have to go," said Abdul. "Starving to death is not my idea of fun. I'd rather go quickly."

Cesar spoke up. "I would like to remind everyone that just over three hours ago, all of us would have experienced a quick death if it had not been for the efforts of the two cheela, Admiral Steel-Slicer and Engineer Cliff-Web, who now ask for our help."

Pierre waited for more discussion. There was none, so he passed out blank sheets of paper.

"Write 'Yes' if you agree to let the cheela use Otis, and 'No' if you think the risk is too high." Then Pierre collected the ballots and went through them quickly.

"There are four 'Yes' votes and one 'No'. I will inform Admiral Steel-Slicer that they will have to find another way of getting down to Egg. Then I will program the herder rockets to change Otis's orbit so we can go home."

"Just a minute," Abdul spoke up. "I change my mind. Switch my vote to a 'Yes.' It wasn't the fault of the cheela that Amalita was taken away and it's stupid to be mad at a neutron star. It doesn't care."

10:25:02 GMT TUESDAY 21 JUNE 2050

Steel-Slicer and a newly rejuvenated Cliff-Web watched from a scout ship as the cargo ship brought the first batch of north monopoles from the distant monopole factory and dumped them into the human deorbiter mass. The monopoles scattered into a diffuse cloud from their mutual repulsion as they were released from the hold of the cargo ship. The cloud was sucked up by the gravity field from the deorbiter mass and disappeared beneath the fuzzy surface of the kilometer-sized ball. Later they would have to shoot the monopoles into the magnetized ball with an electromagnetic accelerator.

"One," said Cliff-Web. "And an infinity more to go." He sucked on a chewy red ball from one of the new food machines.

"It's going to be a long, dull job," Steel-Slicer said. "Forty generations of ferrying monopoles over the same dull stretch of space between the factory and the deorbiter mass. The situation is ripe for boredom, mistakes, and even mutiny. I want plenty of history in the creche-classes, lots of time off from the ferrying job at entertainment centers, and the best and newest of the food machines *on* the ferry ships."

They watched the second ship dump its cargo of north monopoles.

"Let's go over to the refurbishment facilities at West Pole Space Station," said Cliff-Web. "I want to see how they are coming on the conversion of the Abdul from an exploration ship to a cargo ship."

20:55:45 GMT TUESDAY 21 JUNE 2050

It was many greats later when Steel-Slicer and Cliff-Web visited Otis again. Having recently undergone his 34th rejuvenation, Steel-Slicer was now young looking, while Cliff-Web and the scoutship were old and tired. The black hole at the center of the scout ship was now noticeably less massive, as its rest mass had been used up to operate the inertial drives for the past 1300 greats. They watched as a cargo ship unloaded the last of the north monopoles in the holding tank of a long electromagnetic gun. A stream of high-speed monopoles shot from the tube and penetrated deep into the now solid crust of the deorbiter mass. In the center, the monopoles were held by the strong gravity forces of the ten-meter-diameter ball despite the magnetic repulsion from the rest of the monopoles in the ultra-dense core.

As the last of the stream spluttered out, a continuous combination of *'trumming* and dancing for joy rose throughout the communications links. It grew in volume as the image of the last of the monopole stream spread through the space around Egg at the slow crawl of the speed of light.

"We're done!" Cliff-Web's aged tread was trying to keep up with the victory *'trumming* of his engineers.

"That's one giant ripple for cheela-kind," said Steel-Slicer calmly, knowing that they still had much to do. "We'll let it cool down for eight to twelve greats, then we can take the next tread-ripple on our long journey home."

"My new class of gravitational engineers will be ready. Will you have a good gravity-well pilot to take us down?" Cliff-Web asked. "Even though the surface gravity and escape velocity of Otis are only a small fraction of that of Egg, it will be a tricky landing for someone used to flying around in space."

"My next class of pilots are already training on the ring masses around the human spacecraft Dragon Slayer," said Steel-Slicer. "In about two greats they will transition to simulated landings 50 meters up from Otis. You'll get the best one from that group, and he or she will be allowed to choose a new name. Everyone in the class agrees that the name they want is 'Otis-Elevator.'"

Landing

"Everyone out of the southern hemisphere," Captain Otis-Elevator said into his tread amplifier. The command rippled out from the control deck at the "north pole" of the large cargo hauler and echoed back and forth through the hull underneath the deserted cargo holds on the bottom of the spherical ship. The warning was unnecessary. They were rapidly approaching the surface of Otis, and from the southern hemisphere it looked as if the planetoid were falling directly down upon them.

The inertia drive humming vigorously, the mighty cargo ship approached the planetoid. Otis-Elevator hovered at a point fifty meters from Otis while they watched the asteroid slowly turn. The attraction from Otis was now stronger than the attraction from the black hole in the middle of the cargo ship.

"Feels good being under a little gravity once again," said Cliff-Web.

"I wouldn't know; I've always lived in space." Otis-Elevator slowly descended in a vertical trajectory. As they drew closer, the gravity became stronger and began to approach the gravity on Egg. Choruses of groans could be heard through the deck.

"I can't hold my eyes up," said Otis-Elevator.

Cliff-Web looked at the pilot, who was struggling to

223

keep his eyes elevated in the strong gravity field. The eye-stubs were thin, and wavered as they attempted to balance the heavy eye-ball on top of them. Cliff-Web's eye-stubs had automatically thickened into the proper exponential shape. They ached slightly from generations of little use, but at least the automatic balance reflexes kept the eyes steady.

"I didn't realize that you might not be able to function in high gravity," said Cliff-Web. "Shall I take over the controls?"

"No, I can handle it, but I'm going to have to switch to tread-screen control." He pulled his eyes in under his eyeflaps and concentrated on the taste image on the deck beneath his tread.

They dropped quickly down the last few meters, then, very slowly, Otis-Elevator put the cargo ship down on the crust. The hemispherical top flattened noticeably as Otis pulled hard at the black hole at the center of the cargo ship. Squeals and pops could be heard through the deck plates. The stabilizing fields that held the black hole at the center of the spacecraft finally reached their limit and the black hole fell through the bottom of the hull into the center of Otis where it evaporated. The hull rebounded a little, then stabilized.

Cliff-Web had thought they could begin work as soon as they landed, but it took a dozen turns and a lot of food to build up the space-bred cheela to the point where they could function in the strong gravity field. Cliff-Web had returned to normal rapidly and had taken a prospecting trip out on the ten-meter ball while the others were build-ing up their strength.

"The portable analyzer says that the crust has a high percentage of high-strength metals," he said upon re-turning. "The volcanic regions where we inserted the monopoles have ejecta containing some of the rarer neutron-rich isotopes that we might need for alloying, but other than that, the composition of the crust is pretty much the same everywhere. Let's set up the power generators and start the mass separators and foundries going.''

Within half a great, the mass separators were pouring out powdered raw materials that were turned into working stock by the foundries. The first structure they constructed was a simple space fountain. It only had one stream of rings and only went up 50 meters to a crude top platform, but it sufficed as a landing dock for other spacecraft in the fleet. Soon, most of the space cheela were on Otis, working to make the gravity machines that would enable them to return from their enforced exile from Egg.

Their next task was the construction of a large gravity catapult capable of accelerating the lander at many times Egg gravity so it would reach the escape velocity of Egg after less than 10 centimeters of travel. Unlike the ancient gravity catapults now lying dormant on Egg, which had only to toss small spacecraft into the sky, this gravity catapult had to be big enough to toss a miniature copy of itself to those speeds. It took nearly four greats of turns to fabricate the twenty-centimeter ring with its meters and meters of high-strength tubing full of ultra-dense liquid and the battery of pumps to accelerate the fluid to high velocities rapidly. The uniformity of the resulting gravitational repeller field was important.

"Run it up again," Cliff-Web ordered. He was monitoring the display of the array of gravity sensors spread across the center of the gravity catapult ring. The ring was large in diameter, but small in thickness. Cliff-Web had pushed every rule of gravitational engineering to make it. It only had to work once, but if it worked, it was worth it. The tests they were doing now were at fractions of its operational power levels. That would do—until the final blink when full power was applied. The machine hummed, and the sensors displayed a contour map of gravitational force levels.

"There is only a difference of a billion gravities across the central centimeter portion," Engineer Push-Pull announced. "Surely the lander can handle that."

Cliff-Web looked carefully at the contours, made minor adjustments to some trim loops and closed down the display.

"The launch ring is ready. Next is the lander," he said. "We have passed apoapsis, so we have only four greats of turns to build it."

"It will be ready long before that," said Push-Pull.

"I'm sure," said Cliff-Web. "But there is someone else we must consult with before it is properly delivered." He reset his tread screen, treaded a brief formal message, then left without waiting for a reply. The reply would come later, much later.

21:02:03 GMT TUESDAY 21 JUNE 2050

The call that Pierre had been dreading came.

"Request asteroid O-1 be reprogrammed to arrive at space-time point given by following coordinates," said the image of Cliff-Web. There followed an $x,y,z,\theta,\phi,\lambda,t$ listing of coordinates in the Dragon's Egg space-time system. The requested orbit went far down in the gravity well of Egg so that the ten percent time rate and frame drag difference between deep space and the surface of the neutron star was significant.

Cliff-Web was not used to talking to humans. He forgot to always assume the same position each time he checked in at the screen for a reply, so his image flickered every fifth of a second.

Pierre hesitated. The image flickered.

The real decision had been made long ago. Pierre touched the screen in front of him, and the coordinates were transferred to the herder rockets that kept Otis on its desired path. Pierre then pushed the *execute* square on his touch screen. The engines on the herder rockets flared. Within seconds Otis was on a new trajectory that would take it within a few meters of the surface of Dragon's Egg.

21:02:20 GMT TUESDAY 21 JUNE 2050

Push-Pull looked up from his testing apparatus to stare out at the herder rockets that swarmed around Otis. "There seems to be some activity in the large human spacecraft surrounding us."

"I noticed," said Cliff-Web. "What is the status of the high flow-rate tubes?"

"They passed flow tests at twice design pressures, and failed just above that," said Push-Pull.

"Good, but too good. Reduce their thickness by a half-dozeth and test them again. I want this machine light enough to jump itself 40 meters off Egg."

The construction of the four-centimeter-diameter self-levitating gravity lander took significantly less time than the larger machine. They were finished with nearly a great of turns left before Otis reached periapsis.

Steel-Slicer came to see the completed lander. It was a torus sitting inside a larger torus.

"What's its name?" Steel-Slicer asked.

"It's just the lander," Cliff-Web replied with obvious annoyance. "It doesn't have a name except Egg Surface Descent Craft, if you want to be formal."

"All ships have to have a name," said Steel-Slicer. "Since it flies above the surface of Egg it should have the name of some flying animal."

"There *are* no flying animals on Egg." Cliff-Web was even more annoyed.

"There are flying animals on the human planet Earth," Push-Pull interjected. "One of them is the eagle."

"Eagle it shall be." Steel-Slicer declared.

"If you say so," said Cliff-Web.

"Is there anything else we should do?"

"I would do some thinking," said Cliff-Web. "Once we have landed on Egg, there is no way to get off again until we have rebuilt civilization. We are mass limited and must only take the things we will need. If we forget to take something, there is no going back. Tell me. What is the minimum list of skilled technologists and equipment you need to rebuild a civilization?"

"I don't know," said Steel-Slicer.

"Neither do I. But 122 turns from now we had better know."

The turns passed as the members of the landing party were selected and their equipment was packed in the compounds constructed on the topside of Eagle. Egg grew larger in the sky, then disappeared behind the horizon of their miniature planet as the human herder rockets turned Otis until the gravity catapult was facing back along the orbital trajectory. With the light of Egg gone from the sky they had to make do with the dull glow from the surface of Otis. The cold reddish light put a pall over their last turnfeast together.

The food preparers had done their best. Besides the large mounds of artificial foods from the food machines, there were a number of whole pet Slinks, especially fattened for the occasion and beautifully garnished with fresh nuts and fruits from the gardens that had been started on Otis from artificially fabricated seeds shortly after they had arrived. The center of attention, however, was a whole roast cheela. The body was badly flattened from a fall off the scaffolding around the gravity catapult, but that didn't hurt the taste. Steel-Slicer and Cliff-Web decided not to try to push through the crowd and settled for one of the Slinks.

"Excellent Slink," Steel-Slicer said, sucking the eye off an eye-stub chunk.

"Not as good as food Slinks back on Egg," said Cliff-Web.

"I've been trying to forget they exist."

"Back when I was on Egg, I never really paid much attention to my food," Cliff-Web said. "At turnfeast I would just stuff my pouches as if I were recharging a machine. Now that we are getting close to returning to Egg, my pouches are beginning to ache for a decent chunk of food Slink or a squirt of South Pole singleberry juice."

"It has been so long. . . ." Then Steel-Slicer turned silent as he thought of the agony and hopeless despair the two separated groups of cheela had undergone over dozens and dozens of generations. Although he had just undergone rejuvenation again, he felt old and tired.

The following turn passed rapidly. The elevator on the Space Fountain was in continuous operation as the base on Otis was abandoned and most of the cheela returned to their spacecraft. All that were left were the brave 144 that were to fly down to Egg on Eagle.

On the crust of Otis, Cliff-Web watched the cargo ship pull away from the top of the Space Fountain. Once it was clear, he flicked his eye-stubs at an engineer who was waiting at the controls. The engineer made an adjustment, and the high-pitched whine coming through the crust started to drop in tone. Slowly the tower grew shorter and shorter. Soon the tower was reduced to a pile of metal rings and a stack of platforms. It might have been simpler to turn off the stream of rings and let the tower fall, but Cliff-Web didn't want any stray projectiles orbiting around Otis and dropping on Eagle.

Their next task was to charge up the flow tubes on Eagle.

"Attach the power cables to the pumps on Tube Array 1," said Cliff-Web. Large masts rose from holes in the crust and coupled to two dozen pumps spaced around the periphery of Eagle. The pumps hummed to life, and the ultra-dense black-hole dust circulated faster and faster in the array of tubes. The hull of Eagle creaked as the fluid reached relativistic velocities; still the pumps pushed. The fluid became heavier instead of moving faster, and the gravity potentials inside the torus became so intense that they could no longer be described by the old Einstein theory. The rate of change of flow rate had been slow, however, so the gravity repulsion forces generated in the hole of the torus had been negligible.

Cliff-Web felt the whining of the pumps reach a peak and level off. Eagle now had one of its two multi-tube arrays charged with energy in the form of high speed ultra-dense mass. It was time for them to leave.

"Switch to internal power," he said. There was a hesitation in the sound as the pumps were switched from the outside power connectors to internal stored power. The stored power to compensate for friction and gravitational radiation losses would only last a few milliseconds, so they had to be on their way. He watched as the huge power conductors that had energized Eagle were retracted from their connectors on the hull and lowered down into holes in the crust. Eagle, perched on its launching pad, was now free to fly.

Cliff-Web, his engineer's part done, stopped the normal wave motion of four of his eye-stubs and stared at Otis-Elevator.

"Eagle ready for launch, Captain," said Cliff-Web.

Otis-Elevator waited as the motion of Otis took the dot on the tread screen beneath him along its plotted path. The orbit would take Otis within 100 meters of the surface of Egg, where it would pass over the surface at one-third the speed of light. There were rumblings in the crust of Otis as the tidal forces from Egg attempted to pull the planetoid apart. Cliff-Web anxiously looked out in all directions, hoping that the crust in this region would hold together for a few more microseconds.

Just before the planetoid reached its periapsis, the captain acted. "Launch!" commanded Otis-Elevator. His tread moved rapidly over the touch screen beneath him and neutrino beams sent out coded signals from Eagle to the machinery sitting around it. The power generators had been storing their power in temporary accumulators while waiting for the launch command. When the signal came, all the stored energy plus all the power that the generators could produce was switched into the pumps that drove the ultra-dense dust in the bigger gravity catapult.

The pumps, shrieking from the high loads, pushed the dust in the twenty-centimeter-diameter torus at unbelievable accelerations. The moving stream of black holes generated a rapidly increasing gravitomagnetic field inside the torus. The increasing gravitomagnetic field in turn generated a repulsive gravitational field at the center of the torus. Eagle was repelled upwards at many times the gravity of Egg, but the crew felt nothing, for the forces were gravitational. Eagle reached a third of the speed of light in two nanoseconds and left the surface of Otis to find itself hovering motionless 100 meters up over the outskirts of Bright. It started to fall.

"Divert one-twelfth flow in Tube Array 1 to Tube Array 2," said Otis-Elevator.

There was a pause, then the First Officer replied. "No response, Captain."

"Try it again." Eagle built up speed as it fell.

"I did, sir," First Officer Space-Treader responded. "The signals are being sent and received, but the diverter valve is not responding. It must be stuck!"

"It's not stuck," interjected Cliff-Web. He transferred an image of the diverter valve from his engineer's screen to that of the two officers. "Someone forgot to remove the safety pin. You can see the glow-tab at the end." He flowed off the screen and headed for the inner railing that surrounded the hole in the torus.

"Use some of our accumulator energy to slow the flow in Tube Array 1," he said as he squeezed his body beneath the railing. "We can't land using that, but it will slow our fall and give us more time."

"Where are you going?" Otis-Elevator asked. The reply was distant and muffled, for the vibrations set up by Cliff-Web's tread had to make a circuitous path from the tubular engines of Eagle up to the command deck.

"I'm going to pull that pin," said Cliff-Web.

Cliff-Web found Tube Array 2 and made his way along the gigantic bundle of pipes that wound in layers around the toroidal body of Eagle. Fortunately, Eagle had enough self-gravity that he was in no danger of falling. As he neared the central hole in the ring he could see the crust of Egg below him. The captain had the pumps to Tube Array 1 on, but Eagle was still falling rapidly. Cliff-Web reached the juncture where Tube Arrays 1 and 2 connected through the diverter valve. As he got near Tube

Array 1 his tread started to slip as the rushing ultra-dense dust inside the tube tried to drag him along in its inertial reference frame. He clenched his tread tighter against the smooth surface of Tube Array 2 and carefully made his way to the diverter valve. He pulled the pin and held it up to the video monitor.

"Divert flow!" he shouted, hoping that they could hear him over the long distance through the hull.

"I will wait!" roared the captain's amplified voice from the ship's general announcement system. "Hurry!"

Cliff-Web looked at the rapidly approaching crust. Somewhere down there were dozens and dozens of bags of South Pole singleberry juice that he would never get to taste.

"Too late!" Cliff-Web shouted. "Divert flow!"

The diverter valve slammed. The ultra-velocity, ultra-dense dust switched from one Tube Array to the other. The change in gravity potential created an ultra-strong repulsive gravity field that pushed Cliff-Web from his perch near the diverter valve and threw him toward the crust below. There was a bright streak of incandescent plasma, and he was gone.

Eagle's repulsor gravitational field reached out from the central hole in its hull and shoved against the mass of Egg below it. The spacecraft slowed its fall, Captain Otis-Elevator finally gained control. They couldn't afford to hover for long, since they would soon have diverted all the flow. Eagle had drifted over a small mountain range, and he would have to move them to a flatter landing place.

Flying on the repulsive gravitational forces, Eagle coasted down the mountain slopes, causing minor crustquakes as it made its own valley down a mountainside. They passed over a herd of animals grazing in the plains, scattering them in all directions. Then, with the last bit of stored energy surging through the pumps to augment the last of the diverted flow, they floated down to a landing. First Officer Space-Treader monitored the sensors and video monitors on the bottom of the hull.

". . . 200 millimeters . . . four-and-a-half down . . . contact indicator . . . engine stop. . . ."

There was a pause as the heavy machine sank slightly into the crust, then *'trums* and electronic whistles sounded as Captain Otis-Elevator announced through the neutrino communication link to the waiting ships in orbit.

"East Pole Station! Dragon's Egg Base here. The Eagle has landed!"

Cheers vibrated throughout the hull of Eagle and were echoed by the communications console under Admiral Steel-Slicer's tread. He did not join in, however, for all of his eyes were looking upward at the fragmented remains of the deorbiter mass, Otis. They had saved a world, but at the expense of sentencing five innocent friends to a slow death.

21:02:46 GMT TUESDAY 21 JUNE 2050

The first warning Letter-Reader had of the catastrophe was the rumbling in the crust from the direction of the low hills nearby. His eye-wave pattern hesitated for a blink, then resumed as his brain-knot identified the sound as just another crustquake. Four of his non-pink eyes then returned to their task of reading the ancient scroll that lay unsprung on the crust. The scroll contained instructions for the operation of a magical machine that could talk to the stars in the sky. There were many words that Letter-Reader didn't know, but he hoped that by reading the scroll again and again they would become clear.

The crustquake continued to rumble and seemed to be getting closer. The hunting reflexes built into Letter-Reader's pink and white speckled tread alerted his brain-knot, and he stopped reading to analyze the vibrations coming through the crust. It didn't sound like the approach of a wild Swift, so his herd of food Slinks were not in danger of attack. It was something new, however, and it was coming his way.

Letter-Reader looked off in the direction that his tread had indicated. At first he saw nothing, then he noticed a disturbance in the crust. The disturbance was coming down the side of one of the nearby hills. He then looked up to see that one of the stars was falling from the sky. It was coming straight for him! His screaming tread carried him along as he and his herd ran away in panic.

Steel-Slicer waited until Otis-Elevator had closed down the pumps on Eagle and had stabilized the energy accumulators.

"Excellent landing," said Steel-Slicer. "How much energy do we have left in the accumulators?"

"Only a quarter of what Cliff-Web had planned," Otis-Elevator replied. "But it should be enough to keep ship operations powered for a dozen turns."

"We will need to have a new power generator up and operating by then," said Steel-Slicer. "Call the senior engineering staff up to the control deck. I will want your senior officers there, too. Place four spacers at the outer rail as lookouts. We are far from any city, but we did pass over someone on the way in." The crew deck on Eagle was compact, so it was not long before the senior staff gathered.

"Now that we are on the crust, we spacers are out of a job until you engineers get this gravity catapult reactivated and bring down a ship for us to fly," said Steel-

Slicer. "With Cliff-Web gone, I am going to assume the responsibility for management of the engineering contingent. I want Captain Otis-Elevator to assume responsibility for the spacer contingent. Unless one of the spacers has a technical ability that the engineers can use, their job is support, security, and interaction with the Egg cheela. It is a long way from flying about in ultrasophisticated spacecraft to preparing food and interacting with barbarians, but the sooner the engineers can rebuild technology in this Bright-Afflicted spot, the sooner we can be back into space."

"We are all in this together," Otis-Elevator said. "My spacers will do anything that needs to be done."

"It would help if we didn't have to use any energy for the food generators," said Steel-Slicer. "I noticed that we scattered a herd of animals as we landed. If you can form a food-gathering crew and find a few of those animals to feed us, your crew would not only help our energy crisis but be real heroes to a hungry group of engineers."

"We will return shortly." Otis-Elevator lead his senior officers off.

"Our first task will be to get power," Steel-Slicer told the engineers. "Who is in charge of the miniature power plant?"

"I am," answered Engineer Power-Pack. "My team is loading the parts on the elevator now."

"I will go down with them," said Steel-Slicer. "What else will you need?"

"A mass separator and a monopole generator," said Power-Pack. "We will need hundreds of meters of high-strength pipe to reach the neutron-rich magma below the crust."

"They will be ready when you need them," Engineer Delta-Mass assured him. "Guaranteed leakless."

"I think managing a Web Construction Company project is going to be the easiest job I ever had," Steel-Slicer said. "Let's ripple treads."

"The elevator seems to be moving very slowly," said Steel-Slicer. "Is it because of the weight of the power plant parts?"

"No," said Power-Pack. "Cliff-Web programmed the elevator controls for maximum energy extraction rather than maximum safe descent speed. As we offload Eagle, the elevator motors will recharge the energy accumulators. Cliff-Web always liked to find ways of lowering the cost of projects."

"In this case, he may have saved our hides," said Steel-Slicer. "He certainly was a remarkable engineer."

"Yes, he was," Power-Pack agreed. The elevator deck remained silent for the rest of the ride down.

When they reached the crust, Power-Pack slid aside the low gate and moved back. Steel-Slicer paused, then glided off onto the crust of Egg.

"I have returned," Admiral Steel-Slicer declared softly into the warm, yellow-white crust. He paused as the others flowed off the elevator to surround him on all sides, awed by their return to their homeland. Then he spoke.

"Call me Admiral Steel-Slicer no longer," he said. "I used to be called Star-Glider, but from now on call me Crust-Crawler. For I am tired of space, and I am tired of rejuvenations. I shall stay here until I flow."

Letter-Reader was tending one of his remaining food Slinks, which had been acting sick. He pulled in his normal, dark red eyes and allowed only his three pink eyes to scan the creature. The ultra-red glow from one side of the food Slink indicated a problem. Thankful that his speckle-vision had saved another of the herd, he held it down, reached into one of its feeding pouches, and took out a number of small pebbles that the stupid creature had mistaken for ground nuts. Then he set the food Slink back to grazing.

Thereupon he heard the strangers far off in the distance. They were very noisy. Letter-Reader flattened himself down behind a crust-rock, pulled down his eye-stubs, and let his tread do the seeing. He was glad his hide had some speckles; that made him harder to see.

It was too early for the arrival of the dothbute takers from Bright Center. Besides, they rode Swifts, and even off their mounts they never would have made as much unnecessary noise as these cheela.

He listened carefully and could make out a few voices. The accent was clipped, and he didn't understand a lot of the words.

"Eagle really plowed a furrow in the crust when we came down," Otis-Elevator said as they pushed single file through the disturbed crust dust raised by their passage.

"I see something up ahead," said Lieutenant Star-Counter. "It has black stripes."

"It must be one of the herd animals." M.D. Len-McCoy looked at her scroll. "I prepared a list of the types of animals and plants that were said to have survived the starquake." She rolled quickly through the scroll and stopped. "Here it is. It is a food Slink. The stripes go through to the meat inside. The dark meat has the taste of groundnuts, while the white meat has the flavor of singleberries."

"My pouches are juicy already," Star-Counter said. "Let's capture it and take it back to base."

"I don't think we'll have too much trouble," said Otis-Elevator. "It doesn't seem to be moving. But let's surround it anyway."

Letter-Reader pushed one eye up. The strangers had found one of the food Slinks that had died when the flying star landed. They moved cautiously, as if they thought the food Slink were still alive. The animal was obviously dead, since there was no pulsing in the crust from the creature's fluid pumps. There must be something wrong with the treads of the strangers if they couldn't feel that.

Len-McCoy approached the motionless black and white striped food Slink, then finally saw the large wound on the topside where a falling piece of crust had struck it on the brain-knot.

"It's dead, Captain."

"Good. Let's cut it up and haul it back to base."

Len-McCoy removed her medical bag from her carrying pouch, and soon a surgeon's scalpel was serving as a butcher's slicer.

"I wonder what food the Slinks eat?" Star-Counter pouched a large chunk of food Slink. "I don't see much except those prickly-looking shrubs." His manipulator was dripping juice and he stuck it in an eating pouch to suck it clean. "Mmmmm. Delicious! Tastes like ground-nuts."

"That plant is a groundnut shrub." Len-McCoy told him. "These food Slinks have been bred to dig up the crust near these plants and feed on the nuts."

"We ought to take some of them home, too," said Otis-Elevator. "While the doctor is cutting up the meat, the rest of you can be digging for groundnuts. They will make a good dressing when mixed with white meal-mush from the food generators."

"Anything would be better than plain meal-mush," said a spacer as he started to dig.

Letter-Reader finally felt that he had to do something. After all, it was his job to protect the herd for the clan, and it looked as if the strangers from the flying star were going to take the Slink away and eat it. A lot of hungry younglings back in the clan camp could use that food. He finally unflattened himself and moved to the top of the rise that had kept him hidden. He didn't try to keep his movements silent, but still the strangers didn't sense him. He readied his herder's pike and loosened a bag of tread-pricks in one of his pouches in case they tried to chase after him.

"Greetings, great strangers," he said, announcing himself. They didn't hear him.

"GREETINGS," he said, louder. One of them finally saw him.

"It's a native," said Otis-Elevator. "Gather back here and let's talk with him. This is probably his food Slink we're cutting up. How did he sneak up on us? Keep some eyes looking around. There may be others."

"Greetings, great strangers," Letter-Reader said. "If you are from Bright Center you are early for your doth-bute. I am sorry for the loss of the animal, but it was damaged by your new mount that moves with the stars."

Otis-Elevator was relieved that he could understand most of what the youngling was saying. The tread accent was broad and drawling, and he didn't get some of the words. The phrase "Bright Center" must refer to the central portion of Bright's Heaven, while "mount" used a root word that implied that someone rode on something; although there were no machines to ride here. He didn't understand the word "dothbute" at all.

"Greetings. I am Otis-Elevator," said the captain. "We are not from Bright Center. We are from the near stars. The ones that do not rotate."

"I am Letter-Reader," the youngling replied. "I have read that there were cheela living on the near stars, but I never believed it until now. If you are not from Bright Center, then you cannot take the Zebu Slink. The Taker from Bright Center will be angry with you for taking his dothbute."

"Who is the Taker?" Otis-Elevator asked. "And what is a dothbute?"

"Each 72 turns the Taker for the Emperor comes from Bright Center and commands us to gather the clan herd. We then give them a dothbute for the Emperor and they leave with the animals. They give us 144 more food Slink eggs of the type that they want for the next harvest, and we tend them until the next taking."

"They take a dozeth of your herd and don't even pay you?" Otis-Elevator was incredulous.

"No," Letter-Reader replied. "We get to keep a dozeth of their herd if we have taken care of them properly."

"Why don't you raise your own herd?" asked Otis-Elevator.

"We have no Slink eggs," said Letter-Reader. "The Emperor does not allow us to have animals that might eat his groundnuts. We ourselves must only harvest groundnuts in the hilly areas where the food Slinks are not allowed. I am afraid the clan will go hungry this great of turns. We lost six Zebu Slinks to wild Swifts, then your machine killed two, and six were scattered and lost. The meat you have belongs to the Emperor. The Taker for the Emperor will be angry that it is not fresh."

"Tell the Taker that we will pay for the food Slink," said Otis-Elevator. "Right now we need food, but by the next dozen turns we will have plenty of food. The Taker and all your clan can come and have as much as you want."

"You do not tell the truth. You cannot grow food in a dozen turns."

"We make the food," Otis-Elevator said. "We use a machine. It makes foods with many different flavors. Come in a dozen turns and taste them."

He reached into a pouch, pulled out a glow-jewel eye-ring, placed it on the ground, and moved back away. "That is a present for you. We are sorry that our flying machine scared you and your herd. Tell your clan leader we will not let the clan go hungry."

Letter-Reader was not looking at the glow-ring. Instead four of his eyes were looking at the silvery metal scroll that Len-McCoy was still holding.

"Is that a scroll?" asked Letter-Reader.

"Yes," said Len-McCoy.

"With letters and words on it?"

"Yes, and some pictures, too."

"The ring is very pretty, but I would like something new to read," said Letter-Reader. "I would trade you my scroll for your scroll." He reached into a pouch and pulled out a soiled and wrinkled scroll. "It is old, and not shiny like your scroll, but you can still read the words on it." He held it out eagerly.

"I'll give it to him," said Len-McCoy. "I can have the computer print out a new list when we get back to base."

The trade was made, with the captain adding the glow-ring to the bargain. He looked carefully at the ancient scroll.

He unrolled it until he came to the personal sign at the bottom. "It is a portion of a daily log. It was written by Qui-Qui!"

"We must find out where he got it!" whispered Len-McCoy.

"Later. Right now we have to get a gravity catapult activated, make sure that a clan doesn't starve, and some-how make friends with a dictatorial Emperor that seems to own every last food Slink and groundnut on Egg." He stopped his electronic whisper, and his tread moved again as he spoke once more to Letter-Reader.

"Who is this Emperor you speak of?" Otis-Elevator asked.

"He is the Mighty One, the Terrible One, the Unforgiving One. The cheela that never flows—Attila-the-Speckled," said Letter-Reader, his speckled tread trembling at the name.

Meanwhile, back at the base, Engineer Power-Pack was setting up the power plant that would give them the energy they needed to survive.

"We are about twenty centimeters from base," he said. "That should give us enough separation so that crust cracks developing about the power plant won't interfere with the foundations for the gravity catapult, while the stray gravity fields from the gravity catapult don't disturb the power plant. My crew will set up the bore rig here and start drilling."

"You have enough hole liner pipe to get started," said Engineer Delta-Mass. "By the time you get down six centimeters my crew will have made the first dozen centimeters of liner for you. After that we can make it faster than you can drill."

"We will see," Power-Pack said. "That antimatter-jet drill that Cliff-Web designed will poke through this crust like a black hole through a human."

Delta-Mass returned to base, traveling slowly as she planned the route for the power lines that would have to be run over the twenty centimeters between the site of the power plant and the base. By the time she arrived at the base, her crew had the mass separator operating and were feeding it with ground-up loads of crust. Most of the crust emerged from the machine as dust, which was piped away to a dumping site. Rare elements and useful metals and compounds were collected, while the high-strength metals were combined into a strong alloy and extruded as a large diameter pipe.

"The first three centimeters are done," Delta-Mass told her crew as the end of the long pipe fell to the crust with a ringing clang. "Let's take an early break for turn-feast. My eating pouches are wet from thinking about the food Slink that is waiting for us. Groundnuts and single-berry together in the same chunk of meat. I can hardly wait." She led her crew off while the finished pipe was lifted onto cargo-gliders by a transportation crew and hauled off to the distant power plant site.

Delta-Mass stopped at the outskirts of the base to ask directions. In the turn that she and her crew had been getting the mass separator into operation, the base construction crew under the direction of Metal-Bender had nearly dismantled the cargo and living platforms on Eagle and had reassembled them on the crust as a walled living compound.

"Do you have the eating area made yet?" Delta-Mass asked.

"It's the first thing we built," replied Metal-Bender. "Go through the east gate in the outer wall, then straight through to the center. That is the combined eating and meeting area."

"Great!" Delta-Mass started to lead her crew to the east gate.

"You'll enjoy the food Slink," said Metal-Bender.

"I hope you and your crew of Swifts didn't devour it all," Delta-Mass replied.

"No, the food-service crew wants to make the food Slink last, so they only give you a small piece after you have eaten a big portion of meal-mush."

The mention of meal-mush brought groans from the treads of the crew. The artificial food generators were quite versatile and could produce a great variety of flavors and textures, but after dozens of greats of eating nothing but artificial food, their pouches ached for something that was different.

The antimatter drill moved rapidly through the crust, and the hole went down millimeter by millimeter as Power-Pack's drilling crew developed a rhythm. They finally approached the magma layer. The temperatures, pressures, and densities were so high that the outer casing of the drill began to show evidence of transmutation by neutron drip from the surrounding near-fluid of excess neutrons.

"Lower the last section of liner and put a pressure seal on the top," said Power-Pack. "Then put an antimatter bomb on the end of the drill string in place of the drill and lower it. We are going to make a volcano—a tame volcano."

The antimatter bomb was lowered to the bottom of the hole, and the drill string was removed. Set off by a coded pulse of acoustic waves, the bomb fractured the remaining few centimeters of crust and the high pressure neutron fluid in the mantle pushed upward to the surface. As the fluid rose into regions of lower pressure, some of the neutrons decayed into electrons and protons, releasing energy and lowering the density of the fluid, so that it rose even faster.

"Here it comes!" Power-Pack shouted over the deep rumble in the crust. "Open the valve to the power generators."

The high speed, high density, high pressure, high temperature nucleonic fluid rose up through the drill hole and whirled through the power generator where its free thermal, kinetic, and nuclear energies were extracted. The resulting warm crust dust was piped to a nearby depression, while the power extracted from the bowels of Egg flowed over the transmission lines to energize the machinery at the base some twenty centimeters away.

Admiral Steel-Slicer, now Crust-Crawler, met with the senior staff. "We're on our way," he said. "But we still have a long way to go. What is next on Cliff-Web's schedule?"

"The gravity catapult needs a power plant two dozen times more powerful than the one we just got into operation," said Power-Pack. "My seismic survey team has found a promising upwelling of energetic magma forty centimeters to the Bright-west. We have moved the drilling rig there and are already down a meter on the first hole, but we will need a power plant built."

"My crew has finished with the living quarters at base," said Metal-Bender. "We've also installed magnetic barriers around the perimeter to keep out wild Swifts. We're now ready to build the power plant. We have plenty of computer controlled robot welders, nibblers, and cutters for the precision parts, but we need a forge for the larger components. We are ready to go as soon as we get enough metal."

"The mass separator has been generating plate for the last few turns," Delta-Mass told them. "But we will have to shift back to liner pipe at the rate Power-Pack's crew is going. Perhaps the first thing you should build is another mass separator."

"You're right," Metal-Bender replied. "I'll get my team busy on that."

"Anything else?" asked Crust-Crawler.

"Don't forget that I promised the nearby clan we would give them food once we had power," said Otis-Elevator. "We have visited them a number of times in the past turns and know them pretty well now. It is obvious that they are living at a subsistence level. We have taken them samples of various flavors of meal-mush. They call it the 'food of the gods.'"

"Good," said Metal-Bender. "Let's trade them a mush-maker for a herd of food Slinks."

"They won't do that," said Otis-Elevator. "They let us have the ones we killed during the landing, but the herd belongs to the Emperor. In fact, I think I notice an increased anxiety in the leader of the clan as the time comes for the arrival of the Taker to take the herd."

"What did the leader say?" Crust-Crawler asked.

"She won't talk about it. But every time the subject comes up, I notice a strange twitch in her eye-wave pattern. Of course, it could be my imagination. The clan leader, like a number of the clan elders, is missing some eyes. The old injuries could be causing the twitch."

"We must certainly keep our promise," Crust-Crawler said. "Let's start off by inviting them here for next turn-feast and turn it into a real feast."

"It will certainly be a pleasure feeding someone that appreciates my food," said Chef Pouch-Pleaser. "If the engineers can arrange a power pack, I can give the clan one of our food generators and teach them how to operate it."

"I'll give them a glider," said Power-Pack. "They can use it to transport the mush-maker back to their compound, then use the power pack on the glider to run the food machine. When the power pack gets low, they can just glide back here and recharge it."

"I've gotten to know the clan pretty well," said Otis-Elevator. "They are very proud and will insist on bringing food to the feast."

"Good!" said Pouch-Pleaser. "I want to learn all about the native foods. Not only how to prepare them for serving, but the best way to grow them. Anything to stop the groans at turnfeast."

"You are right, Chef," said Crust-Crawler. "We can't live on artificial food forever. Don't forget, our main objective is to become natives of Egg once again."

"I will invite the clan to the next turnfeast," said Otis-Elevator.

Emperor

The long procession from the distant clan compound started to arrive well before the end of the turn. Every clan member except those in charge of the herd came. Dented-Shield, the leader of the clan, led the procession, carrying her battered shield high in front of her. Right behind her came her warriors carrying a freshly killed food Slink. It was pink with glowing white spots. Next were younglings with pouches full of nuts and berries. Then came the Old Ones. From their pouches peered the eyes of tiny hatchlings. Bringing up the rear were the herders who were not out taking care of the herd.

"Where did they get the pink and white food Slink?" Crust-Crawler whispered as the procession approached.

"There is a clan farther east that is charged with growing that flavor of food Slink," Otis-Elevator replied. "I notice that most of the glow-jewels that I have given them are missing. They probably traded the jewels to the other clan for one of the food Slinks the Emperor allows them to keep."

"Welcome, friends of the Dusty Crust Clan," said Captain Otis-Elevator. "Your gifts of food for our meager turnfeast are most welcome. While we wait for the turnfeast to start, perhaps you would like to taste these pre-turn samples we have set out on the food mats."

249

"Let us give thanks to Bright for our new friends and their marvelous food machines," said Dented-Shield. "May we all never be hungry again."

The warriors and the younglings dropped their loads of food, which were picked up eagerly by Chef Pouch-Pleaser's crew. The members of the clan, having just finished a long trek, were hungry and wandered about between the foodmats, sampling the large variety of foods that the food machines could produce.

"Aren't you spacers going to eat any of the food?" Letter-Reader asked Otis-Elevator, who picked up a dark red ball of chewy meal-mush and put it into an eating pouch to reassure Letter-Reader.

"We would rather wait to taste the food that you brought," said Otis-Elevator.

"The food Slink isn't bad," said Letter-Reader, putting a couple of golden yellow crystals into a food-pouch. "But I don't understand why you would want to eat groundnuts and singleberries instead of these tasty chunks."

"You will see after a few greats of eating nothing but meal-mush from the machine we will give you," Otis-Elevator told him.

"I'll never get tired," said Letter-Reader, sucking on the end of a yellow and silver stick. "I'm going to try everything on the instruction scroll."

"Are you going to be operating the machine?" asked Otis-Elevator.

"Yes. I'm the only one in the clan who can read, so they put me in charge of running it."

"The turnfeast is ready," 'trummed Chef Pouch-Pleaser loudly into the crust. They all went into the compound to the eating area where the pink and white food slink, perched on a dressing of chopped groundnuts and fresh singleberries, was waiting for them. It was soon surrounded by spacers, while the members of the Dusty

Crust Clan gathered around their new food machine. Letter-Reader almost forgot to eat as he operated the machine, producing piles of golden yellow crystals, dark red balls, blue-white eggs, and yellow and silver cylinders, each one tasting better than the next.

"It is truly a miraculous machine," Dented-Shield told Crust-Crawler as they shared squirts from a bag of singleberry juice. "It causes me to worry, though. My workers will become restless if they do not have to hunt for food."

"They could come here and we could teach them other things. We will teach them to read letters, work with numbers, and how to operate machines. We will even teach them how to make machines of their own."

"An excellent idea!" said Dented-Shield. "I will leave some of them here when we depart. Perhaps while you are teaching them, they may be of service to you in building your giant machine that will pull down the starships from the skies."

Suddenly, three herders came into the eating area, moving as fast as their treads could take them. One of them had dropped his herder pike in his panic.

"The Taker has come!" the first shouted.

"She counted the herd and was very angry," said the second, coming up to Dented-Shield. "She said for us to take her to you, and we came as fast as we could."

An alarm rang through the crust. "Five Swifts approaching from the east," said a computer voice. "Magnetic barriers are activated."

"Swifts?" said Crust-Crawler.

"The Emperor's warriors do not crawl on the crust," said Dented-Shield. "They ride on the backs of trained Swifts." Dented-Shield rose from the resting pad next to the eating mat she had been sharing with Crust-Crawler and started to leave. Crust-Crawler joined her.

"This is no concern of yours," said Dented-Shield. "I shall go out to meet them myself. They are angry with me, not you."

"I want to meet them and explain that the loss of the food Slinks was an accident," Crust-Crawler said.

"The Emperor does not accept excuses," said Dented-Shield.

"Perhaps he will accept payment. Or perhaps the Taker will accept a bribe. Besides, I think I should turn off the magnetic barrier before one of the Emperor's tame Swifts burns a tread."

"That would be wise," said Dented-Shield.

Crust-Crawler turned off the magnetic barrier and stood beside Dented-Shield as they waited for the Taker and her party to approach. The five Swifts each carried a heavily speckled cheela. The random dark red and yellow-white speckled pattern even extended to their eyeballs. Behind the five Swifts plodded a line of porters, their pouches overloaded with cargo. Some were speckled, but nowhere near as much as the five warriors. The warriors kept their eyes looking in all directions, since they were in strange territory, but they seemed unimpressed with the huge gravity catapult off in the distance and the shiny machines scattered about the base.

"I don't see how they can see out of those pink eyeballs," Engineer Thermal-Conductor whispered. "That would put them at a great disadvantage in a battle."

"They can't see well," Dented-Shield explained. "But the speckled ones make up for it by their control over animals. It is rumored that the Emperor can talk to animals."

"I can see how riding on a Swift would be a significant advantage in a battle," said Otis-Elevator. "One warrior on a Swift would be more than a match for a dozen warriors on the ground."

"Two dozen," said Dented-Shield quietly. "I know." Her eight eyes looked down at the deep dents in her shield. She dropped the shield on the ground and moved forward to meet the Taker, unarmed.

"Greetings, Taker of the Emperor," she said. "I am Dented-Shield, Leader of the Dusty Crust Clan."

"You failed," said the Taker. Her harsh voice was slightly muffled by the body of her Swift.

"We have come to take the 132 Zebu Slinks that belong to the Emperor. You are four short. You know the penalty."

"Yes, Taker." Dented-Shield moved closer.

"What is the penalty?" Crust-Crawler whispered to Letter-Reader, who was standing next to him.

"An eye," said Letter-Reader. "One eye for each Slink."

"But she only has eight eyes now!"

"I will move forward with you, Dented-Shield," said one of the elders of the clan.

"I will too," said another.

"Wait!" said Crust-Crawler. "We are visitors from the stars in the sky. When our great ship came down from the stars we accidentally killed some of the Zebu Slinks that the clan was guarding. We would be more than willing to pay the Emperor for his loss."

"It is good for you that you admit your crime, slave," said the Taker. "You are indeed a stranger. Otherwise you would know that the Emperor has no need of money. Money is for trade between slaves. What the Emperor wants, he takes."

"We can give him a machine that makes food," said Crust-Crawler. "It will make more food than a great of food Slinks."

The Taker paused, her eye-stub waves switching from one pattern to another as she considered. Crust-Crawler took advantage of the hesitation.

"I have some samples right here," he said, moving over to the food mats. He picked up a half-dozen each of the red balls and the golden cubes and brought them back. Forming a strong manipulator he reached up over the back of the Swift and handed them to the Taker. The Taker took one each and looked them over carefully. Then she glared down at Crust-Crawler.

"Eat them!" she commanded. "Now!" She watched carefully as he took them back from her and put them in a feeding pouch. After a few sethturns he opened his pouch to show her that they were gone. He then raised the rest up for her to choose another. She sucked carefully at the golden crystal, then dropped it in her eating pouch.

"The Emperor will take the food machine," she said.

"I will place it on another machine that will carry it for you," said Crust-Crawler.

"I had better give them a cargo-glider," said Power-Pack. "It has a large accumulator. We don't want the Emperor to run out of food."

Within a few methturns a cargo-glider was loaded with a second food machine and brought before the Taker.

"This is the box that controls the glider," said Crust-Crawler. "I have set it for automatic. Wherever the box goes, the glider will follow."

The Taker took the box, then called over the leader of the porters.

"Here, slave," she said. "You carry the box. Be careful you do not damage the Emperor's food machine. The penalty will be severe."

"Yes, Taker," said the porter. Crust-Crawler noticed that he only had nine eyes.

Crust-Crawler then handed up a scroll. "This scroll contains the instructions for the operation of the food machine. In there the Emperor can read how to produce over a dozen greats of different kinds of food with the machine."

The Taker took the scroll and placed it in a pouch without deigning to look at it. "The Emperor has more important things to do than read," she said. "I do his reading for him."

"There is plenty of room left on the cargo-glider," said Crust-Crawler. "Your porters could unload their cargo and let the glider carry it for them."

"Ah! Yes. The cargo," said the Taker. "Unload the eggs!"

Each porter emptied three or four pouches, and soon there was a pile of black and white striped Slink eggs on the crust. The porters were still fairly bulky, however. They were probably still carrying the food supplies for the party and the Swifts, as well.

The Taker looked down at Dented-Shield. "Here are 144 Zebu Slink eggs. They belong to the Emperor. In 72 turns I will return. If you have taken proper care of the Emperor's 144 Zebu Slinks he will magnanimously give you twelve of them to feed the clan. If you fail, you know the penalty."

"Yes, Taker," said Dented-Shield.

"Speaking of penalties," said the Taker. "You have not yet paid your penalty for the last failure."

"But we gave you the food machine!" Crust-Crawler objected loudly.

"Silence, slave!" the Taker roared. "You do not *give* the Emperor anything. The Emperor *takes*."

The Taker brought her eyes to focus on Dented-Shield. "The Emperor also does not accept excuses," she said, pulling a long whiplike sword from its scabbard along the flank of her Swift.

"I understand, Taker." Dented-Shield raised four eyes up on elongated stubs.

"I will stand beside you," said an elder.

"I will too," said another, moving forward with an eye-stub erect.

"I, too," said Captain Otis-Elevator. He moved bravely forward to stand next to Dented-Shield. He held up an eye-stub, the eye glaring at the Taker.

"This affair is no concern of yours!" whispered Dented-Shield so loudly the electronic wave tingled Otis-Elevator's hide.

"I was pilot when my ship caused your clan damage," said Otis-Elevator. "I will cleanse my clan's honor by sharing in your punishment."

"I care not where the four eyes come from," said the Taker, cutting off the conversation with an expert whirl of her whip-sword. Four eyes fell to the crust and burst open from the fall. The Taker then stowed her whip-sword and urged her Swift up onto the cargo glider. Her four silent bodyguards did the same.

"Our Swifts are tired from much travel," the Taker said to the lead porter. "Take the box and lead this floating machine back to Bright Center." She left without looking back.

Dented-Shield waited until the Taker was far in the distance. She then turned her attention to Otis-Elevator beside her. His remaining eleven eye-stubs were rigid with fury, the eye-balls riveted on the distant speck on the horizon.

"It is useless to fight the warriors of the Emperor," said Dented-Shield. "Fortunately, they do not come often." Instead of reaching over to touch his hide with a tendril, she reached over with one of her good eye-stubs and rubbed the rigid base of one of his stubs. The subtle sexual overtones of the touch helped him come to his senses.

"Your clan and my clan have participated in a feast of friendship. I know I speak for the rest of the Spacer Clan" said Otis-Elevator, "when I say that we wish to be more than a friend of the Dusty Crust Clan. Although we are not bound to out-clan relations by exchange of partners and eggs, we can be bound to out-clan relations by mingling of body juices in combat."

He raised a stump of an eye-stub, body juices still dripping from the end. She brought her fresh stump forward and touched his, their juices blending. There was a hesitation, then the two elders of the clan that had shared in the sacrifice moved toward them and added their two stubs. Crust-Crawler took a sharp object from one of his pouches, deliberately slashed the side of one of his eye-stubs and pushed forward to join the group.

"You were very brave to come forward as you did," said Dented-Shield as the group broke apart. "I would be honored to share an egg with you, for I am sure the hatchling would bring honor to our clan. Would your clan become our out-clan by exchange of partners as well as mingling of combat juices? That is, if you are willing to mate with a female that only has seven eyes."

"None of us is perfect." Otis-Elevator waved his stump.

"Then if your clan leader will permit, you will come with us as we return to our clan compound," said Dented-Shield. "I am sure we have a lot to learn about each other."

"I have no objection," said Crust-Crawler. "Do you, Captain Otis-Elevator?"

"None," he replied. "But I think this is time for a name change. From now on, call me Captain Otis-Elevator no longer. Instead, call me Avenging-Eye!"

Dented-Shield gathered her clan, the clan's clutch of Slink eggs, and headed east toward the clan compound.

Letter-Reader operated the glider carrying the food machine while Avenging-Eye moved alongside, giving instructions through a rapidly rippling tread. Not all the clan left, though. A number of the younger members stayed with the "Spacer Clan" to become apprentices to the engineers and learn the secrets of reading and computing.

The word of the strangers from the stars and their marvelous food machines spread across the crust. The leaders of other clans came to visit and were greeted warmly by Crust-Crawler and fed the delicious "starfood" from the machines. The members of the clans were eager to learn more about the miraculous machines of the spacers. The memories of a life of ease and plenty in the ancient days before the starquake had been passed down verbally from the tales of Old Ones in their hatchling pens, so they were not afraid of the technology, but embraced it.

It wasn't long before the clans abandoned their homesites and resettled around the spacer's base. They were careful to bring along the Emperor's herds of food Slinks; but instead of being allowed to wander, the herds were kept in pens made of magnetic barriers and fed from food machines that had been adapted to manufacture a feed for the food Slinks that produced optimum growth in the animals. But they weren't eaten, for Chef Pouch-Pleaser and Engineer Metal-Bender had worked together to make food machines that could produce chunks of food Slink meat that were indistinguishable from the real thing.

"It seems like my crew is spending half its time building food machines," Metal-Bender said one turn at the meeting of the senior staff.

"One-dozeth is more like it," said Crust-Crawler. "Besides, with all the clan apprentices, your machine construction team is twice as large as it was."

"My crust engineering team is five times as large as it was," Engineer Crust-Cracker told the group. "We already have the support foundations under the gravity catapult and have excavated and lined the crust under the central hole. We are now moving into road building. We will have all the roads in the base camp plus clan compounds paved in the next four turns and the road out to the power plant site will be widened to Flow Slow size in a dozen turns."

"With the extra crew and the road, the construction of the main power plants is way ahead of schedule," said Power-Pack. "The first plant will be sipping magma in six turns."

"Good," said Push-Pull. "My crew has finished reconnecting the tubing on the gravity catapult to turn it from a flying machine into a standard catapult. One power plant should allow us to test it at one-quarter power."

"When you think you are ready, I'll send a message up to East Pole Orbital Station to send down a lightly loaded scout ship," said Crust-Crawler. "I want to bring down a rejuvenation machine. Some of these clan leaders are getting old and nearly eyeless from their encounters with Taker. Their experience is too valuable to lose at this stage."

"We can make our own rejuvenation machines," said Delta-Mass. "If the precision shops on the interstellar arks can fabricate the delicate inner machinery, Metal-Bender's crew can do the rest of it."

"We still have the problem of getting the rare catalyst to promote the formation of the rejuvenation enzyme," Crust-Crawler reminded his colleague.

"That's no problem," said Delta-Mass. "We have been shoving so much crust through the mass separator machines to make metal stock that as a byproduct we have collected enough of the catalyst to activate four dozen rejuvenation machines.''

"How are our relations with the clans, Avenging-Eye?" asked Crust-Crawler.

"Excellent," said Avenging-Eye. "The members of the Dusty Crust Clan now almost consider themselves spacers. They mix willingly with the other clans and have even taken over all of the beginner reading and computation classes. There seems to be a tenseness in the actions of the elders, though. I think it is time for the Taker to come again.''

"The thought makes *me* tense," said Crust-Crawler. "Are we ready for her?"

"I hope so," said Avenging-Eye.

21:03:12 GMT TUESDAY 21 JUNE 2050

The Taker came out of the west. She and her four warrior-guards rode their Swifts down the center of the paved road while the porters plodded alongside on the crust, carrying their heavy loads of Slink eggs. Even at the great distance Crust-Crawler could see the annoyed twitch in the Taker's eye-wave pattern as she passed by the clan compounds and food Slink pens.

"The timing is nearly perfect," Crust-Crawler said as one eye looked up at the sky. A large object was falling out of the sky directly toward them. A low groan started in the crust, rose to a piercing shriek, then tapered off as the gravity catapult brought the spherical scout ship to an abrupt halt in midair, then lowered it gently onto the landing platform.

The clan cheela and the food Slinks had seen a dozen landings already and were not disturbed. The porters accompanying the Taker, however, back-treaded and scattered, some of them pushing eggs out of their pouches as they fled. Two of the riding Swifts bolted, and it took expert handling by the warrior-guards to bring them under control, but not before one of the Swifts scooped up three of the dropped eggs.

The Taker got her mount under control, glared angrily at Crust-Crawler, then with harsh commands and flickers of her whip-sword, reformed her expedition. Three eyes were left lying in the road.

The Taker moved her Swift forward and pulled a scroll from her pouch.

"Clan Leaders! Come forward!"

The leaders of the eight clans that had come to live around the base gathered in a group in front of the Taker. Dented-Shield moved forward from the rest. She had no weapons, but she carried her shield by her side.

"Greetings, Taker of the Emperor," she said. "I am Dented-Shield, Leader of the Dusty Crust Clan."

"I have come to take the 132 Zebu Slinks that belong to the Emperor," said Taker. "Why did you leave your assigned grazing place and bring them here without permission?"

"The Emperor's Slinks are protected from wild Swifts here. If you count them you will find we have lost none of them. The Emperor's Slinks have better grazing here. If you look at them you will find them all in prime condition." The Taker had already counted the black and white striped Slinks in the pen when she had ridden by earlier; in fact, except for one yellow and pink Slink missing from the herd belonging to the White Cliff Clan, all were in excellent condition.

"I will take 132 Slinks from each herd for the Emperor," said the Taker. "The Emperor magnanimously gives you the rest to feed your clan." She waved her eyes at the porters, who started to unload their cargo of Slink eggs from their pouches.

"Here are the eggs for your next herd. They are the Emperor's property, guard them carefully. You know the penalty."

Dented-Shield's tread hesitated as she spoke, but she finally *trummed* out the reply.

"We do not wish to have the remaining food Slinks. We willingly give them to the Emperor."

"You do not *give* things to the Emperor, slave," said the Taker angrily. "The Emperor takes! For your insolence I shall take *all* of the food Slinks, and your Clans can grub for groundnuts. Now pick up those Slink eggs and take care of them."

"We do not wish any more of the Emperor's Slink eggs." Dented-Shield sounded braver this time.

"Insolent slave!" the Taker roared. "The Emperor owns everything. Every food Slink, every groundnut, every fruit on every plant, even the meat on the wild Swifts he owns. Pick up those eggs, or I shall banish you all from the Emperor's lands and you shall starve."

"We give to the Emperor all that which belongs to the Emperor. We have no need of the Emperor's food. We have the food machines to feed us."

"I will take the food machines, slave. Everything belongs to the Emperor. Even you." Taker pulled out her whip-sword and flicked it menacingly. "When I am through with you, insolent crust-slug, there will be no more talk of refusing to raise the Emperor's food Slinks."

Dented-Shield raised her shield as Taker urged her riding-Swift forward. Crust-Crawler rapped a short command into the crust and a nearly invisible magnetic barrier sprang up across the road. The riding-Swift slowed and reared as its tread touched the magnetic barrier. The ultra-strong magnetic fields stretched the molecules in the tread of the Swift to the breaking point. The Swift roared and backed off, favoring the burned edge of its tread.

Crust-Crawler moved forward to stand next to Dented-Shield.

"There is no need to raise food Slinks anymore," he said to the Taker. "The food machines can now give us Slink meat as well as all the other foods it did before. Now that we have nearly finished our task here, we would like to meet your Emperor. We will give him many, many food machines, cargo-gliders, personal gliders, road pavers, and other machines, as well as the power plants to run them. All of Egg can become prosperous, and there will no longer be a need for slaves."

Crust-Crawler noticed that Taker's eye-wave pattern almost stopped as she contemplated the thought of not having slaves to do her bidding.

"If the Emperor will guarantee me safe conduct," said Crust-Crawler, "I and my machine makers will be glad to visit him in Bright Center. Otherwise, he may come here. As you notice, we have not attacked your party and have given you more than you came for. We would welcome the visit of the Emperor. If he wishes, he can ride in our starships and look down on all of his domain at one time."

As if to punctuate his offer, there was a rising whine in the crust and the gravity catapult threw the scout ship back into the sky.

Faced with a barrier she could not overcome, and awed by the technology around her in spite of herself, Taker decided to retreat.

"I leave to report your behavior to the Emperor," she said. "He will decide what you will do next."

Crust-Crawler had the barrier around the herding pens lowered, and the porters, now reloaded with Slink eggs, drove the docile herds off on the long journey to Bright

Center. Before Taker left, however, she and her warriors used the treads of their riding-Swifts to push over all the low walls outlining the clan living areas and tread the meager contents into the crust.

"I hope the Emperor is more reasonable than the Taker," said Metal-Bender.

"If the Emperor is the original Attila," Crust-Crawler replied, "even two dozen rejuvenations wouldn't be enough to make him reasonable. I think we had better work on our defenses."

The Taker got back to Bright Center just as Attila finished his latest rejuvenation. His compact, muscular body was stronger than ever and just as speckled as before. He had a holding pouch of golden yellow crystals and was popping them one by one into an eating pouch.

"Good haul, Crazy-Eyes," he said, looking at the food Slinks flowing past. "I want one of those striped ones."

"I will have the servers prepare it for turnfeast, Terrible One," said the Taker.

"I want it *now*!" demanded Attila. "I'm hungry." He waved at a nearby server. "That stupid rejuvenation robot kept feeding me mush and telling me to eat slowly. Had to dent it with my sword before it would let me go."

"I had some trouble in the eastern provinces," the Taker said after a long silence.

"Some slaves holding out on you?"

"No. They not only gave us back all the food Slinks they were supposed to, but they even refused to take their dozeth."

"I thought the herds looked bigger. What's the matter with them?" Attila asked. "They can't survive long on just groundnuts."

"They have also refused to eat your groundnuts or plant fruits," said Taker.

"You sound like your brain-knot has stopped working, Crazy-Eyes," said Attila. "If I didn't know you better, I would say you are getting too old to be Taker."

"I am still the strongest of your warriors, O Terrible One," said the Taker fearfully. "But I have even worse news, O Terrible One."

"Stop that 'O Terrible One' nonsense, Crazy-Eyes. I'm feeling great in this new body, and you know and I know that no other warrior of mine would be as good as you are for Taker-of-the-Emperor." He paused for a moment as a server brought in a raw chunk of Zebu Slink.

"That is, unless you don't come out on top at the next combat trials." Attila stuffed his eating pouch with the meat and started to suck on it noisily. He then tossed a few golden yellow crystals in on top of the meat.

"Excellent combination," he said. "Now, tell me the bad news."

"They refused to take the new batch of Slink eggs."

"You sliced up the Clan Leader and a few Elders until you found someone in the clan who *would* take the eggs rather than die, didn't you?"

"I tried to, O Terrible One," said Taker, her tread stuttering in fear. "But we were near the compound of the strange clan that made the food machine. They created an invisible barrier that stopped my riding-Swift." She paused as she saw his eye-wave pattern take on a slow, thoughtful motion. "I did my best, Terrible One," she said.

Attila finally broke his silence. "Did your Swift have a burned tread?" he asked.

"Yes!" she replied, amazed at his question. "I could not understand it. I could see no heat radiation coming from the barrier."

"That strange clan makes more than food machines," said Attila thoughtfully. "You ran into a magnetic barrier.

It takes more than a Swift to cross them. What else did you see?"

"They have many machines. Some cover the crust with smooth roads, some spit out long tubes and bars of metal, and others crawl around cutting the metal into pieces to make other machines. They have even turned their giant flying machine into a machine that catches metal spheres that fall from the sky."

"Those are Old One tales from the days before the big crustquake," said Attila. "Next you will be telling me that there are cheela that live among the stars."

"I saw two cheela get out of the sphere and unload some small machines," the Taker told him. "Then they got back in the sphere and it was tossed back up into the sky."

"I don't like the idea of someone being able to come and go from Egg without my permission. What if all the slaves decided to go to live in the stars?"

"The leader of the strange clan offered to give us all the machines we wanted, including new food machines that would make any kind of food Slink meat," she said. "He said we wouldn't need herders or gatherers for food, and all the work could be done by machine. There wouldn't be a need for slaves anymore. I didn't like the sound of that."

"If there weren't any slaves," said Attila, "there wouldn't be a need for an Emperor and his warriors." He jammed another hunk of raw Slink in his eating pouch. "There is rebellion falling from the sky," he said. "I shall crush it under my tread just as I did long ago." He wiped his manipulator on the crust and started moving toward the ancient Maze Temple in the middle of Bright Center.

He found no guard around the maze. The slaves were so afraid of the place that they never came near. Attila ignored the entrance and circled around the outside until he came to a wide breach in the tall walls. As he flowed up over the crumbled blocks of rock, Taker lagged behind.

"Come along, Crazy-Eyes," Attila ordered. "You are not letting the Old One tales get to you, are you?"

"I have heard there are death-traps in there," said Taker.

"You heard correctly." Attila continued to follow the path of destruction into the interior. Taker came to an abrupt halt. "But the death-traps stopped working when I reached the power generator."

They finally came to the last broken wall. It opened into a large room. In the middle was a pile of metal plates and old Flow Slow bones. Attila pushed the bones aside and picked up a metal plate as big as a large shield. He gave it a tap and it rang loudly.

"Feels solid," he said. He placed it on the floor of the room and flowed onto it, pulling the edge of his tread up until none of it touched the crust. He held the position for a moment.

"Did you hear my whisper?" he asked. The metal plate gave his tread an echoing sound.

"I didn't hear a thing," said the Taker.

"Good," said Attila. "It's still superconducting."

He started moving more bones and stacking up the plates.

"Get some slaves in here to gather up all these plates," he said. "You may have to persuade them a little with a whip-sword." Just then Attila felt a sharp pain in his tread. He looked down to see the blade of a pricker and a few crystallium eye-stub bones.

"Had to get one last cut, didn't you Qui-Qui," he said. His tread flicked, and the bones scattered across the room.

"Who's Qui-Qui?" the Taker asked.

"Someone I knew long ago," said Attila.

As they exited the breach in the maze wall Attila said, "I remember ordering a zoo some time ago. I wanted to see all the animals that lived on Egg. Where is it?"

"There has been a zoo in Bright Center since long before I was a hatchling," said the Taker.

"Take me there," said Attila, flowing up the tail of his riding-Swift.

At the zoo, Attila rode rapidly by the holding pens until they came to the Flow Slow pen. He dismounted and slid through the narrow passage crack in the thick wall.

"They are dangerous, O Terrible One," warned a keeper.

"Quiet, slave!" Attila said as the Flow Slow started toward him. "Crazy-Eyes. Come here."

The Taker got down from her mount and, short-sword at the ready, entered the cage.

"You keep moving right in front of it, tempting it on," said Attila. He moved to one side and held still. The attention of the Flow Slow shifted to the Taker. She moved away and the Flow Slow followed her. Attila rushed the animal from the back side and caught the leading edge of a plate as it rose from the crust and started to flow up to the top of the rolling animal.

The Taker alternately poked and hollered at the front of the Flow Slow. The huge plates appeared over the top of the animal and looked as if they were falling directly down on her. Suddenly it sounded as if the Flow Slow were calling her name.

"Crazy-Eyes," came the muffled voice. "Look up here!"

The Taker backed away to see Attila on top of the Flow Slow, his tread moving backward as the plates of the Flow Slow moved ponderously forward.

"I haven't forgotten how to do it," Attila said proudly. He thumped the animal hard on the top and it stopped moving, bewildered. He thumped it in another place, and it started flowing again.

"It's a stupid way to ride," he said as his tread started to move again to keep him on top of the animal. "You don't get to rest your tread as you do riding a Swift. You have to walk as far as it does, only backwards." He prodded the Flow Slow until it was moving as fast as it could go, then nimbly rippled down the trailing edge onto the crust.

"Get some slaves and nail those superconducting plates to it. No magnetic barrier is going to stop me!"

"It is so slow; it will take a great of turns to get to the stranger's compound," Taker said.

"I see you have never moved an army," said Attila. "A few warriors on Swifts can move rapidly across the crust; but an army of warriors moves with the speed of a Flow Slow and, like a Flow Slow, eats everything in its path." He reached into a pouch and pulled out some dark red balls. He popped two into his eating pouch then rolled the rest into the path of the approaching Flow Slow.

21:03:45 GMT TUESDAY 21 JUNE 2050

"Say, everybody," said Abdul. "There's something funny going on down on Egg." He pushed an override switch and the image showed up on all the screens.

"It looks like column of driver ants," Cesar said.

"An apt analogy, Doctor Wong," said Seiko. "I have been monitoring the condensed news briefs from the cheela. The landing base is expecting an attack by Attila. That must be his army."

"They'll be there in thirty seconds," said Pierre. "If only we could do something."

"The speckled cheela have pink eyes," said Seiko. "Remember how the Prophet Pink-Eyes was affected by our laser?"

"Focus the laser on the landing base, Abdul!" Jean chimed in.

"Okay. But a laser beam isn't going to do anything to a cheela except titillate it."

21:04:15 GMT TUESDAY 21 JUNE 2050

The whine of the pumps on the gravity catapult changed pitch as they caught the heavily laden cargo ship and lowered it gently down to the off-loading platform. Dozens of space cheela poured down the curved off-ramp and started unloading the cargo hold. Star-Counter left the control deck and came down to greet Crust-Crawler.

"Had trouble getting volunteers to stay in space where it's safe," Star-Counter told him. "Everyone wants to be down here where the action is."

"I see you brought some weapons." Crust-Crawler was pleased.

"Positron beamers, fountain howitzers, antimatter mines, slicetop gliders, and a couple of meters of super-mag barrier coils."

"I'll get the barrier coils to Engineer Electro-Magnetic immediately," said Crust-Crawler. "The Speckled Horde is only a few turns away."

"I could see it as we were coming down," said Star-Counter. "The column stretches out for hundreds of meters. Are you sure we have a chance against all of them?"

"Most of them are porters and support personnel," said Crust-Crawler. "The only ones we really have to fear are Attila himself and some three dozen greats of his speckled warriors. If we can defeat them, the rest will give up."

"Three dozen greats against two greats," said Star-Counter.

"But our 288 have technology on their side."

"We have something more than that on our side," Star-Counter added.

"What is that?" asked Crust-Crawler.

"We know we must not lose. Boost me up a few meters at low power so I can report on what they are doing."

21:04:16 GMT TUESDAY 21 JUNE 2050

Attila rode his Swift at the head of his army. Group after group, each led by a greaturion who commanded a great of mounted warriors, stretched out down the long paved road toward the west. Beside Attila rode the Taker.

"A nice road the strangers have made for us," the Taker said. "The quicker to hasten their deaths."

"It looks freshly paved," said Attila. "I don't understand that, or the warm spots either."

"Warm spots?" asked the Taker.

"Shove those black eye-balls under your floppy eye-flaps and use the pink eyes Bright gave you," Attila snapped.

The Taker lowered all her normal eyes and looked with her pink ones at the road. She could see ragged spots of ultra-red along the road, as if something warm were underneath.

"What are they?" the Taker asked.

"I don't know. And I don't like things I don't understand."

They reached the outskirts of the stranger's compound. The lead warriors halted. It would take nearly a turn for the rest of the long column to gather.

Attila had been looking forward to this battle. It was the first time in many generations that he had felt the tingle of danger rippling over his hide.

"Bring up those Flow Slows!" he commanded. "And the first dozen greaturions report to me." The twelve group leaders rode up on their Swifts and gathered around him.

"I will ride the first Flow Slow over the barriers at the main entrance," said Attila. "The first four groups are to follow me in." He turned to the greaturion of the Fourth Group. "Torn-Tread!"

"Yef, O Terrible One." Torn-Tread's tread was lisping because of the massive scar from the bite of a Swift.

"You will ride the second Flow Slow over the barriers to the right, and Groups Five through Eight will follow you. Eleven-Eyes will take his Flow Slow to the left.

"Bring up my Flow Slow!" he ordered, sliding down off his Swift. The Swift stayed with its mate, which was being ridden by the Taker.

"It is almost turnfeast," reminded the Taker.

"We will not stop for turnfeast," said Attila. "My warriors will eat the meat of the strangers for their turnfeast."

Attila scampered up the trailing edge of the Flow Slow and took over control of the great animal. The greaturions whirled their mounts around and raced back to gather their groups. The warriors saw Attila on the Flow Slow, heard the shouts of their greaturions, and immediately dashed forward, their war-cries mingled with the roars of their Swifts.

"They're attacking!" yelled Crust-Crawler. "He's not even going to talk to us first!"

"It has been a long time since the Terrible One has had an excuse to fight," said Dented-Shield. "He was afraid you would surrender."

"We'll give him a fight," Crust-Crawler promised. "Fire the antimatter mines!"

Engineer Power-Pack closed a switch and in a rippling roar, the road to the west exploded under the treads of the Speckled Horde. Swifts and their warrior mounts were torn apart by the explosions and tossed to the sides of the road. Those that had been along the edges of the road or between the mine emplacements immediately left the road, only to be met by two more rippling roars as two more strings of mines on either side of the road went up.

Attila felt a dull thump through the body of his Flow Slow as the antimatter mine went off. The Flow Slow gave a deep rumble of pain, but continued on under the pricking from the creature above it. Attila could sense the animal was hurt. But, except for a cracked plate underneath its armor cover, it was still functional.

He looked out from his vantage point on top of the Flow Slow and surveyed the damage that had been done to his army. Unlike the Flow Slow, the army had been badly hurt by the sneak attack. The warriors had not panicked under the attack and were still moving forward toward the enemy, but they were not in their usual group formations. They all had at least one eye fixed on their Emperor.

Attila pulled out his limber-swords and flashed them in a complex pattern about his body. The warriors halted their disorganized rush and looked about for a greaturion. The greaturions, limber-swords signaling, gathered the warriors that were around them, then signaled their leader. There were only six groups now—half the warriors had been killed by the antimatter mines. Limber-swords flashing, Attila lined up the groups behind the three Flow Slows and the attack continued.

"Let's get this beast moving!" Attila called, as he jabbed the point of a pricker between the cracks in the Flow Slow's armor. He marched backward as the Flow Slow ponderously moved forward. He looked upward at the large sphere hanging in the sky above him. He refused to be awed by it. The sphere would fall once the fort fell and the power was turned off.

High above the battlefield Star-Counter watched the developing action and reported down to her friends below.

"First two groups now within range of the fountain-tubes," she said. "Coordinates one-three and one-six."

"One-three fired," said Metal-Bender, throwing small switches on his console. "One-six fired." Racks of long, nearly vertical tubes fired in salvos and dozens and dozens of tiny heavy balls shot up into the sky to fall like tiny avenging meteorites on the Speckled Horde. The crust vibrated with the cries of punctured warriors and Swifts, but the attack moved on.

"Coordinates one-two. Coordinates one-seven. Coordinates two-three," Star-Counter reported from above.

Down below, Attila took out his limber-swords and flashed another signal. The greaturions now switched their advance to a zig-zag pattern. Many of the deadly falling balls missed their targets. Attila heard a grunt as the warrior next to him took a ball through the brain-knot. His dead body, carried over the front of the Flow Slow by the moving plates, was crushed into the crust beneath.

"Three-three. Four-seven. Four-two. Five-seven. Six-seven. Seven-seven," said Star-Counter.

"My tubes are empty," Metal-Bender said.

"Attila's Flow Slow has almost reached the barrier and the other two are not far behind," Crust-Crawler told them. "We have got to stop those Flow Slows! Activate the robots."

The tubes that acted like fountain plants had finally stopped shooting pellets. They were approaching the barrier. Attila slowed his Flow Slow, wary of new surprises. Lying in front of the nearly invisible magnetic barriers were complex chunks of metal. Suddenly, they seemed to come alive. Each one had a number of large manipulators that pinched, cut, or burned. The robots had been programmed to go after the Flow Slows, especially the riders on top. Some were crushed under the massive armored plates, while others scurried around to the trailing edge and started to ride up on top. They were impervious to sword blades; and once a Swift had encountered one of the cutting, burning, pinching robots, they refused to go near them again.

"Use your quirrls!" Attila shouted to the mounted warriors around him.

The warriors loaded their specially adapted pouches with short heavy quirrls and used their internal muscles to throw the quirrls in a short arc from their perches high up on their Swifts. The quirrls punctured the metallic hides of the robots, leaving a glowing wound. Some stopped working; some were pinned to the crust; but the others kept on.

"Two are climbing the Flow Slow!" said one of the warriors next to him.

"Throw quirrls!" Attila was thumping the Flow-Slow hard to make it reverse itself. The robots now had to climb against a down-flow of moving plates, and they slowed their advance. First one, then the other was picked off by quirrls. The Flow Slow groaned again. One of the quirrls had found a chink in its armor. The Flow Slow was now surrounded by a swirling mass of Swift-riding warriors that had silenced the rest of the robots as they tried to attack.

"The robots got two of the Flow Slows," Star-Counter said.

"We can hear that through the crust," said Crust-Crawler over the bellows from the Flow Slows. "It can't be pleasant having a construction robot cutting and burning its way down to your brain-knot."

With a wailing cry, the bellows stopped. The remaining Flow Slow echoed the cry of its dying mate, then returned to its usual complaining groans as the mite on its topside pricked it into motion once again.

"They didn't get the important one," said Crust-Crawler. "Attila is going to breach the magnetic barrier."

"Follow me," Attila shouted. Limber-swords whirling a victory flourish, he urged the armored Flow Slow up onto the magnetic barrier. The crust groaned as the generators attempted to maintain the field, then the barrier fell. With shouts of triumph, the vanguard of the Speckled Horde poured through the opening. They fell back as they were met by a barrage of positron beams that ate holes in their hides. The positron beamers had limited range in the tenuous atmosphere, but the range of the beamers was longer than the range of the quirrls. The quirrls, however, could be thrown in any direction, while the positron beams spiraled along the east-west magnetic field lines. The spacers with their beamers and the warriors with their quirrls sparred with each other at long distance like knights fighting bishops in a weird end game.

"Herders! Spread your stickers!" Letter-Reader shouted to his clan. He then ran out between the knots of fighters and threw tiny tread stickers in the path of the Swifts. His actions were followed by others. The moving Swifts ran into the stickers and roared as they came to a halt. Their riders cursed and slashed at them to get them moving again, but many were caught by the stinging positron beams.

Slowly, relentlessly, the defenders were driven back. Attila again raised his limber-swords and signaled a command. The warriors about him cursed with anger, then fought all the harder.

"What happened?" Crust-Crawler asked Dented-Shield.

"Attila has decided to call in the rest of his army," said Dented-Shield. "The first echelon is angry that they did not finish the battle by themselves."

"They are coming fast," Star-Counter told them.

Attila signaled again, and the warriors about him disengaged and retreated to set up a guard to protect the gap in the magnetic barrier. As the rest of his army approached, Attila slid down the backside of the Flow Slow and mounted his riding Swift. Limber-swords flashing, he triumphantly led the Speckled Horde through the gap.

"Let loose the slicer-gliders!" Crust-Crawler yelled. "Be careful how you point them, they can't tell friend from foe."

Dozens upon dozens of small powered gliders zoomed across the crust. On their topsides glistened three long razor-sharp blades, which caused many a warrior to abandon his damaged mount. But even an unmounted warrior from the Speckled Horde was a formidable foe. Great upon great, the Swifts and their riders flowed through the gap. The fountain tubes had been reloaded and belched once again. Positron beams flickered through the atmosphere to eat holes in flesh, and glide-cars driven by reckless spacers spewed antimatter bombs from each side until the driver was stopped with a whip-sword or a quirrl to the brain-knot. The defenders were driven back of their last magnetic barrier. The armored Flow Slow was moved forward once again.

A battered glide-car slid to a stop beside Crust-Crawler and Dented-Shield. The driver was Avenging-Eye. His pouches were stuffed with heavy objects.

"We've got to stop that Flow Slow," said Avenging-Eye. "Lower the barriers while I get across." Without waiting for a reply he jammed his speed control into high and headed directly for the barrier.

"Stop!" cried Crust-Crawler after him, then signaled to Engineer Electro-Magnetic. The barrier dropped; the glide-car shot across, and the barrier popped back up again.

"A crazy fool," Eleven-Eyes told Attila. "Advance with quirrls!" he commanded to his warriors behind him.

"He's after the Flow Slow!" shouted Attila, slapping his Swift into action. The Taker's Swift was already past him, and she was unsheathing her whip-sword. Avenging-Eye feinted a turn and rolled an antimatter bomb toward her, but she knew his target and could not be fooled. He increased the speed of his glide-car to maximum, trying to get by her, but her whip-sword caught him in the side. Avenging-Eye exploded as the antimatter bombs in his stuffed pouches went off in a gigantic explosion. The remains of the glide-car slid under the plates of the still advancing Flow Slow.

A dazed Taker wiggled out from under her dead Swift, ordered a warrior off his mount, and was pulling out a new whip-sword from her weapons pouch when Attila arrived.

"Only a miracle can save us now," said Crust-Crawler.

Suddenly a cry of anguish arose from the advancing army. The cry was repeated by some of the friendly clan warriors nearby.

"Attila and his warriors are pulling in their eye-balls," Dented-Shield observed in bewilderment.

"It's too bright!" Letter-Reader shouted, pulling in three of his eyes.

"What's too bright?" asked Crust-Crawler.

"It's an ultra-red beacon from the center of the Eyes of Bright. It makes my pink eyes ache."

"The humans have turned on their laser!" Crust-Crawler exclaimed.

"Most of the Horde have only a few eyes up," said Dented-Shield. "They are having trouble controlling their riding-Swifts."

The Taker pulled in her speckled eyes and looked out with her two common eyes. She had to sweep them back and forth to find out what was going on around her.

"Stop that light!!!" Attila roared, all of his eyes under their flaps. He had been proud that none of his eyes were common, though it meant that he could never read the small writing on a scroll.

Both the Taker's and Attila's riding Swifts were struck by slicer-gliders and stopped to tend their wounds. The ultra-red light glared on.

"These stupid Swifts are useless," Attila shouted. He drew his three limber-swords and slid down the back of his Swift, the flickering swords protecting his flanks from unseen enemies as he tried to peer out from under his eyeflaps at the glaring hostileness. The Taker slid down to stand beside her leader.

A screaming shriek passed by one side of them, then another seemed to pass under them. It was only after the tiny missile with the supersharp vertical blades had passed that the Taker realized her tread was slippery and the muscles didn't work well anymore. Attila screamed again and leaned his small muscular body against hers as he tried to lift his tread from the torture of another slicer-glider.

The riding-Swifts were easy to kill, Crust-Crawler recalled later. Without their riders to protect them, they were easy targets for a positron beam. The speckled warriors were tougher, even though they were mostly blind; for once on the crust, they could sense an enemy coming through their tread and most of them had one or more common eyes to see with. Attila, however, had none.

The battle grew old, but the ultra-red light from above glared on and on.

"Will it never end!" shouted Attila, his limber-swords flickering about him in an interwoven shield. The Taker had moved away from him to avoid the blades.

"The humans take forever to do anything," Crust-Crawler said from a short distance away. "For once let Bright delay them some more."

"Come and get me, slaves," said Taker, her whip-sword flickering on the crust. The muscles in her weapons pouch fired a quirrl, but the bolt fell short and vibrated in the crust. She flashed her whip-sword about her body menacingly.

"With pleasure," Dented-Shield said, raising her shield and pike. Taker's whip-sword whirled faster as she advanced on Dented-Shield.

"Wait, Dented-Shield," called Crust-Crawler.

Standing off at a safe distance, far from the reach of the whip-sword, he shot the Taker with a positron beam. It made a large hole.

Juices oozing from tread and hide, the Taker snaked out her whip-sword to take an eye from her tormentor.

A dented shield blocked the slash. Another bolt from the antimatter weapon burned deep into her brain-knot.

The Taker flowed.

The crust around Attila grew silent, but the ultra-red glared on. Attila stopped waving the limber-swords a moment to allow his tread to hear what was going on. The manipulators holding the limber-swords felt a vibration coming down the haft. When Attila waved the swords again, there was nothing to wave. The sword blades had disintegrated.

Attila pushed a pink eye out into the ultra-red glare and saw a speckled hide!

"Give me your sword," Attila demanded.

"Yes, O Terrible One," came the voice, and Letter-Reader's sword sliced through the protruding eye.

"Avenging-Eye is avenged!" Letter-Reader boasted.

Attila screamed in agony.

Crust-Crawler raised his positron beamer. "Let's get this over with."

"No!" Dented-Shield said. "He is mine!" She ran up on top of Attila. His body twisted and almost flipped tread upward in an attempt to shake off his assailant. She held him down and drove her short-sword into his brain-knot. Attila's eyeflaps relaxed, and the pink eyes flowed out on the crust as the ultra-red glare from the Eyes of Bright finally faded.

Dented-Shield picked up a lifeless eye-ball and lopped it from its stub. She went on to the next one.

"One. Two. Three. Four. Five," she said. "That takes care of what you owe me. Now for the elders that stood with me." She continued around the flowing body until she came to the last eye. Crust-Crawler was holding it in a manipulator and had a small slicer ready.

"I am tired," Dented-Shield said. "You can have that one."

"This is for Qui-Qui." And Crust-Crawler sliced the last eye-ball from the Emperor of Dragon's Egg.

"Who is Qui-Qui?" Dented-Shield asked.

"Someone I knew long ago," he said.

21:04:17 GMT TUESDAY 21 JUNE 2050

"Excellent choice of frequency, Jean," said Seiko. "Short ultraviolet. Too long for normal cheela vision and too short to cause sexual side effects. It definitely affected the battle."

"What is happening?" Abdul asked.

"Happened. It was all over in a tenth of a second."

"But who *won*?" Abdul shouted.

"The space cheela did, of course." Seiko was monitoring the snippets of condensed news from the crust below.

"With a little help from their friends," said Abdul.

"They need a little more help," Seiko said. "Their libraries were wiped out by the starquake, and they want us to send back some of the information on our library HoloMem crystals. They don't want all of it, but they will let our computer know which sections."

"I'll bring up the first crystal." Pierre, seated at the library console, reached up to the HoloMem rack and pulled out the first crystal. It was still labeled *A* to *AME*, but that human dictionary content had been replaced long ago with knowledge from the cheela. The crystal would transmit faster if it were in the communications console on the Main Deck, so Pierre pushed himself up the metal ladder as fast as he could go, knowing that no matter how fast a human moved, it was too slow for a cheela.

Escape

"That's the last of the HoloMem storage crystals, Pierre," Jean said as she turned away from the communications console. "Most of the material on that one was encrypted. I hope they have the crypto-keys." She swiveled back as the image of Sky-Speaker flashed on the screen.

"Keys obvious," said Sky-Speaker. "Goodbye."

"I liked the old Sky-Teacher better," said Pierre. "He talked so verbosely that it gave you time to think."

"We have plenty of time to think now," Jean said quietly as she shut down the communications console. She reached under the counter and extracted the HoloMem crystal that had come from the library and replaced it with the regular console crystal that kept a log of everything that went through the console.

"Too much time," said Pierre. He followed Jean as she ottered her way down the passageway to the crew deck. Jean went to the library console and restored the HoloMem to its place in the storage rack. Pierre, driven by his command responsibility, returned to the galley and stared at the listing of the food supplies on the food storage lockers. There was food for eight more days at normal rations, sixteen days at half-rations, thirty-two days at quarter-rations . . . only one month. It would take five more months after that before Oscar returned from its long elliptical orbit around Egg. His eyes didn't look at the bank of lockers with the blank label. Bouncing lightly in the low gravity, he passed Jean at the library console and turned into the lounge. Doc was talking with Seiko and Abdul was looking pensively out of the viewport in the floor.

"HoloMems done?" asked Abdul, looking up.

"Yep," said Pierre, floating lightly to the cushion beside him.

"Anything left for us mere humans to do?" Abdul asked.

"The cheela don't need us anymore. They should be well on their way to recovery by now." A tiny white-hot speck appeared outside the viewport window and stopped.

"Smile," said Abdul. "You're about to have your picture taken by some tourists."

The speck released a shower of sparks. There was a flickering of light, then the sparks rejoined the glowing speck and it sped away.

"What are your plans for the rest of the mission, Pierre?" Seiko asked.

"I have no plans."

"You must!" Seiko sounded disturbed. "We must not waste our lives doing nothing until we die!"

Pierre raised his gaze from the viewport. The anguish in his face showed through the ragged, unkempt beard.

"I can't find a way to save us," he said, tears starting to well up in his eyes.

"Of course you can't," said Seiko. "There *is* no way to save us. It is simple mathematics. There are five people to feed and only eight days of food rations. We might be able to stretch that out using our body reserves, but we will be out of food in a month. We could even consider eating Amalita's body. At best, we could only get about 50 kilos of meat from it." She turned to Doc Wong.

"How many calories in meat, Doctor Wong?" she asked him.

"I can't believe this conversation!" said Abdul. "There is no way I'm going to be a cannibal! I'm leaving!" He started to dive out the door to his private quarters, but Pierre held him back with a hand on one shoulder. He kept it there as he nodded at Doc to answer.

"Use the values for pork, Doc," Abdul blurted. "I hear from my cannibal friends that you can't tell the difference."

"Most meats have about 4000 calories per kilogram," said Dr. Cesar Wong. "The average person could live on a half-kilo of meat per day if the diet were supplemented with vitamins."

"So 50 kilos would only last us 20 days at full rations or 80 days at quarter rations," said Seiko, "We are still short by two months." She paused for a second. "As I said, there is no way to save us."

"I thought for sure that the next thing you were going to suggest was that we draw straws," said Abdul to Pierre.

"Abdul!" Pierre said severely.

"I have calculated that option," said Seiko. "There is a problem. If we wait for a person to die of hunger, then there is very little nourishment left on the body."

"There'll be none left on mine!" said Abdul.

"If, however, a person dies at the beginning of the period, then not only does his body become a source of significant nourishment, but he is not consuming food as time goes on. Using Doctor Wong's calorie estimate, while two carcasses would allow quarter rations for four people over the same period, three could supply adequate nourishment for the remaining three for six months."

"Great!" cried Abdul. "Why stop at cannibalism when we can have ritualistic murder?"

"Although such an option is technically feasible," continued Seiko, "I personally have no intention of suggesting or participating in any such option."

"What's the matter?" Abdul asked. "Afraid of drawing the short straw?"

"No. The long one," answered Seiko. "Neither you, nor I, nor any of the others, could return to our respective cultures if we had to survive using that solution. I, for one, am going to spend my last days completing my scientific studies, preparing my work for publication, and transmitting it back to St. George. It will be the culmination of my career. When I am done, I am ready to go." She turned to Dr. Wong again.

"We do have termination capsules on board, Doctor Wong?" she asked.

"Of course," Cesar replied.

Seiko then turned back to Pierre. "It will be difficult to stay rational as time goes on," she said matter-of-factly. "I would recommend that you consider consigning Amalita's body to space now. That way we can avoid temptation later." She dove out the door and pulled herself up through the passageway to the Science Deck.

Pierre looked around at the others.

"She's right," Jean said.

"I'll help take her out," said Cesar.

"If you don't mind, I'd rather be somewhere else," said Abdul. "I don't think I could take it."

"Sure," said Pierre. "Doc and I can handle it, and Jean can run the EVA controls for us."

Amalita had been placed in the storage locker in a fetal position, so she was relatively easy to move around on the deck, but it was a close fit through the passageway holes. She was still in her spacesuit, since Doctor Wong had not bothered to examine her further after he had removed her helmet and found the broken neck. Seiko closed down the star physics console and dimmed the star image table as they brought Amalita to the Science Deck.

"I'll hold Amalita while you get your suits on," she said softly, taking the frosty burden from them.

"The EVA lock is ready," said Jean. She got up from the EVA console, helped Pierre and Cesar with their suits, and took them through the checkout sheet, trying to be as careful and thorough as Amalita had always been.

"Magni-stiction boots . . ." said Jean. Pierre flicked a switch in his chest console that rearranged the pseudo-random pattern of the magnetic monopoles in the soles of his boots so they matched up with the hexagonal pattern of monopoles built into the inner plates and hull of Dragon Slayer. His boots clanged onto the deck, twisted outward at a 30-degree angle.

"Check," he said, then clumped into the EVA lock. He turned around and helped Cesar maneuver Amalita's body in through the door.

"Don't forget your safety lines," said Jean. "There are some weird gravity fields out there." Pierre attached a line to himself and another to the ring in Amalita's suit. Just then a dark head appeared in the passageway hole in the deck.

"I had to say goodbye," said Abdul. He forced himself to look at Amalita's badly burned face. His left hand reached into the singed hair and held it lightly, while his right hand took two kisses from his lips and placed them softly on the frosted blisters of Amalita's closed eyelids. He turned and dove down the passageway, leaving behind clusters of teardrops moving upward in the swirling air.

Jean cycled them through.

"The best place to release her is near the viewport window," Pierre said as he climbed out the outer lock. He carefully attached his magni-stiction boots to the hull, then shifted his safety line to a tiedown. "She'll be pulled outward to the ring of compensator masses and be gone in a flash of plasma. The last thing we want is to have her, or 'pieces' of her, in orbit."

They moved carefully over the hull to a point near the viewport. They were standing at the south pole of their little moon that circled around the neutron star five times a second. The hull of Dragon Slayer did not spin while it orbited, however, but stayed oriented with respect to the distant stars. To the two humans standing on the hull, the white-hot neutron star seemed to be rotating around the equator of the ship five times a second, while above and below them whirled a ring of six red masses that passed over the two poles of the spherical ship while it rotated to always be tangent to the direction to the star. In this configuration, the gravity tides from the ring of masses cancelled the dangerous gravity tides from the star and allowed the humans to survive.

"I'll give her a slight push while you pay out the safety line," Pierre said.

He let go of Amalita's body, and the uncompensated tides started to pull her outwards. The further she got away from the ship and the closer she got to the massive bodies in the ring, the stronger the forces became. A sprinkling of white-hot sparks gathered off in the distance to observe.

"She is getting heavy," said Cesar.

"It looks stable," said Pierre. "Let her go."

The last of the safety rope whipped through the tiedown and followed Amalita as she accelerated rapidly toward the ring 200 meters away. Just before she reached the ring her body was momentarily surrounded by a swirling cloud of white-hot specks. There was a flash, and she was gone.

When Pierre and Cesar came inside, Jean and Seiko helped them out of their suits.

"Unless somebody is going to use the console library, I think I'll get back to working on my book," said Pierre.

"Which one?" Jean asked.

"The popular version that covers everything that happened on the trip. I was going to call it *Dragon's Egg*, but the editors at Ballantine Interplanetary said that they already had a title of that name in their inventory. Besides, they wanted something more personal, so they chose, *My Visit With Our Nucleonic Friends*. I think it's a dumb title, but they are the ones buying the book."

"I don't think money is a consideration anymore," Seiko reminded him.

"Hmm." Pierre glanced down at the star image table and noticed that there were a number of new features on the surface of the neutron star.

"There have been some changes in the last hour," he said to Seiko.

"Yes," she replied. "While you and Doctor Wong were outside, the cheela have reestablished a highly technological civilization on the ground and have resumed extensive space travel activities. They have rapidly caught up to where they were at the time of the starquake and are continuing on at a rapid pace."

"I'd better get busy writing if I am going to stay up with them." Pierre reached down and pulled himself through the passageway hole in the deck. He stopped when he came to the main deck. Abdul was there. He had opened the metal shield on one of the equatorial viewports and was looking out through the tinted glass.

"Hey! Look at the sightseers," Abdul hollered across the deck. "It's like being one of the heads on Mount Rushmore. Why don't you come over and pretend to be Teddy Roosevelt? You've got the beard for it." As Pierre approached the window, the number of specks outside increased dramatically.

01:30:04 GMT WEDNESDAY 22 JUNE 2050

Busy-Thoughts moved around the creche-classroom critiquing the work of the students. Although most of the youngling's education was done through holovid connections to the "Master Teacher" program in the central computer, there were still some topics that were best handled by live teachers in central classrooms. Plasma art was one of them, especially since the generators were massive and expensive.

"Excellent structure, Lovely-Eyes," said Busy-Thoughts. "But the colors are a little weak for such a bold form. Perhaps you should try more current in the ion generators."

The student adjusted the controls under his tread and increased the intensity of the ion beams shooting into the shaped magnetic fields. The ions spiraled along the magnetic field lines, giving off a glow of synchrotron radiation. With the increased current, the interior of the magnetic sculpture glowed brighter. Lovely-Eyes then increased the strength of one of the magnetic field generators in the base and adjusted some transparent superconductor guides attached to the top. The sculpture was now a floating form of brightly glowing colors. The shape was bisymmetric. There was an intense inner violet structure that was basically spherical, but had large rough holes penetrating it. Two circles were set side-by-side in the violet sphere, with a triangle and a rectangle below them. Covering the violet structure was a lumpy blanket of softer plasma in blue-white with patches of yellow-white.

"It looks strangely familiar," said Busy-Thoughts.

"It is a portrait of one of the humans," said Lovely-Eyes. "This one is Pierre Carnot Niven, the Commander of the Expedition."

"If you say so. The Slow Ones all look the same to me."

"Not once you know them better," said Lovely-Eyes. "Pierre has hairs on the bottom side of his head-lump as well as the top side." Lovely-Eyes went on eagerly, "I've been learning all about the humans in my holovid courses. The Master Teacher program says I do well in that subject and has allowed me to take a special advanced program in humanology."

"That's very nice, Lovely-Eyes, but this is an abstract art class. As strange as humans look, they don't qualify as abstract art. In the next class I want you to concentrate on doing your assignment."

Busy-Thoughts moved to the center of the classroom and '*trummed* the class to attention.

"Everyone finish his sculpture and set the control pattern in memory. When you finish I have an announcement."

There were whispered exchanges between the students as they made last minute adjustments to their pieces and closed down their generators. As they gathered around the teacher, Busy-Thoughts momentarily felt the instinct to reach out and cover them all with his hatching mantle. He shook off the feeling, then made a resolve to apply for rejuvenation again. He had been putting it off too long.

"The White Rock Clan has prospered this year," said Busy-Thoughts. "With the decrease in our egg quota from the Combined Clans Population Control Board, we have had fewer creche expenses. The elders of the clan have decided to send the entire creche-school on a trip to see the humans. After all, we are in a unique period in history, when all five humans can be seen, up close, at the same time."

Lovely-Eyes was ecstatic at the announcement. For the first time he would be able to see the humans he had been studying.

The class took a glide-carrier to the West Pole and rode up the West Pole Space Fountain to the top. Busy-Thoughts had arranged a special hookup to the Master Teacher. On the way up the class was given a lecture on the geographical features of the West Pole hemisphere they could see below them. At Topside Platform they switched to a tourist ship especially made for viewing the humans. It had artificial gravity generators and tiers of platforms so that everyone had a good view, yet the human spacecraft wasn't uncomfortably "overhead."

"Oh my! They *are* huge," Lovely-Eyes said as the tourist ship floated to a stop a meter away from the porthole that held the motionless visages of Pierre and Abdul. He formed a tendril and pointed it at one of the humans. "That's Pierre. You can tell because of the yellow patch all over the bottom of his head. The other one is Abdul. He only has a thin yellow patch under his nose."

"What is the yellow stuff?" one of his classmates asked.

"Hairs. Humans are mostly hairless like us, but they have hairy patches like Slink hide on their heads."

"Ugly!!!" she replied.

The tourist ship moved on to the next porthole where Jean Kelly was looking out.

"They all look the same," someone said. "I thought they had hides of different color."

"They do, in the long wavelength portion of the spectrum where the human eyes work," said Lovely-Eyes. "But they all look the same to X-ray vision."

The tourist ship set up a holovid projector with a time-lapse sequence. First they saw Abdul at the porthole calling Pierre, the appearance of Pierre at the window, then Abdul and Pierre talking and looking at the visiting spacecraft. The jerky time-lapse photography had everyone rumbling their tread.

"Stop laughing!!!" Lovely-Eyes shouted into the deck. "Those brave humans have given up their lives to save Egg, and you laugh at them like Slinks in a zoo!"

"Lovely-Eyes!" Busy-Thoughts' tread rapped in the distance. "Behave yourself!"

Lovely-Eyes' tread fell silent, but his brain-knot was still seething. "There *must* be a way to save them," he thought. "And I will not change my accursed egg-name until I find it. When I do, the name I shall choose will be a better name, a *noble* name."

01:30:05 GMT WEDNESDAY 22 JUNE 2050

"Look at those spaceships!" said Abdul. "They are almost 10 centimeters long and have multiple decks. They must be the equivalent of cruise ships, coming up to see the sights."

"They are no longer spherical." Seiko was peering out an adjacent porthole. "They have found an efficient method of producing gravity, so they no longer need to carry along miniature black holes. Their technological capability is increasing at an astounding rate."

"I wonder if they'll ever be able to move asteroids," Jean said wistfully.

"They have plenty of energy to do the job," said Pierre. "It's just that Oscar is so fragile, and they and their machines are so dense."

"Superman may be able to lift icebergs in the holo-vids," said Abdul. "But if he tried lifting a real iceberg he would end up with nothing but a pile of ice cubes."

"There is no way they could bring Oscar back any sooner than six months," said Seiko in her authoritative Teutonic tone. "We might as well stop wishful thinking; it's counterproductive. We're going to die, and there is not much we can do about it. I'm going down to the galley for something to eat. Anyone care to join me?"

"I'm not hungry just now," said Cesar. The others kept looking out the windows at the blizzard of visiting space-craft.

03:54:50 GMT WEDNESDAY 22 JUNE 2050

The turn eventually came when Lovely-Eyes at last gave up on his quest and returned to White Rock City, the homeland of his clan. He found the creche-master and asked for a position tending the young ones.

"Few positions left," said Creche-Master/71. "PopCon Board decreasing cheela, more robots instead."

Lovely-Eyes didn't like the abrupt language style that had developed in the last 60 greats of turns. Now that nearly every cheela had a horde of robots at its beck and call, and seldom interacted with other cheela, politeness had nearly dropped out of the language. After all, robots didn't have feelings and didn't have to be persuaded to do anything, just told to do it. Since he was talking to a cheela, however, he thought that perhaps he would do better if he used the old style.

"I would really appreciate it if you could find a position for me," said Lovely-Eyes. "I have worked hard for 300 greats of turns and am looking forward to tending the hatchlings."

"Experience?" asked Creche-Master/71.

"I have advanced degrees in Humanology, Human Medicine, Expanded Matter Science, Inertial and Gravitational Engineering, and Science Administration. I was also Leader of the Fourth Segment in the Legislature of the Combined Clans."

"Successes?"

"Not many, I'm afraid," Lovely-Eyes said. "I have spent most of my life trying to find some means to prevent the eventual starvation of the humans. I have studied human medicine to find some method like deep sleep to keep the humans alive without food. I have studied expanded matter science to find a way to make food with the equipment the humans have on Dragon Slayer. I have studied inertial and gravitational engineering to find a way to return the distant asteroid sooner. I was unsuccessful.

"I went into politics, became leader of the fourth segment, pushed through the funding to form a special task force to solve the human starvation problem, then left the legislature to run the task force. I had the brightest minds, both cheela and robotic, working on the problem for two generations. They were unsuccessful. When the funding for the task force was terminated I gave up and came here. I have no successes to tell the younglings about. I'm afraid I wouldn't be a good choice for that job."

"No," Creche-Master/71 agreed. Her tread was manipulating her touch screen. "One egg available for hatching in 18 turns."

"I'll take it!" said Lovely-Eyes.

The driven soul of Lovely-Eyes was, at last, at peace. The egg had produced a near-perfect hatchling, exactly as the geneticists had predicted. The hatchling had the official name of White-Rock/207891384, but Lovely-Eyes, recalling an old story he had read in his humanology studies, called him Grandest-Tiger.

Grandest-Tiger was dodging in and out from under Lovely-Eyes' hatching mantle, playing peek-and-chase with its robotic hatchling-mates. While Grandest-Tiger played, Lovely-Eyes picked up one of the hatchling's learning toys. It was quite expensive for such a simple toy, but the hatchling psychologists felt it was important for the young ones to have experience with the paradoxical phenomena early in their life.

The toy was a simple ring. It came with a dozen tiny metal spheres. When a sphere was pushed through the hole in the ring, it didn't come out on the other side immediately. Depending upon which side the ball was put through, it would come out at some different time, either in the past or the future. Right now there were six spheres lying on the crust. Idly, Lovely-Eyes picked up five of the spheres and poked them, one at a time through the ring. There was a long pause, then the five spheres popped out again.

Suddenly, Lovely-Eyes pulled back his hatching mantle and rushed out of the pen, leaving a bewildered Grandest-Tiger behind. The robotic hatchling-mates diverted the attention of Grandest-Tiger from the disappearing Old One while they sent emergency messages to the creche-master for a replacement.

03:55:03 GMT WEDNESDAY 22 JUNE 2050

The screen on the communications console flashed on to show the image of Sky-Speaker. Above the electronic chitter of data being transferred there came a calling signal. Seiko went to the console, and the image of Sky-Speaker started talking as she approached.

"You read fast," the image said. "You listen slow. Read."

The image was replaced by text that scrolled rapidly up the screen, keeping in pace with the scan of her eyes. Seiko didn't know how the cheela had done it, but they had taken over control of the communications console display program.

"Pierre," said Seiko, still reading. "They are going to try to rescue us."

"Did they find a way to move Oscar?" he asked, floating over next to her.

"No," she said. "They found a way to move us."

Pierre read the screen along with her, then said to the rest of the crew, "Everybody get into the high-G protection tanks," he said. "The cheela are going to take us for a ride."

04:02:35 GMT WEDNESDAY 22 JUNE 2050

Neutrino-Maker/84 watched as his swarm of robotic workers approached the gigantic viewport window at the south pole of the human spacecraft. They stopped a few meters away from the hull and set up three neutrino generators that flooded the interior of the spacecraft with beams of neutrinos at carefully selected frequencies. He then took his crew around to the other side where they set up a dense array of neutrino detectors. Each robot had the ancient cleft-wort symbol of Web Construction Company emblazoned on its back.

"One more imposs-proj for Web-Con," said the engineer proudly. Once the detectors were in place, a computer generated holo-image slowly began to build up in the display.

"Air, water, humans, steel, all like vacuum," said Neutrino-Maker/84 as he waited impatiently for the image to build up. If they had done a neutrino scan on a decent density object, the image would have formed almost instantly.

After a half-turn, the image was good enough for him to see that the humans were all in their tanks and the last of the air was being replaced by water.

Neutrino-Maker/84 switched his console to communicate with Void-Maker/111. An old and experienced Web-Con disinto engineer, she had been assigned the delicate job of removing the laser communicator from the human spaceship while leaving it in operating condition. The communicator was going to be delivered to another group of Web-Con engineers to calibrate some machines that would allow the ultra-dense cheela to power and control the tenuous human equipment without damaging it.

"Humans in tanks," said Neutrino-Maker/84. "Proceed."

"Proceeding," Void-Maker/111 replied as she set her crew of disinto robots to work.

The communicator had two connections through the hull to the electronics inside Dragon Slayer. One was an electrical power cable for the laser power supply, and the other was a fiber-optic modulator cable that carried the information. Moving carefully, the disinto robots formed a microthin fan of disintegration rays and cut the two cables right at the connectors. Being careful to avoid the free ends of the cables as they waved slowly back and forth in the variable gravity fields outside Dragon Slayer, the disinto robots then attacked the mechanical support structure. The laser communicator came loose.

Void-Maker/111 rubbed her tread screen, and the image of another Web-Con engineer appeared. It was Graviton-

Maker/321. His engineering badges had a circle for gravity instead of a triangle for disinto.

"To you," said Void-Maker/111.

"To me," replied Graviton-Maker/321. "Next to electromagnetic-makers."

"Don't touch!" chirped Void-Maker/111 at the screen.

"Nor you," said Graviton-Maker/321 as the screen went blank.

Graviton-Maker/321 set his crew of gravity robots in the path of the slowly tumbling laser communicator. His job was to get the laser under control and bring it to a halt. He had to catch it without touching it, for the fragile human instrument could not stand the lightest touch by any cheela machines.

His squadron of Web-Con gravity robots were specially designed for this job. They were spherical in shape, and each had a small black hole in the center. The black hole provided the basic gravity field that the robot used. The hull of the robots contained powerful gravity exchangers and diverters that modified the shape, strength, and even the direction of the gravity forces coming from the black hole. Staying carefully off at a distance, the robots pushed and pulled at the tumbling laser communicator until they brought it under control. They then took it out through the whirling ring of compensator masses to a safe place where the electromagnetic-makers could try to operate it.

Electromagnetic-Manager/1 was waiting patiently for the arrival of the laser communicator from the Slow Ones' orbital position. He had his team of electromagnetic engineers ready. There were young ones who would provide the drive that they needed and experienced ones who would provide the caution, for they were treading on new crust when they tried to couple their ultra-dense nucleonic machines to the expanded matter electronic machines that the humans used.

The electromagnetic-makers were a strange breed. It took a perverse type of personality to specialize in a field like electromagnetic engineering where there was almost no opportunity to practice the craft. In general, electromagnetic engineers just talked to themselves, devised exotic experiments involving electromagnetic conductors that stretched hundreds of meters across the surface of Egg to measure the ultra-long electromagnetic waves coming from space, and worked on improving the instructional programs in the Master Teacher Program in case some other student was strange enough to want to become an electromagnetic engineer, too.

This was the first time there had been a need for the management of a team of electromagnetic engineers and Electromagnetic-Manager/1 was the first of his profession.

Graviton-Maker/321 and his crew of robots brought the laser communicator to a halt near the electromagnetic-makers' strange machines floating in orbit some distance away from Dragon Slayer. He stacked up most of his robots, but left a few at the job of keeping the laser communicator in place. Electromagnetic-Manager/1, his team of engineers, and their hordes of specialized robots were waiting for him.

"To you," said Graviton-Maker/321.

"To me," said Electromagnetic-Manager/1.

"Don't . . ." started Graviton-Maker/321.

". . . touch," chirped a chorus of treads from the team of electromagnetic-makers.

The power cable for the laser was brought near an electron generator. It was difficult for the electromagnetic engineers to generate large currents at such low voltages, but soon four amperes of electrons at 500 volts were shooting from one end of the electron generator and four amperes of positrons from the other end. The Web-Con electromagnetic robots steered the beams with the electric and magnetic fields emanating from their bodies and directed them at the conductors in the cut end of the cable.

"Laser photons detected from end of human instrument," said Electromagnetic-Maker/32, who was monitoring the response of a long-wavelength photon detector in one of his robots that he had positioned in front of the laser communicator.

"Positron erosion?" asked Electromagnetic-Manager/1.

"Ten picometers per methturn," replied Electromagnetic-Maker/25.

"Good," said Electromagnetic-Manager/1. The technique for extracting the electrons from the return conductor seemed to be working. A set of ultraviolet generator robots kept the return conductor illuminated with ultraviolet photons which knocked electrons out of the metal. The electrons billowed up in a cloud over the end of the positively charged conductor where they were annihilated by the stream of positrons. Most of the annihilation gamma rays were scattered by the electron cloud, but some high energy photons reached the metal and caused the loss of copper ions.

"Wire temperature?" Electromagnetic-Manager/1 asked another engineer.

"Stablized at 352 K," said Electromagnetic-Maker/28. "Electromagnetic cooling working." His team of robots were monitoring detectors that estimated the detailed spectrum of the heat phonons excited in the surface of the metal where the beam of electrons penetrated. The electron beam was then modulated to produce heat phonons that had the same estimated spectrum but with the phases reversed, so that on the average, the new phonons would tend to cancel the old phonons. Being a statistical technique, it didn't work perfectly, but it did keep the wires well below their melting point.

"Modulation!" ordered Electromagnetic-Manager/1.

Electromagnetic-Maker/55 tapped his control console, and his 20,736 robots each started emitting long-wavelength infrared radiation from their bodies. The robots were arranged in a 144 by 144 array, and their infrared output was phased so that it focused down into a narrow waist just as it entered the optical fiber in the cut end of the communications cable.

"Modulation detected," Electromagnetic-Maker/32 reported.

"Good," said Electromagnetic-Manager/1. He was now sure that the cheela could find a method of getting information on and off the human electrical wires and optical fibers. He contacted Graviton-Maker/321.

"Turn laser toward St. George . . ." said Electromagnetic-Manager/1.

No reply was needed. Graviton-Maker/321 proceeded to manipulate his crew of robots by treading touch-blocks on the sides of his touch-taste screen.

". . . and . . ." continued Electromagnetic-Manager/1.

". . . and?" queried Graviton-Maker/321, puzzled by the verbosity.

"Don't . . ." started Electromagnetic-Manager/1.

". . . touch!" rumbled Graviton-Maker/321, greatly amused.

St. George was far away from the dangerous neutron star in a 100,000-kilometer orbit a third of a light-second away, so it took three turns before Electromagnetic-Manager/1 established contact with the computer on St. George using the laser communicator taken from Dragon Slayer. Once the computer realized that it was communicating directly with cheela instead of the slow-thinking humans, it rapidly repeated the message that it had been sending. The image was that of a female human with yellow hair bound into a single long braid over one shoulder. It reminded Electromagnetic-Manager/1 of a ridiculous type of inbred pet Slink that had hair so long that the pet needed a robot attendant to hold its hair up, out from under its tread when it wanted to move. His console computer link identified the human as Carole Swenson, the Commander of the Dragon's Egg expedition.

"Dragon Slayer! Your last laser communicator is dead. Switch to alternate links! *Dra . . .*"

Electromagnetic-Manager/1 thought for a while about answering the anxious human in order to reassure her that the crew was in no immediate danger. But by the time she had finished saying the word "Dragon Slayer," he would have obtained permission to proceed with the rest of the mission and he could tell her the better news that the cheela were going to try to return the crew to the command ship, St. George. He erased the image of the human from his screen and set up a call to the Administrator of the Slow One Transport Project.

Two turns later, Electromagnetic-Manager/1 received an in-person visit by the administrator of the Slow One Transport Project. Electromagnetic-Manager/1 didn't like working with the Ancient One, who insisted on being addressed by his archaic egg-name, instead of his position.

"I am Lovely-Eyes," said the administrator. The wrinkled hide and erratic eye-stub motion contrasted with the intense gleam from the dark red eyes.

"Coupling experiments successful," reported Electromagnetic-Manager/1.

"Excellent!" said the administrator.

"Excellent!!" the administrator said again, unnecessarily repeating himself.

"Excellent!!!" said the administrator once again.

Electromagnetic-Manager/1 began to be concerned. The eye-stub wave pattern on Lovely-Eyes accelerated, and his hide changed color as his emotions reached the breaking point. His tread started to move again.

"Pro . . ." Suddenly four eye-balls fell sightless to the deck. Electromagnetic-Manager/1 immediately realized that the ancient one had suffered a stroke affecting one of the trilobes of his brain-knot.

"Lovely-Eyes!" Electromagnetic-Manager/1 rushed over to assist the Ancient One. His tread 'trummed an emergency call into the deck as he moved.

Eight, intense, dark red eyes stared him to a halt. They were not "lovely eyes," they were fanatical eyes.

"Pro . . . Pro . . . ceed with project." The treading was weak, but distinct.

"Lovely-Eyes," said Electromagnetic-Manager/1. "I stay until medicos come."

"Go!" came the reply. "And call me Lovely-Eyes no longer. Call me Human-Savior."

The great wrinkled hide shuddered and collapsed. The body of the Ancient One flowed in all directions. When the medical robots tried to enter, their way was blocked.

After checking with Manager-Director/5, the Web-Con supervisor of the Slow One Transport contract, Electro-magnetic-Manager/1 returned to the laser communicator. The human, Carole Swenson, had finished her sentence and was now looking wide-eyed at the screen as she read the message from the cheela. There wasn't time to wait for the human to react, so Electromagnetic-Manager/1 left a long message for the St. George computer and a shorter one for her.

"Dragon Slayer will be disintegrated. Six Eyes of Bright will be collapsed. Return for crew in six months."

He turned off the laser communicator, gathered his engineers and their robots, and headed for Dragon Slayer.

Void-Maker/111 arranged her robotic crew with care around the periphery of the large viewport window in the south pole of the human spacecraft. When she received the signal from Manager-Director/5 she activated her console and the robots disintegrated the hull around the window. The viewport blew away as the air emptied out of the ship. She touched her tread screen and the image of another Web-Con engineer appeared. It was Graviton-Maker/321.

"To you," said Void-Maker/111.

"To me," replied Graviton-Maker/321.

"Don't . . ."

"Won't." Both of their screens rippled with laughter.

Graviton-Maker/321 set his crew of gravity robots in the path of the slowly tumbling plate of glass. This piece of high-strength glass was one of the many parts of the spacecraft that the expanded matter scientists wanted to examine. As soon as his robots had the viewport under control, he sent some of them off with the window while he and the rest of the crew returned to Dragon Slayer. By the time he had returned, Void-Maker/111 had cut a large circular sample out of the spacecraft hull. The task of capturing the circular piece of hull was so similar to the task of catching the viewport that Graviton-Maker/321 did not even bother to monitor the robots. They were faster thinking and more intelligent than he was when it came to doing their job.

Electromagnetic-Manager/1 and his team had arrived and Graviton-Maker/321 joined them as they entered the hole where the viewport had been. They all felt a little uneasy as they entered the dark interior of the ship. Not only was the friendly glare of Egg gone, but they could no longer see the sky.

"Human Protection Tank 6 ahead," said Electromagnetic-Manager/1 to his team as they floated into the center of the cylindrical room. "Take over control."

A team of electromagnetic engineers brought up their generators. Each team was assigned a disinto engineer whose crew of robots were used to clear a path through the walls and cut the cables. In a few dothturns they had cut free tank 6 containing Abdul from the main hull, had replaced the ship's power to the tank with their own, and had inserted their own optical link in the fiber optic connection to the rest of the tanks.

Electromagnetic-Manager/1 monitored the video transmission channel and looked once again at a human as seen in their own region of the visual spectrum. This human was very different from Carole, the Commander of the human expedition. The hair on top of this human's head-lump was short and black instead of long and yellow. But instead of the ridiculously long thick braid coming out of the top of the head-lump, this human had a ridiculously long string of hair in the middle of the head-lump. The face was dark colored, and the pupils of the eyes seemed very wide open. Electromagnetic-Manager/1 wondered if the look of the human was due to the breathing mask that the humans had to wear under water, or whether something else had caused it.

04:02:39 GMT WEDNESDAY 22 JUNE 2050

"I lost power for a second!" said Abdul, just short of panic. "What's going on?"

"The cheela have breached the hull and are wandering around inside Dragon Slayer," said Pierre.

"I sure hope they know what they are doing!" Abdul replied.

04:02:40 GMT WEDNESDAY 22 JUNE 2050

Manager-Director/5 set up a conference link with her team leaders.

"All tanks separated," said Void-Manager/18.

"All tanks powered," said Electromagnetic-Manager/1.

"All samples obtained," said Science-Manager/23.

"Monopole generators ready," said Monopole-Manager/4.

"Inertia pushers ready," said Graviton-Manager/53.

"Proceed," said Manager-Director/5. She returned to the task of braiding the long hair on her prize-winning Slink. She could have had robots do it for her, but Rapunzel deserved personal care.

"Cut away," Void-Manager/18 told his team of engineers.

Void-Maker/111 and her robots sliced off the science tower at the north pole of Dragon Slayer, and it floated upward in the residual gravity tides. There it would be held in place by gravity robots while the disinto robots reduced it to stored energy.

"To you," said Void-Maker/111.

"To me," said Graviton-Maker/321. He paused, waiting for the next phrase from Void-Maker/111. There was a long pause.

"Touch," said Void-Maker/111, holding off her disinto robots for a while.

"Touch!" said Graviton-Maker/321. He sent his personal flitter directly at the gigantic structure. He pulled his eyes in under their eyeflaps to avoid the glare as the cold metal turned into a hot plasma as it was torn apart by the strong gravity field surrounding his spacecraft. There was a breeze of ionized gas that rapidly settled to the deck and he was through to the other side.

"Touch!" he hollered again on his screen as he swooped his flitter around and dove once more at the mountain of nothing.

Soon, most of the engineers had put their crews of robots on automatic and joined in the fun. Manager-Director/5 was notified of the disruption by the contract performance program, but she did nothing about it. The robots would probably get the rest of the job done in half the time, now that the cheela engineers were out of the way having fun.

It took five long seconds to reduce Dragon Slayer to five spherical steel tanks, bobbing gently in the center of the ring of six condensed asteroids. The cheela electromagnetic engineers brought back the laser communicator, attached it to Pierre's tank, and set it up so it was pointed out to St. George.

04:02:45 GMT WEDNESDAY 22 JUNE 2050

"Am I glad to see you!" Carole Swenson said as Pierre's face appeared on her screen. "Is everyone okay?"

"So far," said Pierre. He reached to his control panel and set up a split screen display format that combined the images of the remaining crew members of Dragon Slayer with that of Carole.

"I'd sure like to see what those busybodies are doing to us," said Abdul. "But the monitor cameras went with the rest of the ship."

"We have the large telescope trained on you," Carole told him. "At this distance, each of your acceleration tanks is just a blob, but we can resolve the compensator asteroids easily. We can even detect the activities of the cheela. Although they and their machines are too small to see, they are white-hot and we can get a lot of information from speckle interferometry. Except for a few machines near you, they seem to be concentrating out at the asteroid ring. Let me transfer a picture.''

The screen blanked and a visual image overlaid with computer graphics appeared on the screen. The computer had strobed the picture at the rotation rate of Egg so the asteroids looked as if they were standing still.

''One of the asteroids is smaller than the others,'' said Jean.

''According to the plan they left with me,'' Carole explained, ''they are going to shrink all the asteroids by dumping magnetic monopoles in them. Then they are going to shrink the radius of the ring until the asteroids coalesce into a solid rotating ring of magnetically charged, ultra-dense matter. I don't like that. The tides from the gravity field of the ring are going to get orders of magnitude larger than the tides from Egg. I don't think even your acceleration tanks are going to help you survive that.''

''You forgot the augmentor masses,'' Seiko told her.

''What are those?'' asked Carole.

''The augmentor masses were well covered by the cheela in their briefing to us, Commander Swenson,'' said Seiko. ''I'm sure the information was in your briefing.''

''I just scanned it quickly,'' admitted Carole.

''The augmentor masses are dense masses just like the compensator masses, but there are only two of them. Instead of being placed in a ring around the point to be protected, they are placed above and below the place to be protected. In that position the two masses add to the tides of the neutron star.''

"But that would just make the tides worse," said Carole.

"Not in this case. When they shrink the size of the ring of compensator masses, the tides from the ring get stronger than the tides from the star, so the star tides have to be 'augmented' by the augmentor masses."

"The cheela are bringing them now." Cesar was looking out the porthole in his acceleration tank. The augmentor masses were modest-sized, old-fashioned cheela spaceships about the size of a softball. They had black holes in the middle of them to provide enough gravity to keep the cheela in their condensed state.

"Looks like we each get two augmentor masses," Abdul said as he watched the activity outside his porthole. "I thought there would be two big ones."

"Because of the way that tidal forces add," said Seiko. "They can do a better job if they null out the tides for each one of the tanks individually."

"The asteroids are now tiny dots," said Jean.

"And the ring is starting to shrink," Pierre added.

"I'll never complain about a mere 200 gees per meter again," said Abdul. "Hey! The ultrasonic pressure drivers have started. This is getting serious!"

"The ring of asteroids is now at 50-meters radius and has coalesced into a solid ring," said Carole. "Things seem to have halted."

Suddenly the screens blanked and a message appeared on all their screens.

NEXT PHASE STARTS IN 10 SECONDS.
DRAGON SLAYER CREW WILL RETURN IN SIX MONTHS.

The ten seconds passed slowly. The next two milliseconds were full of activity. Each tank was jerked upwards away from the center of the ring. The ring was collapsed until it was only a few meters in diameter. As it shrank, its glowing surface turned redder and redder, finally turning into a deep, dark, impossible black. It did not even reflect the yellow-white light from Egg. Then, one by one, the tanks were thrust through the hole in the center of the invisible ring. The heavy steel tanks distorted visibly as they passed through.

They did not come out the other side.

04:03:01 GMT WEDNESDAY 22 JUNE 2050

Pierre screamed as his arms slammed against the creaking walls of the heavy steel tank. Just as he thought that his fingers were going to be pulled off his hands, it was over. He coughed up some water he had inhaled, cleared his mask, and tried his control panel. The video display was dead, so he looked out his porthole.

He could make out the presence of three of the other tanks from the light coming from their portholes. Egg and its ever-present glare was gone.

Most of the sky was black and starless. In the distance was a small elliptical patch with a few dozen stars in it. The stars in the patch of sky were blue to ultraviolet in color. What was most confusing was that the patch of starlight seem to be rotating, while he and the rest of the tanks were standing still.

"That was a Kerr space-warp!" Pierre said out loud.

"That is correct," came a voice. The image of Sky-Speaker was on the screen.

"That can't be!" said Pierre. "I remember from my gravitational engineering courses that a Kerr ring with the mass of a sun would have a one-kilometer hole. The compensator asteroid masses are orders of magnitude less massive than the sun. The biggest ring they could make would be less than a micron in diameter. According to Einstein, that was impossible. . . ."

"Einstein was intelligent, but human," said Sky-Speaker. "He failed to combine gravity and electromagnetism. We have. The unified theory agrees with Einstein for large masses. For very small masses, the diameters of magnetized space-warps are larger than Einstein predicted."

While Sky-Speaker was talking, Pierre noticed that the string of free-floating spheres was being moved. The tanks with their clouds of robot-tended equipment had moved back under the rotating patch of sky. The cheela robots formed the tanks into a circle and accelerated them until they were moving in the same direction as the whirling patch of sky above them. The acceleration continued.

"We're moving in time," said Pierre.

"Yes," said Sky-Speaker. "The rate is one month normal galactic time per ten minutes proper time for your crew. You will return through space-warp in one hour. Six months will have passed in normal space. The asteroid Oscar will have returned."

The cheela robots now had communication links set up between all the tanks, and Pierre could see each of the remaining crew members on one of his miniature screens.

"Is everyone okay?" he asked.

"Yes," said Abdul. "But I'm not looking forward to going back through that meat grinder again."

"The engineering check program indicates a problem," said Jean.

"I'm surprised it is still functional after the drastic changes the cheela made," said Seiko.

"What's the problem?" Pierre asked.

"There is a leak in Tank 6," Jean replied.

"Whose tank is that?" asked Pierre.

"Mine," replied Abdul. "She's right. I've lost some pressure. The water must have frozen and plugged the leak, though. The pressure seems to have stabilized."

"The tank must be repaired!" Cesar said. "It surely cannot withstand another trip through those extreme tidal forces."

"The cheela can work miracles. But I don't think they can weld the mist we call steel. I'll just have to risk it." Abdul paused, looking puzzled, then turned away from the video pickup and put his hands against the back wall of the tank.

"Hey!" he said. "I feel little tiny tugs of gravity near the wall. They keep zipping back and forth."

"I can see some activity outside your tank," Seiko told him. "It looks like an electric arc. I think they are attempting to weld the leak shut."

"I hope it holds," said Abdul.

05:06 CREW TIME WEDNESDAY 22 JUNE 2050 (00:01 GMT SUNDAY 25 DECEMBER 2050)

"Ten seconds to reentry," said Sky-Speaker.

Pierre saw the view outside his porthole tilt and shift as the circle of tanks turned into a line of tanks that swooped away from the patch of sky in a large arc, then dove headfirst through the Kerr-warp at high speed. The next few milliseconds passed too quickly for the tortured humans to follow.

As Oscar neared the space-warp the five tanks popped, one by one, out of the flat circle of black. After the passage of the second tank, the diameter of the ring expanded a little, then shrank just as the third tank passed through. The oscillations in the ring grew larger, and the fourth tank was highly distorted by the tides of the contracting ring. The cheela obviously hadn't expected this instability. They managed to slow the last tank down so that it wasn't trying to get through the ring at its minimum radius, but it wasn't enough. The tank ruptured, spewing a human being and gobbets of water into the vacuum of space.

The cheela robots assembled the remaining four tanks in a line just below the periapsis of the plunging asteroid, Oscar. The asteroid passed rapidly over the tanks, and one at a time its gravity field jerked the tanks upward in a high trajectory that took them quickly away from the tides of Egg.

The cheela attempted to help the remaining human. They moved a piece of tank to shield him from the radiation from Egg. They kept him from being torn apart by the gravity tides by making a miniature compensator ring of dense spacecraft that circled around him. However, they couldn't prevent him from being dragged back toward the massive space-warp. His eyes temporarily protected from the vacuum of space by his underwater mask, Abdul looked up and waved goodbye to his departing comrades. Then, pushing off from the heavy piece of steel tank, he dove headfirst into the whirling black ring to join the atoms that had once been Amalita. Just before he reached the ring his body was momentarily surrounded by a swirling cloud of white-hot specks. There was a flash and he was gone.

05:15 CREW TIME WEDNESDAY 22 JUNE 2050 (00:10 GMT SUNDAY 25 DECEMBER 2050)

The four tanks were met at the top of their trajectory by a flitter from St. George that took them in tow. While one spacesuited figure secured the tow line, another came over and peered in Pierre's porthole. It was Commander Carole Swenson. He saw a big grin on her face as she put her helmet against the outer wall of the tank and hollered a greeting.

"That's the last time I let you have a spaceship to drive," she said. "Did you get the license number of the truck?"

She knew Pierre couldn't talk underwater except through his throat mike, so she shouted one more message and pushed back to the flitter for the ride in.

"I've got a surprise for you," she said. "See you in the air lock."

Pierre couldn't understand why Carole was so happy. Perhaps it was because at least four of the crew of Dragon Slayer made it back. All Pierre could think of, however, was that two of them didn't. They had been his responsibility, and now they were dead. He dreaded what he had to do next. He would have to let their families know. How do you tell someone that their loved ones had been torn to atoms?

05:50 CREW TIME WEDNESDAY 22 JUNE 2050 (00:45 GMT SUNDAY 25 DECEMBER 2050)

The four tanks were crowded into the cargo air lock on St. George, and soon the lock was full of balls of water and sloppy, wet, sobbing people.

"I'm sorry about Amalita and Abdul, Carole," Pierre said as he took off his mask. "If only there was something I could. . . ."

"Hush. . . ." Carole was smiling happily. "Come! I want you to meet a couple of friends of ours." She grabbed his hand and pulled him down the corridor to the communications room. The room was empty except for the communications operator. Pierre was completely baffled.

"Hello, Pierre." It was Amalita's voice.

"Did you have a nice ride up from Egg?" Abdul's voice asked.

Pierre whirled around to face a communications screen at one end of the room. He saw video images of Amalita and Abdul in two segments of the screen.

"Surprise! Surprise!" Abdul yelled.

"It *really* is us," Amalita said. "Or at least all of us that counts."

"I even have a moustache to twirl." Abdul lifted his hand to twirl the end of his long moustache. "And it feels like the real thing even though it's made of software instead of hardware."

Carole squeezed Pierre's arm in reassurance as she spoke. "The cheela scanned them thoroughly just before their bodies were destroyed," she said. "Their intellect patterns now reside in cheela supercomputers."

"But Amalita was irradiated and frozen," Pierre protested.

"I admit I have a lot of missing memories," said Amalita. "But the basic personality is still there."

"Yeah!" said Abdul. "She's just as bossy as ever."

"Hush!"

"See?" said Abdul, raising his eyebrows and shrugging his shoulders. "She'll be even more bossy when we get into those walk-around bodies they're building for us."

"We have slowed ourselves down so we can say goodbye to all of you and our families," said Amalita. "Then we had better get back up to normal cheela rates if we are going to stay up with what is going on down here. . . ."

"Doc! Seiko! Jean!" Abdul called. "Over here on the screen."

Pierre turned around to see astonished looks on the remainder of his crew as they came into the communications room. His chronometer chimed the hour, and he looked down at it. He started to reset it to make it agree with the clock on the wall, but decided against it. Not many people lived on a time-line six months shorter than the rest of the universe.

06:00 CREW TIME WEDNESDAY 22 JUNE 2050

The long day was over.

Technical Appendix

The following sections are selected extracts from the book, *My Visit With Our Nucleonic Friends*, by Pierre Carnot Niven, Ballantine Interplanetary, New York, Earth and Washington, Mars (2053). This is the only book to win the Nobel, Pulitzer, Hugo, Nebula, and Moebius prizes in the same year (2053).

DRAGON'S EGG

The home star of the cheela was given the picturesque name Dragon's Egg by the humans because it is a star right at the end of the constellation Draco (the Dragon), as if the Dragon had left an egg behind in its nest. The cheela coincidently also called their home Egg because it is the source of lifegiving heat and light, and glows warmly like the eggs they lay.

Egg, like most neutron stars, rotates rapidly because it is a small, compact body only 20 kilometers in diameter that condensed from a large, slowly rotating red giant star many millions of kilometers across. Most of the mass, magnetic field, and angular momentum of the original star ended up in the neutron star. Dragon's Egg has a surface gravity of 67 billion Earth gravities, a magnetic field at the poles of a trillion gauss, and a rotation rate of 5.0183495 revolutions per second. Thus, one turn of Egg is roughly one-millionth of an Earth day. This approximate million-to-one relative time scale also seems to apply to the cheela life processes. Our nucleonic friends think, talk, live, and die a million times faster than we humans.

RELATIVE TIME SCALES

The cheela use a base twelve numbering system since they have twelve eyes. The cheela units of time are given in the following table, along with the roughly equivalent time span for humans, taking into account the average lifetime of the cheela compared to the average lifetime of a human.

Human Time	Cheela Time	Remarks
1 day	3,000 g	100 cheela generations
1 hour	126 g	4 cheela generations
45 min	94 g	cheela lifetime
15 min	31 g	cheela generation
29 sec	1 g = 1 great = 144 turns	(equiv. to human year)
0.2 sec	1 t = 1 turn of Egg	(equiv. to human day)
17 msec	1/12 t = dothturn	(equiv. to human hour)
1.4 msec	1/144 t = grethturn	(equiv. to human 10 min)
115 μsec	1/1728 t = methturn	(equiv. to human minute)
10 μsec	1/20736 t = sethturn	(equiv. to human 4 sec)
800 nsec	1/248832 t = blink	(equiv. to human blink)

OUR NUCLEONIC FRIENDS

One can hardly imagine a more alien life form than a cheela. A typical cheela weighs the same as a typical human, about 70 kilograms; but the nuclei in the cheela body have lost their electron clouds, so the nuclei are condensed into a tiny body that is squashed by the high gravity and stretched by the high magnetic field into an oval pancake shape a half-centimeter in diameter and a half-millimeter high—a little larger than a sesame seed.

The body is tough and flexible, with a tread on the bottom like that of a slug. Unlike a slug, a cheela can move equally well in any direction. The cheela have twelve eyes spaced around their periphery, giving them 360-degree vision. The eyes are up on stalks like those of a slug, but because of the high gravity the stalk is thicker. The cheela see using the ultraviolet and soft X-rays emitted by the 8200-K glowing surface of Egg.

Despite their alien appearance, the cheela are not thought of as ugly, terrifying monsters. Instead, they have become our friends. One suspects that their small size may have something to do with it, as well as the fact that they cannot use anything on Earth, or even the Earth itself. Anything made out of normal matter would collapse at a touch from their ultra-dense nucleonic bodies.

LIFE ON A NEUTRON STAR

Living on a neutron star is very different from living on the Earth, but our friends, the cheela, find it very pleasant. The very high gravity field of 67 billion times Earth gravity means that everything must be built low to the crust and very sturdy. The very high magnetic field of a trillion gauss tends to elongate objects along the magnetic field lines and makes it difficult to move things across the magnetic field lines. The two magnetic poles of Dragon's Egg are on opposite sides of the neutron star near the equator. They are called the "East" and "West" Poles. Midway between the two magnetic poles the magnetic field lines are parallel to the surface, and the cheela find it easy to move east and west but difficult to move north and south.

There are things lacking on a neutron star that we take for granted. There is no sun. The light and energy that keep us alive on Earth pour down from the Sun during the day, while at night it is dark and cold. Thus, most life-forms on Earth go to sleep at night. On Egg the light and energy that keep the cheela alive come upward from the crust. It is never dark, so the life-forms on Egg never developed sleep. They do not have a moon, so they have no months. They do not orbit a star, so they have no year. Their only natural unit of time is the rotation of the fixed stars in the sky. Thus, their equivalent of a day-night cycle is a turn of the star.

The cheela don't have lamps, candles, fireplaces, or flashlights, for there is no dark and no cold on the glowing surface of Egg. Even the inside of a cave is brightly illuminated by the glow from the walls. The cheela don't have hanging pictures, hinged doors or windows, leafed books, rooftops, or tops to anything usually, for the gravity is too high. They don't have airplanes, balloons, kites, whistles, fans, straws, perfume, lungs, or breath because there is no air. What atmosphere there is consists of a few electrons and ions of iron or other typical crustal nuclei. They don't have umbrellas, bathtubs, showers, or flush toilets because there is no rain nor are there streams, lakes, or oceans.

Life for a modern cheela is not drab. Although cheela do not wear cloth to cover their supple, elastic, and variable-shaped bodies, they do dress up. Even uncivilized cheela wear body paint to cover their nakedness, and the modern fluorescent, liquid crystal, and variable-emittance paints make the city streets bright with color and patterns in the pre-turnfeast rush. Civilized cheela also never leave their compounds without first inserting into the holding sphincters in their hide a set of six badges that indicate their profession and their rank in that profession. For more festive occasions, jewelry can replace or augment the badges on the hide, while jewel-rings encircle each of their twelve eye-stubs.

A corner of a typical cheela home compound is shown in Figure 1. There are paintings on the wall, but they are painted right on the wall. There are books, but they are rolled up scrolls that are stored in scroll-walls. There are soft pads and pillows, but they are for resting and reading, not sleeping, for cheela don't sleep. There are windows, but they have no glass, for there is no cold or hot air to keep out. If a cheela wishes privacy, he pulls the horizontally sliding window blind shut. There is a door to the compound, which also slides in a track. Although modern cheela now use nuclear-power chronometers to keep track of time, the old-fashioned pendulum clock works as well on Egg as it does on earth, provided a sturdy frame is made to hold the pendulum in the strong gravity. On Earth, a one-meter pendulum ticks a slow once a second, whereas on Egg a one-millimeter pendulum ticks a fast three times a blink. On the right is one of the favorite pets of the cheela, a long-haired Slink.

Since cheela are egg-layers that leave their eggs at the hatching pens of their clan, they do not form family units, and each cheela lives alone with its pets. Most cheela choose a Slink for their pet. There are as many different breeds of Slinks on Egg as there are different breeds of dogs on Earth, and apparently for the same reasons.

A typical mongrel Slink is a small hairy animal with an oval shape, an undertread for moving, and twelve eyes up on stalks. Although most cheela don't admit it to themselves, except for the hair and the significantly lower intelligence, a Slink looks and behaves much like a young

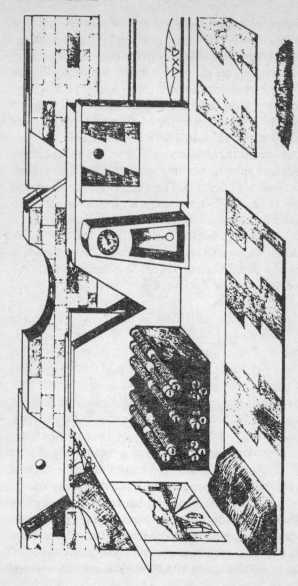

Figure 1. Typical Early Cheela Home Compound

cheela hatchling. On Earth, it would be as if the most popular pets were monkeys rather than cats or dogs.

Cheela bodies are very wide compared to their height so they take up a lot of area. To accommodate these wide bodies without the aid of basements or multiple stories, the home and workplace compounds also take up a lot of area, so the walls go right out to the street as they do in old towns on Earth.

An architect's version of a typical cheela street in the town of Swift's Climb is shown in Figure 2. The East Pole mountains can be seen in the distance, while to the right rise the South Side cliffs marking the South Side fault line. The main street is east-west, with compounds on each side abutting the slidewalks. Near the East Pole, the magnetic field comes up out of the ground so all directions are hard-going, and the cross streets are at right angles to each other. In cities far from the poles, such as the capital, Bright's Heaven, the "cross" streets are at an angle of thirty to sixty degrees to the easy-going east-west streets. When moving along these cross streets the cheela brace their bodies against the slippery slidewalls and push their way at an angle to the prevailing magnetic field to get to the next east-west street where the rippling is easier.

The cheela learned about traffic problems from the humans long before they had cities big enough to have traffic problems. This street, with its double yellow line down the middle, is ready for the turnfeast glide-car rush.

Each compound usually takes up a separate block to itself. (In Bright's Heaven, the "blocks" are diamond- or triangle-shaped.) The street name markers are built up from the corners of the compound walls, while the entrances to the compounds are identified with street numbers in the wall and the name of the owner in the slidewalk plate. The home compound on the left is a modern version

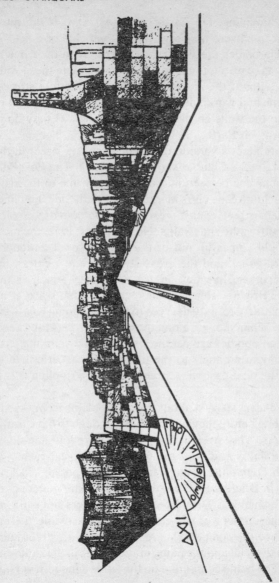

Figure 2. View Down Typical Street in Swift's Climb

Figure 3. Parasol Plant

with half-circle window cutouts and an inner walled patio area with a tri-poster tree. The home compound on the right is an older version with simple square windows and no inner patio.

PLANT LIFE ON EGG

The plants on Egg make food by extracting energy from the hot crust of Egg with their root system and rejecting their waste heat to the cold temperature of the sky. One major form of plant life is the parasol or petal-pod plant shown in Figure 3. It has a single taproot buried deep in the crust. From the single root grow twelve strong, curving compression members or "trunks," tied together with tension threads to a central post. Between each trunk and across the top of the plant is stretched a membrane "skin." The top membrane, facing the cold sky, is highly emissive and dark. At the end of each of the twelve trunks are the pollen shooters and collectors.

The cheela evolved from the parasol plant and still contain the genetic code for the plant form in their genes. Under proper manipulation of their "hormone" balance, they become immobile, dissolve their internal muscles, and re-form into a very large version of the parasol plant

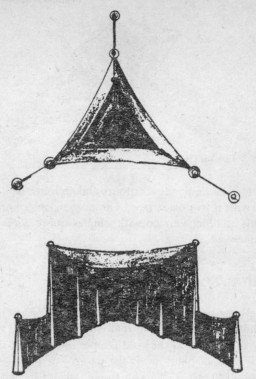

Figure 4. Tri-Poster Plant

called a dragon plant. Upon reversal of the process, they
regrow a new, young cheela body to house their brain and
nervous system, which has been unaffected by the trans-
formation. This animal-plant-animal process gives the
cheela a method for rejuvenation of the body.

Another form of plant life is the tri-poster plant shown
in Figure 4. It puts out secondary trunks like the banyan
tree on Earth, then grows an interconnected triple trunk
system with membranes and tension fibers completing the
structure.

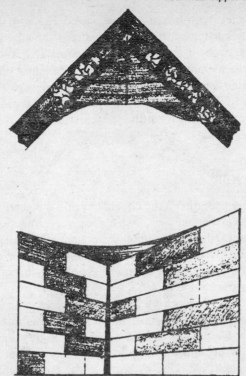

Figure 5. Cleft-Wort Plant

A third form of plant life is the cleft-wort, well-known trademark of the Web Construction Company. It is found mostly in crevices in rocks in the mountainous areas at the east and west magnetic poles, although the hardy mountain plant also thrives in the nooks and crannies of the homes and offices in the cities and towns. As can be seen in Figure 5, the cleft-wort plant uses the rocks and ledges to provide mechanical support. A taproot at the base of the cleft climbs up the corner of the crevice to the upper surface where it attaches onto opposite sides of the cleft with broad surface roots. The surface roots then anchor tension fibers in a pattern similar to that of a spider web in the corner of a room. The web fibers support a membrane between them. The upper surface of the membrane is highly emissive to allow waste heat to escape to the cold sky, while the lower surface is silvery to reflect the heat from the hot crust below.

STARQUAKES

The only "weather" the cheela have on the nearly airless Egg is earthquakes or, more properly, crustquakes or starquakes, depending upon the magnitude. While a large quake on Earth has a Richter magnitude of 8 or greater, large starquakes on neutron stars can reach an equivalent Richter magnitude of 16!

Having experienced a starquake at close quarters with a number of different instruments active and measuring, we now have a better idea of what a large starquake is like. Our present understanding is summarized in a recently published book by some of the crew members on Dragon Slayer.[1] Our findings are not significantly different than the older publications in the field that discussed how the vibrational energy in the crust gets transferred into the magnetic field and then into the electrons and ions in the sparse atmosphere,[2,3] how the smaller quakes can be used to predict the larger quakes,[4] and how a large quake can trigger a core collapse or starquake. Unfortunately, being able to predict a large quake from smaller quakes was of little help to us humans who were there. The whole quake sequence takes place in less than a second.

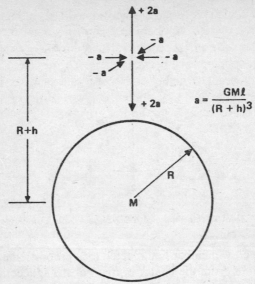

Figure 6. Tidal Accelerations Above a Mass

ULTRADENSE MACHINERY

Being ultra-dense themselves and living on an ultra-dense world, the cheela have developed a technology of ultra-dense machines that is way beyond our present understanding, although Einstein and others have given us some clues. Of course, even to approach Dragon's Egg with our spacecraft, Dragon Slayer, we humans had to construct some simple ultra-dense machines ourselves.

Figure 6 shows the basic problem of getting to know a neutron star better. If our spacecraft is in orbit at an altitude h above a neutron star of mass M and radius R, then only the center of the spacecraft is in free fall. The rest of the objects in the spacecraft (like the crew) are subjected to tidal forces. The amount of tidal acceleration

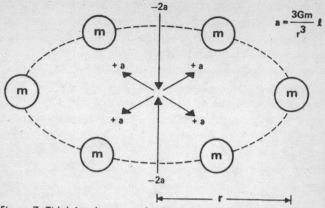

Figure 7. Tidal Accelerations of a Six-Sphere Tidal Compensator

a each crew member is subjected to is proportional to the distance ℓ from the center of mass of the spacecraft.

We wanted Dragon Slayer at a 406-kilometer altitude above Egg so it would be in a synchronous orbit about the star (with the orbital period equal to the rotation period of the star). At this distance from a neutron star, even though the orbital motion cancels the gravity attraction at the center of the spacecraft, the acceleration due to the tidal effects is 200 Earth gravities per meter outward in the radial direction to the neutron star and 100 gravities per meter inward in a plane tangent to the star.

To counteract these tides the crew of St. George constructed a tidal compensator made of six ultra-dense masses arranged in a ring around the spacecraft. As can be seen in Figure 7, the tides in the middle of a ring of masses have a tidal pattern that is exactly opposite to that of the tides above a single mass. By adjusting the mass *m* and spacing *r* of the ring masses, we were able to compensate the tides of the neutron star and get close enough to the star to collect good scientific data.

Later, when the cheela wanted to shrink the ring of masses, the tides from the compensator masses became stronger than the tides from the neutron star and it was necessary to "augment" the neutron star tides to keep the combined tides near zero. As is shown in Figure 8, this was done with a two-mass tidal augmentor. This mass configuration gives no net gravity force at the point between them, so the orbital parameters of the object between the masses are not changed, but the accelerations at points away from the zero-force point increase in exactly the same way as the tidal accelerations above a single mass. A full explanation of tidal forces and how they can be compensated and augmented by arrangements of dense spheres can be found in an old paper on producing picogravity regions near the Earth.[5]

The tidal forces of a neutron star, and the compensators and augmentors needed to cope with them, could have been understood by Newton, although he would have been amazed that such ultra-dense stars and machines could exist. The cheela have ultra-dense machines that are even more amazing. We know that the cheela machines use technology that goes beyond the Einstein theory of gravity, especially at the ultra-high densities, fields, and velocities that the highly advanced cheela are able to generate.

The secrets to the fabrication of the ultra-dense machines of the cheela are still locked up behind their cryptographic code in the HoloMem Crystals at the Smithsonian Museum. However, just as Newton's laws of gravity are still valid at low mass densities, Einstein's laws of gravity are still valid at high mass densities, and they can be used to give clues as to what might happen in the ultra-high density regions where the Einstein laws fail.

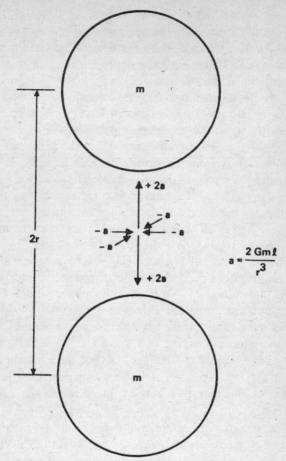

Figure 8. Tidal Accelerations of a Two-Sphere Tidal Augmentor

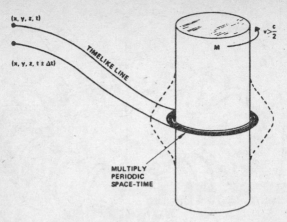

Figure 9. Two-way Time Machine

The cheela had a time machine that allowed messages to be sent backward and forward in time. The Einstein General Theory of Relativity can be used to show how such a machine might be built, despite the paradoxes that such a machine would bring if it *were* built. As is shown in Figure 9, if a long, ultra-dense cylinder is somehow rotated about its long axis until the peripheral velocity of the cylinder is greater than half the speed of light, then a simple analysis[6] shows that there should be a region near the middle of the cylinder, but outside the surface of the cylinder, where space and time are mixed up. By choosing a proper trajectory, an object or photon can be sent circling around the cylinder with or against the spin of the cylinder to emerge either in the past or the future. How the cheela managed to make a spinning ultra-dense cylinder and keep it elongated long enough to send messages is unknown.

The workhorse of early cheela space transportation was a gravity catapult. We are not sure exactly how it works, but again the Einstein General Theory of Relativity gives

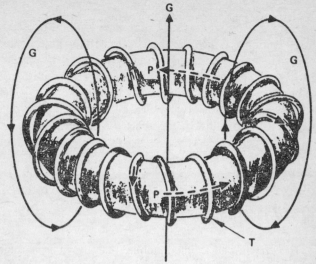

Figure 10. Gravity Catapult

us a clue. It has been shown[7,8] that the Einstein theory of gravity has a number of similarities to the Maxwell theory of electromagnetism. In electromagnetism, the basic source of all the forces is the charge on the electron. The charge generates an electric field. If you move the charge to form an electric current, the current generates a magnetic field. It is also known that if you increase or decrease a magnetic field, that changing magnetic field in turn generates an electric field.

The same thing happens in gravity. The basic source of all the forces is the mass of whatever particles you are using. The mass generates a gravity field. If you move the particles to form a mass current, the current generates a new field that is the gravitational equivalent of the magnetic field. In Figure 10 we show a torus wrapped with tubing carrying a mass current T and generating the new field P called the protational or Lense-Thirring field. If you increase or decrease the protational field, it will generate a gravity field G at the center of the catapult that will push any object at the center of the ring in an upward direction. The cheela gravity catapults must work in somewhat the same manner, but it is also obvious that new physics must be involved. The Einstein theory would predict that a machine using neutron star density material could not make a strong enough gravity field to catapult a spacecraft off Egg.

The most amazing ultra-dense machine the cheela constructed was a miniature space-warp. The Einstein General Theory of Relativity can give us a clue to its formation, but only a clue, since the size of the space-warp that they made was much larger than what the Einstein theory would have predicted. There is a relatively simple exact solution to the full Einstein field equations that describes the exterior field of a dense spinning mass. It is called the Kerr metric solution.

If you assume that the spinning mass is in the form of an ultra-dense ring as is shown in Figure 11, with mass M and electric or magnetic charge Q, then using the Kerr metric, it can be shown[9,10] that if the spinning ring is dense enough and spinning rapidly enough, it acts like a space-warp and a time machine combined. When a small object is sent through the center of the ring, it does not come out the other side!

Instead, the mathematics predicts that the object enters a hyperspace where time and space have been interchanged. If the object is moved with or against the spin of the ring, it is moved backward or forward in time. To return to our universe, the object is merely moved back through the hole in the ring once again. Such a rapidly rotating ultra-dense ring is obviously unstable and it took

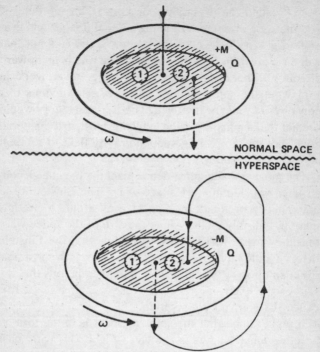

Figure 11. Kerr Metric Space Warp

all the advanced technology of the cheela to keep the ring stable long enough to attempt a rescue.

REFERENCES

1. S. K. Takahashi, J. K. Thomas, and P. C. Niven, *Neutron Star Dynamics,* McGraw-Hill (2053).

2. R. Ramaty et al., "Origin of the 5 March 1979 Gamma-Ray Transient: A Vibrating Neutron Star," *Nature* **287,** 122 (11 Sept 1980).

3. E. P. T. Liang, "Inverse Comptonization and the Nature of the March 1979 Gamma-Ray Burst Event," *Nature* **292,** 319 (23 July 1981).

4. V. Trimble, "A Successful Glitch-Hunt," *Nature* **353,** 666 (31 Oct 1991).

5. R. L. Forward, "Flattening Spacetime near the Earth," *Phys. Rev.* **D26,** 735 (1982).

6. F. J. Tipler, "Rotating Cylinders and the Possibility of Global Causality Violation," *Phys. Rev.* **D9,** 2203 (1974).

7. R. L. Forward, "General Relativity for the Experimentalist," *Proc. IRE* (now *Proc. IEEE*) **49,** 1442 (1961).

8. R. L. Forward, "Guidelines to Antigravity," *Am. J. Physics* **31,** 166 (1963).

9. B. Carter, "Complete Analytic Extension of the Symmetry Axis of Kerr's Solution of Einstein's Equations," *Phys. Rev.* **141,** 1242 (1966).

10. B. Carter, "Global Structure of the Kerr Family of Gravitational Fields," *Phys. Rev.* **174,** 1559 (1968).

ABOUT THE AUTHOR

DR. ROBERT L. FORWARD is a Senior Scientist at the Hughes Research Labs in Malibu, California. One of the pioneers in the field of gravitational astronomy, he participated in the construction of the first antenna for detection of gravitational radiation from supernovas, black holes, and neutron stars. Those of his far-out ideas which can be accomplished using present technology he does as research projects. Those that are too far out he writes about in speculative science articles or develops in his short stories and novels. Contributing to the unreality of his views are his wife and four children.

Introducing...

The Science Fiction Collection

Del Rey has gathered the forces of four of its greatest authors into a thrilling, mind-boggling series that no Science Fiction fan will want to do without!!

Available at your bookstore or use this coupon.

____THE BEST OF LESTER DEL REY	32933	3.95
____THE BEST OF ERIC FRANK RUSSELL	33223	3.95
____THE BEST OF L. SPRAGUE DE CAMP	32930	3.50
____THE BEST OF LEIGH BRACKETT	33247	3.95

 BALLANTINE MAIL SALES
Dept. TA, 201 E. 50th St., New York, N.Y. 10022

Please send me the BALLANTINE or DEL REY BOOKS I have checked above. I am enclosing $.................(add 50¢ per copy to cover postage and handling). Send check or money order—no cash or C.O.D.'s please. Prices and numbers are subject to change without notice. Valid in U.S. only. All orders are subject to availability of books.

Name_____

Address_____

City_____State_____Zip Code_____

08   Allow at least 4 weeks for delivery.   TA-131

27 million Americans can't read a bedtime story to a child.

It's because 27 million adults in this country simply can't read.

Functional illiteracy has reached one out of five Americans. It robs them of even the simplest of human pleasures, like reading a fairy tale to a child.

You can change all this by joining the fight against illiteracy.

Call the Coalition for Literacy at toll-free **1-800-228-8813** and volunteer.

**Volunteer
Against Illiteracy.
The only degree you need
is a degree of caring.**

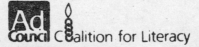

Ad Council C🕯ꞏalition for Literacy

LV-3

THIS AD PRODUCED BY MARTIN LITHOGRAPHERS
A MARTIN COMMUNICATIONS COMPANY